THE
Queen's
Dwarf

THE
QUEEN'S
DWARF

Ella March Chase

THOMAS DUNNE BOOKS
St. Martin's Press
New York

This is a work of fiction. All of the characters, organizations, and events portrayed in this novel are either products of the author's imagination or are used fictitiously.

THOMAS DUNNE BOOKS.
An imprint of St. Martin's Press.

www.thomasdunnebooks.com
www.stmartins.com

Design by Kathryn Parise

LIBRARY OF CONGRESS CATALOGING-IN-PUBLICATION DATA

Chase, Ella March.
    The queen's dwarf : a novel / Ella March Chase.
        p. cm.
    ISBN 978-1-250-00629-5 (hardcover)
    ISBN 978-1-250-03852-4 (e-book)
    1. Hudson, Jeffrey, 1619–1681—Fiction.   2. Henrietta Maria, Queen, consort of Charles I, King of England, 1609–1669—Fiction.
3. Buckingham, George Villiers, Duke of, 1592–1628—Fiction.
4. Charles I, king of England, 1600–1649—Fiction.   5. Dwarfs—Great Britain—Fiction.   6. Courts and courtiers—Fiction.   7. Great Britain—Kings and rulers—Fiction.   I. Title.

    PS3553.A845Q44 2014
    813'.54—dc23
                                                        2013030262

St. Martin's Press books may be purchased for educational, business, or promotional use. For information on bulk purchases, please contact Macmillan Corporate and Premium Sales Department at 1-800-221-7945, extension 5442, or write specialmarkets@macmillan.com.

First Edition: January 2014

10   9   8   7   6   5   4   3   2   1

To *Owen Muir Bautch*, the beautiful, earnest little greenwood lad who made springtime forever brighter. I will always remember you on the day after your first birthday, riding in your mom's backpack, your wide-eyed gaze fixed on the redwoods, your fingers reaching toward dogwood blossoms as we hiked on sun-washed trails. May you find peace and beauty and many delightful adventures in the forests your namesake cherished. I am so grateful to have you in my life.

In loving memory of my father, Warren Ostrom, who loved the wilderness. He never gave up.

ACKNOWLEDGMENTS

·

A *gifted editor* is a treasure. I've been fortunate enough to share Jeffrey's journey with three. Karyn Marcus's vision helped breathe life into the images captured in Van Dyck's famous painting of Jeffrey Hudson and Queen Henrietta Maria. Karyn's passion for Jeffrey's story and her faith in my ability to tell it offered me an opportunity to reach and grow as a writer, which I will always be grateful for. I could not have taken this journey without her. When Karyn accepted another career opportunity, Margaret Smith leapt into Jeffrey's world with delightful enthusiasm. *The Queen's Dwarf* became her baby, and she shepherded Jeffrey through the edits, honing the story until it sparkled. When adventure beckoned, Margaret, like any worthy heroine, seized the opportunity. She gathered all her notes and her plans, passed Jeffrey into the capable hands of Anne Bensson Brewer, then embarked for a new life in Canada. The swashbuckling cavalier era is famous for heroes who dash in at the last moment to perform seemingly impossible feats. Anne swept into Jeffrey's world the week before the book's in-house launch and dazzled me with her fierce championing of this novel. Not only did she read the manuscript and prepare her presentation, she sent me her own edits on the manuscript, polishing it even further. Jeffrey and I thank you from the bottom of our hearts.

I've been so lucky to share this journey with agents extraordinaire: Andrea Cirillo and Christina Hogerbe, as well as the rest of the talented crew at Jane Rotrosen Literary Agency. Your excitement over this project and your help in making this book the best it could be is a gift beyond price.

My amazing daughter, Kate, her wonderful husband, Kevin, and their irrepressible boys, Sam and Owen, bring me joy, make me laugh, and love me no matter what. Thank you for teaching me how to play again.

To David, who shares memories, bright and dark. You tamed the chaos of moving Dad from our childhood home to an apartment, then to his final resting place with our mom. You faced tough situations with a dignity and decency that made me proud you are my brother. I love you more than ever.

My critique group: talented writers Leslie Langtry, Janene Murphy, and, as always, Susan Carroll (the woman I've "shared a brain" with for nearly thirty years). Jeffrey and I raise countless cups of highly caffeinated coffee to salute you.

Thanks to dear friends Maureen Dittmar, Eileen Dreyer, Elizabeth Grayson, and Tami Hoag. You were always a phone call away.

To Bob Bradley, the talented, tenderhearted man who shares my passion for writing, reading, history, and a neurotic collie named Oliver. Thank you for playing "train songs" for Sam over the phone, for coffee in the morning, and making sure I remember to eat when I'm on deadline. Thank you for music that makes every day magical and for your unselfishness in caring for my dying father so I could go to Owen's first birthday. Thank you for conversations that delight my heart, your poet's vision which makes each fallen leaf beautiful. Thank you for understanding me. Thank you for loving me.

THE QUEEN'S DWARF

$\mathcal{P}$ROLOGUE

•

Jeffrey Hudson, the Queen's Fool
Seventeen Years Old
March 1629
Greenwich Palace

It is easy to assassinate a queen. The thrust of a dagger in the midst of a masque, the blast of a pistol as she walked to chapel or some invisible poison applied to her spaniel's collar. Queen Henrietta Maria could never resist burying her nose in her beloved dog's fur. An ingenious assassin could apply some elixir over time, making her seem to sicken, then die of natural causes.

Such murders had happened in her native France, the legacy of her de Medici ancestors.

Any one of us in the queen's "Menagerie of Curiosities and Freaks of Nature" could have administered the venom or found some other means to murder our mistress on countless occasions.

But it was the teeming humanity around her that chilled me. More people wished her ill than I could count—too many to guard against and control. God himself could not have kept an eye upon them all.

Besides, there were many ways to kill. The only implement you really needed was hate—or love. I could not guess which of those emotions the queen now felt for me. Did it matter? I braced myself against the chair the queen had had joiners build to fit my undersized frame and wondered. The chamber courtiers call the "Freaks' Lair" spilled before me—the room appointed with the tools of our trade, the haven where we awaited the queen's pleasure. Around me, my fellow performers were beginning to move toward the door on their way to the Great Hall. Anger burned beneath my ribs.

The royal menagerie was leaving me behind. I felt their furtive glances as they passed, regarding me with the fascinated horror of those who find a plague cross painted upon their neighbor's door. They feared that whatever ill luck had driven the queen to exile me might strike them down, as well. A year ago, I would have considered the irony of rejects sitting in judgment rich meat for jest, tossing their desertion of me back in their mismatched faces. But I could no longer attempt a battle of wits. What use was my skill in satire if Queen Henrietta Maria would not allow me to use it in her defense? I frowned at the mechanism in the clockwork bird I hoped to include in a trick I was working on and tried to drive my thoughts away from the masque to be performed that night.

The scenes enacted from myth and legend would delight the queen's favorites, her costumed courtiers dancing upon scenery whose "magic" feats of engineering would awe anyone lucky enough to be in the audience. Tonight's fare was just the latest in the endless stream of court entertainments that delighted the queen. Yet such sinful pleasures horrified the Puritans who drudged through joyless lives beyond the palace walls. Other queens had danced in masques without such outcry. But they had played silent roles, not spouted lines like a common actress. Queen Henrietta Maria adored delivering speeches. Her playacting offered one more opportunity for those who hated the French-born queen to maneuver her into saying something reckless that could cost her her life. England is not kind to cast-off queens. I should have remembered that when I came to court.

Now forcing my thoughts away from the things I could not change, I fixed my attention on the preparations of the troupe of players I had lived among for over three years.

Boku, our master of illusions, murmured a sonorous blend of English and his exotic native tongue, searching for accents that would give the words the most effect. The turban bound around his head looked like a red jewel against black-velvet skin.

A fellow dwarf named Robin Goodfellow retrieved filigreed balls from spaniels wearing sapphire-studded collars. He began sending the spheres flying to the limit of Simon Rattlebones's reach, cheering our animal trainer's exaggerated leaps, laughing when Rattlebones missed.

A ball rolled against my boot. Once I would have tossed the sphere back with a quip. Now I doubted anyone would take it once it touched my hand.

Rattlebones snatched the ball up, the cadaverous acrobat's face angled away from me. I could see the toothsome grin stiffen until Simon was once again at a safe distance, bantering with Goodfellow.

Only one person seemed oblivious to the tension: Deborah Martin, the rope dancer our giant had rechristened Dulcinea after hearing courtiers discuss Cervantes's *Don Quixote*. She seemed to float above our world with butterfly grace, her body swathed in gauze the hue of Valencia oranges. Her tip-tilted eyes fixed on something none of us could see.

It seemed cruel that Little Sara, the dwarf woman, had to follow in such beauty's wake. The tambourine Sara held jangled without rhythm as she tried to straighten her headdress with fingers too thick to be nimble.

Silent amid the clamor of this family I had once laughed with, fought with, depended upon, I braced myself for the sensation of being abandoned.

A year ago, I would have been lord of these revels, the member of Her Majesty's menagerie that every man, woman, and child in England was most eager to see. Jeffrey Hudson, Lord Minimus, the angel-faced freak who barely reached a man's thigh. Queen Henrietta Maria's marvelous dwarf, whose face and form rivaled that of the most exquisite cherub painted in Greenwich Palace.

Foreboding clutched me, and the urge to follow the menagerie was more than I could resist. I knew how vulnerable the queen would be during a masque, with pools of manufactured mists that could conceal an enemy, trapdoors to slip through, scaffolding behind the scenery that was easily climbed, and a host of masked players in flowing costumes that could disguise a weapon.

I started to rise, but a huge paw engulfed most of my arm, keeping me in my seat. It could only be Will, my overgrown friend. The seven-foot six-inch sergeant porter was the one person within the menagerie still willing to offer me companionship—and tempt the queen's wrath for my sake. The bearskin that transformed him into the villain of the upcoming masque gave off a musty scent. I tried not to resent his kindness. No small struggle while knowing he was about to experience everything in this life that I loved.

His voice rumbled. "You must not give up hope, Jeffrey." How many times in the past months had he offered just this comfort? "Her Majesty will remember all you have been to each other. She will forgive you."

"I don't think that likely." I remembered the loathing contorting her features as she forbade me her company. *Your spirit is as unnatural as your form, just as the surgeons say. You are a monstrous creature unable to love or give loyalty even to those who have shown you nothing but kindness.*

How many times these past years had I feared that was true?

Will pulled me from my dark thoughts. "Whatever is amiss between you and the queen will mend in time. I know you refuse to explain what happened to upset her, but I am sure you meant no offense. You've always been her most loyal supporter. She can't have forgotten that you were her first true friend in the English court."

I pulled away from the comfort his hand had offered, wishing I could rid myself of my sins as easily. "It would only make matters worse if I were to tell you what angered her. But Will, if you knew what I did . . . Queen Elizabeth would have locked me in the Tower. King Henry would have demanded that my head roll. If you had seen Queen Henrietta Maria's horror, even you would not torment me by holding out hope."

"Whatever happened, you are her most loyal defender. I would stake my soul on it."

I knew he was hoping for me to confide in him and shift the secret burden I carried onto his willing shoulders.

"By God, Jeffrey," Will insisted, "if the queen knew what you risked for her . . ."

I chuckled without mirth. "Don't speak of it. I will not be made ridiculous, Will," I said, my voice cracking. "Not in front of *her*." Kind Will. He did not remark that it was my profession to play the fool in Her Majesty's presence. I had made myself the butt of jests from the moment I sprang into her presence garbed in a miniature suit of armor and waving a blue-and-gold pennon above my head. That moment was locked in my memory—her sorrowful dark eyes growing wide, light dancing beneath thick fans of lashes. The way she clapped her hands and laughed—a surprised, throaty sound.

"You could win an honored position in any one of a hundred noble households," Will prodded. "If you believe the queen will never summon you again, why not ask Her Majesty to release you so you can find another situation?"

"Because the queen is surrounded by people who will destroy her if they can. Even now I fear someone is plotting to kill her. What happened with the dogs at Hampton Court—" I stopped, swore. "I know what you are thinking. Dogs attack every day with no grander reason than stealing a scrap of meat." I could see by the flush across his cheekbones that I had guessed correctly. "People behave as if I have conjured up the danger as a ploy to regain the queen's favor. Even you doubt me, Will."

"I do not doubt you believe the threat is real. You spend so much time alone, it is no wonder your imagination spins danger into every shadow. But the queen is guarded by the strongest men the king can command, men stout enough to protect her." Will lowered his gaze to spare my pride, not needing to tell me that I was in no position to help the queen, even if she let me.

"I must go before Robin tries to fasten up Dulcinea's dancing rope," he said. Robin Goodfellow's thick fingers painted scenery so real, I had once witnessed a child weep when she could not take a bite of a canvas pomegranate. But he could never get the knots tight enough, and Will did not like to wound the man's pride by retying them in front of the other performers.

Will paused at the door. "I will do what I can to plead your case to the queen." His face, with its craggy brow and off-kilter chin, grew unbearable in its tenderness. "Jeffrey, Her Majesty is lucky to have the devotion of a subject like you."

I listened to the thump of his boots on the marble floor, the sound growing fainter until it disappeared. Silence lowered iron bars around me. It had become my constant companion these past weary months, but it felt more ominous this time. Will had unwittingly loosed other memories. What would Will say if he knew that the queen's enemies had used me to inflame the threat looming over her? I had urged her onto the path of defiance that led so many of her subjects to hate her.

I was no better than the trained monkey, Pug. I was a pet forever poised on the razor's edge between gaining a sweetmeat or the blow of a master's fist. I had learned that terrible trapped feeling three and a half years before, when I first met the man who would be my patron. Before life at court taught me that words could wound deep as any sword and even a man small as I was could bring about the downfall of the mighty. Before I sensed the stealthy tread of a murderer in the corridors behind me and knew that if I failed to expose the assasin who stalked my queen, Henrietta Maria would die.

ONE

·

April 1626
Three Years Earlier
Fourteen Years Old
Oakham, Rutland

I was sure I would not sleep my last night in the shambles. I had lived my whole life amid the butchers' shops that lined the narrow street. The strangely human screams that rippled through the animals when their fellows' throats were slashed became my lullaby. But the eerie silence that fell when the men put down their knives seemed filled with frightening possibilities. Never more so than tonight, when I had no more knowledge of my fate than the beasts barred in the holding pens.

I burrowed under the frayed blanket my younger brother, Samuel, and I had shared since we could climb the ladder to the cottage loft. I wondered why his conversations with God always took longer when I needed to talk to Samuel myself. The rest of us Hudsons dealt with prayers the way we scrubbed our faces in winter, rushing through the ordeal as quickly as possible, jumbling forbidden Catholic Latin with lawful Anglican English, and not overly fastidious about either. Grumbling loudly enough for my kneeling brother to hear, I punched a lump of straw in Samuel's side of the pallet to smooth it in case he ever decided to come to bed. Not that I expected my show of irritation to do any good. It never had before.

But tonight should be different, I thought. Once we climbed out from under this blanket in the morning, everything would change. Next time I returned to the cottage, I would be a visitor. I wouldn't know all the little happenings of Samuel's day. He would know nothing of mine.

My stomach lurched and I wondered if my older brother, John, had felt this sick dread when he had left home to become an apprentice three years ago. It seemed strange to think of him as a grown man, wielding a butcher's knife for the master he served five shops away. I remembered Mother weeping as she stitched him a shirt out of her wedding petticoat, and Father's wide grin when he returned from the secondhand clothing man with a pair of boots. John had drawn them on and paced the cottage floor, every sinew in his lanky frame determined to show he was officially a man.

Our sister, Ann, had tied up John's bundle—two pairs of stockings she had darned, a leather apron, and three scorched ginger nuts Samuel had earned by sweeping out the baker's oven. The preparations for my leave-taking would not be so elaborate.

"I convinced His Grace to take Jeff with nothing but the clothes on his back," Father had said, congratulating himself, the night he announced I was to be handed over to the duke. "Made His Grace wary that some sickness from the shambles might travel to his mansion on the hill."

I had been tempted to remind Father that *he* traveled from the shambles to the duke's holdings all the time in his position as trainer of the nobleman's bull-baiting dogs. But why bother? Even if the duke had permitted me to bring a whole wagonload of goods to my new life, my take-leave would have been nothing like John's. Of all my family, only Samuel would mourn my leaving.

I closed my eyes for just a moment—not because they were suddenly burning, but to rest them until Samuel's prayers were finished. I must have dozed, for I started awake, panicked at the absence of Samuel's warmth on the pallet beside me.

Moonlight trickled in through the hole in the roof that Father had not gotten around to mending. A white-robed ghost seemed to take shape in the silvery glow: Samuel, sitting cross-legged in the moonlight, my mother's sewing basket at his side.

"What are you doing over there?" I asked.

"Thinking," Samuel said. "When John left home, it was a comfort to picture the place he'd sleep near the master butcher's hearth. But no matter how I try, I cannot imagine what life will be like for you once you leave Oakham behind."

"I'll still be staring at people's knees, but the stockings will have fewer holes in them."

Samuel did not even try to smile. I climbed out of bed and crossed to where my mother had laid my costume the night before. But the garb that turned me into a Fairy King was not where I remembered it, one side of the green cloth more crumpled than I recalled.

I had worn it scores of times dancing for pennies at the market fair. Is that how the great ones heard of me? I wondered as I smoothed out a wrinkle.

"Do not pretend to jest, Jeffrey. Not tonight." Samuel's face clouded. I could not bear it if he cried.

"I'll not jest if you promise not to get melancholy. After all, there is a chance that I might be stealing your blanket again by nightfall. The duke might take one look at me and decide I am not worthy of his attention." I meant to soothe Samuel. Instead, he grew alarmed.

"Never say that!"

"So you are eager to get rid of me after all?"

"You know I am not. But Father has already been bragging at the pub, and I fear his temper. I fear the duke even more. People say such horrible things about how wicked he is. Are you afraid?"

There was no use lying to Samuel. He'd always been able to see right through to the truth in me. "A little."

"So am I. That is why I had to protect you."

I looked at my slight, fair brother with his tousled golden ringlets and eyes far too gentle for the shambles and I thought how John would have laughed at Samuel's claim.

"Protect me?" I echoed. "How?"

"I sewed Our Lady in the seam of your tunic while everyone was sleeping."

That holy medal was Samuel's most beloved possession, a gift from the half-mad old woman who kept a statue of the Virgin Mary under her floorboards. Much as his generosity touched me, it unnerved me, as well. Holy relics had been outlawed in England, along with the Catholic faith. Five monarchs had ruled since Henry VIII had broken with Rome, and factions were still warring over England's immortal soul—Anglicans, Puritans, Catholics, and whatever other sects sprang up in between.

John gets ginger nuts. I get a chunk of tin that could land me in Fleet Prison, I thought with wry humor, but I curbed my tongue, saying only, "Samuel, you should not have given me your medal."

"It was the only way I could think of to remind you when I am not around," Samuel insisted.

"Remind me of what?"

"That what people say of you is not true. You weren't born of dark magic. You are good. A gift from Heaven."

I shook my head and turned away. Samuel's hand drifted down on my shoulder. "Whenever you doubt yourself, touch the medal and remember Our Lady loves you, Jeffrey, and so do I."

My eyes burned. I nudged him with my elbow to disguise my emotions. "If you'd given me ginger nuts, I would have shared them with you."

Samuel punched me back, and I knew he understood what I could not say. I've shared everything—my whole life—with you. Until now.

We climbed into bed and stared at the ceiling as the night slipped through our fingers and morning dawned in a hurly-burly of preparations. I had never been bathed and combed, trimmed and polished with more vigor, never hammered with more instructions of how I was to behave in the duke's presence. The bathing was women's work; Father's work: barking out orders. But I could see Samuel outside the mad circle. He stayed close, watching me, until the only thing left to say was good-bye.

⁓⁕⁓

It seemed I had barely blinked before I was standing in my new master's withdrawing room at the center of a world I had never known.

Sweat trickled beneath my leaf green tunic, burning skin scrubbed raw. The handwoven cloth scoured my ribs as Father hefted me onto the writing table that dominated the duke of Buckingham's privy chamber. From here, George Villiers ruled my village and much of England besides. Not that he ruled it well, I had heard men in Oakham's shambles grumble. Buckingham had just limped home after squandering the greatest fleet England had ever sent to sea. His intent: to reprise Drake's famous raid upon the Spanish port of Cádiz.

The duke's failure had not cost him any of the king's love, from all reports. Charles Stuart had welcomed Buckingham back. The rest of England loathed Buckingham more than ever.

I stood before the most powerful nobleman in England and tried not to tread on the inked pages that littered Buckingham's table, or smudge wax still soft on the letter stamped with his seal. The candle he'd used to melt that wax flickered so close to me, I could feel the curls my mother had pressed into my hair wilting. I remembered the blisters she had burned into her hands while holding my golden brown locks around a hot poker, and I wondered if winning this nobleman's favor could make my mother love me.

Buckingham crossed his arms over a doublet sprinkled with jewels, and I fought the urge to rub my eyes. Every surface in the room gleamed in the late-afternoon sun, even the tapestries draping the walls threaded with gilt. I remembered the tale my father had told me as we trudged from his butcher shop to His Grace's estate of Burley-on-the-Hill.

"Nothing but a lowly knight's son was George Villiers, and a second son at that. His family was poor, but that lad was prettier than any ever seen. Aped the ways of his betters and used his fair face to make two kings love him. Rose to be court favorite to slobbering James. When the old king started to wither, Buckingham turned all that charm on James's stammering runt of a son, our new king, Charles."

It was easy to see how the royals had fallen under Buckingham's thrall. I could not remember when I had first made a game of picturing myself in other people's skins—striding on the legs of a running footman, or inhabiting a tall man who cut through the crowds that swallowed me up. But as I stared at the duke, my imagination failed me.

Never had I seen a man knit together with such perfect pieces. White hose clung to the finest legs I had ever seen—and God knew I had been lost in a forest of legs my whole life. Sable hair tumbled in curls to broad shoulders garbed in peacock blue cut velvet. My heart beat faster as Buckingham approached me.

"A pretty plaything you will make, Jeffrey Hudson," he said. "I hardly believed the rumors I heard regarding your appearance. Seldom does a specimen live up to expectations."

Specimen. The word sounded as if I were not human. "Thank His Grace, Jeffrey," my father ordered.

I did not know what I was supposed to thank him *for*. "I am honored—" Buckingham cut me off with a gesture, pacing around the table to observe me on all sides. My skin itched where his gaze touched it.

"I must know what tricks you have used to achieve such perfection." Buckingham grasped my thigh, kneading the flesh as if he expected it to peel away. I willed myself to hold still no matter how he pinched. The duke inspected first one leg, then the other. My cheeks burned when he pulled up my tunic. Cold air flooded over my naked belly as Buckingham spoke to my father. "Hard to believe you have not padded his clothes with sawdust to mold such attractive lines."

My parents have not padded me, I longed to say. But they would still be wrapping me in bandages so tight that I'd have no room to grow if I hadn't learned to twist my body into impossible angles and pull the knots free with my teeth.

"My son is as God made him," my father said. "You will never see Jeffrey's like again."

I tried not to flinch as the duke peeled back my lips, examining my teeth.

Father grasped curls at my nape and pulled my head back until my mouth fell open. He turned me so the candle light could probe deeper to teeth that had been hidden. "Jeffrey is keen as the edge of my cleaver. He learned French when Huguenots moved next door."

"A butcher's lad speaking French? It will stand him in good stead, since the queen makes little effort to learn English."

"My lad hears something once and he remembers it forever."

"That is a skill I can make use of at court." Buckingham laid one finger along his cheek. I stared at his face, fascinated. The duke's beard was groomed to a meticulous point, his mustache feathered broad at each end. The chestnut whiskers drew my eyes to the mouth they framed—his upper lip a trifle fuller than his lower, something oddly feminine in their shape. I had never seen anyone so clean.

"Jeffrey, I will make you king among court fools," Buckingham said. "In return, I require absolute loyalty. A trumped-up charge of treason is the most expedient way to be rid of an opponent at court. Such affairs are notoriously messy. If I fall, a servant like you might end up on a scaffold along with me. But we will speak no more of such gloomy possibilities. You will unravel the plans of whoever schemes against me. No one will suspect you, even after their villainy is exposed. You look innocent as angels, freak though you may be."

I did not wince at the word. I was fourteen years old, well-used to being labeled a freak. It no longer made me cry. "Enemies, Your Grace?" I asked.

"You may have heard of some little difficulty in Cádiz?"

Returning with a third of the ships he had set out with did not seem "little" to me.

"The court is filled with people determined to use that misfortune to destroy me. They tell the king lies about me. They did the same with His Majesty's father when King James loved me. My enemies were certain that when Charles ascended to the throne, I would fall from favor. Instead, I became his dearest friend, his brother in all but blood. Now those enemies believe I hold too much influence over His Majesty. There are even those who wish me dead."

I tried to imagine the duke suffering such a fate. He seemed above such physical limitations. I wondered what would happen to the families who lived on his estates if such men stole the duke's holdings.

Buckingham smiled thinly. "The queen herself would rejoice if I were to disappear. But, then, she is not yet seventeen. Too inexperienced to realize someone else would rise up to take my place. Someone who might use the king's favor in less amiable ways than I do. It is our duty to save the queen from herself."

"Yes, Your Grace," I replied.

"It is settled, then. I will take you to court, where the queen has made collecting rarities such as you her favorite amusement. She is behaving like a petulant child, playing with her particular friends and using her curiosities in the masques she loves to put on while she ostracizes those of us who would bend her attentions to unpleasant matters. If you do your work well, Her

Majesty will delight in taking you for a pet. I have never seen anyone so quick to lavish affection. You will be vigilant and carry everything you hear back to me."

I tried to sort out my feelings about a woman who would collect people for pets. Buckingham fingered strands of my hair.

"Her Majesty is a charming woman, Jeffrey. Not beautiful, exactly, but she is so spirited, it scarcely matters." Buckingham frowned. "You must not be fooled. She is the French king's eyes, the Pope's instrument. If she has her way, England will bow to Catholic masters. Do you understand how dangerous such divided loyalties can be?"

"I do." Cold prickled my neck, and I thought of the medal my brother Samuel had sewn into the seam of my tunic.

Buckingham's eyes narrowed. "Never forget that you are my dog, Jeffrey. Have you seen what your father does to dogs that will not fight when they are thrown into the bull pit?"

"Answer His Grace, Jeffrey," my father said.

"Father flings them to the pack to be torn apart, Your Grace." I had seen that ritual and had held Samuel while he retched all over my shoes.

"It is unpleasant, but it must be done, or the pack will run wild," Buckingham said. "You understand?"

He spoke with such tender regret, I found myself agreeing with him. "Yes, Your Grace."

"I trust you will not need an example of this lesson. You have a wealth of other things to learn. Have you ever felt the kiss of silk upon your back?"

He knew I was garbed in my best. "Never, Your Grace."

"You must have all new clothes." He touched my sleeve, then rubbed his fingers together to crush any fleas he carried away from me. "The moment the first garment is finished, you will cast this rag into the fire."

I thought of the medal. "My clothes are precious to me. My family sacrificed much so I might—"

"Jeffrey!" Father jabbed me with his finger. "Be glad of your master's generosity. Your Grace, I will tear those clothes off him now, if you say the word."

"Do not concern yourself, John. Your son shows loyalty to the place he came from. I hope he shows as much on my behalf when the need arises."

Buckingham gestured for my father to lift me from the table. The duke's signet ring glittered.

Father swung me to the floor, his grip so tight, my ribs bruised. If the duke sent me back to the cottage on High Street, I would suffer other bruises, as well.

"I did not mean to offend," I said. "I will do better."

"You will have to. The royal court is no place for a butcher's son. You will have to create a new Jeffrey Hudson, one worthy to associate with the greatest nobles of the land. They attend the most lavish banquets, dwell in the finest houses, and find even the most costly entertainment dull. It will be your duty to make yourself so vital to the queen's happiness that she cannot bear to be without you, even in her most private moments. You must win a place—not as her court fool, but as her shadow."

I could barely bring myself to speak to a milkmaid for fear she would jeer at me. Now I was to invite the mighty to laugh at me, including the greatest lady in the land. What if the queen took a dislike to me?

The duke laid steepled hands against his lips. I was struck by how delicate those hands were. "Now we've one last question to resolve, Jeffrey Hudson. How much will you be worth? Your father has advised me on the purchase of dogs and bulls that would provide the best sport. What kind of sport will you bring to the baiting ring we call court?"

"Jeffrey earns a pretty sum when he dances in his Fairy Cage," father said.

"A Fairy Cage?" Buckingham queried.

"That is how Jeffrey earned his bread. Brought him to the square in a birdcage his sister decked with flowers. Hung the cage from an iron hook and claimed he was the King of the Fairies. When people put forth enough coin, we'd open the door. He'd dance while his brother Samuel played a tin whistle."

Much as I'd hated being poked by the crowd, I would have welcomed the cage's familiar confines now. It would mean that once night came, I would be sleeping under the eaves with Samuel.

The duke reached into his purse, then dumped a handful of coins into my father's hungry palm. Father's eyes widened as he curled his fingers over the shining mass, his fingernails black with blood he could never scrub clean.

"Go back to your dogs, John Hudson," Buckingham told my father. "There will be more coin in your purse if this whelp I have purchased performs well in the ring."

Panic pricked me. I edged toward my father, my last tie to the life I had known. "Father, tell Samuel that I will not forget my prayers, and Ann that she may have the ribbon from the Fairy Cage, and John—"

I did not know what farewell to send my eldest brother. John seemed a stranger since he'd left home, worn down like our father.

"You have more important things to attend to than shambles folk now," Father said. "Mind the duke, Jeffrey." He leaned down to pat my shoulder, but his hands were full of coin.

He cast me an apologetic glance, then stumbled out of the duke's presence, leaving me behind. Buckingham settled at his desk and took up his quill. My hands clenched as he started to write. It was obvious the duke was finished with me. What was I supposed to do now? The gilt clock in the corner chimed. I gasped, startled. Buckingham looked up with a scowl. "Be about your business."

"I do not know where I am to go, Your Grace."

"You cannot expect me to lead you by the hand! Go prepare yourself to be companion to the queen. There are clothes to stitch, protocol to be taught, alliances to be explained. There will be more subtle skills for you to master once you've proven trustworthy."

What would those skills be? I still had no idea how to proceed, when I heard a scratch at the door.

"Enter," Buckingham ordered. The door opened, revealing a servant in fine livery.

"Your Grace, a lady begs your indulgence. She is early for your appointment." I glanced at the door, watching for a chance to slip out.

Buckingham's mouth curled. "Has my wife gone to deliver alms at St. Coppices, according to plan?"

"The duchess is well on her journey, Your Grace. Shall I send a footman to fetch her?"

"No," the duke said too quickly. "I would not interrupt her ministrations to our tenants. She takes tender care of them."

I heard a silvery laugh as a woman in gold satin swept in, blocking my escape. Her gloved hand held a doeskin pouch. A hood concealed all but one dark brown curl. A winter white mask starred with blue gems concealed her from nose to brow. Was there something wrong with her face?

I had seen people scarred by smallpox around Oakham shrink into their skins. However, this woman took up more of the room than her lithe figure seemed to warrant. The part of her face that remained visible was unforgettable. Full lips were painted a deeper scarlet than I had ever seen in nature, a dimple dancing at the corner of her mouth. Her eyes sparkled through catlike slits in her mask, as if she knew a secret the rest of the world was too dull to understand.

"You act as if you are surprised by the duchess's attentions to the Rutland poor, Your Grace." She cast the pouch upon the nearest chair. "Once her brothers died of Mother Flowers's witchery, your wife knew Rutland's wretches would fall to her charge."

I had heard the earl of Rutland's sons had withered away because of a spell cast by a vengeful servant. The duchess had nearly died, as well.

"The estate would fall to her husband's charge, you mean," Buckingham said, correcting her.

"A fortune is a great beautifier to an ambitious man," she said as Buckingham rose and moved toward her. "It is no wonder that the earl of Rutland was determined not to let his beloved daughter fall prey to a fortune hunter. How relieved he must have been to see his fond Kate settled with a worthy man like Your Grace." Buckingham swept up the lady's hand to kiss. She captured his wrist.

"Do you like my mask? I was eager to bring you this packet from London, but my husband did not want your enemies to know I carried it." She skimmed Buckingham's knuckles against her breasts and rose up on tiptoe to claim a lingering kiss. "It has been too long."

I edged toward the door, but just as I was about to escape, I trod on her trailing skirts. The woman whirled toward me, startled. Slippery fabric wrenched my feet out from under me. I tumbled to the floor. Humiliation surged heat from my collar to my brow.

"Clumsy child!" she scolded as I scrambled to my feet. In spite of her mask, I could see her eyes widen in surprise. "Why—that is no child. Buckingham, what witchery is this?"

Dread kindled in me. I had been weaned on my mother's fear that someone would claim I had been sired by the devil and would burn us at the stake, as they had two witches blamed for the deaths of Rutland's sons.

"I am no sorcerer," Buckingham told the woman. "A wizard's daughter like you should know that."

A wizard's daughter? The woman made no attempt to deny it. Did they not know how dangerous jests about dark arts could be? Or did the duke and this lady not care? *Why should they?* I could hear my father scoff. *A pack of misery-grubbing Puritans could never harm great ones like these.*

"I found him in the shambles," Buckingham said. "This little man is to be a gift for your mistress, the queen. How fares Her Majesty in my absence?"

"You would have to ask the ladies she brought from France. We English ladies the king appointed to her household are exiled from her chambers. She dislikes me most of all, almost as much as she dislikes you. I wonder she lets you get close to her at all."

"It hardly matters what she thinks of me. It's the king who counts, and he's been in my pocket since he was a stammering little boy barely visible in his older brother's shadow."

"Did he find you captivating in the same way old King James did?" she asked, her lips pursed in a way both lovely and mocking.

Buckingham's face flushed ever so slightly and the muscles in his jaw tightened as he held tightly to his composure. "I took notice of him. That is all. You would be surprised how much return is paid on a little kindness."

"Especially when the stammering little boy's brilliant brother dies," the wizard's daughter mocked. "And he finds himself hauled out of the shadows, those sad, bulging eyes so unaccustomed to the light. Very lucky for you the Prince of Wales died, Your Grace."

There was fire in the duke's eyes, but he kept his voice level, if cold. "You may find this hard to believe, my dear, but I genuinely like the king."

I could sense that this strange woman was pulling at the ends of the duke's patience. Apparently she could also, for she lightly turned the subject back to me. "Nonetheless, Her Majesty will never trust any gift that comes from you."

Buckingham frowned. "Have you any thoughts how I might remedy that situation?"

The wizard's daughter placed hands on her hips. "Do not let the queen know your little man is meant for her. Present him as your own plaything. Once Henrietta Maria is enthralled by his performance, you can oh so reluctantly surrender him to her. Think how impressed the king will be with your effort to please his quarrelsome queen."

"The question is, How to make the dwarf irresistible to Her Majesty?" Buckingham said.

The masked woman clasped her hands. "I know what you must do! Your little man is quite the most delicious tidbit I have ever seen. Serve him to the queen in a pie."

It was a jest, I told myself, though my heart skittered.

"A pie." Buckingham stroked his beard to a finer point.

"The plan is not without risk," the woman said. "I *have* heard of mishaps: a kitchen lad returning the pie to the oven or someone being overzealous with the knife." A nasty glint showed in her eyes, and I knew she was hoping for a reaction. I had seen the same expression on apprentices in the shambles who loved to torment Samuel and me.

I strained to stand as tall as possible. "I am not afraid." I did not know how the duke would react to my impertinence. My father would have struck me.

The lady leveled her clever gaze at me. I would not give her the satisfaction of seeing me squirm. "You had best teach your monkey manners before you introduce him to the queen, or some kitchen accident will be the least of his worries," she said.

"I have summoned the perfect man to train Jeffrey in the skills court requires. Uriel Ware."

"An interesting choice, my Lord Admiral. Is not Master Ware in Bristol, attending to Your Grace's interests? The East India Company men are becoming quite belligerent in regards to their shipping fees, as I understand."

"Ware will be an exacting master."

"Indeed. What remains a mystery is why such a grim Puritan stays in the employ of a sensualist like you." Her face dimpled. "Perhaps he hopes to reform you."

"God burdened my wife with that particular labor of Sisyphus."

I wondered who Sisyphus was. Perhaps some master of childbirth.

"As for Ware," Buckingham continued, "he scorns Puritans since his return to my family's employ. A mind like Ware's cannot find challenges worthy of him among the dour crows at prayer meetings. A man of superior talents must have an outlet for them."

"The same might be said of a clever woman, but she is not allowed to pursue her talents, no matter how exceptional they are. People will praise Ware for his resourcefulness. A woman with a keen mind will be condemned by high- and lowborn alike."

"Dearest lady, a man who could not find use for your *talents* is a very unimaginative fellow," Buckingham said.

I saw frustration flit across the woman's face before she smiled and busied herself in straightening the fan that dangled at her waist. "We are not here to debate my talents. As for your dwarf, only time will tell whether Ware can make a courtier out of your Shambles Doll. But even if this pet bungles things at court, he will give the queen pleasure. Seeing the mighty duke of Buckingham publicly humiliated is her favorite pastime. She's developed quite a taste for it since you returned from Cádiz."

I saw Buckingham's mouth tighten. He smoothed the dangerous expression away. "Nothing great is gained without risk."

"So speaks the man who visited Queen Anne's bedchamber when last he was in France." The woman laughed. "You were there to negotiate with the king. Declaring your passion for his wife was not the most diplomatic move you have ever made."

"Why should I not enjoy the queen's bed? Everyone knows King Louis has no use for it. Let lesser men exercise restraint. History will not remember them. But the duke of Buckingham will hold a glorious place in the annals of time." Buckingham's eyes gleamed. "I will send word to York House and have my surveyor of works begin preparations for an entertainment the like of which London has seldom seen. When I return to court, I will host a great banquet for Their Majesties. Jeffrey will be the final course."

Two

·

The year I turned eight, a pack of apprentices tossed me headfirst into a rain barrel to "wash my devils out." Buckingham flung me into the aristocratic life at Burley-on-the Hill the same way. I fought to get my head above water, battering myself against the boundaries of a world I could not understand.

I had never imagined such wealth. Just one lady's clothes billowed with enough fabric to clothe my whole family. Mounds of broken food from the duke's meal were piled upon the servant's tables after the great ones had supped. But my stomach cramped so tightly at the unfamiliar smells of lampreys stewed in cinnamon and sauces thick with saffron that I could not bear to taste anything at all. I fled the table the moment I could, guilt choking me. All I could think of were the thin faces of my family as father parceled out food to each in order of importance—the largest portion to himself, then John, then Samuel, then mother and Ann, the servings shrinking on each plate until only scraps were left for me.

Are their bellies full tonight? I wondered. Did Father buy a joint of meat to celebrate the sale of a son?

After the duke's household supped, I was left to my own devices. I had no spirit for exploring, only peered out the windows, hoping to glimpse some flicker of light from town. Weary at last, I trudged to the wing where servants slept. Buckingham had said Uriel Ware would seek me in the northernmost room come morning. When I opened the door in question, a dozen pairs of eyes fixed on me.

A man some years older than I was approached me. "Been expecting you, Jeffrey Hudson. We're to share this bed under the window."

I would rather have curled up on the floor like one of father's dogs than sleep with a stranger, but I could not say so. With a hitch in his step, the man guided me to the finest bed I had ever seen. The other servants peeped at me from the far side of the room. "Name's Clemmy Watson," the man said as I removed shoes stained from walking past the slaughterhouse, in spite of my effort to stay out of the blood and filth.

The stranger scratched a patch of dry skin beneath his chin. "Lads meant to draw lots, with the loser taking you as bedfellow. They fear you've been marked by the devil."

At least I needn't dread some attempt to eradicate my "evil" by suffocating me with a pillow tonight. They would not risk Buckingham's ire. "How unfortunate you drew the short straw," I told Clemmy.

"Didn't draw straws. Stepped up and offered to share my bed with you."

"You're not afraid of me?"

"I might be once it gets dark." He grinned, showing a front tooth broken off, so that it resembled a saw.

I stripped off my hose, hoping that he would return to his fellows and leave me in peace. I decided not to shed my tunic and risk it being swept away under Buckingham's orders. I would have to snip Samuel's medal out and hide it if the duke insisted on burning my clothes. But I wanted to keep the garment. It smelled like home.

Clemmy gave me a measuring glance in spite of my efforts to ignore him. "I suppose the devil *could* have shrunk you. But I owed it to the Tadpole to take you in."

He waited, clearly expecting me to ask who bore that ridiculous name. In the end, I could not resist. "Tadpole?"

"The youngest of my sisters, born so tiny that Grandmam told Ma to give me the teat instead, save the cost of bread. I refused to eat unless Tadpole got a sip, so they gave me the keeping of her. Lucky thing your ma fed you."

I thought about the nights hunger had gnawed my belly until Samuel slipped me crusts he'd hidden from his portion.

"Old Gabby Yates said my sister was touched by demons," Clemmy said. "Not that I'd have cared if demons *did* save her long, as she got to stay alive.

Would've hated to see a pack of fools scrabbling away from sharing a bed with her."

"What happened to her?"

"She died. But Grandmam said I sent her to the angels knowing that her brother loved her. That was more than most babes get. Not many folk like us cry over the loss of one more mouth to feed."

The man was kind in his way, but I feared he would jabber all night if I let him. I curled up on the bed. "I am very tired."

"Course you are," Clemmy said. "You'll be having a busy day tomorrow, being in Master Ware's charge. Didn't even know Master Ware was back until he sent word you were to sleep here. He's always off running about on the duke's business. Wouldn't be decent not to give you one word of warning, though. Got a great scarred-up hole where his eye used to be. People claim Ware lusted after a whore, so he cut his own eye out with a knife."

I had seen children crippled by their parents to make them better beggars. For a week one summer, I had even befriended a foundling a traveling troupe had taken in. His master had carved the boy's lips away to bare teeth, the horror of the gargoyle smile making the lad into an attraction. I had never heard of a man who mutilated himself of his own free will.

"Some people think that bit about Ware is just a story, but—" Clemmy muttered an oath. "What a fool I am, rattling on. You probably just want peace. First night away from home hurts worse than the toothache."

It was true. I could never remember a night without Samuel beside me, his prayers lulling me to sleep. Clemmy and I lay there as the candles sizzled out, extinguished as men licked their fingers, then pinched the wick between.

When the last flame was crushed to death, Clemmy spoke so softly, I could barely hear. "You can cry if you want to. I won't tell."

⇜⇝

I cannot say if I slept at all, disturbed by the clamor of my bladder and images of eyeballs bursting on the point of a knife. When dawn dislodged everyone from their beds, I dressed quickly, spying a chamber pot the moment before it—and the single washbasin—vanished behind a jostling wall of men. Fearing I would piss myself by the time the crowd thinned, I searched for a way to keep from humiliating myself.

When I heard lark song drift through the open window beside the bed, I hauled myself up onto the sill. Balancing near its edge, I pulled out my pizzle. I was just beginning to ease myself when I heard someone hiss, "Master Ware."

Fumbling to cover myself, I wheeled to face the newcomer and nearly stepped backward into nothingness. A severe gray doublet and wine red cloak garbed a figure that would have been far less imposing than my father's were it not for the eye patch that sliced across a clean-shaven face. Beneath the fringe of black hair cropped level with his jaw, his remaining eye regarded my damp hand in distaste.

I wiped my fingers on my tunic, my cheeks warm. "I could not reach the chamber pot."

"There are going to be a great many things you will not be able to reach at court. One hopes you can devise ways to remedy the situation without pissing on the queen, should she be passing beneath a window. In fact, the duke himself was strolling beneath that window when I rode in. A pity you did not splash him. I could have sent you back to your family and saved us all a good deal of aggravation."

⚜

Twice in the weeks that followed, I almost stole away to see my brother, my loneliness too heavy to bear. I would have been willing to suffer any punishment my father or the duke chose to deal me, but the possibility father would take his ire out on Samuel was too great a risk.

Trapped as days tumbled past, I tried to find my balance in a world where everything I did was wrong and there were always people eager to tell me so. I spent hours under Uriel Ware's inescapable eye as he made me practice the skills I would need. I walked backward toward doors I could not see, because a courtier must never present his back to the queen. I mastered intricate dance steps and memorized words to French songs Her Majesty favored. I familiarized myself with the rattle of dice that ruled the gaming table where the queen pursued one of her favorite pastimes. Not that a queen whose dowry had not been paid had any business gambling, Ware complained.

But I would have wagered upon dicing forever to spare myself an encounter with the dining table. I fumbled with that Italian contrivance called a "fork" and tried to keep from spilling on my new regalia. Glass goblets mystified me, their slippery surface too broad for my hands to get a secure grip.

On my eighth day under Ware's critical gaze, he determined I should not get a drop of moisture unless I drank as a gentleman should. Parched, my fingers aching, I longed for talons to sink into the glass surface—the only hope I had of holding on to the vessel. Despite my efforts, the goblet started to slip. Exasperated, I trapped it between two hands, as I had the pewter flagon Samuel and I shared at home. I gulped wine, then thumped the goblet down on the table before Ware could snatch my glass away.

Ware's voice grew deadly quiet. "I do not think you grasp the gravity of your situation. The favorite sport of the French courtiers is finding fault with Englishmen—including the king. How do you expect to succeed in your mission if you cannot do something as simple as raise a goblet to your lips?"

I struggled to keep my voice calm. "My hands are too small to encircle the goblet. There is no help for that unless you can lengthen my fingers."

I remembered the times John had attempted to stretch me so I could be like other boys. My brother would sneak me into the butcher shops and lift me so that I could hold on to the iron hooks sunk in the ceiling beams. I would dangle like the haunches of meat, my limbs nearly pulled from their sockets when he grabbed hold of my middle. He'd add as much weight as he could, until my burning fingers surrendered and we both slammed down onto the stone floor.

"Hudson!" Ware's voice pulled my attention back to the gleaming tableware. But despite such luxury, I could still feel the hook slickening under my hands, my arms shaking with the effort to hold on. I could still hear John's voice: *Do you want to stay a freak? I cannot help you if you lie there on the floor, crying like a babe!*

"You cannot clutch the glass like some clodpoll the shambles has shaken off its hoof!" Ware poured more wine, then pulled my hand from the glass and slammed my palm flat on the table. His face was so close, I could see puckered skin at the rim of his patch. "Try again, and this time use one hand, or I will nail your sleeve to the table."

I wanted to fling wine into his face and storm off as other men might do, but I had learned from experience that such gestures were futile for one of my size. They only embarrassed me more.

I grasped the goblet as if I were hanging from John's hook, the sweat on my hand mingling with the dampness beading the side of the glass. My fingers pinched the glass so tightly, it sprang out as if from a slingshot.

I had never heard glass shatter—had never touched glass until I joined the duke's household. Ware wrenched around, nearly breaking my wrist before he released it. We both stared at the shards on the floor.

"Fool! Do you have any idea how much that was worth?"

I gawped at the ruined goblet in horror. "What will happen to me?"

Ware turned back to me, every line of his body agitated. "You won't be flogged, no matter how much you deserve it. I reprimand you harshly for your own good. It is vital for this enterprise that you charm the queen, and I have only days to teach you what the families of courtiers spend years drumming into their children's heads." Ware paced away. "His Grace is demanding the impossible of me. But when has he ever done anything different?"

Seeking some brief respite from frustration, Ware delivered me to the man charged with fashioning the costume I was to wear when I was presented to the queen. I gave myself over to a new torment.

My ears rang from the blows of hammer on iron as the armorer fitted the helmet and breastplate. Once the smith released me from the hot forge, the torture grew even grimmer. Tailors trussed me up in whalebone-stiffened doublets and boots that chafed. When they finished, Ware greeted me with a lump of cream-colored doeskin with sausage-shaped swells front and back and straps and buckles that hung about the middle. "It is a gift from the duke," he said just as I noticed the child-size stirrups. "The king and queen spend hours upon horseback when hunting. You will have to ride with them."

"It is a lovely saddle," I said. "But I prefer my own feet."

"On a horse, you will be swift as other men," Ware said.

"I'm sure it will be gratifying for the handful of minutes before the beast tramples me to death."

Ware almost smiled. "This is no ordinary saddle. Place your hand here." He indicated what I assumed must be the front of the saddle. The doeskin had been pleated into diamond shapes fastened with metal studs. I did as he told me.

"There is a slit where you will be able to conceal messages. Can you find it?"

I felt wadded wool padding, then wiggled my fingers and was surprised when they slipped into a natural hollow formed by the saddle frame.

"Even if you are searched, it is unlikely anyone would think to dismantle your saddle. I had the slit placed in front, so that if anyone notices you fiddling about there, they will believe you are adjusting your prick."

The idea of riding a horse was terrifying enough. But to fumble with a missive that might condemn me while the animal was prancing around was unthinkable. "What if I drop the message?"

"If you are fortunate, I will kill you quickly. A necessity to spare you torture and to keep you from betraying His Grace. If I do not reach you first, you will suffer the rack and a traitor's death. I suggest that you practice concealing the messages so neither of those possibilities come to pass."

I nodded, my throat dry.

He escorted me to the duke's stable yard and left me in the charge of the riding master who instructed His Grace's children. A groom cinched the new saddle upon a horse whose nostrils looked like wet flame. The fellow plopped me astride the animal and strapped my legs into place with leather bands.

"Cling to the beast with your knees," the riding master ordered. But how was I to accomplish this with my legs sticking straight out on either side like fire pokers?

Riding was difficult enough. But when I tried to get off of that mountain of equine muscle, only a groom stood between me and a horse eager to take vengeance for times my riding master had insisted I apply the crop. On my fifth day of lessons, I dragged my leg across the horse's back, depending on the groom to catch me beneath the armpits to slow my drop to the ground. But just as I slid past the point of no return, the steadying hands vanished, and I was falling into a maze of stamping hooves.

I struck the ground so hard, I couldn't breathe as I tried to scramble out from under the horse.

I heard an angry shout. "You fool! Help him!"

The groom grabbed the tail of my coat, flinging me out of the way. I skidded across the ground, then crashed into a waterfall of pink. It took me a moment to realize that I'd collided with a woman's skirts. I arched my head back, the world still seeming to spin around me.

"I ordered you to teach him to ride, not to kill him!" Buckingham's voice roared. "If you have marred his face, I will take a whip to you myself!"

The groom babbled apologies, but I heard gentler tones above me. "Are you hurt, child?"

I did not have to correct the woman before me. Buckingham broke in, a trifle impatient.

"That is no child, Kate. It is the creature I told you about."

I had caught glimpses of Catherine Villiers's coach on occasion, but I had never seen her up close. Her crimson riding hat seemed to have sucked some of the richness from her brown hair. The features framed between shoulder-length curls were pretty enough. But everything around her—from the palatial stable to the husband at her side—conspired to overpower her.

The duchess tucked her gloved hand into the crook of Buckingham's arm, then nodded. "You are John Hudson's son. Your father's dogs have provided my husband with hours of sport. I am grateful for whatever gives His Grace rest from burdens of state." She looked at Buckingham, love naked on her face. I thought of the masked woman I had encountered in the duke's privy chamber—her sly smile, her dimpled cheek, her hand on this woman's husband.

"As you see, Jeffrey, my wife is concerned with my happiness rather than her own." Buckingham patted his duchess's hand, then scrutinized me. "This groom has not damaged you, Jeffrey. No bruise is going to mar your face."

It was not a question, as if he could order wounds to vanish. Parts of my body felt bludgeoned, but they would be hidden beneath my costume. I squared my shoulders. "I am fine, Your Grace."

"In your appearance, perhaps. I am less confident regarding your manners. We leave for London day after tomorrow. I have gone to a great deal of expense to launch you properly, and I begin to fear my coin wasted. You have not applied yourself as diligently as I had hoped. It would be difficult for you to repay me, should you fail. You cannot afford the price of one goblet. The cost of an entire royal banquet would be beyond your imagination."

"He will not be able to mind his lessons if you keep pricking at him," the duchess chided.

"Do you believe I am 'pricking' at you, Jeffrey? Or am I in earnest?"

"A little of both, I think."

"Exactly. Unlike my wife, I was not born to wealth. My mother struggled to give me a gentleman's education after my father's death. I brought all my efforts to bear on those lessons. You must do the same. Look at what I gained—a dukedom—title once given only to princes of royal blood. I rule over vast lands and have the best wife in England." He cut her the same kind of glance the butchers gave a prime haunch of beef. I felt sorry for Buckingham's Kate, having a husband far more beautiful than she could ever be. *A fortune is a great beautifier for an ambitious man,* the wizard's daughter from the privy chamber whispered in my head.

What woman would ever love me with such devotion? I wondered as Buckingham led his wife away. I had watched John dance at the fair with girls, their breasts bobbing against the front of their dresses. I had dreamed of mapping the shape of them with my hand. But John was strong and tall. Girls looked at him in ways they would never look at me.

I had only my strange size and a face some claimed looked like an angel's. I decided I must make the best of my assets, as the duke had done.

When I returned to the quarters I shared with the other servants that night, my bruises showed in patches. Clemmy insisted on sharing some salve his mother had sent for him. "Not easy, hauling heavy trays of food about the Great Hall. The other lads made the job even harder, taunting me about these ugly scales upon my chin. My muscles ached so much that first month here, I'd cry when no one was looking. Now, whenever His Grace needs a kitchen page to serve at one of his fancy meetings, who does the steward send but Clemmy Watson? Don't know what would have happened without my mam's salve." He held the clay pot out to me. I smeared the foul-smelling stuff over my bruises in hopes that he would stop harping.

Instead, he filled my ears with tales of the wonders we would see in the city. "There is no place like London when it comes to putting on shows, be it in the theaters or the Tower's menagerie, Southwark's bear pits or horses racing near St. James's Park."

Suddenly, Clemmy's brow darkened. Perhaps he thought once we reached the city it would be too dangerous to be friends with someone labeled "devil spawn." His kindness to me in my patron's own household had already caused gossip among his fellow servants.

"I will not have time for such excursions," I said, surprised by my regret. "Besides, you have risked enough ill will on my account."

Clemmy seemed to shake himself inwardly. "I was not thinking of those superstitious fools. The mention of St. James's brought back memories I wish to forget."

If Samuel had been in my place, he would have fallen silent to avoid jarring a wound. John would have changed the subject. I hesitated, aware that my place in Buckingham's employ depended upon coaxing the queen to reveal incidents that pained her. Would it not be wise to test my skill?

"I am told London is full of dangers. Your expression when you spoke of your memory has made me more nervous than ever." I saw Clemmy flush, the patch of scaly skin on his chin white. "I would not want you to recount something unpleasant," I said soothingly. "I only wish I did not have so vivid an imagination."

"No harm easing the mind of a friend," Clemmy said. "Not like I had any part in it, except seeing something I wish I could scrub out of my head." I felt both triumph and shame as Clemmy spoke.

"I'd just finished serving the sea captains Master Ware had brought to speak to His Grace. See, my grandda had sailed with Raleigh, and the captains were all agog to hear the tales Grandda passed on. Ware was so pleased with me that he gave me the rest of the day off. Met an old friend wandering near St. James's Park and he took me to see two Jesuit spies executed at Tyburn Tree. Suppose I should not have been so surprised the prisoners showed such nerve when the executioner put the knives to their bellies. The Pope's minions are trained by people who want to bring the Inquisition to England. My friend cheered with the rest of the crowd, raging that Jesuits plotted with other Catholics, wanting to make good Guy Fawkes's plan to blow up Parliament and old King James. Said loyal Englishmen had to keep such deviltry at bay. The priests were getting the punishment they earned, but it didn't sit well with my stomach to watch it. Broke down, I did, and begged the executioner to put an end to them quick."

"Not wishing a fellow creature to suffer cannot be such a bad thing."

"You don't know how dangerous it is to sympathize with Jesuits in the city. Lots of Puritans there. The crowd got mad as snakes at me for trying to cut their fun short. Don't like having the Roman faith rubbed in their faces."

I could never understand why so many Catholics seemed eager to do just that. Why not be reasonable, as my family was? Like most country folk, we leaned toward the old ways, but we did as the law commanded and filled an Anglican pew every Sunday. Even Samuel, the only devout one among us, agreed it did not matter if you sat through the Anglican service as long as you were loyal to the true faith in your heart.

"Only a fool would think arguments about the sacraments were worth risking beggary or imprisonment or the death those priests were dealt," I said.

"Still have nightmares about those Jesuits choking down their silent screams." Clemmy shuddered. "Guess you'll think me weak for hating blood-letting, you being raised around your father's trade."

"I didn't like bloodletting between dogs and bulls," I said, made smaller by his admission and my part in extracting it. "My older brother, John, never minded, but Samuel . . ." Clemmy's talk of Jesuits made me think of Samuel's medal and what the angry crowd at Tyburn might do to the boy who had sewn it there. "My brother Samuel has a tender heart," I said, finishing my sentence.

"Guess we think alike, Jeffrey Hudson."

I slipped under the covers, surprised that the bed Clemmy and I slept in no longer seemed strange. I had become accustomed to the bed and the man who shared it just in time to leave them.

⚜

Six years ago, John had boosted Samuel and me into a tree to watch the noble household of Burley-on-the-Hill stream out of the manor's gates. Heralds and gentlemen at arms forged the way, a small army to guard the riches highwaymen would covet. Great lords rode glossy horses beneath fluttering pennons. Coaches carrying the noble ladies rumbled past, running footmen striding ahead of them. In the rear, two-wheeled carts labored beneath all the goods needed to set up household in grand estate. Servants were stuffed among the furniture in much the same way, choking on the dust raised by their betters.

It seemed impossible that I was to be part of that procession on the pink-tinged May morning Ware hoisted me into one of the first carts. "I cannot let you go bouncing into the road to be trampled after the trouble I've taken to train you." Ware almost smiled as he settled me into a nook he had formed out of trunks.

By the time the cart jolted down the hill, I had squeezed myself in as securely as I was able. I peered over the cart's edge, watching everything I'd known melt into the distance.

Upon arriving at the manor, I had memorized every wonder I saw so that I could describe them to Samuel next time I saw him. But as the carts wound through the village of Stamford and onto the Great North Road, I could not imagine when I would see my brother again.

Loneliness knotted in my belly, despite the people who filled the road as far as I could see. But by the time we crested the hill and rumbled into the village of Hampstead three days later, even loneliness for Samuel could not hobble my curiosity. A forest of windmills spun over our heads. Buildings sprawled in the distance, stitched together with a web of roads.

More steeples than I could count pierced smoke from chimneys that honeycombed the sky. Clemmy climbed into my cart, daring his master's anger. "That's Westminster and the City." He fairly quivered in his eagerness to point out the Tower of London's stout yellow walls.

St. Paul's was next, floating like an ark in God's great flood. Small houses scrabbled like drowning sinners against the cathedral's walls.

"Isn't just worshipping goes on there," Clemmy said as we wound down the hill. "Place of business, it is. Bell ringers will let you climb to the top of the steeple if you've got the coin. They keep pebbles up there that people can throw at folk below. See that black snake coiling through the city? That's the Thames. Ships sail in from places where oliphants and pygmies and dragons eat folk like us as if we were mutton."

All too soon, the crushing traffic of the city surrounded us, its noise louder than the rattle of the duke's carts. I could not suppress a shudder as I imagined what would happen if I tumbled into that chaos. Most of my life,

I had avoided being trampled in crowds by riding on someone's shoulders—my father's or John's. When I turned twelve, I devised a way to clear my own path by whittling the end of my blackthorn walking stick to a point and jabbing the ankles of anyone who traipsed too close. Samuel had laughed when children warned that "the Fairy King bites." But even my sharpened stick would not protect me in London's vast crowd.

When we stopped at a water gate, the important members of the duke's party boarded a fleet of barges to finish the trip down the Thames, abandoning lesser servants to a city whose jaws seemed ready to grind flesh from bone. I almost wept with relief when Ware herded me onto one of the boats.

Oarsmen in Buckingham livery set to rowing, and I fought to keep my balance as the oak hull began to sway. When I dared look up again, I marveled as the filth and furor of the city thinned, huge gardens rolling from the shore to the grand houses lining the Strand. It was hard to believe that I would belong to these palaces, people.

I strained to look at Buckingham's family in the barge some ways ahead of mine. Beneath a canopy embroidered with falcons, the duke's mother, the countess of Buckingham, peered out with avaricious eyes. I remembered something Clemmy had said.

Beware around that one, friend. After old Queen Anne died, the countess shoved herself into her place, as the mother of the king's dearest "friend." She had been strutting through the court as if she were consort to King James, having her way in everything until the new queen arrived. Sure she figured a little French chit would march to her drumming like everyone else, but the princess has more spine than that. Not one to like being sent down a step, the countess. When James gave her a title, she made sure he did not raise her husband to earl alongside her. Might as well have nipped off his pizzle and dressed him in a petticoat.

The countess looked just the kind of woman who enjoyed cutting men to size. Proud and frightening, she sat rigidly on the edge of her bench. Buckingham's wife perched beside her like a songbird assured the hawk would not eat her—yet. The duchess's gaze was solemn, except when she looked at her husband. Then her cheeks warmed. I wondered about the masked lady who had scorned her. Buckingham's wife would cut herself on that woman's sharp edges.

We had barely docked at the water gate when Ware hastened me through a small door in the walled courtyard. If Burley had been glorious, York House was like tumbling into Heaven.

The Great Hall was full of workmen preparing for the celebration to come. A huge dais where the queen would sit was being decked in cloth of gold. A vast canvas cloth was painted the blue of a sun-washed sky. Workmen gathered drifts of muslin into billowy clouds, hammering them into place upon what seemed to be wagon beds attached to ropes and pulleys.

"Is this where I will perform?" I surveyed the setting with unease. How could I possibly speak loudly enough to fill such a space?

"No. The duke and his guests will dine on the main courses here, then repair upstairs to the banqueting hall, where sweet stuffs will be served— along with you. When the old king reigned, the guests would have been too bent on debauchery to care about your performance. But King Charles is fastidious regarding his manners and expects his courtiers to be the same." Ware chuckled.

"What amuses you?" I asked, risking being called impertinent.

"I was only thinking how foreign dignitaries wrangle for invitations to Buckingham's banquets. It is a shame battles and negotiations cannot be held amid floating clouds and coffin pies, or Buckingham would be the greatest statesman of our age."

We walked deeper into the building. My steps slowed as I stared at paintings lining the walls. "That angel's limbs seem to move," I whispered.

"Not even the king has a finer collection of art than His Grace," Ware said. "You're not to wander about to gape at it. You go nowhere except in my company, now we are in London."

Under different circumstances, I might have liked staying out of the confusion, but the fact that Ware had ordered me to do so made me chafe. "Why should I not look about if I choose?"

"His Grace does not wish anyone to see you before your unveiling. It would spoil the surprise for the queen. I will fetch you to the palace kitchens in an hour. The master cook will be awaiting you in the Pastry House." Ware's mouth tipped up at one corner. "It is time to measure you for your coffin."

THREE

•

I had never imagined people could eat gold. I had only seen the precious metal rarely, decking the few wealthy folk who crossed my path. But when Uriel Ware marched me into the Pastry House of Buckingham's London Palace, the master cook was applying gilt to the crust of the pie I was to inhabit that evening.

Fluted pastry edges caught sparks of light, making the trestle table appear battle-scarred in contrast to the edible wonders being constructed everywhere I looked. As Ware herded me toward the table, I wondered if the workers would notice if I broke off a flake of golden crust to taste it. The master cook wiped his sweaty brow.

"This is the dwarf who is to fill up your crust," Ware said.

The cook gave me that slack-jawed look I had seen my whole life. I glanced at the crust warily. "Do you think I will fit?"

The master cook surprised me with a chuckle. "I've not built it with your comfort in mind. The tight fit is part of the illusion. We don't want anyone to guess there is a little man beneath the crust. Not that anyone would. I rolled out the crust myself and I can hardly believe it."

"How long will that take? From the time I am closed in?"

"You have a long wait. We'll nest you in here, then fasten the top crust tight and finish decorating it. Once all is dry, you'll be carried from the kitchens to the Great Hall, then wait until the great ones are ready."

"You are in service to nobles now," Ware said. "You will spend the rest of your life waiting and be expected to thank them for it. Now, your hair must be dressed, the last touches put on your costume, and we will take one more chance with the goblets before His Grace sets you before the queen. Then someone else will have charge of you." Ware glanced at the cook. "Perhaps if he vexes Her Majesty, she may feed him to Will Evans."

"Who is Will Evans?" I asked.

"The queen's pet giant. What do you think, cook? Would Hudson even make Evans a mouthful?"

"Tiny birds are the most succulent," the cook said.

I thought of tales John had used to scare Samuel. Perhaps this giant had jagged teeth and bloody claws. Perhaps Ware and the cook were behaving like asses.

"I do not think His Grace has gone to all this trouble so I could be someone's dinner."

Ware sneered. "Then he should have presented you in something other than a pie."

᠅᠅

Ware had just left me at the back stairs, so he could go make his own toilette before the banquet, when I heard a familiar voice. "Jeffrey!" Clemmy gasped, rushing toward me. "I feared I would not catch you before you got too big to talk to me."

I saw him wince as he realized what he'd said. "Too great in *station,*" he explained. "For what would the brightest star of Buckingham's banquet have to do with a kitchen page like me?" He hitched up his hose, which always sagged. I should have reassured him, but I was too much on edge.

"I have been in the Great Hall these past hours, practicing floating down from the heavens." He grinned. "It is a dangerous business to balance trays of food while those cloud platforms are lowered to the ground. Twice the gears have gotten stuck and jerked to a stop so rough, I nearly dropped a tray on Uriel Ware's head. You should have seen him jump!"

I pictured the clattering tray, the dour face startled. "Too bad your tray missed," I said.

Clemmy smiled, his broken tooth catching the light. "You'd not be wanting me to lose my position," he said. "Especially since I might be of use to you. My master has a soft spot for my older sister, so he lets me go back to Burley on errands now and then. I might carry word to your home folks if ever you wanted me to. It's hard to be far away from your own hearth—even if it is crowded."

I felt a strange ache at his kindness.

I heard someone shout Clemmy's name. Clemmy glanced over his shoulder. "I had best get along. Have my own duties to attend to, though not as grand as yours. By the time the banquet is over, you'll be able to bite your thumb at Ware. We'll steal away and toast to it tomorrow morning."

If all went as planned, I would not be at York House come morning. I would be a spy in the queen's court—or else a failure, bracing for Buckingham's wrath.

He loped off.

"Clemmy!" I cried.

He stopped, turned.

"I was born the same size as other babes, but my mother ate a surfeit of pickled gherkins," I said solemnly. "The midwife says that is why I did not grow."

Clemmy's eyes went wide. "Gherkins. Who would guess they could cause such mischief?"

I had not believed anything could make the Pastry House more uncomfortable for me, but when I left the twilight-cooled garden for kitchens crazed with preparations, I felt as if I wanted to jump from my own skin. Heat from the ovens blasted my breastplate, making the metal hot to the touch. Every servant rushing about heightened my anxiety. If they feared the consequences of oysters not stewed to the great ones' liking, how much more calamitous it would be if I should fail to delight?

I glanced at Ware, tempted to ask him to count off the steps of my performance one last time, but the master cook snared his attention, grim.

"One of the queen's underservants came down to scrump a saffron cake. Said that the queen is scratching like a cat, not wanting to attend the banquet."

Ware gave a snort of disgust. "Those French she-snakes encourage rebellion. Look what happened during the king's coronation. The queen wouldn't even set foot in a Protestant church. Buckingham had to drag the woman through the rain and force her to stand at the window so the people could see her."

The master cook wiped his hands on his apron. "Could you not convince His Grace to save Jeffrey for a more auspicious night?"

"His Grace has spent a fortune on this banquet. Besides, I have better things to do than drill dance steps. Once tonight is over, His Grace will let me get back to matters worthy of my attention."

"We're all wondering why he called you back from wherever you go about the duke's business. Folks say you convinced His Grace to invest in a voyage that did not end well, so he set you to herding about this dwarf to punish you."

I saw a tiny tick at the corner of Ware's mouth. "The duke disposes of his servants as he chooses. It is not our role to question."

The cook wiped his nose with the back of his hand. "I applaud Buckingham's desire to scoop up the riches the New World offers. Every Englishman born would swell up with pride if cinnamon and sugar arrived aboard English ships. But the French and Spanish hold the Spice Islands in mighty fists. You'd know that if you'd ever sailed yourself."

"I have sailed enough to know that even the mightiest of fists can be broken if the right pressure is applied. The Inquisition has proven that. Now, let us apply ourselves to concluding this night's business."

The cook led Ware to where a piecrust was cooling in two separate pieces, the bottom crust upon a silver tray. The master cook signaled and two of his underlings lifted me above the bottom crust

My feet instinctively searched for purchase. "Do not move under your own power!" the cook snapped. "Go limp so we can fold you up tight." Hands began to wedge my limbs into positions that made them ache. When I grunted protest, the cook ignored me. "I do not care how you force his leg to fit. It must seem impossible that this dwarf emerged from such a tiny space."

My breastplate gouged my armpit and my teeth all but embedded in my knee. I could taste silk and hoped my spittle would not leave a blotch on my blue hose. When I could not be wedged any tighter, the Cook jammed in the red-and-gilt-striped pole on which pennons were strung, the man forcing it between my legs and the curve of my arms like a bodkin.

"You must not spring out until the perfect moment or the effect will be spoiled," Ware warned. "Burst from the crust with these pennons waving and march up and down the table."

With apprentices tucking fabric around my legs, I was more likely to stumble around like a prisoner in shackles. "My foot is going numb," I said, my hands slickening with sweat where they gripped the wooden pole. "Could I—"

Ware ignored me, continuing his lecture. "Every courtier in the chamber will have learned French, or be too ashamed to admit the lack of it. Conversing around Her Majesty is done in her native language. Anything in English is translated by those near her. Tonight, Buckingham has enlisted the countess of Carlisle's toady, Sir Tobie Mathews, for the task. He is so adept at it, one barely notices it anymore."

"But I speak French."

"The king would prefer the queen cease this childish stubbornness and apply herself to learning the language of the subjects she rules. Once you join the queen's household, you may gabble in French as much as you like, but here at York House we will honor the king's wishes."

"Seal the coffin lid, boys," the master cook commanded.

Two underlings scrambled to do so. I watched, helpless as the crust blotted out the smoke-blackened ceiling, the stone walls, then all the world. It forced all the air from the tiny space allowed me, entombing me in darkness.

The pennon tickled my nose, and I struggled not to sneeze. If I did, would the pastry above me crack?

Muffled sounds crept through slits in the crust and the surface beneath me heaved. They were carrying the tray my pie was perched on, but making a bad job of it. The slight lurching, the darkness, and the strange closed-up smell of my prison made the wine I'd managed to swallow earlier slosh in my stomach.

Had they mounted the platform yet? The machinery had been laboring all night under heavy loads of food and people. Were the lads manning the ropes and pulleys exhausted from the weight? I heard a sizzle and crackle of fireworks bursting and I stiffened as gears made grinding sounds. I felt a sudden weightless sensation of being lowered.

I forced my mind away from the picture of my brains dashed on the marble and turned my thoughts to what would happen if—no, *when*—I reached the floor. The sounds of a crowd grew louder; then I felt the rocking sensation of being carried again. My bearers must have moved into the hall, for I could pick out Buckingham's voice among the others. I strained to listen but could only catch snippets of the duke's French and the higher-pitched translations of the man whom Ware had told me about.

". . . be so bold as to beg the queen's help with . . . symbol of our regard for her . . . by presenting her with . . ."

"A knife?" I heard a woman exclaim in French. A blur of affronted voices, also French, rose. My left foot began to quiver.

"That peacock would have the daughter of Henri the Fourth do a servant's task?" The second Frenchwoman's outraged muttering was close enough for me to pick out. "Henrietta Maria should fling the thing in Buckingham's face!"

Did she think the duke was so intent on the queen's reaction that he would not hear her insult? Or did she see him as such a lowborn upstart she did not care if he did? What kind of woman would dare abuse the most powerful courtier in England in front of the king himself? I cringed to think of Buckingham's reaction. But if the queen did fling the knife, I hoped she would take the outraged lady's suggestion of target and not fling the blade into the pie.

"Madame Saint-Georges, Her Majesty is far too gracious to hurl things at a humble courtier who only wishes to please her," Buckingham said in effortless French.

I wondered at Buckingham's arrogance, not only letting the queen's courtier know he had heard her spiteful comment but announcing it to the entire company, as well.

A haughty stranger intruded with a bit of a stammer, which made his French sound clumsier. "His Grace is my most loyal and generous subject. As the queen would know if a wise councillor could silence those forever criticizing His Grace in her presence."

Madame Saint-Georges hastened to speak, her voice young in spite of its hauteur. "Your Majesty, I was saying only that it is demeaning for a queen to carry out a servant's task."

"The queen is the only one who can judge that," Buckingham said. "I fling myself upon her mercy. Your Majesty," he said, addressing the queen, his tone almost cozening. "Will you indulge me?" I held my breath, waiting for the blare of horns. It did not come.

The platter beneath me shifted again, then thudded and went still. I braced myself for just a heartbeat before I heard it—a fanfare.

I thrust my fist through the crust and launched myself upward, bursting through the pastry. A chorus of gasps erupted as I yanked my pennon upright and leapt onto the table, blinking gilt from my lashes. I waited for my vision to clear after the darkness of the pie, not wanting to knock over some serving piece or spill upon the queen. Yet Ware had stressed it was vital that I snare the queen's attention.

As the last crumbs dropped from my face, I found myself staring into the face of the queen. Every detail burned into my memory with a clarity created by awe and fear. This dark-haired woman was the queen I was to spy upon. My future depended on learning every nuance of expression so I could wring out her secrets and spill them into Buckingham's hands.

Could any emotion ever remain hidden in the queen's face? She stared as if she expected me to whir like a clockwork marvel instead of draw breath. Her dark almond-shaped eyes were red from earlier tears, a wistfulness about her that I had not expected to find in a queen.

I felt a twinge of sympathy but fought it by bounding over the edge of the crust. I landed—blessedly—between the saltcellar and her gold-trimmed goblet. My boots, embroidered with dragons, fought for a hold on the linens, the staff that held my pennon aiding my balance as the satin flag unfurled over my head. Feeling jolted back into my foot, but I did not let the queen see the needlelike sensation sewing its way up my calf.

She laughed in surprise and delight, clapping more like a girl pretending to be a queen than the daughter of royalty and a king's wife.

"Greetings from the fairy realm, most gracious Majesty," I said in English, sweeping a bow so deep, I almost overset myself. "I have left my magical kingdom behind in quest of the most elusive prize any man mortal or fairy-born might win." I pasted on an impish grin as the toadlike man behind her began to translate between us so naturally that it astonished me. He was no more intrusive than an echo.

"What reward do you seek?" she asked.

"Grant me one of your smiles, Queen of my heart." I struck my breast-plate with my fist. "I shall wage any battle for it, fight any foe."

She tilted her head, listening to Sir Tobie. Her lips trembled. "I am in need of a champion." Henrietta Maria's gaze flicked to Buckingham. I saw the lady-in-waiting standing to her left level Buckingham a bitter glare.

Did the queen know what a formidable opponent she faced? The rubies crusting Buckingham's doublet sparked red. For an instant, I thought of hell's flames.

A melody swelled from the musician's gallery, my signal to perform. But fear had wiped the intricate melding of dance and battle from my memory. Panic rose until I discerned a pipe trilling among the other instruments. I imagined the reed clamped between Samuel's lips, his fingers flying along the pipe's length.

I thrust and feinted with my pennon stave, swirling the banner into shapes, leaping through the circle of color as if it were a hoop. The assem-blage cried out in amazement, the applause turning my feet into springs. Never had I leapt so high, my heavy breastplate now lighter than the muslin clouds. I glimpsed the duchess's worried face and Buckingham's mother's contemptuous sneer as I danced on.

At last I finished, sweeping down to one knee to pay homage. My breath came in gasps despite my effort to calm it. The silk shirt beneath my breast-plate was soaked with sweat, but the glow in my cheeks was pure triumph. If I had been at the market fair, pennies would have rained into my father's pocket.

The queen rose in a gown green as a meadow, starred with gems. She was small in stature, delicate. Her quick, grace-filled movements and eager gaze reminded me of a sparrow.

My gaze shifted to the man at her side. The queen's husband stood only a little taller than she did. I stared, unable to believe that I was an arm's length from the king. A most disappointing figure of a king. Garbed in sober black, Charles Stuart held himself apart, his shoulders stiff, his legs too thin. Ru-mor said he had not even learned to walk until he was four years old.

His dark hair was forced into curls that tried—and failed—to match the natural lushness of Buckingham's. Thin wisps of mustache and beard could not disguise a weak chin. His overlarge eyes were so aloof, they made me want to find a brazier to get warm.

I wondered if His Highness knew what anyone who saw him next to Buckingham was thinking: Buckingham looked like the king, and Charles, his servant.

"You have outdone yourself, Buckingham!" The king praised the duke with the eagerness of an awkward younger brother trying to please the heroic elder one he adored. "What a droll little man!"

"I would wager even the queen, with her renowned menagerie, has never seen my freak's equal."

"He is the most wondrous creature I have ever encountered," Her Majesty said, Sir Tobie's voice a murmur behind her. The queen reached toward me, then curled her fingers into her palm and let her hand fall to her side.

Buckingham laughed, addressing the assemblage in English. "Her Majesty looks at my freak as if he were honey cake and she wants to take a bite."

The queen flushed at Mathews's translation. "You overstep yourself, Your Grace."

"You always take Buckingham's jests too seriously!" the king said. "He has gone to great trouble to please you tonight."

"Yet, I have offended Her Majesty somehow." Buckingham appeared crestfallen. "I suppose there is a reason God fashioned women to be jealous of their dignity. How else can such frail vessels bring men to our knees? We husbands must chasten them for their tempers, even though they cannot help misbehaving. I vow I would go to any length to prove my goodwill to the queen."

It was the signal I was to listen for. "I know a way!" I burst out, then shrank back, appropriately appalled at my own boldness.

Buckingham gaped as if the golden deer decorating the saltcellar had spoken, the queen startled, yet leaning closer to Sir Tobie, eager for his translation.

"Your Grace, forgive me," I rushed on. "But I could suggest a gift you might offer the queen."

"I would grant Her Majesty anything in my power," Buckingham said with an ominous undertone, as if I would be punished for my impertinence.

"You think a dwarf knows how to please the queen better than a nobleman of the realm? By all means, enlighten my guests. What would you have me give the queen?"

"Me." I did not have to pretend I was fighting to master my nerves.

"You?" Buckingham echoed.

"To act in her masques and caper about and make jests. If Her Majesty would have me." I turned to the young queen, silently pleading that she would rescue me from Buckingham's patronage as Sir Tobie repeated my plea. I had not known I was such a fine actor. But perhaps my success didn't rest in my ability to perform. My fear of Buckingham was real.

"It is a fine idea if you are willing to part with your pet, Buckingham!" the king exclaimed. "I have never seen greater delight on the queen's face than when that dwarf leapt from the pie."

The duke hesitated a long moment, feigning reluctance. He cast his duchess an uncomfortable look, then turned to the queen. "Your Highness, I wish you would feel such joy always. Will you accept this little man as a token of my devotion?"

Her breath caught, her face reminding me of my sister when the whetstone lad had offered her a kitten.

"See how generous Buckingham is," the king cried. "Thank His Grace, wife."

The warmth in the queen's face cooled. "Your Majesty, please tell His Grace that this is a most welcome gift."

The king's lips compressed. "That is an unsatisfactory way to address our truest friend!"

I could feel anger building. Knowing I must reclaim their attention, I wiggled my stave to make the banner ripple. It brushed her skirts. I snatched it away, afraid I had gone too far. But the queen's gaze turned to me.

"Have you a name, little pet?" she asked in French, her accent as musical as the instruments that had bewitched me. I caught myself before I replied, waiting for Sir Tobie's translation.

"I was christened Jeffrey Hudson, Your Majesty," I replied.

"Jeffrey." She plucked my name out of the jumble of English even before the rest of the reply was transferred into French. She touched one of my curls, feather light. I imagined her in her chapel, running Ave beads through her fingers.

"You must take pains your new plaything is not trampled underfoot," the king said in French. "Put him in the care of your giant."

"Jeffrey could make his bed in Will Evans's shoe," Buckingham jested. "Let us hope Evans does not get jealous and put the shoe on with Jeffrey in it."

What could one so tall know of the fear he had touched in me? I had spent my whole life afraid of being crushed, had experienced enough near misses to guess what it would feel like. A trill of laughter from the crowd sounded surprisingly familiar, and the king turned toward the sound.

"It seems as if someone is amused by your quip, Buckingham," His Majesty said.

"The ever-witty countess of Carlisle, unless I miss my guess," Buckingham replied. "Pray come and share your jest with Their Majesties, Your Ladyship."

The duke beckoned and a stunning beauty in ice white swept toward us from another cluster of ladies, English I guessed, from the barely veiled distaste on the queen's face.

But neither that nor the sudden stiffening of the duchess of Buckingham's shoulders dampened the Englishwoman's amusement as she laid siege to the queen's bastion of French courtiers. I knew where I had seen the woman before. Masked at Burley-on-the- Hill.

She sank into a curtsy before the queen. "I was only musing that I shall be eager to see what happens when you place Jeffrey in the cage with your other pets, Your Majesty." The woman's French was flawless, just as Ware had claimed an English courtier's should be.

My parents had displayed me in the Fairy Cage, but only for show. Surely the queen did not keep her curiosities imprisoned all the time.

"Dogs will attack the runt in a litter," the courtier said in English as she fingered the silk of my pennon. "A cage might be the safest place for Jeffrey."

I bit my lip, only half aware of Sir Tobie's murmured translation. What other curiosities might the queen have in her collection? Dangerous ones? She would have to keep her "specimens" somewhere.

"I do not find your jest amusing, Your Ladyship." The queen's eyes sparked with temper.

"Forgive me. The jest is between Jeffrey and me. He was raised alongside his father's dogs, and when we first met, he smelled of the kennel." A dimple appeared at the corner of her knowing smile.

"Well, he will never be so lowly again! Jeffrey will have the finest of everything." The queen clasped her hands. "What fun it will be to order things up—tiny chairs and miniature tables!"

The duke laughed. "Even his chamber pot must be small, lest he fall in."

The royal party returned to their seats, taking me with them. While the duchess dealt with her sour-faced mother-in-law and guests picked bits off of spun-sugar castles, Buckingham and the queen discussed roles to cast me in: devil's imps and cherubs and pygmy kings. It was as if they were playing with a rag poppet.

I forced myself to swallow the bits Her Majesty fed me from her marrow-bone pie. When she saw my amazement, she struggled in halting English to explain its mysterious tastes. With the help of her more fluent ladies and the stout man behind her, she described layers of artichokes and dates, sweet potatoes and sea holly roots, and marrow sweetened with sugar. More courses followed—swans roasted, then dressed in their feathers; sea creatures the queen told me were called "porpoise" but which sailors once believed were mermaids; sturgeon, flaking off thin bones.

Horror at the waste filled me as the guests sent full platters back to the kitchen. If I'd been closer to home, I could have made a pouch of my pennon and smuggled delicacies to the shambles so my family could share my feast.

My eyelids grew heavy as the hours passed. My face ached from hardening it into a smile.

It was nearly three in the morning when the duke signaled another fanfare. Sincerity dripped from his face as he addressed the queen. "Majesty, I have one more tribute offer: a tableau in your honor."

Music poured forth, so exquisite, I was sure nothing human could make such sounds. Layered beneath, I heard the grinding of gears, the creak of ropes. How dare the fools interrupt the magic sound? Against the painted sky, the clouds shivered into motion, but this time I watched with the guests.

The clouds reached the floor and parted to reveal what looked to be statues frozen in different poses. Ermine swathed royal forms, crowns glinting on brows. Leopards and French lilies embroidered every scrap of cloth.

I could not guess who the figures were meant to be, but the queen gave a tiny cry. Her eyes grew bright with tears. "My father! My mother! So like life, they might speak."

As if by magic, the statues began to move—and I realized they were dancers made up to look the part. The other guests exclaimed over the spectacle in a mixture of French and English, Buckingham's words lost to them in the rising tide of music and voices.

"You were a babe when your father died, so you have never experienced the love between father and child. A bond I cherish, being a father myself." The duke smiled. "I look forward to the time when I share that role with my dearest friend and his kingdom."

Henrietta Maria blushed. "It is my fondest hope to provide an heir."

Buckingham's voice dropped lower still. "It is difficult to conceive when a husband is forbidden his wife's bed by priests who guard the door."

I saw the king's gaze darken, but he was looking at the queen, not the man who had spoken so bluntly.

Henrietta Maria evaded the king's glare, something in her expression reminding me of Ann when she was trying to avoid a bitter tonic. "Even a queen has no power to circumvent holy days. I do not forget that my greatest duty is to become mother of a prince."

"A very Protestant prince when he is born." Buckingham pressed his fingertips together. "A soul girded to wage war against Rome."

And France? The question hung in the air, unspoken.

"Since the age of Solomon, wars have come," Buckingham said. "Fate demands men choose sides. We must crush the enemy or be crushed ourselves."

I peered up at the trio around me—king and queen and duke. Where my breastplate had been so hot, I was suddenly chilled.

FOUR

.

F our in the morning . . ." I heard the king say. But even after the dancing stopped, rainbow doublets and gowned figures whirled before my eyes, chasing one another in my memory. From my seat upon the arm of the queen's chair, I watched as the duke and his duchess bade farewell to the king and queen.

I raised my gaze heavenward in thanks. My buttocks hurt, as if the griffin carved into the wood was gnawing its way to my bone. The breastplate had come askew, digging under my arm. I wondered how I would reach the buckles and leather strips that fastened it. Would I have to sleep in the thing? I remembered the king's suggestion for my bed and wondered if the armor would fit inside a giant's shoe.

"The lateness of the hour is testament to your skills as a host, Buckingham. It is time Her Majesty and I depart." The king stifled a yawn behind his delicate hand. I sensed he was a man not accustomed to reveling until dawn.

I watched as the duchess of Buckingham approached the queen, certain she did not please Henrietta Maria yet not certain why. "It is a long journey to reach your own beds, Your Majesties. Would you do us the honor of spending the night here?"

"No, we must not."

The duchess went still, and I saw the queen realize that her hasty refusal edged toward rudeness. Henrietta Maria glanced at the king.

Buckingham's smile did not reach his eyes. "Would our accommodations not be to your liking, Your Majesty? We have done all in our power to please you."

"You have pleased me too greatly, Your Grace." The queen attempted to salve the insult without surrendering her pride. "I cannot wait to fit Jeffrey alongside the rest of my menagerie, and speak to Master Jones about using Jeffrey in my new masque."

"That is an event all of court will look forward to," Buckingham said. "Perhaps Master Jones could find a role for my wife."

"I admire Your Majesty," the duchess said. "There is much you might teach me."

"The masque is cast already with my own ladies."

"*French* ladies," Buckingham said.

As if summoned, one of the French women swept up to the queen and curtsyed. "Your Majesty, you are looking pale. Are you getting one of your headaches?"

"I am, Mamie. You take such good care of me." The queen signaled for Sir Tobie to translate, then turned to me. "Jeffrey, Madame Saint-Georges is the daughter of Madame Montglat, my childhood governess. We were raised together as little girls at the Palace of Saint-Germain-en-Lae."

"I understand there were many children there." Buckingham switched effortlessly into French. "Some whose birth might be frowned on by the Church."

The queen's chin rose. "My father adored his children," she said. "We were lucky to be together—*all* of my brothers and sisters." The queen addressed her husband. "Your Majesty, I beg your leave to retire to Denmark House."

I could see the king hesitate, looking first at Buckingham, then the queen. But it was the duchess who smoothed the waters.

"Majesty, women are not like men, who are happiest galloping off to explore new places. We crave our own nests."

The king's expression changed to gratitude, her intervention sparing him from having to choose between Buckingham's will and the queen's. "You are a pearl without price, my lady. You must join the queen's household and give her the benefit of your wifely wisdom."

The French ladies' scowls turned thunderous, the queen appearing a heartbeat away from stamping her royal foot. The duchess pretended not to notice. "I would be honored to serve the queen when the time is amenable for us both."

Buckingham glared, but she continued. "I must remain in my own nest at present, and tend my children. Moll has her father's charm, and I fear her nurse allows her more freedom than is good for her."

"Why should she not have it?" Affection warmed the king's eyes. "I have never encountered a more winning little sprite."

"She is all too aware that Your Majesty is fond of her. She told poor Madam Linley that you would chain the woman in the Tower dungeon before tonight was done."

"For what infraction?"

"Not allowing Moll to wear the gown you gave her."

"A reasonable-enough request."

"The child wanted to wear it to bed."

The king chuckled.

"Will you indulge an old friend, Your Majesty, and allow me to stay with my children until a more favorable time?"

"It shall be as you wish." The king kissed the duchess's hand.

I could feel the queen's resentment burn hotter. "Madame Saint-Georges," Her Majesty ordered, "tell Griggory to alert my bargemen. I need them to ferry me to Denmark House."

I could tell neither Frenchwoman was grateful for the duchess of Buckingham's interference. In a swirl of satin, Madame Saint-Georges crossed to a footman who was staring at me so hard, he did not hear her call. When she snapped her second command, he stumbled toward the door, glaring as if it were my fault she had caught him off guard.

The rest of the queen's party prepared to depart. Velvet capes, plumed hats, and soft hoods appeared as if by magic. I thought of the trunk Uriel Ware had provided for my trip to London. Would anyone remember to send it with me? The queen had been eager to dress me. Would she want to shed all evidence I had once belonged to Buckingham?

I glimpsed Uriel Ware standing some distance from the throng. His hands were clasped behind his back, as if to make certain no one could guess what he was feeling. I could not wait to be free of the man. Yet, if I inquired after my trunk, I could compel him to admit I had done well in my performance.

I wound through the crowd to where he stood. "The hero of the pie,"

Ware said. "From the crowd's reaction, one would think you decimated the whole French army single-handedly."

"The queen seems pleased."

"She will spend a fortune on you, money the treasury can ill afford. But the king will wrench it out of his subject's hands by any means he can."

I wanted to charge Ware with disloyalty to the Crown, but folk in Oakham also complained that the royals squeezed poor men's purses to fund their excess. I had not realized how true it was until I had come to serve Buckingham.

"Did you enjoy the tableau of the queen's family?" Ware asked. "Note they did not show the part where her brother the king cast her mother, Marie de Medici, out of her post as regent and watched from the window while his guards murdered her Italian adviser. Nothing like sending one's mother fleeing for her life to liven up a tranquil family scene."

I thought of the queen's impassioned response to the tableau. Her father had been murdered, her mother ousted from power in a bloody coup. Twice her world had crumbled beneath her feet. Now, if Buckingham had his way, it would crumble again.

"Did you have some purpose in seeking me out, or did you just wish to gloat over your triumph?"

"I wish you to send my trunk to the palace," I said.

"I cannot imagine that you will need it. But delivering it will give me an excuse to visit you at Denmark House the first time."

"I thought you were anxious to be off messing about with ships."

Frustration sparked for a moment in Ware's eye before he shuttered it away. "I am as eager to get away from court as you are to be rid of me. It seems we must tolerate each other a while longer. You will be gratified to learn we have become good friends, Jeffrey. The duke is so pleased with our combined efforts that I am to visit you when business brings me to London."

My dislike must have shown on my face. Ware's lip curled. "I am no happier about this arrangement than you are. But I suggest you learn to hide your reactions now you are at court; otherwise, you might as well bare your throat to wolves. Speaking of such, Madame Saint-Georges seems to be searching for you. Weave around a bit so she cannot trace you to me."

I darted in a roundabout way to the queen's party. We spilled out into the night, halberd-wielding guards before us and behind as we made our way by torchlight through Buckingham's famous gardens to York House's water gate. The scent of flowers gave way to the smell of fish and sewage from the river lapping against the landing. I could feel the city, menacing as the lions carved in the water gate's stone. Streets and waterways would be deserted by honest folk. Only those bent on mischief would still be marauding under cover of darkness.

"I wish to be alone," the queen said. "Only Madame Saint-Georges shall attend me." I was certain Henrietta Maria meant to exclude me, as well. I watched the footman called Griggory assist her descent into the ornate royal barge, Madame Saint-Georges managing the royal skirts.

The drop to the step proved more challenging for me. With legs aching from being crammed in the pie, I clambered onto the boat's deck, fighting to keep my balance. Cold wind skimmed off of the river. No one had thought to provide me with a cloak for this trip. I hoped Denmark House was not far, or I would be miserable by the time we reached it.

I clunked into the side of the boat. The hollow sound drew the queen's attention.

"Why does Jeffrey have no cloak?" the queen inquired of her attendant. "Ask him."

The woman repeated her question in stilted English.

I thought of answering in French but was too tired to go into some lengthy explanation. Instead, I replied in kind. "I did not dare ask permission to fetch a wrap,"

The queen touched my cheek. Even through her gloves, her hand felt warm. "Griggory, give Jeffrey your cloak at once."

The footman's fingers tightened on the folds at his throat, as if he wanted to refuse. But in the end, he stripped off the heavy garment and flung it around me. It swallowed me up, pooling on the ground, as if I were a tall man whose legs had melted. I did not show how much more comfortable it made me. If I continued to behave as if I were cold, the queen might invite me into that private circle she and Saint-Georges would share near the brazier meant to warm Her Majesty's feet.

I must have looked forlorn. I certainly felt so. The queen beckoned me as she moved to her throne in the vessel, Saint-Georges at her side.

"Majesty, do you think it would be wiser to send the little man to the front of the boat with the others?"

"He looks so exhausted, he will be asleep before we are three boat lengths beyond Buckingham's wharf. Let him be, Mamie."

The queen patted one of the damask cushions strewn around her. I hauled myself onto the slippery mound. With one last, wary look, Mamie Saint-Georges settled in next to us, the footmen shooing everyone else to the prow of the barge, as if closing a door behind us.

Link boys wedged torches into iron holders to light our way and the bargemen cast off their lines, a drum beating rhythm as the oars dipped into the water.

Madame Saint-Georges spoke as soon as the other women were out of earshot, her French more biting than the wind. "What arrogance for Buckingham to thrust his wife at you that way!" Madame Saint-Georges huffed, no doubt certain I could not understand. "His Majesty was no better—instructing *her* to teach *you* how to be a good wife?"

I expected temper from the queen, but she grew pensive. "I fear Buckingham is right. I am not very good at being a wife."

"The duke is hardly qualified to advise you! That scoundrel abducted Catherine Manners after her father refused to consent to his beloved daughter marrying such a fortune hunter. Then, after Buckingham had ruined her reputation, he forced her father to *beg* him to marry the little idiot. Imagine! One of the greatest heiresses in England being handed over to such a man!"

"Yet the duchess adores her husband."

"She deserves what she gets. Buckingham dallies with any woman who can gain him power or wealth or merely diversion. They say the duke is hand in glove with that sly witch Lucy Hay and the earl of Carlisle encourages his wife in the affair so he can benefit from Buckingham's power."

"It is easy to see how the countess of Carlisle fascinates men," the queen said. "I am sure she does not flinch from the unpleasantness of the marriage bed, no matter how embarrassing and painful and clumsy the act is. I heard so many great love tales and thought my bedding would be different. Perhaps if I learned from her, I might win the king's affection."

"All you would learn from her is harlot's ways! His Majesty *does* care for you. If Buckingham would stop interfering, the king would care even more! *Why* cannot some obliging assassin thrust a knife in him?"

"Mamie!" the queen exclaimed, hushing her. I thought she would remind Saint-Georges of my connection to the duke. But I might have had no more wit than the pillows they sat upon. "I cannot wish Buckingham harmed. The loss would devastate the king. Besides, I cannot bear talk of such violence after what happened to my father."

"Your life would be easier without the duke to plague you," Mamie insisted.

"His would be easier if he were rid of me. Rescuing those Huguenot nobles in New Rochelle like he craves would mean war with my brother, while Rome hopes to use French armies to force England back into the true faith. A French Catholic with an empty womb can serve neither side."

"My mother says anxiety keeps a woman's womb too bitter to feed a babe. If King Charles wants a son, he should make Buckingham and the others stop tormenting you. As for the English Catholics, you have done all in your power to ease their burdens. You've made Denmark House into a haven where they can come to Mass and confess. The chapel Inigo Jones is building there will be magnificent."

Sorrow knit the queen's brow. "How many of my subjects will be able to seek comfort there? A handful with enough wealth and power? What of the poor scattered to the corners of this island? Even those few who do use my chapel—what happens once they walk out of my door? The hatred and suspicion toward Catholics grows. I cannot tell you how many letters I receive from France demanding to know why I do not accomplish what I was sent here for."

"That fop Buckingham is no match for a daughter of France," Madame Saint-Georges said. "Be merry, chase roses back into your cheeks, laugh and dance. You will win the king in the end. No one can resist you when they see you thus."

"If I was without you and my menagerie, I would die of loneliness. I did not think my life would be like this. Not when Charles rode out to meet me, so eager that he could not wait for protocol. He seemed so delighted with me the first time we met that I thought . . . well, it hardly matters now. The king and I even argue as to whether or not it is raining." Henrietta Maria gave a sad little laugh. "Was I foolish to hope for love? My parents did not love. I cannot think of any royalty who found love with their husband or wife. But the first time I saw the king's picture, I felt as if he were locked behind that coldness everyone speaks of and I could release him."

Madame Saint-Georges gave her a hug that flew in the face of all the royal protocol Ware had drilled me in. But the queen accepted the caress with a sigh and leaned against her friend. Mamie kissed the top of her head. "Sweet Etta, you were always hungry for affection. In our *petit troupeau* at Saint-Germaine, you were everyone's favorite. It is no wonder you are lonely here. Just close your eyes and think of the flowers and sunshine and your brothers and sisters playing at hoodman-blind."

"Buckingham wanted me to be ashamed of them. He would have called them bastards and cast them out of the palace walls. His heart is too small, while my father's . . . I wish I had known him, Mamie. I have only the memories you and *le petit troupeau* shared with me. I begged for tales of him so often, they almost seem my own."

I leaned back so I could see the sadness that pooled with the shadows around the queen's mouth. I remembered the duke's warning that I must not be drawn in by the queen. "She has a certain charm," he had claimed. I braced my feet against the deck and pushed to put more space between us.

I watched as Madame Saint-Georges stroked the queen's hair. "Close your eyes, *mon ame*," Madame Saint-Georges murmured. "Tomorrow things will look bright again. We will play with the puppies in the garden and see what antics that dreadful monkey of yours gets up to. And we shall dress your new little man. Think what fun we shall have."

The rhythm of oars in water lulled me. The queen's voice drifted to my ears. "It is so cold here, Mamie," she said. "I begin to fear I will never get warm."

I shivered as wind gusted across the water again. Yet it was not the weather outside that chilled me, but the loneliness I felt within—that hollow place where someone's love might have warmed me.

FIVE

·

The ground was moving. I tried to lift my eyelids, but some wicked brownie had knotted my lashes together. Foreign fairies, it seemed, for I heard melodious French and a sonorous accent speaking a kind of English far from what I had heard in Oakham.

My body wedged against a craggy wall of wool, which made it impossible to move my legs or arms. I tossed my head, thumping against something metallic. The sting made my eyelashes come untied at last, torchlight splashing hell glow across the face of a monster. Slabs of granite formed cheekbones longer than my whole head. Brows jutted over eyes that seemed aflame from reflected torchlight. Ivory teeth gleamed in a bristly nest of beard. I would have screamed if I'd had enough room to suck air into my lungs.

"Easy, there, man," rumbled the deepest voice I had ever heard. "You'll hurt yourself thrashing about, and then what will I tell the queen?"

I craned my neck, glimpsing Her Majesty a little distance away, her flock of ladies adjusting her cloak as she started toward the palace. I wanted to escape the monster who imprisoned me, scramble over to the women, who were at least somewhat familiar, but one arm was trapped against my captor, the other so tangled in my wrappings, I gave a cry of frustration. "Let me go."

"I can't be doing that," the monster replied as we fell into step behind the royal party. "Her Majesty ordered me to carry you up to my rooms until the steward can make you a place of your own. Griggory is to valet you. My fingers are too clumsy to work fastenings tiny as the ones on your clothes."

"Who are you?"

One thatched eyebrow arched higher. "My mother would smack me with a broomstick if she knew I have forgotten the manners she taught me. William Evans, sergeant porter of the queen's back stairs at your service."

This was the giant I had been taunted about, until the "curiosity" loomed like a bogey in a child's night terror. I struggled to get a better look. His was as homely a countenance as I had ever seen. A prominent brow made his eyes seem buried in caves. His shovel of a nose must have collided with a door lintel and healed askew. Everything about Evans was forged on a scale to intimidate the most stalwart man. I felt like a nit he might crush just by flexing his hand.

"I was having a walk when I saw the queen's barge approaching," Evans said. "I came to see if I could lend a hand. Wasn't on duty, but no one at Denmark House is better at lifting and carrying things than Will Evans."

"You were taking a walk at this hour?"

"The world doesn't fit me, so my legs need stretching now and again. Good thing for you I was about. Griggory would have dropped you once you started to squawk. Man's scared of anything that's not common-looking as mud on a rainy Sunday."

The queen's party veered away from us, Her Majesty lifting a hand in farewell. Evans kept walking, and I noticed a hitch in rhythm that kept his stride from being graceful. I could scarce believe how his legs ate up the ground as we turned into what were obviously the servants' quarters.

A fortune in wax candles lit the way, whomever we met drawing a word from the giant. "How goes it with the new babe, Maude?" "Did the patch on your mam's roof hold, Donald?" It was as if Evans knew everyone. The smiles they gave back were real. Who was this man beyond a hulking form and harsh features? If I had been his size, no one would have dared to grope me or move me around as if I were a basket of carding wool. I imagined switching bodies with Evans. Grim satisfaction filled me at the thought that even Buckingham would be awed by my anger, though the nobleman would never show it. Would I even need to be seven feet six inches tall if Will Evans became my friend? Or would those who harassed me be cautious because they feared the giant would settle my debt?

When we reached a stairway, Evans shifted me onto his shoulder and pinned me with one arm as if I were a babe. He bent down, and I saw a thin girl hunched under the weight of two buckets of coal. Evans grabbed both handles with one platter-size hand, hefting the buckets as if they were filled with goose down. I could not see the maid's face, but I heard her, prickly with pride as she scurried along beside us. "I am strong enough to do it myself, Sergeant Evans."

"I'm capable of scraping up my arm while fetching my stockings when they roll under the cupboard. But every time I've lost one thus, it magically reappears, folded on my bed. You'd not know how that happens, would you, Becky?"

She grumbled a reply, but she did not protest as Evans hefted both the buckets and me up stairs that seemed to go on forever.

"What have you got in the cloak, Sergeant Evans?" the girl asked.

I braced myself to be shown, as if I were still in the Fairy Cage. Instead, I heard Evans's voice, kind but firm. "This bundle has nothing to do with you." He set the buckets down on the landing. "Now, run along and don't be listening to Riley's flattery. He's trouble for a good girl like you."

"Yes, Sergeant." She took up her burden and went off.

Evans's reticence puzzled me. People were usually eager to display me and impress whoever they encountered. "Why did you not tell her who I was?" I asked.

He shifted me so he could see my face. The eyes set in those bony caves of his were cornflower blue and kind. "A man doesn't like to be introduced to a lady unless he's standing on his own feet. Here we are, at my quarters." He opened a heavy wooden door and doubled over to pass through it.

He closed the door, then straightened and carried me to the stone fireplace. My legs nearly buckled when he stood me in front of its cheery warmth. "There now," he said, hunkering down so he could steady me. "I'd wager the queen danced you off of your feet. I'd be tipsy, as well, after such a night."

I glanced around the chamber as fingers thick as sausages began untangling the cloak that cocooned me. A lone taper guttered in a pewter branch. Walls were hung with weaponry meant to be used, not arranged in decorative sunbursts as in Buckingham's residences. Evans's swords, shield, and halberd were kept within quick reach for a man who might need them.

Furniture crouched like oaken beasts. Not one piece was set squarely, as if Evans had bumped into things so often, he had quit bothering to straighten them. Patches of raw wood showed at the chairs' joints, where someone had made crude attempts to repair damage likely caused in bearing Evans's weight.

A once-fine tapestry, now in disrepair, seemed out of place in a giant's room. Israel's David stretched almost to the floor, his sandaled foot planted on a fallen Goliath. Something, likely a rat, had gnawed one corner of the tapestry into a ragged mess and snagged the lower portion with scrabbling claws.

When Evans finally worked Griggory's cloak free, he tossed it onto a stool with such unintended force, the wooden legs skittered across the floor.

"Griggory would have had your costume off you a long time ago and you'd be tucked in bed, where you belong," Evans grumbled. "Where the devil is the man?"

I wedged my fingers under the place where my breastplate was grinding its way into my flesh. Evans must have seen me wince.

"You'll be wanting free of that armor, friend. Probably blistered or bleeding underneath it, the way it's wrenched to one side."

I unfastened what I could reach, while Evans set himself to defeating the buckles I could not. The long process cost several muttered oaths, but when the giant peeled the plates from my torso, I sighed in relief. Air struck me, cold on the damp shirt. Sometime during my acrobatics, the breastplate reduced the thin silk to shreds.

Evans frowned. "Can't have you wearing soaked rags to bed." He tossed me a length of towel. "Strip down and dry off before you catch your death."

I curled inward, my cheeks on fire at the idea of baring my shrunken body to this behemoth of a man. But Evans had already turned away. He went to a trunk and took out a stocking and a pair of scissors. As I rubbed myself dry, he snipped holes for my head and arms.

"This will keep you warm." He tossed the makeshift garment toward me, keeping his eyes averted. I pulled the fabric over my head, and wondered at a man who would ruin perfectly good stockings for someone he'd just met. He flung back the blankets on a bed wide as meadows. "I'll boost you up, then under the covers with you, lad."

He scooped me up onto a bed so high, it seemed like a cottage loft. The moment he let go, I rolled down into the giant-size hollow Will Evans had made in the feather mattress when he slept.

Evans chuckled. "I'll throw you a rope to help you climb out later. Just sleep while you've the chance. Her Majesty always throws herself into play-acting after she's had a night with Buckingham. Trying to drive all his devils away." For the first time, I saw Will Evan's frown and understood why children feared giants in the tales their elders told. He looked in my direction.

"Forgive me, lad. I do not mean to brood over things no one can cure. You will come to grieve Her Majesty's troubles yourself. She is such a winning little sparrow."

He cocked his head. "How did you come to serve the queen?"

He would find out the truth soon enough. "I am a gift to Her Majesty from the duke of Buckingham."

Warmth drained from Evans's face. Before I could tell him the lie Buckingham had concocted to disguise my true loyalties, the door swung open and Griggory edged into the room.

"Her Majesty said I was to attend the dwarf." Griggory made it sound as if she'd asked him to coddle a snake. Yet since I'd mentioned Buckingham's name, even Evans regarded me as if he wanted to scrub everything I had touched.

"Griggory will set bread and cheese in your reach in case you wake before I return. I am to take you down to meet the others at dinner." Evans straightened the badge of livery at his shoulder.

"The others," I echoed.

"The rest of the queen's menagerie," Evans said. "Griggory, see if you can find him something more appropriate to wear than my sock by then."

The giant lumbered to the door, and I saw why his gait was uneven. His legs bowed inward, his knees knocking together. There were patches stitched where holes must have rubbed in his hose.

I pulled the covers over my head, imagining Evans striding down the stairs. Would he raise the alarm among other members of the queen's household? *Jeffrey Hudson is Buckingham's man. Do not trust him.* Would he even put suspicion in the mind of the queen?

I intended to pick at my predicament until I could find a way to ease it. But the rich food of the banquet, the excitement of my performance, and strain of ceaseless training had taken their toll. I drifted to sleep, dreaming of glowering giants and grotesque shadows of the human curiosities serving a prisoner queen.

When I woke, the sun was streaming in the window and Will Evans sat brooding by the fireplace. He'd chosen the most uncomfortable seat in the room—a three-legged stool, which groaned under his weight. I wondered how long he had been waiting, his shaggy head bowed, his elbows braced on his knees. His clasped hands seemed the size of boulders. Scenes from our last encounter rekindled in my mind and I could not forget his expression when he heard I was linked to Buckingham.

For a brief time before that revelation, I had felt as if this big man and I might have become friends. But I would need to find a way to keep my distance, no matter how much I craved a kindred soul.

"Sergeant Evans?" I said.

"So you are awake. The menagerie will be glad. They're all lathered up with curiosity."

The prospect of facing another battery of suspicious stares was daunting. A lump of misery formed in my middle. "No doubt they'll want to see what Buckingham's coin has purchased."

Evans raised his head, his unkempt hair falling away from his features. Somehow, the daylight softened their ugliness. "Jeffrey, I've been sitting here the past two hours. It gave me time to think."

"Think what?" Whether to drown me like a kitten if the queen could not be convinced to let me go?

Evans fastened his sober gaze upon me. "How did you come to be Buckingham's man?"

I should have feared Evans had uncovered my purpose here and would hobble me before I had even begun. But something in his words set my chest burning.

"I am no man at all to Buckingham. I am a thing with no will of my own. My father sold me to the duke. The duke gave me to the queen. When the queen tires of me, she will dispose of me where she will, and there is nothing I can do to stop it." Did my voice sound as hollow as I felt?

Evans stood. "Most of us in the menagerie came here at someone else's pleasure. But we are not as helpless in our fate as it first appears. A man cannot help the place he comes from, only how he chooses to walk once the path becomes his own."

I thought of how much better Samuel's life would be if I did as Buckingham wished. "Denmark House is a long way from Oakham."

"True. But this can be your home." Evans gathered a soft bundle from the table. "No sign of your trunks yet, so I borrowed some clothes from Archie Armstrong, King Charles's fool. With some tinkering, we can make them work, and at least you'll not have to go to dinner in a sock."

"Is Archie a dwarf?"

"No. He won the clothes in a game of cards from Robin Goodfellow, the queen's other dwarf. Archie makes it a point to fleece someone in the menagerie's lodgings when he comes to visit a cousin who works in the queen's wardrobe. Hamish is as honest as Archie is sly. Archie won his position at court by stealing a sheep right under King James's nose and could never break the habit."

"Shouldn't a thief be branded or hanged?"

"Any other man would have been. King James and his men gave chase, thought they'd trapped the thief in a cottage. But when they went inside, Archie was not to be found. Just an ugly old woman hovering over a babe swaddled up in a cradle. The crone told the king's men she'd not seen the thief they sought. They left the cottage, save one man, who went and looked at the babe. It was the stolen lamb wrapped up in a shawl, and Archie the thief in a petticoat he'd found. Made the king laugh so hard, he took Archie on as his fool."

"I will have to thank Archie for loaning me the clothes."

"Don't," Evans said. "I had to force his hand. There is no reason for you to be trapped in this room while Archie hoards clothes he cannot even wear. He already has twenty years' worth of the finest garments the royal treasury can buy after playing court fool to this king and the last. Not that he appreciates either one of his masters. Tells anyone who will listen that England would be better off if the king's brother had lived to inherit and Charles had died."

"The king allows such talk?" I asked in surprise.

"A court fool is the one person who gets away with saying almost anything to the royal he serves. But in this case . . ." Evans sobered. "I suspect His Majesty agrees with Archie. King James most certainly did."

I could imagine what my father's reaction would be if John died. Father would wish it was anyone but John in that grave.

"Prince Henry *was* as noble a prince as ever dwelt on this island," Evans said. "A true Arthur reborn."

"Who was Arthur, another brother?"

Evans's jaw dropped. "I did not think there was an English lad alive who had not heard tales of the greatest king who ever ruled. There are a hundred legends of the Round Table and the knights who gathered about it."

"Legends?" I took the clothes around the corner of the bed to obscure Evans's view while I changed. "My father says people use such stories to dupe fools into charging into the path of blazing muskets. He told tales of fairy realms to charm coins out of the crowds that watched me dance at market fairs. They could not afford to waste those coppers. Should have bought a meat pie or boots from the secondhand clothing man."

I peered around the bed. Pity crowded into Evans's deep-set eyes.

"That is the saddest thing I have heard," Evans said. "A lad growing up without tales of valor to brighten his life. Those tales were like food for me when I was growing up in Wales. My mother claimed I gobbled legends down like my brothers gobbled oat cakes. That is what made me grow so tall—to give such stories room to stretch their wonders."

Evans's tales tempted me, but anything he might share about the king could prove useful. I began to put on my borrowed stocking. "I would rather hear about King Charles's brother."

"From the moment Henry Stuart was born, he seemed forged of brighter mettle than other men. No one could best him with a sword or on horseback, and no matter how fierce his father and the royal council pressed Henry, he would not wed a Catholic. Not for a hundred alliances would two religions sleep in his bed, he said."

"Considering the discord religion fired between the king and queen last night, perhaps Prince Henry was wise."

"I am not an educated man," Evans said. "But I know that Catholics and Protestants are knit into England as tightly as the threads in that stocking you are donning. Could you pull out one strand or the other without unraveling the whole garment?"

He did not seem to want an answer. I wondered whose God Will Evans bent his patched knee to.

"Prince Henry was only a lad when he set off to visit the most famous traitor imprisoned in the Tower of London. Spent hours with Sir Walter Raleigh to learn science and hear tales of Virginia and other uncharted territories. Even realms of alchemy, all the secrets of the brotherhood called the School of Night."

"The School of Night?" I echoed.

"A wizard's school made up of atheists. Men like Raleigh and the earl of Northumberland, the playwright Christopher Marlowe, and Dr. John Dee."

The idea of a wizard's school sent a delicious shiver down my spine as I pulled the borrowed shirt over my head and did up the laces.

"Of course, wizardry is a crime. King James himself wrote a book about how to root out witches." Evans adjusted the queen's badge on his livery as I stepped into Archie's breeches. "The prince did not consider Raleigh's doings wizardry. He saw science as deciphering God's fingerprints upon the world. Prince Henry made those around him believe it was God's intent that we explore His mysteries. Everyone in England loved him save one."

"Who was that?" I asked, plunging my arms through the holes in the doublet.

"The duke of Buckingham. He favored Prince Charles. Tutored him in manly arts and the sports that helped him grow strong."

I thought of the duke's single-minded determination to keep the queen beneath him in the king's esteem. Buckingham would have loathed rivalry with the king's gifted son.

"How did the prince die?"

"A fever. It struck so suddenly, some people say . . ." Evans hesitated.

"Say what?"

"That Prince Henry was poisoned."

I froze, the doublet half on, remembering the first time I had met the countess of Carlisle. Her pursed lips, the slyness in her voice as she addressed my master: *Very lucky for you that the Prince of Wales died . . .* Was it possible

Buckingham was somehow tied to the prince's death? If he was willing to poison the king's son, would it not be easy to use the same method to rid himself of a widely loathed French Catholic queen? When the time for the fatal draft came, who better to administer it than the fool at the queen's side every day?

Evans bent down to help me with the last fastenings. "Ah, but what does such gossip matter?" he said. "Prince Henry is dead and Buckingham has risen so high, even the queen is in his shadow. You are dressed once I tie these laces. We'd best feed you and introduce you to the others before the rehearsals begin."

"Rehearsals?"

"For the queen's great passion, the masque. Playacting of sorts. She tries to shape the world into something prettier, where she can be beloved, heroic—all she dreamed of when she crossed the seas from France. Sometimes, I think she considers her masque world more real than the one she shares with the king."

No wonder, with her life so full of snares. I wished I could escape this world, as well. "I see," I said, doubting Evans could guess how much I meant it.

"Even after last night's fete, grand as it was, you can only imagine." Evans fumbled with the laces, drawing them tight as he was able. "The whole court is a world of make-believe, Jeffrey. The courtiers may seem like papier-mâché dragons. But the dragons breathe real fire, and even seas made of silk will drown you. Sometimes even the most astute man cannot tell what is real. If you have not heard of King Arthur, you cannot have heard of the Colosseum."

"What is that?" I asked.

"The Romans had menageries like the queen's. Tigers and lions, and gladiators, as well. Slaves who fought one another and the beasts for the amusement of their betters."

"Like the bull-baiting ring my father has charge of."

"Very much like. Archie will want you to believe the queen's other curiosities are all tooth and claw in the court arena. Promise you will judge for yourself."

I slipped on shoes—the one bit of my costume that had not been shredded or ruined beneath the armor plate. "I am ready," I said. But I doubted I would ever be ready to meet the queen's famous freaks.

Will Evans crossed to the door. He swung it open and held it with one huge arm. I forced myself to walk out, the maze of chambers making me wonder how I would ever find my way back. Will snipped the length of his stride and paused so often to point out paintings of Greek gods and statues of legendary heroes that it took time for me to realize he was making certain I could keep up.

I tried to stir up resentment at this new evidence of his kindness, determined not to risk liking someone I knew I would have to betray. "There is no reason to dawdle over every lump of marble we see."

I saw confusion, then temper spark in Evans, reminding me of the bulls just after father chained them in Buckingham's ring. The moment the first dog lunged for no reason and sank teeth in the bull's tender nose.

Had I been in Evans's place, I would have told the ungrateful wretch I was "dawdling" so he could keep up. But Evans only regarded me with those probing eyes.

Evans no longer stopped, but he still slowed his steps. I all but ran in an effort to force him to speed up. Bedraggled, more than a little breathless, I entered a corridor, sensed a change in the giant ambling beside me. "These are Her Majesty's privy quarters," he said, "the place where she seeks refuge with only those she loves and trusts about her."

I did not think I could walk any faster, but I did.

"Jeffrey, Her Majesty has not asked for you yet. There is no reason to race about."

I could hear muffled voices—the queen's, then a man's, a burred Scots accent garbling in French so impassioned, I could not understand it. "Someone sounds angry with the queen," I said.

"We can often hear the queen and her ladies through the wall. Makes it easier to answer the summons and to gauge what mood Her Majesty is in."

And it would make it easier for Buckingham's spy.

"Do you know who her visitor is?"

"It is your job to distract her from such unpleasantness, not add to it with questions about things that are none of your concern." It was the sharpest Will Evans had been with me. I was surprised how his tone stung.

"You are right. I just . . ." I fumbled for a lie and settled for an unrelated truth. "I do not like to hear any woman spoken to thus. It reminds me of my mother and how my father plagues her."

The storm in Evans's eyes receded. "I do not like to hear the queen plagued, either, but I do not believe her visitor is angry with her. They are both angry about something else."

I started to say "What?" then stopped. Too much curiosity would stir up his suspicion.

"They are trying to decide what to do about an injustice," Evans continued. "But that is their burden to shoulder. You will find your own employment on the other side of this door."

He nodded toward the carved wood panel. "Courtiers call this 'the Freaks' Lair.' It is where we await Her Majesty's summons. We keep whatever tools our trade demands—dancing ropes, props for magic tricks, beribboned hoops and such. Practice new tricks. Sometimes we take our meals when not performing or at our other duties."

"What other duties?"

"I'm porter of the queen's back stairs. No one gets past my guard to see the queen unless I give them leave to."

You cannot be a very good guard, I thought. You know I come from Buckingham, but you trip over your own feet to make me comfortable.

"You will be spending many hours in this place with these people," Evans said. "I hope you will be happy here."

"In a 'Freak's Lair'?" I asked, incredulous.

Will Evans looked down at me with such sadness, it surprised me. "We are all twisted somewhere, Jeffrey. Some are freaks on the outside, where everyone can see; others are twisted inside."

I wondered what Will Evans saw when he looked at me. All at once, I would have given anything to water down his pointed gaze. I hitched up my borrowed breeches, steeled my nerves, and stepped into a chamber stranger than any I had ever known.

Six

•

The chamber I stepped into was more like a shipwreck than a palace. A battering ram of gazes nearly pushed me back out. Rigging swooped from a hook driven into one wall to a second hook on the other side of the room. Ribbon-trimmed barrel hoops hung over the back of one chair, and costumes lay about the room like colorful corpses after a battle. A war the gigantic fowl on the platter had lost.

The "curiosities of nature" were in the midst of devouring their roasted enemy. Five souls clustered around a long table, hands frozen midair, jaws stilled in the midst of chewing.

Time seemed to stop as I attempted to take the whole company in. One man of middling height might have played Death in one of the church paintings the plague had inspired. His skin stretched so tight, sharp bones seemed ready to slice through. The knobs of his jawbone stuck out like the knuckles on a stonecutter's hand. Set in that death's-head were the merriest eyes I had ever seen. A small red-and-white spaniel was helping himself to the meat on the man's plate as if it were his due.

Two dwarfs were seated at the table. One was a woman in crimson with hair as intricately dressed as the queen's. The other was a man spattered with paint, the leg of fowl in his hand so large compared to his size that it might have come off of a bear.

I had seen other dwarfs of their kind at the market fair, their faces strangely fascinating, world-weary eyes trying to hide their pain. Their heads were so large for their bodies, the weight threatened to overset them. Their arms seemed to have gotten distracted in the womb and quit bothering to grow. Even fine clothes could not make their stout bodies look graceful.

The moment I had been able to escape my parents, I had run over to their troupe of traveling players, delighted to see little folk like me. But the people who had been watching the dwarfs' comic antics thronged around me. The dwarfs had thrown rotten eggs at me in hopes of regaining the crowd's attention. I could still remember the snotlike goo dripping down my neck.

A monkey capered in the middle of the menagerie's table, seeming ready to fling the ripe peach it clutched in humanlike hands. Revolted, I stared as the creature bared its yellow teeth and chattered a fiendish curse.

More spiteful still was the man teasing the monkey. He was about the same height as the skeleton, but gnarled as a burl oak and so bitter when he glared at my clothes, I knew it could only be the king's fool.

At the end of the table sat a woman as out of place as a butterfly on a dung heap. Exotic eyes regarded me with vague interest, white fingers picking at food, as if she preferred sipping nectar from the cup of a flower. Yet her beauty possessed a cruel magic, her perfection making the flaws of the table's other occupants all the more apparent.

Was I like these people? Once I stepped through this door, I would be *embracing* the fact that I was a grotesque, repellent as the living corpse or the aged fool who seemed constructed of nothing but bile and gristle.

Still, what did it matter what outcasts such as these thought of me? I took a bold step into the room, trying to seem confident, though my breeches were bagging. My cheeks warmed and I could not keep myself from hitching the waistband higher. It only made the garment more lopsided, one knee bared, the other lost in a puddle of black damask. No wonder they were all staring.

"Look at the shape of him!" I heard someone murmur.

"An angelic freak," another marveled.

"This is Jeffrey Hudson." Will said, interrupting. "His ears may be small, but they work just fine."

The dwarf woman stammered. "There were rumors you were beautiful, but no one believed it. Even Archie had never seen a dwarf like you."

"The rest of us had better keep our traveling clothes ready." The unpleasant fool glared at me with personal venom. "Their Majesties will have no more use for ugly gits like us." I glimpsed very real fear in the faces around the table. "Took you so long to get here, the rest of us could have starved," he grumbled.

"Pay no attention to Archie, Master Hudson." The dwarf woman climbed down from her seat and came to greet me. "Pardon us for forgetting our manners, but none of us would have believed someone like you could exist at all if Will Evans had not given the rumors credence. He is the most trustworthy man in England."

"You would think serving as the queen's sergeant porter would cure him of believing everyone is as honorable as he is," Archie crabbed.

"I do not *believe* it," Evans said, correcting him. "I *hope*. There is no crime in that."

"Only inevitable disappointment," the thin man said softly.

"I'm called Little Sara," the dwarf woman said, tucking a shining curl behind her ear. "Welcome to the Lair."

I executed a bow as Master Ware had taught me. "Little Sara," I echoed.

"Moves as graceful as he looks." Curiosity curved the butterfly's cherry lips. "It is uncanny."

Little Sara pointed to each person in turn. "The fellow who has done his best to spoil your appetite is Archie Armstrong. He belongs to the king's household, so he's not here all the time. When he does visit, none of us takes his grousing seriously."

"I'll remember that."

"I'm sure you can guess which one we call Simon Rattlebones." She pointed to the jolly skeleton. "He juggles and does vaulting and performs tricks with Her Majesty's dogs."

"Most of the time their 'tricks' involve deciding whether to jump through a hoop or piss on someone's shoe," Archie grumbled.

"They are very discerning dogs and piss only on Puritans, eh, Scrap?" Rattlebones scratched the spaniel's ears. "Welcome to the menagerie, Master Hudson." I nodded in greeting, not wanting to like the dog trainer, yet unable to stop myself from being amused by him.

"The woman you men can't take your eyes off is our rope dancer," Sara continued. "She came to us as Deborah Martin, but we ignored that name once Will Evans christened her Dulcinea—you know, after Don Quixote's love in the book."

I did not know, but I wasn't about to tell them. The rope dancer fluttered her hand in greeting. "Are you afraid of heights, Master Hudson? There are tricks I want to try with a dwarf, but none of the others have the courage to try them." She turned a pointed look on the one person Little Sara had failed to introduce, the other dwarf. I noticed a spot of orange paint under his beaky nose. "Around here they call me Robin Goodfellow, but I sign my paintings Robert Gibson."

"You are an artist?" I looked at his hands.

"I paint scenery, but mostly miniatures."

"Miniatures?"

"Tiny portraits you can carry with you." Little Sara displayed a porcelain oval pinned in the lace at her bosom. It depicted a kind-looking woman with eyes like her own. "Robin painted this of my mother." It was hard enough to imagine Goodfellow's short fingers painting bold brushstrokes. Such intricate work seemed impossible.

"Don't let Dulcinea lure you into peril, Master Hudson," Robin warned. "Last time I aided her in one of her tricks, I flew through the air as if I had been shot from a sling. Will managed to slow my fall or it would have been the end of me."

Dulcinea made a farting noise the butchers' apprentices in the shambles would have been proud of. Will Evans cleared his throat as if to obscure the fact Dulcinea had made such a sound. I was not sure whether he wished to hide it from me or himself.

"Sit down, Jeffrey," he said. "You can eat while you tell us about yourself."

"That is right, *Jeffrey*." Archie made my name sound like an insult. "The queen has cast the menagerie the scraps from her table. You will want to get your share."

Evans pulled out a chair that stood before a clean plate and I could see him trying to decide whether he should help me into the seat. I scrambled up myself before he could ask.

"Part of our allotment is to receive the broken meats from the queen's table," Evans explained. "It is a privilege, not something to complain about. Better food than most people get at a feast."

Archie shoved himself back from the table. "If you listen to Evans, he'll paint life in the menagerie as bright as Gibson's rainbows. I will tell you the truth. We are dogs at the royal table. The royals may claim they love you, that you are part of their family. But you are no more human to them than that performing monkey." Archie snatched the animal's peach. The creature screeched and leapt up and down, frantic.

"Their Majesties keep us scampering about like poor Pug here, that is certain," Rattlebones reached toward the monkey, but it would not be comforted.

"What are our duties?" I asked.

"Rehearsals, costume fittings, designing new tricks. Collecting gossip to work into our performances. There are books of jests to study and make our own. It is no easy thing to choose the perfect moment, the perfect inflection to carry off a jest, and captivate a royal audience. Robin and I sometimes take Scrap and the other dogs beyond the palace walls to perform, as long as the queen has no use for us. Londoners will pay a pretty penny to see the queen's menagerie perform."

"When the queen is busy with other affairs, entertain anyone who crosses your path," Robin said. "People wait for weeks in hopes of an audience with the queen and many never reach her. They will offer handsome bribes to get you to drop a word in the queen's ear."

"Especially ambassadors," Archie said. "You don't even have to put forward their suit. Just pretend you'll speak to the queen, look at the ambassador a good deal and nod."

"But that is dishonest," Sara said.

"You can pray for forgiveness during Mass," Archie sneered. "All that Catholic chanting of spells and incantations should be good for something."

"You go to Catholic Mass?" I asked, thinking of Samuel.

"Whether we want to or not," Rattlebones muttered.

"As the queen's servant, you must go to chapel with her," Sara said. "But beyond these walls, there have been more arrests of Jesuits and those who harbor them. That is what Father Philip has come to the queen about."

Archie spat over his shoulder, narrowly missing the spaniel. "You'd think a Scotsman—even one stupid enough to become a Catholic priest—would have more sense than to whip the queen into a frenzy over it."

"The old ways comfort people," Will Evans said. "You will see them, Jeffrey, slipping in to receive the sacraments without fear of getting arrested for it."

Robin Goodfellow's brow furrowed. "They may not be arrested at Mass, but their names are recorded by Bishop Laud's spies. I am just grateful members of the queen's household are expected to accompany her to her devotions. If pressed, we could use that excuse."

Sara touched the ivory image of her mother. "You would deny faith if put to the question?"

Dulcinea flung her napkin into the air. "Religion is a dispute about trifles, just as Queen Bess said. My family survived through the reigns of five monarchs without burning. We changed our religion as easily as we changed our petticoats. Catholic, Church of England, Protestant, Catholic, then Protestant again. What does it matter to folk like us which religion is in power? We get none of the wealth, whether it goes to Rome or stays in the king's purse."

"That is true enough." Simon Rattlebones took the abandoned peach from Archie's plate. "Any one of the religions would fight to seize England's soul. Some would do murder." He tossed the peach in the air. The monkey leapt to catch it, then ran off, the dog snapping in hot pursuit.

Evans stroked his beard, as if merely by reasoning, the great oaf could sort out the religious tangle of over a hundred years. "The queen says the old King James signed an *écrit secret* that promised the Crown would lift penalties on English Catholics and that the queen could practice her faith freely."

"The old king is dead," Archie said, and I sensed grief beneath the man's harsh tone.

"The duke of Buckingham swore before Parliament that no 'secret writing' was undertaken," Rattlebones said.

"The duke could lie to Saint Peter and not show remorse," Will said. "Her Majesty would never have come to England without such a promise from the Crown."

"I do not envy King Charles," Rattlebones added. "Catholics from one side of Europe to the other are eager to take the queen's side. Bishop Laud insists His Majesty's duty as head of the Church of England is to crush its opposition. As if that is not bad enough, the Puritans mope about, trying to ruin every bit of amusement people have." Rattlebones made a sour face.

"No wonder you train your dogs to piss on them," Goodfellow teased. "Now if you could only teach them to piss on the duke of Buckingham."

"Robin!" Evans warned. Goodfellow's bewilderment made it clear the duke had often been a bone of gossip at table. "Jeffrey comes from one of the duke's holdings. His Grace presented Jeffrey to the queen during a banquet designed to honor Her Majesty."

A hush fell, the suspicion I'd already detected in the company's faces deepening. I needed to allay it. My first real test in the art of lying, since the untruths told to Will Evans did not count. The giant wanted so much to believe the best of everyone, it was no challenge to deceive him.

I tried to shape my face into something like Samuel's sincerity. "I thank God I need never suffer under Buckingham's thumb again. The ordeal he put me through these past three weeks to prepare for last night—" I shuddered. "I never suffered anything like it in the roughest part of the shambles. He could not even spare me the time to tell my brother farewell."

I saw Sara touch the miniature of her mother, empathy softening her face. I had made my first conquest among those at the table. "Buckingham bought me like a blackamoor. My father took the coin. I owe neither of them allegiance."

"Then what do you think of belonging to the queen?" Rattlebones asked.

"I want nothing more than to settle in here where I belong."

"We shall help you get your bearings, Jeffrey. Won't we, everyone?" Evans clapped one hand onto the table. Dishes rattled as Dulcinea and Simon murmured their agreement.

"Of course we will!" Sara's eyes shone. I could see Robin Goodfellow's enthusiasm wane as he noticed her expression. Was it possible the artist felt something beyond friendship toward her?

If Sara *was* attracted to me, she would be more willing to surrender information I could feed to Buckingham. God knew, my features were more pleasing than Goodfellow's, and I was clean of paint spatter. I glanced at Will Evans, fighting my guilt.

I owed these people nothing. It was their choice whether to be naïve fools or be cautious. They had been at court longer than I and had witnessed its intrigues. They knew I had first been Buckingham's *toy*. They could blame Evans if they were gulled into acting as if this were a family. I certainly didn't believe it. Who wanted to belong to a family of freaks? I fought to hide the contempt that washed through me.

I pressed my palm to the space my heart should have filled. "Thank you for the help you offer me. I am eager to get to know your world."

Archie plucked up his knife, examined the point. "A shrewd general must master the terrain he plans to conquer. Who better to show him the lay of the land than fools who already live there?"

I gave him my most winning smile. "I am new to the business of being a court fool, but I am a very apt pupil."

"I can see that you are." Behind the stony hardness in Archie's eyes I saw something new. He speared the choicest piece of meat with his knife. "Perhaps you will be the fastest learner this court has ever seen."

I had little time to meditate on the temper of his words. Approval? Respect? Or a challenge? A page in the queen's livery hastened to the door.

"Ho, Denis," Evans greeted the lad. Did the giant know every person in the castle by name? "How fares Her Majesty this morn?"

"Weeping since Father Philip left." The lad said in heavily accented English. He wiped his nose with his sleeve. A cold? I wondered. Or had he been crying, as well? "Letters from France berating her. A letter from the king scolding because she did not welcome the duchess of Buckingham into her household. Madame Saint-Georges sent me to fetch the new curiosity, in hopes he can make her smile."

I slid off of the high ledge of the chair seat. Archie's breeches caught on the corner. The twine holding them snapped, and I had to struggle to retie it. "I cannot go to the queen looking like this!" For some reason, I looked to Will Evans in my predicament. Irritation at myself flared. What did I expect? That he would loan me another sock? But it was Sara who intervened.

"Robin, give Jeffrey the cloak Dulcinea stitched when you played Puck. It will cover the ill-fitting clothes and suit him better than you. The green velvet will look well with his eyes."

"Would you mind doing so, Robin?" Will asked.

Goodfellow's cheeks darkened, but he left the table. "I told Dulcinea I would not look well in green," he muttered. "You would think she'd listen to an artist when it came to color."

"No one will listen to you now, Goodfellow," Archie said. "You'll not be charming Sara in the pretty roles. Those will be Hudson's domain. Get used to playing Spite and Envy with the rest of us."

Robin tossed me the mantle, and I caught it in midair. From his expression, I feared he might play those roles very well indeed.

SEVEN

•

I flung Goodfellow's cloak around my shoulders as the page led me out of the room, Will Evans looming over us both. "Never mind about your clothes," Evans said. "Just remember, the poor mite is only a young girl far away from home."

Taut nerves made me surly. "Is it hard for you to see clearly from way up there, Evans? Henrietta Maria is a queen, a princess of France. There is nothing 'poor' about her."

"Married by proxy to a cold fish of a man she'd never met, thrust into a country that hates her religion, sees her family as enemies. French and English, Catholic and Protestant all trying to use her for their own designs. You will be doing the work of angels when you dry her tears."

Tears? The implication struck me. The giant was going to thrust me into a chamber with a crying woman and leave me there. I had faced my father when he'd been in a drunken fury. I had endured Buckingham's threats. I had lied to Will Evans, when he could snap my bones with one flick of his wrist. The prospect of facing a weeping queen was infinitely more terrifying.

Those times my mother or sister had cried, I'd dived for whatever hiding place I could find. One Christmas, I had spent the night in the kennel with weanling pups, shivering while the muffled sound of Mother's weeping and my sister's sobs seeped through the cracks in the shutters.

Samuel had stayed behind instead of fleeing as I had done. I had known I was being a coward, but I had not regretted my flight until now. Why had I never asked Samuel how he had managed to quiet them? Was this retribution for my failings then?

I heard the queen's voice, but there was nothing lilting in it now. An usher swept open the door, announcing me. "Master Jeffrey Hudson."

In an instant, I took in the mood of the room. For the first time, I was aware of how skilled at judging people's temper I was—a matter of survival for someone whose size made him an easy target.

The usher motioned me forward and I stepped into a chamber that seemed plucked from Heaven. Rich paintings hung on walls and adorned the ceiling. Cushions on the chairs arranged about the room had been stuffed fat. Gilt shimmered on trinkets displayed about the room. Jewels encircled the throats and nestled on the breasts of the ladies-in-waiting. Small clusters of women had gathered as far as possible from the queen, who was slumped in the most ornate chair of all.

Had Her Majesty banished them so she could grieve privately? Or had they deserted her in an act of self-preservation? I looked into that forest of skirts, instinctively searching for the best place to hide. Plain Jeffrey Hudson could have escaped thus. Jeffrey Hudson, queen's fool, Buckingham's spy, dared not.

The queen bent over a table that had snarling lions for legs. An ornate box sat before her, bone and lapis lazuli inlays gleaming in intricate patterns. The front panel of the box had been lowered on hinges until it lay against the table, revealing the wall of fitted drawers for correspondence it had concealed.

Her Majesty looked as though she wished the lion table could devour the letters strewn across it. Distance made it possible for me to see the tabletop mounded with crumpled correspondence. I could see heavy wax seals broken like the queen's spirit seemed to be, the inked pages splotched with her tears.

Buckingham would want to know what was written on those pages. But my ability to read was crude—a smattering of French from our Huguenot neighbors and English picked up from those I could charm into amusing themselves by teaching me tricks, like Simon Rattlebones teaching the menagerie's monkey.

It would have been a challenge to read the letters at my leisure. How was I to unravel what the words said with people watching? I stiffened, imagining Buckingham's displeasure should I fail.

Madame Saint-Georges's pleading look made panic cinch tighter in my breast. She expected me to fix whatever had driven the light from the queen's eyes.

"Your Majesty, look!" She urged in French. "Your new little man has come."

The queen did not even seem to notice me when she looked up. I could see strands of the brown hair dressed so carefully at last night's banquet now clinging in untidy strands to her temples. Her blue satin skirts were crumpled, as if she had clutched them in her fists.

How I was supposed to entertain someone so far gone in misery? Pull out the antics Ware had concocted to prepare me for this role? Or should I back out of the room and leave the queen to her ladies' ministrations? No. I could not leave without royal permission. But my feet itched to flee.

"Come, Majesty," Saint-Georges urged with brittle enthusiasm, "let us cast all this vexation away and be happy as we were at Saint-Germain."

"How can I be happy when I am a disappointment to everyone?" The queen took up the letter with the most impressive seal. "My brother insists I make my husband honor the terms of our marriage contract and remove all sanctions against Catholics in England. My mother asks why I am not yet with child and sends remedies to cure an empty womb. Both are certain that once I produce an heir, the king will be so grateful that he will be easy to lead back to the Church."

"I do not think you could lead these crude English even if you put rings in their noses and dragged them behind a team of horses."

Her scorn stung. Who were these French chits to hold us in contempt?

"They are stubborn and uncouth and have no sense of style. It is always raining. That alone is a good reason to light candles to the saints they abhor. To get a glimpse of sunshine."

She did have a point about the rain, I had to confess.

"It is not your fault that the king has broken his promise to stop persecuting his Catholic subjects, *me petite*. Can't Father Philip see how hard you are trying?"

"Father Philip was right to upbraid me. I was sent here to turn the king's heart back to the true faith. Catholics in England have suffered for generations and look to me to deliver them. They cannot receive the Euchanst, their dying are refused the comfort of Extreme Unction, and their marriages cannot be consecrated nor their babes baptized. The king's pursuivants hunt them, seize their lands, and imprison any priests who dare to step on English shores."

"It is heartbreaking, but—"

"Yet despite the danger, those priests continue to breach English shores in secret. They brave horrific death to minister to the faithful. When they are captured . . ." I saw the queen shudder. "When I think of the torment those martyrs suffer, there are times I wish I could fling myself on the pyre. The other day when my coach passed Tyburn, I saw an old woman kiss the spot where the martyrs died. I could hear innocent blood cry out to me. *Why do you do nothing?* That moment, I was seized with the strangest impulse. I wanted to make pilgrimage as we did when we were in France. I wanted to walk barefoot to Tyburn, through the streets where secret Catholics might see their queen has not abandoned them. I felt as if God were calling me to pray for those who died for their faith."

"You always had the most passionate heart when it came to injustice."

"My *feelings* are of no use to anyone unless I act on them, Mamie."

I saw the queen's cheeks flush, heard the resolve in her tone. I searched for an opening to speak—about what? I was to make the queen laugh. Priests being hanged, drawn, and quartered were hardly amusing.

"You can do nothing at this moment," Saint-Georges soothed. "Allow yourself time away from this misery. Gather strength so you will better be able to fight."

"I do not know how to fight this, Mamie."

I considered dancing up to her with an imaginary sword, reminding her I was to be her champion, but Saint-Georges stroked the queen's shoulder and the moment for action seemed lost.

"The way will appear, Your Majesty."

The queen laughed without mirth, and I remembered the delight rippling from her throat the night before. "How will 'the way' appear? By magic?"

Instinct shoved me. This time I listened. I swept forward in my strange garb. "Perhaps inspiration will spring from a pie," I suggested in perfect French.

Murmurs of surprise filled the room. "You speak French!" Her Majesty exclaimed. "Why did I not know this?"

"More important, why did the dwarf hide it until now?" Madame Saint-Georges demanded.

"I sought only to honor the wishes of the king. I was told His Majesty preferred English." I feigned confusion, glancing from Saint-Georges to the queen. "Majesty, I beg you, forgive me if I was mistaken." I prayed my explanation would satisfy her. The queen smiled.

"Whatever the king prefers, here in my household we speak French. How beautiful your accent is!" she exclaimed. "Did you travel there? Oh, have you seen how beautiful it is when fields of lavender are in bloom? The way the sun catches on the chestnut trees? And the music in people's voices when they speak!"

"I have smelled lavender. My mother kept a sprig tucked in her chest of clothes." She said Father had given it to her when they were courting. His first wife had died after Ann was born. He had needed a mother for his child. It was the only time he had ever seemed like a lover.

"I had never been beyond the boundaries of Oakham before coming here, Majesty," I confessed. "But I've heard France is a fairyland, and even its castles have spires and elegance far different from England's own."

"Tutors tried to teach me English before I came here, but I am still not very good at it." She made a face. "It is like the thick-tongued lowing of cows. Your French is well spoken, Jeffrey. How proud your tutor must have been of your accent!"

"I never studied under a tutor, only scraped up whatever learning I could. Some Huguenots moved in near my father's cottage. When they spoke, the language sounded so beautiful, I grew hungry to learn it. I was hungry to learn anything." I stopped before I could finish the sentence: anything that carried me beyond the ugliness of the shambles.

I groped for a way to shift the conversation in another direction— something to make her smile and to hide my vulnerability as Goodfellow's cloak concealed my patched-together clothes. My clothes. "Majesty, I know I have only just arrived here. But there is a matter I blush to bring to your attention. It is only a small boon."

A pained line dug at the corner of the queen's mouth, the animation of moments before gone. I was aware how many times a day people must ask for royal favors. "What is this boon?"

"Last night, you vowed I would have the finest the court had to offer."

How weary she looked. "What is it you want?"

Surreptitiously, I slipped one hand to my waistband. Hooking my thumb under the knot I had rigged to hold up Archie's breeches, I gave a tug. The breeches nearly tumbled down and I caught them with comic exaggeration. "I was wondering—might we begin with a ball of royal twine? These breeches are cowardly fellows, determined to flee down my legs to the floor."

Her lovely face transformed, charmingly tender and earnest. "Mamie! My sewing case." That lady rushed to a nearby cupboard, opened it. I saw skeins of embroidery silks and wondered if even artist Goodfellow knew there were so many colors in the world.

Once the elegant box was delivered, the queen laid hold of scissors in the shape of a long-billed bird. I gaped, stunned as she snipped off a length of ribbon that decorated her gown. "Will this do, Sir Jeffrey?" she asked as she tied the sash about my waist. "You did vow to serve as my champion. You should wear your queen's favor."

Her luminous brown eyes sank a hook in my heart. I could feel them drawing me in. I bowed, flinging off Goodfellow's cloak, baring my ridiculousness on purpose. Laughter rose from the ladies and even the queen herself.

"I fear you are shrinking like a sugar cone left in the rain," she said. "Have a care, or there will be nothing left of you!"

The queen clapped her hands, calling for her own seamstresses, and in no time the chamber was awash in materials to fashion a wardrobe worthy of a queen's fool. Mamie Saint-Georges had the gentleman usher place me on the table, this reminder of my first encounter with Buckingham helping me break the spell the queen's sorrowful gaze had cast.

Her women wrapped me in fabrics, touching me in places no woman save my mother ever had. They stripped me to my shirt, then pulled that off as well, despite my protests. I shivered, clutching a bit of fabric like Adam's fig leaf. Plump bosoms swelled above their décolletage as they bent over me. The bare skin brushed my arms; feminine fingers measured from ankle to crotch.

Mamie Saint-Georges strayed far too close, and I could not hide my body's reaction. She giggled. "It seems Lord Minimus's parts are in working order, though they be small!" I fought the urge to dive under the mountain of tawny velvets, green brocades, and blue damasks. I wanted the queen to chastise her. Or defend me? But she played with the single-minded delight of a child, ignoring the unpleasant. I had to salvage what I could of my dignity.

"Her Majesty knows it is not the height of a lover that matters, but his devotion. In that, even Sergeant Evans cannot outstrip me."

"Oh, Mamie! Lord Minimus is a perfect name for him! Think how cunning he and Sergeant Evans will be when they play together in our masques!" The queen smiled as she held a bit of trim near my hair to see if it suited me. "What games we can play with them!"

That was what this all boiled down to, I reminded myself. A game. One I had only hoped to survive. But as I looked at the wealth spread about me— tiny pearls to be stitched on doublets, gold braid and lace like spider's webs, I understood Archie's greed. When Queen Henrietta Maria tired of playing, I would carry away whatever gifts she lavished now.

I would study to learn what made her smile—pry tiny sparkling moments out of the rocky ground the rest of the world forced her to tread. The flash of her smile made me eager to mine for more.

Take care, Buckingham's warning whispered inside me. It was a cliff's edge I walked—one that could crumble should I lean to either side. I knew I must never forget the queen saw me as a toy. I had to see her as a "thing," as well—an object that could move Samuel closer to a decent future. Fill the table back at Oakham, make my mother's life and Ann's not so hard. As for my own—there were valuables I might take with me when I left. Not the hoard of trinkets Archie had amassed, but, rather, skills and knowledge.

I looked down at the letters that were scattered around my feet and sighed.

"Your new fool sounds lovesick already, Majesty," a pretty blonde said. "Have you fallen in love with one of our ladies?"

I chose boldness, battening in place a defense should someone ever see me looking at documents as I was now. "I fear I am in love, Your Majesty. With your writing box and these letters you have about. The ink looks as if it is dancing across the page, and all those mysterious drawers with their tiny pulls—I want to open them and see what lies inside."

The queen gasped, and the other ladies seemed taken aback.

"Not to pry into your correspondence. It is just that I have never seen any box so fine, and imagining what tools you might have inside fascinates me: a penknife, bottles of ink, vellum thicker and finer than anything I have ever seen. And sealing wax. How do they make the impressions stand out so stark? Everything here is so fine, Majesty. I wish . . ."

"What do you wish?"

"I am proud to be known as the queen's fool, Majesty. But I loathe being a fool in life. I may be small in size, but I believe my mind and heart to be big as any man's. If only I had a chance to learn about the world beyond . . . I would rather have that than the finest clothes in England, grateful as I am for these garments."

The queen tilted her head. "You are a strange little man. But why should you not have both wardrobe and wisdom? You shall have the use of my library."

Did that mean I would be left alone there? Even if it were for brief times, it would give me an opportunity to poke around.

"Father Philip will help guide you if you need help with your studies. I shall quiz you and be quite stern if you do not know your lessons."

I could hardly believe my good fortune. I was to have the freedom of Her Majesty's library and to question her confessor. I had come from her enemy, even if she believed I had wanted to escape him. She was a fool to place so much trust in someone she had barely met. Or did she think I had neither the wit nor stature to be a danger to her?

The question haunted me until I was dismissed. I hastened out of the queen's chamber victorious. I had survived humiliation. I had resisted the queen's charm. I had gathered bits of information that might satisfy His Grace when next we met.

I could only hope they would be enough.

EIGHT

.

Archie waited outside the queen's door, his arms folded across his middle. "You had better not have damaged those clothes." He scrutinized the rumpled doublet. "They're going to an East India Company man who fancies rigging his wee son up in garb from court. He'll not pay for damaged goods."

"He'll have no reason to complain."

"Good. Your trunk was delivered by a one-eyed crow. I had him take it to Evans's lodgings. You can change as soon as you rid yourself of the fellow. He insisted on waiting for you."

The notion of Ware alone in Will Evans's chamber unnerved me. "You'll have to show me the way."

Secure in Evans's company, I had not bothered to pick out landmarks to guide me. But if I were to be effective at all, I would have to memorize every secret of this palace. I remembered what the queen had said about Catholics gathering here, about priests in hiding. Were there priest holes carved out even here? Would I go to hell if I betrayed them?

I was still contemplating hellfire when Archie pointed to a heavy door that looked vaguely familiar. "The crow is inside. I'll wait here."

I should have been relieved he was not accompanying me into the room. Ware and I could not speak freely with Archie listening. But even Archie's company was preferable to facing Ware alone.

I entered Evans's room and shut the door behind me. It took a moment to get my bearings. My trunk sat by the window, the lid open, light streaming over belongings that Ware had obviously rifled through. Anger burned in me as I looked for the man who had violated my privacy.

I started as a shadow peeled away from the cupboard that held Evans's things. Ware withdrew his hand from the pouch he held, the queen's badge embossed on the leather.

"What are you doing?" I demanded.

"Seizing the opportunity fate offered. You will learn to do the same. While I waited for you, I learned what I could about the queen's porter." Ware crossed to me. "Evans is a sentimental fellow. He preserves every paper he has ever received so carefully that he does not even break the seal. Fortunately, I have learned how to skin seals off and replace them after, so most people would never know I had meddled with their letters. It is a skill you will master."

I thought of the queen's chamber, crowded with ladies-in-waiting, priests, ambassadors, and servants coming and going. To pry through the queen's state correspondence was treason. I shuddered, remembering Clemmy's description of the Jesuits he had seen die a traitor's death.

"Are you afraid of the lessons the duke insists I teach you, Jeffrey? Good." Ware returned the pouch of letters to the cupboard. "That will cause you to plan your moves on the court's chessboard carefully. Fear can be a great ally. Sentimentality is the enemy."

"I am not sentimental." I never had been, except where Samuel was concerned.

"You save ragged clothes. Your mother's seam work leaves much to be desired."

My throat caught. "She has so much to do by day that she can only stitch by firelight."

"Perhaps your employment with the duke will provide her with enough candles to set a decent seam." He touched the ribbon the queen had given me. "I wager you did not bring this pretty scrap from home. How fares Her Majesty today? Pleased with her new plaything?"

"I believe so."

"His Grace is eager to hear of your first impressions with his own ears."

I heard Archie's voice through the door, then a rumble like thunder.

"It is Sergeant Evans returned," I whispered. My pulse skipped at the possibility that Evans would notice Ware had been sifting through his belongings.

The door swung open and Evans ducked under the lintel. When he straightened, I could see a hopeful camaraderie. "Ho, Jeffrey. I heard your time with the queen went well, and—"

"Sergeant Evans," I said, interrupting. "This is Master Uriel Ware, come from York House."

The porter slammed to a halt, as if I had thrown a snake in his path.

"Your servant," Ware said, sketching the giant a bow. "I was charged with bringing Jeffrey's belongings to him. But I fear I have bungled the task. His ring is missing."

I stared at him, bewildered.

"A ring," Evans echoed, confused.

"I told Jeffrey that Her Majesty will be generous with such baubles—far grander ones than he can imagine—but the dwarf will not be reasonable. Says this ring belonged to his grandfather and cannot be replaced by a casketful of jewels."

"He is right in that," Evans said.

"Hudson has been insisting on going back to York House to search himself. He says there is no better time than now, since he has just finished waiting upon the queen."

I could see the path Ware was leading Will down. I knew what Ware expected me to do. "No one will search as thoroughly as I will," I said. "The longer I wait, the more likely some servant will find it and keep it. I am going to retrieve it now, and there is nothing you can say to stop me, Master Ware."

"You might as well stow away on the wherry that I hauled your trunk aboard. That is, if Sergeant Evans can't dissuade you."

Evans shrugged his massive shoulders. "No reason Jeffrey should not go. Her Majesty is not likely to summon him again until his new wardrobe is ready." He turned to me. "Go look for your ring. It would be hard to lose such a treasure."

"I will be back as soon as I am able," I said, wishing I didn't have to leave at all.

"Sergeant Evans, I will not forget your understanding in this matter,"

Ware said. "I fear the servants took advantage of Jeffrey. I tried to put a stop
to it, but with little success. I will do what I can to help him retrieve his
ring."

"Good luck finding it, Jeffrey. Hasten home when you are finished." He
emphasized *home* just the slightest bit. I started for the door, but Evans
cleared his throat. "You might want to make use of the clothes in your trunk
before you go," he said. "Archie is waiting outside." Yet somehow I sensed
his real motive was kinder: wanting to spare me the indignity of appearing
in front of Buckingham's servants in such disarray, giving them more reason
to torment me.

By the time I had changed and plunked the borrowed clothes in Archie's
arms, I was seething. But I said nothing until Ware and I were on the water.
"That was a ridiculous story. My grandfather was too poor to own a ring."

"Your grandfather has just experienced a rise in fortune, along with the
rest of your family." Ware adjusted his eye patch, and I could see a red line
where it had gouged his skin. "This performance you and I just completed
was a test to see how well you could deal with the unexpected. His Grace will
be pleased that you passed with astonishing grace. You convinced the noble
sergeant you had lost something precious."

"I nearly did. If Sergeant Evans had figured out we were duping him, he
could have crushed me under his boot like a beetle."

"I think the sergeant porter has taken a liking to you. Well done. To have
the porter of the queen's back stairs on your side already is no small accom-
plishment. If he catches you creeping about where you do not belong, he will
want to believe whatever lie you tell him. People generally believe what they
want to. Especially those with eyes like the sergeant's."

I had thought to myself that Evans was gullible. Why did the same opinion from Ware irritate me? "He will not forget about the ring. I am certain
he will ask about it."

"A ring will be provided."

"Fine."

We sat in silence the rest of the way to York House. I had not thought to
see the place again so soon, and I wondered if I might catch a glimpse of
Clemmy. It would do me good just to see his face.

But I did not. Ware escorted me to my old chamber, turned it upside down with me, grumbling the whole time about the incompetence of servants. At length, he claimed we had found the ring where someone had obviously put it because they had gotten wind of my return.

Taking care no one else could see, he slid a floor-length portrait aside, revealing a hidden passage. A few minutes later we emerged in some inner chamber deep in the duke's private quarters, Ware a black shadow beside me. Buckingham paced before the fire, a goblet in hand. He looked up, his gaze almost feverish. "So. The Queen's fool returned to York House. Forgive our little ploy to get you back here, but I sensed something important was happening. I have little patience when it comes to such matters. Tell me, Jeffrey, how fares the queen?"

I did not want to remember the girlish tear-stained face, the dark eyes that had seemed to tie me to the woman I was to betray. But the more I struggled not to think of her, the more vivid my memories of Henrietta Maria became.

"The queen fares ill," I said. "She was weeping over some letters. I could not read what they said—only see that they were from France. It looked like they carried royal seals."

"Probably something to do with a secret treaty Richelieu struck with Spain in her brother's name. That pompous bastard knew the whole point of wedding Henrietta Maria to King Charles was to forge an unbreakable alliance between our countries. Get France to aid us in our war against Spain."

I remembered what Will Evans had said about the "secret writing" portion of the marriage treaty that Buckingham had supposedly witnessed, then denied. "Since arriving at court, I have heard the French believe we have broken promises we made in that treaty, as well. Perhaps they feel that prevents the alliance from being binding."

Buckingham looked at me more closely. "You have gotten people to speak so freely in your presence already?"

"It is easy to overlook someone my size," I said.

"More letters will be coming to the queen. I don't suppose a butcher's son can read."

"I read some. Even a little in French, but not well."

"Memorize the biggest words. Write them down. Ware will decipher their meaning."

Ware compressed his lips in frustration, and I sensed he wanted to be done with Buckingham's court intrigues himself.

"If someone in the queen's household discovers the transcriptions?" I asked.

Buckingham's eyes narrowed. "You would be very sorry for it. If you cannot tell me what is in the letters, you can at least tell me what was said while you were in the queen's presence."

"Her confessor, Father Philip, had just left when she summoned me. She was most upset. He insists she take action to support Catholics beyond the walls. She does not want them to feel abandoned."

"She does come from the land of Joan of Arc," Ware said. "No doubt that is why she wishes to ride out against injustice. Why is it that Catholics tend to gloss over the fact that the affair with Saint Joan ended badly? Nothing like torture and being burned at the stake to delight their grisly sense of God."

"Too true." Buckingham laughed. "And we, like good Englishmen, will do our best to oblige them, eh, Ware? Did Her Majesty say anything more? Come, Jeffrey, think. Any hint she is spying for the French or Spanish? I would delight in catching her servants spying upon England's defenses— anything to implicate them and, through them, the queen. You say Father Philip was there. Of all the vile traitors walking free about England, he is the worst. A Scotsman, no less, pandering to the French king and the Pope! What was Father Philip urging her to?"

I remembered Buckingham's words about saints, and the tale Clemmy had told of his ill-fated visit to Tyburn. "The queen did say something." I fidgeted with my collar, the edge of it feeling sharp as an executioner's knife. "She wants to show Catholics she has not forgotten the promise she made to ease their lot. She said . . ." I swallowed, knowing that this was my first great step toward damnation. "She wished she could go on a pilgrimage to Tyburn, to kiss the place where the Catholic martyrs died."

"Martyrs?" Buckingham grasped the dagger at his belt. "You mean murdering scum! They tried to blow up Parliament, King James! The queen's own husband might have been there if the Gunpowder Plot had succeeded. What kind of woman would honor the very traitors who had attempted to wipe out members of the royal family?"

"A very reckless woman who would incur the wrath of the English people forever—and the wrath of the king whose father was the Jesuits' intended target twenty-odd years ago."

Buckingham spun toward Ware after the one-eyed man's statement. Ware adjusted the patch concealing his empty socket as he continued. "I cannot imagine the king would ever forget such an outrage. If his emotions were ever in danger, a reminder of the queen's trespass would touch a spur to tender places."

"You are right, Ware. Some would say God himself is behind these impulses of Her Majesty's. Her confessor is urging her to do this thing. Henrietta Maria feels moved to go to Tyburn herself. God's voice in her ear—she must heed it." Buckingham smiled. "She just does not realize that God yearns for her undoing."

I could not help but feel the breath of that God on the back of my neck. Feel hellfire, smell brimstone.

"What say you, Jeffrey?" Buckingham asked.

"I would not presume to guess what God was thinking. But if the queen decides to go to Tyburn, I will find a way to send you word."

"You will do more than that," the duke said. "Her brother and mother in France are doubtless putting pressure on her to act, as well. Those French harlots she surrounds herself with are too stupid to dissuade her. When the time is ripe to advance our cause, you will use your influence, as well."

"I have no influence."

"You will have by the time we are ready to act. Let the French and the Catholics feed her sense of outrage. The Pope is declaring 1626 a year of Jubilee, granting the faithful universal forgiveness for sin, God's mercy manifest in exchange for good works. It is a perfect time for Catholics to make a pilgrimage. She will be easy enough to goad to action when the time is right. You are an Englishman," Buckingham said. "If you add your urgings to the others', she will listen. Her Majesty is impulsive enough for anything. During the Jubilee's flurry of superstitious observances, the priests will deny the king his marital pleasures. There is another holy day every time the king turns around. The king and queen will fight about it. If you are there, you will add fuel to that fire."

As Buckingham had done at the banquet? I remembered too clearly the queen's dejected form on the barge, her heartbroken words to the friend she had cherished from childhood. I tried to imagine what it must be like, to have known the fellowship of *le petit troupeau* and then to leave it for a land that had hated your family for generations and loathed everything they stood for.

Buckingham started to pace again, and I could feel his excitement. "I will arrange a hunting party to divert the king from his troublesome wife. Once I have swept him away where he cannot prevent her foolishness, you will remind the queen of her wish to make a pilgrimage to Tyburn. She must heed God's call. You will make certain she cannot do otherwise. And after . . ." Buckingham drained his goblet. Drops of wine clung to his mustache like blood. He waved a hand to dismiss us. Ware cleared his throat.

"Your Grace," Ware said, "there was something you wished to give to Master Hudson."

"Ah, yes." The duke reached into his purse, just as when he had bought me from my father. He withdrew a slender gold ring. I shoved my hands behind my back.

"Let me say I could not find it. My grandfather's finger would have been far larger than mine. It makes no sense that his ring would fit."

"Your grandfather loved you so much, he had it cut down to size," Buckingham said. "Put it on."

I wanted to resist, but I dared not. I slid the ring on my finger. A cross was etched in its surface.

"It will convince the queen you are a godly man," Buckingham said. "Just think how grateful she will be."

It was one thing to deceive her—but to use God Himself as my weapon? I swallowed hard. Perhaps my father had sold my body. Yet as I looked down at the cross on the ring, I knew Buckingham would soon own something only I could surrender: my soul.

NINE

I arrived back at Denmark House feeling as if Buckingham had stuffed me with gunpowder and the touch of a spark might make my whole world explode.

Why had I not noticed the construction going on all about the queen's house before? The homesick Henrietta Maria was building herself a beautiful fortress, complete with a Catholic chapel. A chapel that would be against English law anywhere but the houses of ambassadors from foreign Romish kings. How much would this all cost in the end? How greatly would English Protestants resent their coin being spent to build a lavish safe haven to harbor the religious fanatics they feared most?

I forced myself to mount the stairs, uncertain where I should go once I reached the top. I looked about me, lost. The only person I could think to ask where I was to go now was William Evans. I might even have managed to find my way to the sergeant porter's chamber, but he was the last person I wished to see.

I wandered in search of the Freaks' Lair, aware of people whispering and pointing at me. Had Archie or Evans told them I was visiting the duke? As I twisted the ring on my finger, I could almost hear them scoffing over Ware's preposterous lie.

"Hey-up, Jeffrey!" I heard Simon Rattlebones call. I was never so relieved to see anyone in my life. Six spaniels whose silky ears were combed into love locks scampered up to me, tails flailing air. Only Scrap, the one I had met on my first visit to the lair, hung back, spying on me from between his master's legs.

"Where are you off to?" Rattlebones asked.

"To pitch camp under the table in the Freaks' Lair, I suppose, since no one has bothered to tell me where I am to sleep."

"You needn't get so prickly. Footman came to show you to the room the queen ordered for you. He moved your trunk from Will's chamber and everything." Rattlebones grimaced. "Guess Her Majesty was afraid you'd be trampled on even sharing a room with Goodfellow and me. But then, ever since Will injured Goodfellow with that chair and ruined a performance, the queen has been skittish about accidents. Put Will in a room where he can break furniture without hurting anyone else."

"Sergeant Evans struck Goodfellow with a chair?" I inquired, imagining how fearful the giant would be in a rage. "Is Sergeant Evans's temper so bad?"

"Lord no. Just heavy as a horse and clumsy as bedamned with those big feet of his. Sat on a chair and the thing broke and the chair back flew into Goodfellow. Just like Goodfellow to be standing in the wrong place."

Suddenly, the import of Rattlebones's words struck me. "You mean I am to have a room—alone?"

"The queen's putting you in your own chamber like a jewel in a box."

My own chamber seemed riches beyond imagining. I closed my eyes. God, what I would not give for a little time alone, someplace safe where I could bar the door.

"The footman was surprised when no one could find you," Rattlebones continued. "But Archie said you were off at His Grace's."

I could just imagine Archie's glee, linking me with the queen's great enemy. "I had left something precious at York House," I said. My honor.

"You'll never get it back. Buckingham is the grabbiest of all the noblemen who hang about here, and that dragon of a mother of his is worse. The king's palace is always crawling with Villiers rats—cousins and brothers and sisters, anyone with a drop of blood to connect them. I do a trick with a chain—each dog grasps a link in their teeth and Pug, the monkey, has to haul them around. That's what the Villiers family is like, but you can't shake them off like spaniels. Hang on like bleeding bulldogs on—Od's fish, Scrapper!"

I felt something warm and wet seeping through my shoe, then looked down, to see the spaniel pissing on me, an accusatory wrinkle above his knowing brown eyes.

"Jeffrey's not one of those Puritan toads. I told you we only piss on those who plot against the king."

Scrap kept on pissing.

Simon scooped him up. "I beg pardon for the little rogue. Least I can do by way of apology is to help you find the footman who sought you earlier."

My shoe made a sloshing sound as I trailed Simon to the servant in question, then followed the footman to a door just beyond the queen's privy apartments.

It was obvious someone had worked hard to make my new lodgings pleasant. A pair of footstools sat near the fire. Someone had constructed a chair back on one of them, so I could sit on it and still rest my feet on the floor.

A miniature flight of stairs was pushed against the side of a bed wide enough to accommodate my whole family, as well as Buckingham's fighting dogs. My chest from Buckingham's stood in a corner. Jeremy Griggory stood beside it, in the midst of unpacking. "The queen's steward says I am to be your manservant from now on," he said, working at his task with a dogged resignation, which only made my irritation on finding him worse.

"You sound as if you have been condemned to the scaffold. Anyone in Oakham would be clamoring for the chance to be a servant in this chamber. I wish I could bring my brother here." But I dared not. Samuel would never understand the lies I had to tell, the spying I was obliged to do.

"It's hard to get enthusiastic about serving a master who has already gotten some poor bird at His Grace's turned out in the streets for stealing," Griggory said.

"Where did you hear such a thing?"

"Archie. But it must be true. Will Evans did not deny that there was some fuss about a lost ring."

"I found the ring where I had left it. See?" I held out my hand. "No one to blame for losing it but my own carelessness. Although, I could lose it again and blame you if you want an excuse to end our association."

Griggory looked at me long and hard, as if he were trying to figure out if I was serious. "I suppose there are worse people I might be assigned to. Like that dog trainer who came up to poke around when you weren't here. It's just not right for a live man to look like he belongs in a crypt. And those dogs—I vow I can smell the piss of them even though I scrubbed your floor three times."

"You missed a spot," I said.

Griggory looked around, mystified. I held up my piss-soaked shoe.

⚘

I spent far too much time preparing what I would say if Evans asked how my grandfather had come by a gold ring. Come morning, every explanation flew out of my head when I answered the royal summons for my first rehearsal for the queen's masque.

Henrietta Maria and her ladies flitted about, giggling when they forgot their parts and exclaiming over costumes that slipped down, revealing glimpses of breast. Silk ferns and gauze made them appear swathed in mist; tiny gems had been stitched to sparkle like dew.

This was no Christian court, but a pagan glen where the young queen and her attendants could frolic in ways they would not have dared anywhere else. A world of myth and legend filled Denmark House's banqueting hall. Towering pageant carts were scattered about the vast chamber, minions constructing a dragon so fierce, I half-expected it to roar.

At York House, I had seen only the illusion noble entertainments created *after* the work was finished. This fantasy world was stripped down to its bones—cogs and pulleys and ropes and scaffolds.

At the center of this mayhem stood a preoccupied man garbed in tawny brown, a black skullcap plastered upon his unruly wheat-straw hair. Beneath a bumpy nose, his shovel-like beard rippled in curls that reached his breast. Keen blue eyes peered down at the sheaf of pages in his hand. A stick of charcoal flew over what looked to be plans of some kind.

My curiosity as to who the man was and what he was doing was tempered by nervousness, as the encounter with Evans loomed large. But the giant set me off balance yet again, behaving as easily in my company as he had before Ware's illogical ploy. Relief made me relax my ring-decked hand, and I marveled at my good luck—and Evans's lack of guile. Evans traced the direction of my gaze toward the man who had stirred my curiosity.

"The man's name is Inigo Jones. He is surveyor of works for the king and queen, though he is not overcome with love for Their Majesties. The king is too cold and the queen too frivolous for Jones's tastes, I think. In spite of that, Master Jones has put together a remarkable collection of buildings here in the royal court." Jones barked out an order, and workers constructing a mock balcony rushed over to look at the plans with him.

"What is he sketching?" I asked.

"Might be something to do with the masque. He creates the actors' costumes and the stage they play upon. Or it might be some idea for construction around Denmark House. All the building you see going on here is by his design. He's been at it a long time. Archie was here when Jones began the remodeling for King Charles's mother." Evans chuckled.

"What do you find so amusing?"

"Apparently while out hunting, King James shot his wife's dog by accident. He gave Queen Anne this place as an apology and renamed it Denmark House after her birthplace. She was renovating it when she died. Then our present queen took over, determined to make it her own. Robin Goodfellow has gotten peeks at some of the new designs she has approved. He says Jones is attempting to design stairs without anything to hold them up."

"Goodfellow is just trying to gull you. Such a trick would be impossible."

"People say only a madman would attempt such a feat. Or a man schooled in magic." Evans hunkered down near me, pretending to adjust the knot of ribbon at his knee. "Some say Jones struck a bargain so angels will hold the Tulip Stairs aloft. Others think he stole secrets from the devil. Guess we'll find out when he is finally able to try building them."

I wanted to scoff, but I angled my shoulders away from Evans and made the sign to ward off the evil eye.

"The rumors are nonsense, of course. But Jones had to get his knowledge somewhere, didn't he? No one in England ever created such magic with bricks and plaster before him. As if that weren't amazing enough, I dare you to explain how he makes things appear and disappear during the masques. One moment an entire castle is before your eyes; the next moment it's vanished. . . . Your ring!" he burst out, looking at my hand.

I curled my right hand atop the left to hide the glimmer of gold. "I feel like a fool for misplacing such a keepsake," I said, hoping he wouldn't probe any further.

"It's precious to have something that belonged to someone you loved,"

Evans said. "After my father died, my brother Davey put on Da's coat to smell the pipe smoke on it. If I'd split every seam, the coat wouldn't have stretched over me." Sorrow stole into the giant's eyes.

I tried to imagine what it would be like to find comfort in a father's coat once he was dead.

Evans cleared his throat. "Well, I have my memories. That's all I need, isn't it?" What was it about Evans that made me tempted to tell the truth? I would trade my gold ring to have memories like yours, I wanted to say, but I clamped my mouth shut.

Discordant music drifted from the musicians' gallery, then mellowed into a dancing measure. Will and I both looked over to where the queen was practicing her steps, her skirts scooped up to show dainty feet in pink slippers, her ankles flashing. Curls bounced against her white throat when she tossed her head. I did not want to think how desperate she must be to put on a merry face and forget for just a little while what she certainly knew—that her brother had allied with Spain against her husband.

When she finished dancing, she saw me from across the room. She broke from the chain of ladies and hastened over to where Will and I stood.

"Oh, Sergeant Evans! Little Jeffrey! You will scarce believe how brilliantly Master Jones has rewritten his script. He is not pleased about it, but he rarely is happy unless he is allowed to do as exactly as he likes. I told him I must have a bit about a giant and a dwarf, so, Jeffrey, you are to be a demon in the dragon's service. Sergeant Evans will be Faith and fight to save me. Master Jones is to put a few touches on the mechanical dragon so it looks a trifle like Bishop Laud. The bishop has vexed me so often, the role will be a delicious jest."

"Majesty," Evans began. "It is a fine dragon just as it is. You might do well to leave it alone."

"The bishop will not recognize himself. Only my ladies will understand. How we will laugh when it is done."

"The bishop is an astute man, and the king loves him well. His Majesty would not think such play amusing."

She pouted, her sweet face reminding me of my sister when someone was trying to thwart her. "I *will* have the dragon as I wish. Jeffrey will spring from its mouth in a chariot of flame and try to drag me down to hell."

"Master Jones wrote such a pretty play," said Sergeant Evans soothingly. "Let it stand. Anyone who knows hero tales understands it is not wise to tamper with dragons."

"I hardly think you are qualified to advise me. As for the tales you speak of, William Evans, I have read them a hundred times. Have you?"

Evans looked at her steadily and I felt the current of tension between them. "You know I have not, Your Majesty," he said.

"This much I can tell you: If heroes never tampered with dragons, there would be no story at all!" She flounced off.

I said nothing, though the queen's treatment of Evans stung.

"Jeffrey, you must help me change her mind," he said as we watched her rejoin her ladies.

Why should I interfere? I thought. The queen's stubbornness would only make it easier to spur her to recklessness. She was already determined to behave badly on her own. But Evans was waiting for an answer. "You tried to dissuade Her Majesty and she insulted you."

"She does not know any better," he said.

I set my jaw, looking grim. "Then perhaps it is time she learned."

That night when I returned to my room, I did not have to pretend to be in a foul temper. I raged about a tear in my breeches, sending Griggory scurrying off to get it mended. As soon as I was certain he had gone, I cut off a square of parchment, grabbed my quill in a trembling hand, and scribbled down what had transpired during the rehearsal. The wobbly letters seemed deafening as a scream. I dashed sand across the wet ink and stuffed the writing implements away, straining to hear above the thundering of my heart in case Griggory returned.

I rolled the parchment as small as I could, then sealed it with wax, desperately wondering where to hide it until I could slip it into the nook in my saddle. Hot wax burned my thumb, but I clutched the parchment anyway— a live ember I could not let go, lest I set the world on fire.

⁂

The parchment burned even hotter when I hid it in my doublet the next morning, avoiding Griggory's reproachful eye. I was grateful that we broke our fast with the rest of the servants in the Great Hall that morning, hoping that the presence of so many outside the menagerie would distract my fellow curiosities and keep them from looking at me too closely.

But from the moment Sara slid onto the bench beside me, she sensed something was amiss. She could not bear it when I waved away tray after tray of the food offered. "Jeffrey, have some of these lovely quail's eggs. You must eat something, or you'll not last halfway through the morning ride. Have bit of bread and porridge."

"I'll mind my own porridge, thank you!"

"If you had porridge, I wouldn't have to mind it," Sara argued, a tiny quaver in her voice.

I let her slop some of the foul stuff into my bowl and some quail's eggs on the plate beside it. But when she threatened me with cold mutton, I refused. I had to squeeze the stuff down my throat, after all. I could tell she was going to watch every bite.

I would need to guard my emotions better on days I was to send notes to Buckingham; otherwise, I knew, I might as well take Goodfellow's paints and scribe the words *up to no good* across my brow.

By the time I was able to rid myself of the parchment on our morning ride, I was well and truly sick. Instead of answering a call of nature as I pretended to, I slipped into the woods and retched up a mixture of quail's egg and porridge and guilt.

As the days passed, I told myself it was possible the duke had heard of the bishop's dragon even before some minion of his had plucked my message from its hiding place. He could have learned of the queen's plan from Inigo Jones himself. The surveyor of works' family had come from Rutland, as mine had. Jones had designed entertainments and building projects for Buckingham's family before King James had required his services.

In the weeks we practiced our parts, I tried to soften my own guilt by imagining who else might be taking Buckingham's coin in exchange for information. For all I knew, Buckingham had hired a spy to spy upon *me*.

Yet the queen's fancy to turn the bishop into a dragon had unleashed something unruly in all the French women. They decked Will in Madame Saint-Georges's new hat and made him recite love poems to Little Sara, giggling until I grabbed his halberd. I braced myself against the weight, anger giving me strength to spear through the hat's floppy brim. "Mice might be-deck a lion in flowers," I said with undisguised scorn, "but the lion is still a lion and the mice are still mice." I turned to Little Sara. "Such creatures might gnaw upon a hundred jeweled hats, my lady, but they will never reach a generous heart." Sara's smile and Will's laughter had made me feel a new power all my own.

The "mice" turned their spite elsewhere, teasing any Puritans who strayed into their path and taunting high-church dignitaries who went about the king's business. They might as well have been slipping toads under people's coverlets, so girlish did they seem. By the night of the masque, I feared they might burst from laughing at their game.

Yet as I waited to drive my hell chariot, I could see others playing games of their own. I fingered the reins harnessed to my "horses"—Rattlebones's spaniels dressed in coats stitched with orange-and-crimson silk flames. I saw Bishop Laud folding his hands with disapproval, and the Puritan courtiers did the same as the performance progressed. I glanced at the tight-lipped king and doubted he would see any humor in the masque's jests.

It is not wise to court a king's displeasure, I thought as my imagination conjured up the ghost of the king whose rage had become legend. I could imagine Henry VIII presiding over such an entertainment—the monster who beheaded two wives and gorged on the wealth of the abbeys he pillaged. Royal excess figured large in the tales I had heard of King James, as well. His Scot's retinue had been a grasping lot, greediest of all the pretty, ambitious youths James had slavered over and lifted from obscurity to the highest rank in the land. Young men like Buckingham.

Both former kings—and the duke, as well—were so different from Charles: the short-statured, painfully shy second-born son who was never supposed to be king. How inadequate Charles must feel in the shadow of more forceful nobles, I thought. Even his kinswoman Elizabeth had been more kingly than he, facing down the Armada that had sailed from Spain intending to rip her from her throne and drag England back to the Roman Church.

I thought of how England would have faced the Inquisition had the Spaniards won: torture dealt in the name of God, a faith that seemed the opposite of my gentle brother's. The constant feel of inquisitors' eyes upon you, waiting for you to make a mistake. Terrified victims being put to the question . . . the same question over and over, one you could never prove the answer to.

Did Charles face an inquisition of his own every day? *Are you Christian enough to head God's church? Ruthless enough to protect your people no matter what the cost? Are you even man enough to control your French wife?*

Empathy for Charles Stuart woke in me, though I did not want it to. Is that why the king is so stiff? I wondered. Was Charles's only shield against the debauched legacies of other kings his rigid need for propriety? His desperate attempt to seem kingly in spite of his bowed legs and his stammer was little different from my own habit of stretching myself as tall as I was able.

This mockery of the bishop was no private jest, despite what the queen had claimed. It would humiliate the king before his own court. Infuriate those watching a French Catholic scorning the English Church. The lines and characters shifted, and I saw what those hostile onlookers had obviously discerned. A powerful churchman in England made into a beast, the Catholic queen his victim.

By the time our tableau was finished and we bowed before the court, King Charles was fingering the length of his cane as if he wanted to use it on his wife's backside.

As the dancers mingled with the other guests, I was one of the few who stood near enough to the royal couple to hear what ignited the outrage in Henrietta Maria's remarkable eyes.

". . . Queen Anne—your own mother—performed in the masques!" the queen protested in French, withdrawing into a quiet alcove. "Tonight's work is a play only. Entertainment."

". . . jeer at the church of England, at the bishop . . . insult me as its head . . . Catholic nonsense . . ."

"Your mother was a Catholic and people did not hate her or persecute her for her faith. I am a daughter of France, far above—"

"*A daughter of France?*" the king's voice cut like ice. "That is nothing to pride yourself on when compared to a queen who served her husband and gave him her loyalty instead of throwing tantrums."

The queen recoiled. I could not help but think the king had made a good point.

"You could take a lesson from my lady mother and stop flinging your popery in people's faces," Charles said. "This very afternoon, the bishop told me you and your ladies came dancing through chapel while he was conducting services—the lot of you gavotting about, disrupting people's prayers on purpose. Now you dare behave as if *you* are the one being tormented?"

I saw the crowd around me strain to catch their words. I saw the lips of the queen's enemies grow stiff while trying not to show their pleasure.

The queen's reply to His Majesty was hushed yet filled with outrage. Buckingham shoved his chair back from the table and watched the couple from beneath half-lowered lids.

King Charles's voice rose above her outburst. "I think you had best retire until you learn to speak proper English. This is the court of the king of England, Scotland, Ireland, and Wales. France is your enemy now, as it is mine. We're on the brink of war because of French arrogance. I will not suffer it from my own wife!"

"War?" The queen paled. "No. Sire, I pray you—"

"Yes, pray, pray this—that God will teach you your duty and you will be honorable enough to fulfill it."

Tears streaked Henrietta Maria's face. I could see what it cost her not to turn and run.

"I do not forget where my loyalties lie." She said it so proudly, I had to admire her. "Now, since I have obviously displeased you, I will remove myself from your presence. By your leave, Majesty. "

"Go, go!" He waved his hand and I watched her curtsy, then exit the room. As I followed with the rest of her entourage, the duke of Buckingham thrust his leg in my path so I could not avoid it. I sprawled onto the floor, heard a ripping sound as something on my costume snagged his silk stocking, tearing a nasty hole.

Or had Buckingham torn it himself with the object all but hidden in his hand? One thing was certain, though no one else in the hall might guess: He had tripped me intentionally.

"Fool!" he snapped. "Have you been picking up French tricks? You tore my stocking on purpose!"

I tried to scramble to my feet, but he grabbed me by the collar and forced me back to my knees to look at the damage I had caused. "It was an accident," I said, taken aback by his anger. "Forgive me, Your Grace." Had I really offended him to this degree? I felt the banquet guests watching with intense pleasure.

"Perhaps you should seek absolution the way your new Catholic friends would—mumble over pig's bones or make a pilgrimage to holy wells that are good for nothing but watering a man's horse. Or you could find one of those accursed Jesuits sneaking about and pay a priest coin. Fatten the Pope's purse and he'll forgive murder."

Suddenly, I understood. The duke was creating the illusion that we loathed each other. One more cloak to disguise that he was my real master. I knew I must play my part.

"I do not think I'm in danger of hell at present," I said. "One can hardly murder a shoe."

"But you can make a laughingstock of the bishop of Bath and Wells in front of the king himself! Perhaps this coin might buy you absolution, but it will not buy you the goodwill of any true subject of the king." He pushed something hard into my grasp. I looked down at the object in my cupped palm. A metal token struck by vendors at Tyburn, a souvenir that spectators could flash as they bragged about the executions they had seen. I recalled Clemmy's description of those horrors, could not believe anyone who had witnessed such torture did not want to forget.

I closed my fingers over the medal, my heart sinking. I would have to manipulate the queen as Buckingham desired. I thought of the queen's tear-washed face, her courage, her irreverent humor in capturing the bishop's character so well in the guise of Jones's mechanical dragon. I wished I could work magic as Jones seemed to do—sweep back scenery and scaffolds, strip away costumes—turn back time to the moment Will Evans had begged me to help deter the queen from her reckless course.

I wished I could soften the queen's defiance, veil her fiery Catholicism, muffle her French ways, and coax plain English from her tongue. But I'd stand a better chance dancing the galliard wearing Will Evans's shoes.

Buckingham tugged on one of the silk flames stitched to my tunic, his voice for my ears alone. "You know what to do," he said.

I did.

I bowed to the duke, terrified I would not be able to persuade the queen to go to Tyburn. More terrified still that I *could*.

TEN

·

I had been handled roughly by Buckingham. I fared no better at the hands of Madame Saint-Georges. The Frenchwoman met me at the door to the queen's chamber. "Some court fool you are! The queen is in distress and you are nowhere to be found. She sent Little Sara in search of you."

"I did not see Sara," I said, grateful the woman's sense of duty was so great that she'd not return to the queen until she made a thorough search. The endeavor would take longer than usual, since her awkwardly formed joints pained her after a performance. A decent man would have sent a page out to fetch her, but the possibility of Sara's witnessing what I was about to do was too dangerous to risk.

Mamie glanced over her shoulder at the woman pacing before the fireplace. The costume donned with such merriment hung limp about the queen's slender body. Tears had washed makeup in rivulets down cheeks that had flushed with excitement only a few hours before.

Yet this misery was not enough for the duke of Buckingham.

"Where have you been? Licking the king's boots to remind him you're English?" Madame Saint-Georges grasped my arm and shook me so hard, she lifted me off my feet. "How could you grovel to that man after the way he treated the queen?"

Pain throbbed beneath the vise of Saint-Georges's fingers, and my toes scrabbled but failed to reach the floor. I hated how helpless I was against the court factions battling to control me. *The same way they were determined to control the queen.*

For a moment, empathy filled me and I wanted to snatch Henrietta Maria away from all of them—Buckingham and the king, Madame Saint-Georges and Father Philip and the royal French family pummeling her with their blame-filled letters from across the Channel. I shoved aside the sense of kinship. Samuel and my family were defenseless, not this queen all but drowning in riches, allowed to put on elaborate masques at a whim. At least the queen had some power to fight back.

I bolstered my courage and confronted Madame Saint-Georges. "Actually, Buckingham's shoes were the reason I was delayed. I tripped over them and he yanked me up by my collar to upbraid me." With my free hand, I pulled down the edge of the garment to display a nasty welt. I heard the Frenchwoman draw in a sharp breath. "Now, thanks to you, Madame. I shall have a claw print on my arm, as well."

She released me. The instant I regained my balance, I strained to stand as tall as I could. Not that it mattered. I was still half-suffocated in her skirts.

"Jeffrey! Mamie! I cannot bear your squabbling." The queen tore loose the roses Saint-Georges had woven into her lustrous curls and flung them into the fire. The petals shriveled, the smell of savaged beauty filling my nostrils. "What are you fighting about?"

"I am showing Madame Saint-Georges my battle scars, Majesty. I'm as war-torn as Calais, attacked by two countries. English here"—I displayed the first welt—"and French here." I rubbed my arm. "However, I made certain I left my mark on one adversary, as well," I said with satisfaction. "I tore Buckingham's fine stocking and scuffed his fancy shoe, so he'll not be wearing them again. I made certain that when His Grace's man strips the duke's garments off tonight, he will find bruises as painful as mine."

"Do not say so, Jeffrey!" the queen exclaimed. "Not even inside this room. You must never say you injured Buckingham on purpose. It is against the law for even the most exalted courtiers to strike someone in the palace. You could lose your hand."

"Yet there is no penalty for raging at Your Majesty that way? Perhaps it would be better to cut out men's tongues."

Lines bracketing the queen's mouth softened. I saw the ghost of a smile, but there was no mockery in it, only the tenderness of one as badly in need of refuge as I was. "You look quite fierce, Jeffrey," she said. "I am almost afraid of you."

You should be, I thought.

"A princess is not supposed to show fear," the queen continued. "A queen— never. But here in England, your castles are haunted by fallen queens. You have not yet stayed at Hampton Court, Jeffrey, but the ghosts of Anne Boleyn and Catherine Howard walk the gallery there. They faced a heads- man before a hateful crowd. Catherine Howard was only a little older than I am."

Madame Saint-Georges broke in. "You are the French king's sister! The English would not dare harm you, even if our countries go to war."

I wanted to believe her. Yet, how far would men like Buckingham and the bishop go if the queen clung to her Catholic faith and her French loyalties?

I could not pull my gaze away from the queen's eyes, which were dark and expressive as a doe's. "I would be fierce in your defense, Majesty, were I not trapped . . ." I buried my face in my hands, horrified at what I had almost confessed. Henrietta Maria stroked my hair.

"Trapped by what, Jeffrey?"

I struggled to find some answer that would satisfy. "By things I cannot control . . . this body of mine. I am sorry, Majesty. I am sorry!"

She drew my hands away from my face and kissed my cheek. "Do not vex yourself over what you cannot change, Jeffrey. If your body was not so small and I had not been forced to come to England, our paths would never have crossed. That would have been very sad indeed."

A lump formed in my throat, due to all the things I wish I could have said. Not to the queen, but, rather, to the lost girl who so often broke Will Evans's heart.

Mitte, the queen's favorite spaniel, whined and scratched at her skirts, wanting to comfort her as much as I did. She scooped up the wriggling bundle of fur and buried her face in its neck.

I angled my body away to blot out the sight. God help me, I had to act on Buckingham's orders now or I never would. Only the thought of Samuel gave me strength enough to reach into the pouch Inigo Jones had designed in my costume.

I pinched the token from Tyburn between my fingers, dragged it out. I bowed my head over it and mumbled a prayer, hoping curiosity would be stirred. To betray with a prayer was perhaps an even greater wickedness than Judas Iscariot's kiss.

"What have you got in your hand?" the queen asked as soon as I murmured "Amen."

I pretended to muster my courage and extended my cupped hand. The medal winked, an evil eye against my skin. "A beggar slipped this to me on my way to chapel last Sunday. He said, 'Give this to the queen. Tell Her Majesty that God's faithful beyond the palace walls pin all our hopes on her.'"

"Yet you kept it for yourself, you little thief!" Madame Saint-Georges complained.

"I only wanted to make certain it was not poisoned before I let Her Majesty touch it." I turned to the queen. "I figured if I carried it on my person, any poison would do its vile work on me. Perhaps I was foolish, but you seemed so happy for once. I did not want to trouble you. Was I wrong to do as I did?"

The queen picked up the coin, her fingertips brushing my palm. I had never felt any so soft. The warmth of her melted into my skin. I closed my hand tight on shards of guilt.

"This is not a coin," she mused. "A holy medal, perhaps?" She held it up to the candle. Red glow spilled across the disk and bled between her fingers. I knew she could read the crude letters that had been struck into the medal's surface.

"Tyburn," she whispered.

"Tyburn?" One of her maids of honor turned to question Madame Saint-Georges. At thirteen, what could a protected little French girl know of such a place?

"It is the scaffold where criminals are executed," Saint-Georges explained.

"Not just criminals," I interjected. "Catholics, as well." I had heard of a time when Bloody Mary had burned those of the reformed faith, but I did not mention that fact. "Jesuits and priests also die at Tyburn, suffering a traitor's death."

The maid of honor crossed herself. "God rest their blessed souls."

The clock on the wall ticked so loudly, it hurt my ears. The queen pressed the hand clutching Buckingham's medal against her breast. Amid the gauze of her costume I saw part of a rose she had torn from her hair. The petal stained the fabric, red as blood.

"Buckingham was present at the meeting where King James agreed my marriage would usher in a new age of tolerance. I swear the only reason Buckingham continues to push for the persecution of Catholics is to show his power over me."

"A queen has more important matters to concern herself with than gutter folk," Madame Saint-Georges scoffed, leveling me with a glare. "What do they expect her to do?"

"I do not know what they expect. I think, rather, they hope." I pictured Samuel's fervent joy those rare times we could find a priest. "I know someone who has never gone to Mass in a true chapel or church. His sins weigh on his conscience for months, sometimes even a year, before he can unburden himself to a Catholic confessor brave enough to absolve him. This lad lives in terror that he will die without Extreme Unction and be sent to hell. When a neighbor's babe was not baptized, this lad wept for weeks, thinking of the tiny life walled out of Heaven."

The queen pressed her hands on her own empty womb.

"Jeffrey! Shame on you for troubling Her Majesty with such tales," Madame said. "Can you not see they distress her?"

"I am sorry. But it is hard to be poor. Not even to have hope of Heaven . . ." I looked into the bleak reality of my own future. "Your Majesty, if I were truly brave, I would say what is in my heart. But I do not have the courage of the lad I spoke of."

The queen tipped her head to one side. Dark curls tumbled back, exposing her throat. "What does your heart tell you, Jeffrey? Your heart is big as any man's."

"The day after the banquet at York House, when I first came to this chamber, you said something that has haunted me ever since. You said that you had passed Tyburn in your coach. There, you saw an old lady making a pilgrimage, kneeling where the Catholic martyrs died. You said you wished God would tell you what to do to ease the plight of your English subjects."

"I remember."

My stomach lurched. I dipped my toes into hell. "I believe God stamped his wish on this medal."

"You cannot be serious—" one of the other ladies gasped. Whispers buzzed around me and I could feel everyone in the chamber leaning forward, holding their breath. "It is too dangerous."

I met Her Majesty's dark French eyes. "You told me that a queen must never be afraid. If she is doing God's will, is that not truer than ever?"

Henrietta Maria took a deep breath. Her eyes sparkled—not with wholesome fear, but with a kind of zeal I had seen in my own brother's face. Something full of power and light I could not understand.

"Your simple folk will have their sign, Jeffrey." The queen turned to her ladies. "To honor the Jubilee this summer, we shall garb ourselves in black and make that pilgrimage I spoke of. Walk barefoot from St. James's Palace, through Hyde Park, to where the scaffold waits."

"Majesty," one of her timid ladies said, "will the English not try to stop you?"

"They must not find out until it is done. I will have the oath of everyone in this room that they will tell no one what we have spoken of here today."

"Not even Father Philip?" the little maid of honor asked.

"Father has been urging me to take a stand. I shall ask him to lead us."

"What of the king?" Madame Saint-Georges asked.

The queen twisted her wedding ring around her finger. "I am a daughter of France," she said. "If it is God's will that I make a pilgrimage to Tyburn, how can I refuse?"

It is not God's will, I thought. It is the duke of Buckingham's. Now, God forgive me, I have made it my own.

⌐◦⌐

I had spent my whole life crowded by the sounds of fellow creatures, even in the deepest reaches of night. Not only the noise of my family but also the screams of pigs being slaughtered, the whimpers of dogs Father had brought home to nurse after they survived being in the ring with Buckingham's bulls.

There had been so many times I would have given my allotment of bread for time alone with my own thoughts. But when the queen and her ladies of the bedchamber retired, a weary Little Sara trailing behind them, I could not bear the idea of returning to my own room.

To walk into the chamber was to face reminders of the kindnesses Her Majesty had shown: my small chair, the stairs leading up to the high platform of my bed, the writing table delivered the day after I had expressed my hunger for learning, the wooden surface piled with books for the lessons she had secured for me.

I wandered through the corridors, paused near the entry to the banqueting hall, which the queen had left in such distress. Sounds of music and laughter troubled me as I peeked into the room. The garlands of flowers bedecking the dais where the royals had sat were wilting, the scenery from the ill-fated masque abandoned, a fairyland whose magic had flown. Buckingham and Bishop Laud would be celebrating their triumph over the queen, though neither would admit their delight. They would show the king faces filled with outrage on his behalf or censure toward the queen—those grim, grieved expressions I had seen them adopt other times while they mined the king's good opinion from beneath Henrietta Maria's feet. I could only imagine how thrilled Buckingham would be if I were to seek him out and tell of Her Majesty's plans.

I'd come up with a masterful falsehood to dupe her, one Buckingham would have been proud of. I soothed my guilt by reminding myself that the queen lied every time she dressed up Sara or displayed Robin Goodfellow's paintings or marveled over Dulcinea's uncanny balance. The queen gathered us in as if she were our mother, lavishing caresses on us, spoiling us with trinkets. But in the end, we were playthings to be hoarded and put on display, dressed up and moved about however she chose. As Archie said, we were no more important to her than the trained monkey.

What loyalty did I owe to a woman who regarded me that way? To brand that ugly truth in my mind, I headed away from the festivities and made my way to the Freaks' Lair. It was empty, the menagerie still employed in the hall or off to bed after the excitement of the performance. Only Pug, the monkey, remained, fixed to a gold chain. I crossed to the nest of old costumes where Pug curled up, asleep, one hairy wrist twined in his chain. "Ho there, Pug," I whispered so as not to startle him. He cracked his eyelids open, recognizing my voice. He held up his captive hand with a trust I did not deserve. I untangled him, then grabbed a few dates someone had left in a bowl on the table. I put one piece of dried fruit in my hand and held it out to the monkey. Pug snatched it and took a bite. I expected him to gobble it down, greedy. But he hesitated, looking from his treasure back to me.

Sad, dark eyes peered at me from that ugly face. He held out the half-eaten fruit to share.

Suddenly, I could not bear seeing him chained and alone. I unhooked the leash from its post in the wall, and the creature leaped up onto my shoulder. I reached up to peel him away from me, but—as if he sensed my intention—Pug scrambled across the back of my neck and down into the crook of my arms, pulling his chain with him. He laid with his belly up, his legs kicking the air like an ugly baby.

"Stupid animal," I grumbled without malice, the chain bound around me. "You've got us both so tangled, we'll never get free."

Pug looked up at me, suddenly horribly wise. He laid his hand against my cheek.

☙❧

Next morning as I entered the queen's chamber, I could tell something had altered. The frenetic emotion that had gripped her since I'd joined her household had transformed into an air more unsettling. Every surface seemed draped with black cloth, her ladies under the command of Madame Saint-Georges applying shears with questionable skill. The laps of her little maids of honor overflowed with piles of black frieze to be fashioned into garments as they stitched the mountains of cloth. How alien the coarse material seemed, pillowed against bright silk skirts. Even the queen's face appeared different, no longer frantic with gaiety, nor blustery with tantrums. Henrietta Maria's animated features were as solemn as those of the Madonna that the widow in the shambles kept hidden from everyone but Samuel and me.

Her confessor beamed from a cushion in the corner as he read aloud from a volume of the *Lives of the Saints,* while Will Evans stood guard like a contrary Joshua, determined to hold *up* the walls of Jericho instead of tearing them down.

"Jeffrey!" the queen called out when Will announced me. "We have no time for play today. We have much sewing to do if we are to garb everyone who wishes to take part in my pilgrimage to Tyburn."

"I see, Majesty."

"Sergeant Evans insists he will accompany me. But I would not force anyone to make such a stand unless they chose to." Her black Valois eyes asked what she would not say aloud.

I wanted to stay as far from my handiwork as possible. I imagined the London streets, the city folk who loathed the French. Women who would soon be sending their sons and husbands and fathers to fight the queen's brother in a war her marriage had been meant to prevent, if what the king said was true.

I glanced up at Will Evans, noted his brow furrowed deep with worry. "Your Majesty," he said. "Forgive me for speaking out of turn, but the walk to Tyburn is no place for Master Hudson. I do not doubt Jeffrey's courage or his devotion to you, but I will have my hands full keeping you and your ladies from harm. Master Hudson would be trampled and lost in the crowd. We might never find him."

I felt a new depth of self-loathing as I pictured the queen's bare feet treading the road I had set her upon and Will Evans attempting to shield her.

The queen turned to me. "What say you, Jeffrey?"

"I think I would look well in black." I looked from Henrietta Maria to Will and back again.

It would match the hue of my heart, I thought.

ELEVEN

•

June

I cannot say what it was that deepened the queen's attachment to me during
the weeks that followed. But she stitched me into the fabric of her days as
intimately as she pulled the black thread through the frieze. It unnerved me
to see how openhearted she was; to sense that something in me called to her,
a rare communion I tried to resist.

Yet how could I? She shone at the center of every day, her eyes lighting
up when I came into the room, her laugh spilling over my antics. She needed
me, and I had not imagined how dangerous that sensation could be.

It felt so strange to think of my life before the queen, the journeys I had
taken because of her. I had been glad to put all of the places I had lived behind. But when Griggory packed the contents of my room so we could join
the rest of the queen's household on its trek to Whitehall Palace, I felt a loss
I had never experienced before.

I had heard of Whitehall's size and splendor. When I finally beheld my
new home, I was overwhelmed by the chaotic jumble of buildings. Whitehall might have been one more Gothic beast sprung from Will's imagination. To prepare me for the move, he described the palace as so greedy for
space that it devoured the houses once crowding the suburb of Westminster.
Henry VIII had leveled every building in the area to form his sprawling seat
of government.

I spent the afternoon before my first banquet at Whitehall trying to decipher the muffled voices on the far side of the queen's closed door. Servants hauled steaming copper buckets full of water for the queen's bath, while ladies-in-waiting scurried back and forth with trays of lotions and oils and red silk to buff the queen's hair to a sheen, preparations more lengthy than any I had noticed before.

I hid my spying as best I could, practicing comic faces in the mirror near the door and perfecting the delivery of my jests on anyone who passed by. My banishment was frustrating, the capers I had planned so fitted to the day, I stopped Sara as she darted past with some sweet-smelling lotion. "When will the queen come out?" I demanded.

She blew loose strands of hair from her brow and said, "She is still making ready. She has tried on and discarded half a dozen gowns."

"If she does not want me, why does she not dismiss me so I can go to the Lair?" I grumbled.

"It comforts her to know she can summon you at any moment so you can take her mind off of her troubles. Not that she can speak to any man about the matters that concern her now."

She hastened to the door and a footman opened it. A wave of sweet scent, feminine chatter, and steamy warmth rolled over me before he shut the door again.

Even when the queen emerged from that world of feminine mystery, she did not heed the jests I had labored over to please her. Startled by noises, flushing when I least expected it, Henrietta Maria unnerved me more than ever. I could feel some strange sizzling sensation in the air. When she and Mamie Saint-Georges withdrew from the other women, I edged close as I dared. It astonished me—how adept I was growing at joining the movements of their lips with the half-whispered French words they meant for their ears alone.

"You are exquisite," Madame Saint-Georges reassured as the queen adjusted folds of lace to cover more of her bosom.

"I feel as if there are thorns tucked among the bedclothes when the king visits me," the queen said in a low voice, and I could see the skin of her décolletage flush. "I know I must submit to his attentions, but I cannot like it. I draw my counterpane up over my nose, close my eyes."

I could see the picture so clearly, the queen trying in her girlish way to disappear.

"A husband's love is nothing to be discounted," Madame Saint-Georges said.

"He barely speaks to me. He goes jabbing about and makes the most unlovely sounds. I feel as if I will die of embarrassment. The act is so undignified, it seems more fitted for barnyard animals than a queen."

Saint-Georges softened a laugh with a quick hug. "You will not die of embarrassment any more than other women have. You will grow used to husbandly affection. I believe there are even women who enjoy their husbands' caresses."

Henrietta Maria rubbed her arms. "I cannot imagine enjoying it. It pulls and—and burns and stings inside me."

"Think of France or one of the songs you sing so beautifully and it will soon be over."

When night finally fell, bringing with it my first banquet at Whitehall, I watched the king, catching tiny glimpses beneath Charles's mask of control. He could not take his eyes off of his wife, the warmth she lavished on her ladies, the French dignitaries, and me. Charles stared at her lips, the swell of her breasts above the lace of her gown. He leaned toward her, hunger in his eyes, and I knew he was anticipating bedding his wife.

I remembered snips I had heard about the queen remaining celibate on holy days and other times, as well. I had never stopped to consider how difficult it must be for the king to parade before his servants and the queen's ladies to her bedchamber and be turned away.

I pictured the humiliating journey he must take to return to his own chamber. Everyone he saw would know of his frustrated desire. Most painful of all, he would be attended by the duke, whose handsome face, fine legs, and dangerous charm could overcome the virtue of any lady. Even the French queen, if the rumors were to be believed. Perhaps that was one benefit in Henrietta Maria's loathing the duke. There was no danger of Buckingham bedding her in the king's stead.

Yet the duke of Buckingham's presence penetrated every corridor of Whitehall. I knew I would encounter him often now that we were both in the same palace. I dreaded it, yet I was anxious to get that first meeting over with. When the dancing started, I saw my chance. I caught his attention, then made a show of polishing my ring. With the duke's gaze following me,

I slipped from the hall, the echoing empty chamber beyond offering me a place to wait.

Voices sounded, strident—one the duke's, another a lady's, accented in French. I dived behind an arras to hide until he could rid himself of her. The voices grew clearer. I peeped out and was surprised to see Madame Saint-Georges.

"You wished to share some confidence with me, Your Grace? I cannot imagine why." She managed to give the impression she was looking down her nose at the duke even though he was taller than she. I intended to practice that expression in the mirror until I, too, might "look down" upon giants.

"Madame, do you care about the fate of the queen?"

"What kind of question is that?"

"Tensions between our countries are growing more complicated. A year has passed since the royal marriage, yet your French king refuses to pay the queen's dowry—money we need for our war against Spain."

"Your king promised to stop persecuting Catholics, or France would never have agreed to the marriage."

"King Charles made no such promise."

"His father, then!" Madame Saint-Georges snapped. "Surely such a vow should be honored by a son."

"As your king honors his father's wishes by laying siege to the Huguenots at La Rochelle? Henry le Grande was a Protestant himself. He became Catholic only to gain the French crown. What was the Evergreen Gallant's famous quote, madame? 'Paris is worth a Mass?'"

"Your Henry the Eighth broke with the Church so he could wed his mistress!" Saint-Georges sneered. "A woman later condemned as a harlot and a witch! But once Henry Tudor cut off her head, did he return to the Holy Father in Rome? No. He wanted to keep the wealth plundered from the monasteries. I have seen your Anglican ceremonies. Under the king and Bishop Laud the rites grow more and more like our Catholic ones, with their fine ornaments and ceremonies. Is that not why your Puritans are so angry?"

"The Catholic Church and Anglican one are different enough to make martyrs on both sides of the religious divide since Henry died."

"Like King Charles's own grandmother—the blessed Mary, Queen of Scots."

"The traitor who plotted with Spain and France to steal Queen Elizabeth's throne. Now your king has divided our countries even further—making peace with Spain instead of supporting his brother-in-law's cause against them. But then, diplomacy is an unpredictable business."

"Is that why you persist in tormenting the queen? To punish her for what her brother has done?"

"I could be the queen's greatest ally."

Madame's eyes widened—with interest or disbelief?

"It is obvious the queen values your advice," Buckingham said. "Will you use your influence to benefit your mistress and the king, England and France?"

"I have had Her Majesty's best interests at heart since we were children."

"Children. That is the subject I am most interested in at present. A child who carries the royal blood of Stuart and Bourbon will unite our countries as marriage cannot. Unfortunately, your mistress's flux has come with disappointing regularity since she and the king have bedded together."

From behind the arras, I could see madame's cheeks go red. "Her Majesty's womanly functions are not a proper subject to discuss with any man."

"Someone needs to discuss them with her!" Buckingham said. "Pleasure in lovemaking will increase her chances of conceiving—if only because she will indulge in the act more often. You must convince Her Majesty to return her husband's embraces with more enthusiasm when he visits her bed. If the foolish girl does not bestir herself, she will be more miserable than she can imagine."

Madame's indignation matched my own. "You are the one who makes the queen miserable!" she said. "You scold her and tyrannize her and spread discord between her and the king! Do you think I do not see it?"

"I go to a great deal of trouble to make certain I see things more clearly than you do."

I tensed at the sly edge to Buckingham's tone, knowing I was his eyes.

"I offer your mistress the benefit of my superior wisdom," the duke said.

"Who are you to spout advice to those nobler in blood than you? Her

Majesty is daughter to the king of France! You are nothing but the younger son of a lowly knight!"

"I have risen since then. There is little in this world beyond my reach."

"In England, perhaps, but not in the rest of the world. Everyone knows what kind of scoundrel you are. Do you think France has forgotten your affair with Anne of Austria, the wife of Henrietta Maria's own brother?"

"Rumor only, though Cardinal Richelieu went to a great deal of trouble to prove infidelity. He even listened to someone who claimed I had carried two links from Queen Anne's diamond chain back to England as a love token. When Richelieu got the king to demand she wear the necklace to a ball, he was certain the queen was undone. It was a great disappointment to all of Queen Anne's enemies, and my own, when she appeared with the diamonds around her exquisite throat." Buckingham did not even bother to conceal his smirk.

"Stay away from our lady with your crude English intrigues!" Saint-Georges said. "We do not tolerate upstarts such as you in France."

Buckingham's eyes narrowed. "If you dislike English ways, Madame Saint-Georges, you should go back to France."

She returned Buckingham's glare. "There is nothing you can do to separate me from Her Majesty." Saint-Georges stalked back to the hall.

"We shall see about that," he said as he crossed to the door and shut it.

He looked around the room. "Jeffrey? Show yourself!"

It took all my will to step from behind the arras. "I am here, Your Grace." I looked around to make certain no one else had stumbled upon our meeting place.

"That woman will be sorry she crossed swords with me. You will help me see to it."

I swallowed hard, thinking of the countess of Carlisle.

"Have you got intelligence for me?" Anger only made him look more like Sir Lancelot in Will's tales of King Arthur. "I have not got all night! The king is impatient to bed his wife and will not linger over the dancing. He'll expect me to get him undressed for his wooing."

My stomach clenched, and I thought of the queen, Buckingham's medal in her hand, her face suffused with fervor. I tried to blot out the image. "The queen will go to Tyburn."

Buckingham's eyes glittered. He might have been made of the same stuff as the rings decking his fingers—hard and bright and mercilessly beautiful. "When?"

"To honor the Jubilee. Sometime in summer."

Buckingham slammed one fist into his open palm in triumph. The sound made me jump. "You are certain?"

"I would stake my life on it. Or should I say 'scaffold' my life?" I looked away, sick at heart.

"You have already grown in wit—a court fool's skill indeed. I must draw the king away from Whitehall that day so he cannot discover her plan and spoil everything."

Would it matter? I wondered. Merely knowing the queen intended to go to Tyburn should drive enough of a wedge between the king and queen to secure Buckingham's goal.

Buckingham fumbled at his waist. He held something toward me. He shook it, the clink of silver sounding.

"Take your reward, Jeffrey. You have earned it. Buy something pretty for Little Sara or a coat for that brother of yours—the one who looks as if a bad freeze will put him in the grave."

"Samuel is not ill? You have not heard . . ."

"*Grave* news?" Buckingham chuckled at his own jest. I loathed him for it. "No. But a coat will serve Samuel well. As you have served me. Now, if I could only offer the queen a bag of silver to serve the king in bed. Though why Charles does not avail himself of the countless English noblewomen who would be fiery even in his cold embraces, I do not know."

Because he wants Henrietta Maria, I wanted to tell the duke. How could King Charles not want to bury himself in the queen's fearless zeal, her eagerness, her beauty?

I did.

The confession opened desert wastelands inside me. But it was not until long after the Jubilee passed that I understood the true danger in what I felt.

TWELVE

•

July 7, 1626

The mud of Tyburn Road clutched the hem of the queen's skirt like fingers begging for mercy. But little enough of that virtue could be found at the execution site, where crowds had sated themselves on human suffering for five hundred years.

I peered out the window of the lone coach that was part of the procession that had left St. James's Palace an hour ago and wished we were still winding through Hyde Park, which lay just beyond the palace gates—the Serpentine's chain of shimmering ponds nested in jewel green.

But even the gentry strolling along the water's edge had stared at us with such shock, I would have given anything to stop the queen and her train of pilgrims before they stepped beyond the park's confines and onto the city roads.

I braced myself atop the wooden box placed upon the seat so I could watch the pilgrims filling the street before me and noted that I was not the only one interested in the procession. With each step the queen took, more passersby gathered along the side of the road. I could sense their suspicion as they called to the people in the shops. What had begun as a trickle of onlookers from other streets was growing at a pace that made me grateful the rest of the royal menagerie had remained safely behind the palace walls.

It had been easy for Will to discourage them from participating. Robin was eager for time alone with his paints, Dulcinea was determined to avoid the king's wrath, and Sara had been frightened off by Rattlebones's tales from the city's past.

"I wouldn't send Pug out onto those streets, let alone go myself!" he'd exclaimed. "Londoners form mobs for no reason at all. Since the Armada sailed, they go pure mad every time there has been another Catholic scare. But I would rather face that than the king when he finds out what the queen is about."

My fellow "curiosities" had spent hours discussing what punishment His Majesty would mete out to those foolish enough, loyal enough, or Catholic enough to accompany the queen.

Everyone but Will regarded those potential consequences with horrified fascination as they anticipated the return of the king and the duke of Buckingham. Will hoped the king might grow lonely for his wife and arrive in time to stop the pilgrimage. I knew better.

Buckingham had been true to his word and spirited King Charles away at the critical time. He'd "needed" the king to examine a new ship the duke had commissioned to sail against the French—if he could convince the king to allow it. Being needed by his hero was something the king could not resist. I could imagine Buckingham's secret glee as he showed the king his new plaything, heard the king raining praise down on Buckingham's head. When they were done with the Lord Admiral's business, Buckingham would convince the king to celebrate the triumph with a stop at his country estate at Theobalds to hunt.

No, I knew the king would not return as sure as I knew nothing—not Rattlebones's warnings nor Will's attempts to persuade me to remain behind—would keep me from making this journey with the queen.

I had meant to walk with the others. I still did not know if Will had inserted this coach in the procession so I could be part of the pilgrimage without danger of getting trampled, or if the queen had commanded that I ride.

Either way, I was not sure whether to be grateful or annoyed. I pushed the toes of my boots into the padding of the coach seat, fighting to keep my balance while putting as much distance as possible between myself and the self-satisfied figure of Father Philip. Bone-dry and in the greatest of comfort, the queen's confessor ticked off his Ave beads. What power he must feel, watching the queen and her courtiers trudge through the muck afoot, our coach grinding along behind them. I was nearly willing to risk hell by scooping up mud and smearing it on the good father's face for abandoning her that way. But was it not unjust to blame him when I was also safe and warm and dry? I—the man who had set the queen on this path.

I dashed the thought away, concentrating on the procession before me: the queen's French guards, her French servants, the smattering of Englishmen she tolerated in her household. Clustering nearest the queen were the ladies-in-waiting who usually reminded me of rainbow-feathered birds. Today the little maids of honor straggled through the muck like wretched crows.

Rain had turned the road into a stew of pottery shards and rusted iron perfect for carving up bare feet that had never known anything but the finest satin slippers.

I had begged Henrietta Maria to put on boots, but eyes, which could dance with merriment, had grown solemn. "I want to make certain the people of London will not forget this day," she'd said with a tenderness that twisted like a knife. "The Catholic priests who died at Tyburn suffered hanging, drawing, and quartering for our faith. I can endure walking barefoot, as pilgrims have done since the death of Saint Peter." She had smiled, but I had seen her apprehension, the knowledge of what she dared.

This was not France, where shrines still drew those who sought miracles. This was England, where Catholics risked their possessions, guardianship of their children, even their lives to celebrate Mass in secret rooms, terrified the Crown's priest-hunters would burst through the door and drag them to prison. By honoring those who defied the king's law, the queen spilled a contagion into the London streets that would spread more discord than any martyr who died on Tyburn's scaffold ever could.

I shuddered. If evil things came to pass because of this act of defiance, Henrietta Maria would be blamed. But it would be my fault.

I comforted myself by looking for one keen-eyed figure near the front of the procession. Even at a distance, I could tell Will wore the expression of a shepherd's dog who knows his master is about to do something foolish but cannot think of a way to stop him.

I remembered his expression the night before as he ran the whetstone over the blade of his halberd.

"Do you really think the queen will be in danger?" Sara had asked. "No one outside of the queen's household knows what she intends to do."

"All it takes is one spark to start a brush fire," Will had told her. "A maid of honor boasting to one of the merchants who delivered the black cloth, a gardener's lad overhearing Father Philip and carrying word back to his Puritan family. Someone might be waiting along the route. Even if no one knows what the queen is about, the sight of her will draw crowds on the street. The sight of her at Tyburn might incite them to violence."

I bit the inside of my lip and thought how easy it would be for the duke to raise a crowd if he willed it. But would he need to? The trickle of people had filled in every space along the road, the sight of her French court, parading their Catholic faith so boldly in London firing their outrage. God alone knew what they would do when she enacted the final ritual she had walked all the way from St. James's Palace to perform.

I folded my hands, trying to pay attention to the prayers Father Philip and the courtiers on the road were chanting. But I could not help being aware of the desperation in the grime-smeared faces of London's poor, and the glint in the apprentices' eyes, searching for anything to relieve the monotony of their service—even violence. Yet sprinkled among these underlings and the doughy-faced merchants and their disapproving wives must be the hunted whom the queen hoped to strengthen and comfort this day.

Swathed in drab cloaks, they might be watching her, their fingers surreptitiously making the sign of the cross or perhaps fingering the hard lump where a religious medal had been sewn into the seam of a dress or the lining of a purse—amulets smuggled in with priests who made the perilous journey from Italy or France, or handed down from the time Henry Tudor broke with the Church so he could wed Anne Boleyn.

Foreboding dug into my chest, the damp curls straggling down Henrietta Maria's neck reminding me of the grisly tales Archie had frightened me with. I thought of the ghost of Anne Boleyn wandering the halls of Hampton Court, her severed head trailing blood like ribbons.

But if anywhere in England harbored unquiet spirits, Tyburn must. As the queen reached her destination, the edginess inside me seemed to choke off air and light, causing a horrific sense of being walled off from those I cared for.

Suddenly, I couldn't bear being safe from the seething crowd while the queen was so vulnerable, so brave. I did not take time to pull off my boots as the other pilgrims had done. I forced open the door. Hanging on to the ledge where the window cut in, I swung out in a wide arc, Father Philip's protests ringing in my ears. I released my hold once I was clear of the wheels, my body seeming to fall through the air forever before my boots struck the ground. Only grabbing at one of the wheel spokes saved me from sliding back under the coach. I righted myself and managed to propel myself out of the way as the coach jolted into motion again.

Mist dampened my cheeks. The prayers the courtiers were saying grew louder as I closed the distance between us. I could see the queen standing an arm's length from the post where priests had been tortured. Her face was red, her eyes swollen from tears.

"God, I beg you to grant me the courage to die for my faith if it is your will." She had memorized the words in English, determined her subjects would understand her words. Her French-accented voice flashed in the gray London air like silver before a hungry thief, too bright, taunting her enemies. "I pray for the souls of those martyrs who shed sacred blood in your holy cause," she continued.

Henrietta Maria's prayer was blotted out by a rumble in the crowd, hostility so thick, I could not breathe. I pushed through the maze of people, saw the queen sink to her knees, press her lips to the post dark with bloodstains a generation old.

"Devil's daughter!" someone in the throng shouted. "Traitor queen! Send her to France or hell! No! To Tower Green and the block!"

I saw William Evans stiffen, gripping his halberd in both hands. His glare swept the crowd. Was it possible someone would attack now, as he had feared they might? Some Puritan thinking they were striking down a disciple of the Pope they considered the Antichrist? But the queen had offended more than religious fanatics now. Some of the "martyrs" she honored had tried to destroy the whole English government.

"Back, you knaves!" Will roared above the sound of prayers. "I'll be sending you to Newgate if you make threats against Her Majesty!"

The outcries softened, faces drawing deeper into hoods or beneath hat brims. I caught Will's gaze. The lines in his face deepened as I made my way toward him.

"I will never forget this day!" I heard someone cry.

Was it a Puritan or an Anglican vowing vengeance? A secret Catholic clinging to hope? It might have been my own conscience, branded with the image of the queen of England, on her knees in the muck, kissing the place saints—or traitors—had bled.

I thought of Will's tales—how dragons loved to sate their hunger on a lady fair, a brave lady only the boldest hero could save. I imagined flying to Henrietta Maria's rescue, sword drawn. *Are you going to pinprick her enemies to death?* A voice mocked inside me. *You can barely lift a real sword off the ground.*

I heard a rumble from the direction of the Tower of London. A frisson of alarm shot through everyone in the street, as if it were cannon fire. For an instant, I wondered if it could be some armed force the king had raised, riding down upon the crowd now—to rescue his queen from the angry mob or to arrest her himself?

The booming sound came again, and people began to flee. Yet no armed men appeared. Lightning sent jagged fire across the darkening sky, like God's finger wielding damnation. A stone flew toward me. I jerked my head up, searching the crowd to see where the missile had come from. But rain was pelting us now, the crowd shifting and fleeing for shelter.

"Jeffrey!"

I saw Will Evans striding toward me. I slogged in his direction. Shifting his halberd into the crook of one elbow, Will grabbed the back of my jacket and lifted me until I could scramble astride his shoulders.

"Hold on!" he said. I buried my hands in Will's hair and clung for dear life as he loped back toward the queen. "Keep a sharp eye out for weapons in the windows overhead or anyone in the crowd trying to break through the guard to reach Her Majesty. I depend on you."

He meant it. I twisted this way and that, trying to see past the blur of people to threats beyond. I glimpsed someone disturbingly familiar in the crowd. From the shambles? Surely not. Raised fingers made the sign of the cross in blessing; then he was gone.

My gaze swept too many faces to remember before we entered Hyde Park. The crowd thinned, the verdant beauty a blur as the queen's procession hastened through it. By the time we reached the palace, the onlookers had disappeared altogether. But as the porter opened the gate to let us pass, I could see the scowl on his face and knew. We had not left the conflict at Tyburn. From now on, people would watch the queen in palaces, chapels, in the streets, and at the hunt with the same relentless stare.

***

By the time the queen dismissed me so her ladies could change her clothing and get her warm, I barely had the energy to stagger across to the Freaks' Lair.

Will Evans sat on a stool, drying his hair by the fire. "I posted double the guard on the queen's side of the palace," he said. "I have never seen a London crowd in such a dangerous temper. They would have stoned the queen if they could. I kept searching the crowd, not certain what to do if they attacked."

I had done the same, yet I would have been useless to fend them off. Would Will have fared much better with such a crowd? Especially against zealots, fired by hate?

"I could not think how to guard Her Majesty and keep you from being crushed to death at the same time," Will said. "Tell me you did not get trampled upon."

"Not once. I've spent my life dodging the soles of great clumping boots like yours. You did well, Evans." I tried to reassure us both. "The queen is behind palace gates again. She is safe."

"Is she?" Will raised his shaggy head, drops of water clinging to his beard. "I'm not so sure."

"Of course she is," I protested.

"Her Majesty may be in more danger in her own chambers. Even now someone must be carrying word to the king. Once he hears what she has done, he'll ride for St. James's. I am afraid for her."

"The king will be angry, of course, but she is a queen. Any action taken against her would provoke war with France."

"There are men eager for the glory and fortune they can win only on the battlefield. If those men can convince the king to imprison the queen, try her for treason, even execute her, they will get their war."

My stomach churned. Was it possible the duke's goal had never been to prevent Henrietta Maria from having influence over the king? Did he want to dispose of the queen altogether? Or use her as the flame to touch off an incident that would explode into war?

Fear sickened me. What had I done?

"The queen was only praying," I insisted. "She is allowed to practice her religion by law." I had heard the French say so a dozen times.

"Henrietta Maria was not just praying. She was inciting her subjects to rebel against the law of the land. Charles is the head of the Church of England. The king and the church are one and the same."

"You are saying it might be . . ."

"Treason. I pray the king is too wise to judge it so."

"Thank God the king is away."

"He will return. And when he does, Jeffrey, you will have to stay as close to the queen as possible."

"What am I supposed to do? Fend him off with your pike?"

"Try to soften his anger if you can. Remind him how young the queen is, how far from home."

"I am a court fool. He is the king of England. Why would he listen to me?"

"Because fools can tell kings the truth without fear of reprisal. Sometimes they are the only ones who dare. Because you will be speaking the truth and the king is a decent man."

"Do you think he will arrest her?"

"I do not know." Will kneaded his brow. "But I cannot think of anything that would please the duke of Buckingham more."

I fled to my chamber and drove Griggory out. Alone, I went to my wooden chest. I dug my hand into the darkest corner, heard the coins clink in Buckingham's purse, felt the lump of Samuel's medal in the costume I'd once worn. There, among treasures and secrets, I felt the silk of my lady's token. *If you are to be my champion . . ."* Her lilting voice drifted through my memory.

I thought of the queen's lips pressed fervently against the bloodstain upon Tyburn scaffold and wondered. Was I sending my queen into a future where she would mount a scaffold of her own?

THIRTEEN

•

W hen I woke next morning with aching legs, I thanked God and Will Evans that I had walked for only part of the queen's pilgrimage instead of the whole. I wanted to send word to the queen that I was unwell. Pull the coverlets over my head and annoy Griggory all day, having him fetch hot compresses to ease my stiffness. But I could not bear to stay in my room any more than I had been able to remain in the coach while the queen paced inexorably toward her ruin.

I pasted on my court fool's smile, then went to the queen's withdrawing chamber to face the havoc I had wrought. It hardly looked like a site of disaster. The queen's ladies flitted about in their rich gowns, chattering about how they had defied the heretic English. Father Phillip bent over some documents with a new sense of purpose, apparently embracing the sin of pride.

Henrietta Maria sat near the window with her spaniel Mitte, the queen's animated face a feverish blend of triumph and dread. Everyone else in the chamber was too busy congratulating themselves to notice she was alone.

I crossed the room, hearing her speaking to the little dog, her words cryptic, yet tugging at my heart nonetheless. "We do not need to fret anymore. You got such a worried look on your poor face, I think you have been afraid ever since that she might take you back."

"Majesty," I announced myself, wondering who this ominous "she" could be.

"Jeffrey!" the queen exclaimed as she turned to look at me. "I am so glad that you are here."

"I did not mean to intrude. But please tell Mitte I will not allow anyone to separate the two of you. Just point me toward the villain and I shall challenge her to a duel."

"You cannot duel the dowager queen of France."

"You were speaking of your mother?"

"She gave me Mitte as a parting gift just before I sailed for England. Mitte was in my arms when . . . well, it scarce matters anymore. I have struck a blow for my Catholic subjects at last. No one can believe I have forgotten them."

"You showed great courage," I said.

"Did you see all the people lining the road? Sergeant Evans was most distressed."

"The sergeant guards you from every threat he can see." Unfortunately, he has not guessed I am spinning Buckingham's webs at your feet, I thought.

"Sergeant Evans could not understand why I needed to take such bold action. Yet, now my pilgrimage is over, I feel as if the weight of three kingdoms has rolled off of my breast."

She had best enjoy the respite, I thought, because the king's wrath is about to crash down upon her head.

"Did you know that the Pope sent me a Golden Rose before I left France? He chose me as the prince or princess in all Europe who most embodied the Catholic spirit."

"A nice gesture, since he was about to throw you to the lions," I grumbled.

"Lions?"

"His Holiness had just granted dispensation to send you to a country full of people he considers heretics and wed you to a Protestant king." Anger kindled at the thought. The Pope, the dowager queen, the king of France, Buckingham and Richelieu, even King Charles had flung a fifteen-year-old princess into the center of their religious battles. What had they expected would happen? That this slender young woman would sort out a tangle no one had been able to unravel since Martin Luther had nailed his protest onto a church door?

"The rose is a mark of fatherly affection from the Pope," the queen said. Little wonder she clung so hard to that token of warmth—a child whose father died before she could have memories of him, leaving her with a harsh mother thirsty for intrigue.

I had heard snippets about the queen's mother from the ladies Her Majesty had brought from France. The woman had her son regularly beaten when he was king. What scars had Marie de Medici left on her youngest daughter, this vibrant young queen who so thirsted for love?

I pictured my own mother, the way I sometimes caught her looking at me, dread and fascination in her eyes. There had been love, as well, Samuel insisted. But what is love when it is veiled by a thin layer of fear?

"Your mother must have been proud of a daughter as perfect as you."

"The last thing she said before I sailed was that if I faltered in my faith, she would curse me. Can you think of anything worse than fearing your mother might curse the day you were born?"

"Yes." I closed my eyes; suddenly I was back in the cottage at Oakham. "Knowing that your mother does." Ever so softly Henrietta Maria squeezed my hand.

July 31, 1626

For three weeks after the queen's pilgrimage to Tyburn I felt like a clockwork bird wound too tight, my thoughts flapping inside my head at a speed that made my stomach pitch. We had heard nothing from the king; His Majesty was still off with Buckingham. I tortured myself in the hours I stood at my post in the withdrawing room by imagining the venom my master was pouring into the king's ear.

It was the thirty-first of July. Tomorrow, August would begin. I feared what was happening in the household of the king. Were his privy councillors goading him to set the queen aside? Might they even be attempting to charge her with treason? Surely her enemies would wield her trip to Tyburn like a sword. But where would they strike at her? When?

I picked at my fingernail until it bled as I looked about the withdrawing chamber, which seemed more like a prison every day. The room was a jewel box of color once more, all traces of coarse black cloth banished. A flageolet played hide-and-seek about the lute's melody, the instruments weaving in and out like ribbons around a maypole, the queen's ladies-in-waiting and maids of honor dancing in the space footmen and pages had cleared in the center of the room at Madame Saint-Georges's command.

I had heard Archie tell stories he had gathered from Prince Henry: Sir Walter Raleigh's descriptions of how red-skinned natives in the New World danced mad skirls with war clubs after winning some battle. Despite the perfumes and lace that filled this chamber, this frolic Madame Saint-Georges had got up felt very much the same.

The French court had dealt the English a blow, shown that their princess would not be tyrannized. Henrietta Maria would not shrink her faith into the tiny cell the Protestant lords wished to lock her in, celebrating Masses behind closed doors, hastening her priests out of sight, allowing the king to ignore the terms of the marriage contract without voicing her protest. It was an act of youthful rebellion, I believed. But she had shown her tormenters that she would not be silenced. Little wonder her ladies wanted to exult over her triumph. Yet as I watched their skirts whirl, heard their hands clap in rhythm, I wanted to stop up my ears.

I saw Madame Saint-Georges make a graceful leap, her slippers flashing beneath her primrose skirts. How I longed to trip her. Especially when I stole a glance at the slumped figure in the velvet-covered chair beside me. The bedraggled pilgrim queen of weeks ago had disappeared, and Henrietta Maria was dressed and coiffed as perfectly as ever now her penance was done. But her aspect betrayed a tangle of heavy thoughts; the rims of her eyelids were raw.

The queen's left hand clamped over the side of her jaw, her wedding ring glittering in light that poured in the window. She'd said her tooth ached and made excuses to avoid joining the dance. Even her favorite spaniel sensed something was amiss. Mitte curled in a subdued ball upon the queen's lap, not even licking or wriggling as usual. Instead, the dog peered up at the queen, Mitte's eyes rivaling the worry that had been in Will Evans's when I'd encountered him earlier that morning.

Evans had hunkered down to tell me, "The king's party has been sighted riding in this direction. Servants stationed about the palace will bring word of how His Majesty's temper fares. I hope to warn Her Majesty when the king is coming so she can prepare herself."

"Is his Majesty riding to confront her?"

"It seems so, but I cannot be certain."

For three hours, I listened for Will's heavy tread, but now I feared the infernal music would drown out even Evans's great clomping boots.

Is it better to know when the headsman's ax is about to fall? I could almost hear Archie's cynical voice say. *Or better to remain blissfully clueless until your head is rolling across the scaffold?*

One of the maids giggled, and I saw the queen wince. "Majesty," I said. "Should your ladies take their dancing elsewhere? I never feel like being around merry people when I am unwell."

She rubbed the knot that hinged the left side of her jaw. "I fear I have insulted this joint beyond pardon. I was clenching my teeth when I woke." She paused a moment, then asked, "Jeffrey, do you have nightmares?"

The court fool in me wanted to quip, *I don't bother with them any longer, since I'm living one.*

But such a reply would never do. "Did you spend a restless night, Majesty?"

"I have ever since I visited Tyburn." She leaned closer so that no one else could hear. Not that her ladies seemed overly worried their mistress was in torment. "I dreamed I was on the rack. I was trying to keep from betraying other Catholics, but the pain . . . I kept thinking, I'll tell. . . . I'll tell. I would picture these faces . . . people I know, like Mamie, and I would clamp my jaws shut to keep from screaming out names."

She shuddered. I wished I had the courage to dare the unthinkable. Reach out to squeeze her hand, a hand as tender as a babe's, no callus ever roughening the skin from work. I said, "It was only a dream, Majesty."

"Not for the martyrs who died at Tyburn. It must have been horrifying, knowing you held so many lives in your hands. That if the torture master broke you, they would suffer as you were suffering. Can you imagine?"

I wanted to tell the queen she had nothing to fear. But I was not a clever-enough liar.

"Only a fool would not be afraid to meet the kind of fate you describe. But you are safe from the rack, Majesty. England does not torture aristocrats, and certainly not its queens."

"There are many kinds of torture, Jeffrey. To feel like a stranger so far from home. To know people are suspicious of you, even loathe you for things you cannot help. Things they knew about you before you even met them."

"You are not alone in feeling that way, Majesty. I would guess all of us in your menagerie have felt the same."

"I had not thought that I might have been speaking of you instead of myself. Who would have guessed how alike we are? Perhaps that is why just having you nearby comforts me. You smooth the jagged edges of this country, this palace, the courtiers beyond my own household."

"I would give whatever ease I could," I said. Whatever ease I can sneak past Buckingham, I added to myself.

"I wish . . ."

"Wish what, Majesty?"

"That I could speak to my husband as I speak to you. Without his advisers tearing at me like crows on carrion, trying to force their will on me. Even when the king comes to my bedchamber—" She choked to a stop. "No. I must not speak of such things to any man."

I could hear the censure in her head—her mother's voice, Buckingham's, Madame Saint-Georges, every priest or adviser who had ever ruled over her.

"What if my marriage is a dead thing, Jeffrey? Will they allow me to fly away?"

"Majesty, I do not—"

Suddenly, a sound came, a tramping of feet, the door swinging wide. Will Evans hastened over to us, alarm etched deep in his face.

"The king is approaching, Your Majesty," Evans said. "His Gentlemen Pensioners march with him." The queen turned white as bone.

The flageolet tumbled to the floor with a hollow crack. The lute strings twanged and went silent. Maids of honor stumbled out of the dance and clustered near the older attendants like lambs do when a flock scents a wolf. Even the youngest among the queen's attendants knew what the approach of the Gentlemen Pensioners meant.

They were the king's armed force, made of nobles of the land. What use could the king have for them while visiting the queen unless she was to be arrested?

Henrietta Maria straightened up in her chair. She reached down, caught hold of my hand, and hid our clasped fingers beneath a fold of her skirt.

The door filled with men in bright livery, halberds in their hands, their faces schooled into emotionless masks. But their eyes showed that ugly pleasure I'd seen suffuse my father's face when he knew his dog was going to take down its quarry.

"His Majesty, the king." Will Evans's booming voice did not betray that he had been dreading this moment since the queen decided to go to Tyburn. The announcement brought the queen to her feet. I could see a tremor work through her as her short-statured husband strode through the door. The king's garb of black embroidered with touches of white thread was silhouetted against Buckingham's court raiment of crimson and gold. Buckingham towered above his master, as if the king were a meager shadow of the far more imposing duke.

Bile rose in my throat as Buckingham's gaze flicked to me, then slid past, leaving only the ghost of a smirk to betray his satisfaction. Was it possible someone in the queen's household might guess that the tiny curl of the duke's lip was meant for me? Anger burned in me, a fierce need to protect her.

The Gentleman Pensioners filed in, stationing themselves about the room, cutting off the path to the door. I saw the French courtiers shift their feet like creatures who know they are cornered. None more thoroughly trapped than the queen, caught in the king's furious glare.

"So, Madam, have you nothing better to do than dance today? No riots to incite among our subjects?"

"As you see, I am not dancing."

"Can it be that after three weeks you are still worn out from tromping through the muck to honor the traitors who attempted to murder my family?"

The queen swallowed hard. "I only wished to show my fellow Catholics that I have not forgotten the promises made to them in our marriage contract."

"I have told you—and your brother—that I made no such promise! Do you—my own wife—dare call me a liar?"

For all her boldness, Henrietta Maria took a small step backward. "No, Your Majesty. But there was an understanding—"

Buckingham broke in. "Perhaps His Majesty should follow the example you set by going to Tyburn. He could honor the Protestants your brother has under siege at La Rochelle. Or shall I arrange a parade through the street to honor the fanatic who assassinated your father, my queen?"

Henrietta Maria gasped. "How dare you speak to me of such horrors?"

She turned to the king. "You allow him to gloat over the murder of my father?"

"It is no different from what you have done before all England," the king said. "At least a zealot's knife is tidy. It strikes down only one person. The kegs of gunpowder some of your 'martyrs' meant to set off are a good deal less discriminating. When ignited, they kill anyone unfortunate enough to be in the vicinity. I was four years old when the plot was foiled, but I have imagined my family blown to bits many times since."

I could see the queen flinch. "I had not thought of it that way," she said.

"The death of a few extra people does not trouble a good Catholic, I suppose. In fact, remind me, madam. What religion was your father's assassin?"

"A Catholic," she said in a quavering voice.

"Why would a Catholic kill a Catholic king? Oh, I recall. Henri was not ruthless enough in persecuting the Huguenots. It seems Catholics resort to murder whatever side their target is on. Tell me, wife, whose idea was it to march to Tyburn? Your priests? Your French ladies? Did they spur you to make this grand gesture?"

I wondered if the queen would show the king the Tyburn medal and tell him of my part in her decision. I would have done so if I had been in her position—anything to shift blame off of myself.

Even the king's stammer could not soften his words. "You prayed for the courage to die as those traitors died, madam. Is that what you wish? To be made a martyr? Will that satisfy your brother, the French king? Your flock of priests? The Jesuits who invade my shore on every tide to stir up dissention in this kingdom? Will Madame Saint-Georges finally be happy when she no longer merely denies me your bed on holy days, but sees you locked up in a cell?"

"You cannot understand what it means to be Catholic and be denied the sacraments. I was only—"

"Perhaps if you would speak English, I would have a better chance of understanding your words, if not your actions. If you had taken the duchess of Buckingham into your household as I advised, she would have prevented such madness, instead of urging you to every folly."

"My marriage contract assured me the practice of my faith, and my brother is determined I should have my own French household."

"Your brother's opinion is of no concern, since he has not aided England against Spain as he intimated he would. It seems His Highness and I are both destined to be disappointed. Madam, you will accompany me into more private quarters."

"Majesty, let me attend—" Madame Saint-Georges began.

But the king slashed his hand through the air to silence her. "You have caused trouble between my wife and me for the last time." He grasped the queen and forced her into her bedchamber.

Mitte attempted to follow, but Buckingham shoved the dog aside with his boot. Never before had I heard Mitte growl in anything but play, but the spaniel was in earnest as it barked and snarled, attempting to fling itself at the door. For a moment, I hoped the gentle dog would sink her teeth into Buckingham's ankle. But what would the penalty be for biting a duke? I did not want to find out. I flung my arms around the spaniel to pull her out of harm's way.

Buckingham blocked the door with his broad shoulders, then turned back to the French courtiers. I could see what an avenging angel must look like, surveying the battlefields after Armageddon. "Gentlemen, remove these papist dogs. They are not to set foot upon palace grounds again."

"You have no right to order us away from Her Majesty!" Madame Saint-Georges hands knotted in fists. I knew she would like to strike that sneer off of Buckingham's face. "We serve the queen! We do not bow to a pandering upstart like you!"

I could hear muffled voices beyond the door Buckingham was blocking, the king's hard tones, the queen in distress.

Saint-Georges flung herself at the door, but Buckingham grabbed her by the wrists.

"Be grateful your diplomatic status prevents His Majesty from sending you to the Tower."

"I will speak with the king!"

"Attempt to fill either of Their Majesties' heads with Catholic nonsense again and the king will see you condemned as spies. As soon as ships can be made ready, you will be exiled to France."

"But the queen and I have loved each other from the time she was a babe."

"Her Majesty is no longer a child. It is time she realized that." Buckingham

signaled to the other men and they began to herd the French courtiers from
the room.

"I will not go!" Madam's chin quivered. "I will not!"

"Sergeant Evans." Buckingham signaled to Will. "It seems madam has
lost the use of her legs. You will carry her to the coaches waiting to carry
these French troublemakers away."

I sensed Will's reluctance, but what could he do? He was bound to carry
out the king's wishes. He closed the space between himself and the Frenchwoman. "I do not want to humiliate you as His Grace commands, but I must
if you do not obey the king's orders."

"Do you not love the queen?" Saint-Georges shrilled. "Have you no
shred of loyalty?"

Will's eyes filled with sorrow, but he reached out his big hands to gently
grasp madam by the shoulders. The woman shrieked French curses, swinging her fists in a futile effort to reach him. The distance was too far. He ma-
neuvered her toward the door, the rest of the queen's ladies herded along
behind them by the other guards.

I raced to the window, where I could see coaches waiting. The queen
must have seen them, as well. Her screams grew more desperate as her ladies
and their guards spilled into the gardens below.

Buckingham's voice sounded, low just behind me. "You have done well,
Jeffrey. I predict the queen's new household will be far more amenable to
English interests. My Kate, my lady mother, my sister, the countess of Den-
bigh, and the countess of Carlisle."

He would sic his mother on Henrietta Maria? God help her. And the
countess of Carlisle, his mistress? It offended me, the idea of that ruthless
woman in the service of the queen.

"I can see from your expression I have given you food for thought. Lucy
Hay will make a fine mistress for the king. Don't you agree?"

I had heard of Henry the Eighth making his mistresses ladies-in-waiting to
his wives. But I could not think whom I felt more sorry for in this instance—
the queen or the duchess of Buckingham.

A loud crash sounded from behind the door, Mitte yelping in alarm. I
could not bear it. I ducked around Buckingham, bolted to the unguarded
door. I wrestled the portal open and slipped inside. Neither royal noticed.

The queen was on her knees beside an overturned table, pleading with her husband, who stood, resolute as stone. "I beg you, Majesty. Do not send them away." The queen sobbed. "I will be good. I will be good."

Only the twitch at the corner of the king's eye betrayed how those screams tortured him. He grasped her puffed sleeve to urge her to her feet. "Compose yourself! You are the queen of England."

"You English hate me! You all hate me!" She wrenched away from the king, her gown tearing under his grasp, exposing a crescent of bare shoulder. She flung herself at the window. "Mamie! Oh, blessed Virgin, don't let them take Mamie away!" She pounded on the glass like a bird fighting to get free.

I cried out in horror as her fist shattered the pane, her hand driving through the starlike hole. Glass struck the floor with a tinkling sound, a horrible echo of the dancing measure that had played in the next room what seemed an eternity ago. Terror that she would fling herself to her death shot through me.

I raced to grab her skirts, knowing I was powerless to stop her, but the king circled her around her waist, hauling her backward. A metallic scent filled the room, one that had clung to my father in the shambles.

"Majesty, the queen is hurt!" I cried as she crumpled in his grasp, the fight draining out of her like the blood streaming onto her skirt.

The king's surprise at my presence was tempered with horror—at the queen's wound or her unbridled show of emotion? I did not know. He looked at me with stunned helplessness and I understood. No one had ever dared fight him this way, flailing and screaming, with no guard to step in. He had been surrounded by servants his whole life, could not even make water in the chamber pot by himself. He was no more use in dealing with the queen's wound than the spaniel racing about in frenzied circles, whining.

"The wrist is full of veins," I said, remembering lessons learned near the slicing blades in the shambles. "We must stanch the wound, lest she bleed to death."

Stricken, the king lowered her gently to the floor. I ripped off my white Holland collar to wrap around the wound. But it was not her wrist that was bleeding, thank God. A dagger-shaped shard of glass was buried in the fleshy mound above her thumb. I pulled the shard free, slicing my own finger as I threw the bloodstained glass aside. I barely felt the sting as I pressed the wadded-up collar against the queen's wound. She choked out a pained cry.

"Jeffrey!" Henrietta Maria wept, finally seeing me through the tangle of hair that had tumbled from its pins. Her eyes flayed my conscience, their dark depths wide and sick and haunted. "He sent them all away. He sent Mamie away."

I had to push words past the lump in my own throat. "Majesty, I am sorry I hurt you," I said over and over again. "I am so sorry."

"Now you are my only friend."

I looked up at Charles Stuart, stiff as the wooden puppets in the shows at the Oakham Fair. Beyond him, in the doorway, stood the duke of Buckingham—the puppet master who now held all of our strings in his capricious hands.

FOURTEEN

•

Where do we go from here? The queen? The king? Me? I wondered as I stared across the wreckage my mischief had caused. I could not imagine any future but misery for all three of us.

A surgeon could stitch up the queen's hand, but he could not get to the poison that threatened the queen's world, along with the new household the king insisted upon. I imagined pus gathering beneath the queen's bandage, red streaks traveling up her arm. Briefly, I even feared my mistress might be grateful for the escape death offered.

No. I brought myself up sharp. Even the wound in the queen's hand would heal. Had I not held her other hand and watched as her surgeon stitched it up with care? The king had also watched the shining, curved needle, as if His Majesty was suffering his own brand of penance.

But now that the stitching was done, a more painful ordeal loomed before the queen.

"Majesty, you must collect yourself before you meet your new household," I urged as I heard the duke beyond the chamber door, commanding one of the guards to fetch the queen's new ladies. I leaned so close to Henrietta Maria's ear that her curls brushed my lips. "I beg you, Majesty, do not let Buckingham and these ladies of his see you like this."

Did my words have power? Or was it years of royal upbringing in France that gave her the inner strength? I could see her change from petulant child to courageous woman.

"By Your Majesty's leave, I will receive the ladies in the withdrawing chamber," she told the king. "Jeffrey will accompany me."

"As you wish," the king said, and I could tell he wanted to get as far as possible from female hysterics and painful scenes.

She had no one to pin up her hair, no one to put her gown right. She might have been Joan of Arc facing the Inquisition as she walked past the broken trinkets and overturned table, evidence that she had dared fight against the king.

As she stepped into the chamber that had been filled with dancing maids an hour before, I could hear the ghost of their laughter. Did Buckingham hear echoes, as well? Had the women's helpless cries caused the half smirk on his lips? He stepped into the chamber with an air of invincibility, confident that no one could refuse him anything he desired—surely not the women that trailed in his wake. How long had they known about the plan to eject the queen's French attendants? Long enough to secure gowns that were elegant even by court standards—gowns that rivaled anything the queen might wear. Buckingham bowed so low before Henrietta Maria that it was almost a mockery.

The queen's dignity in the face of her tormenter broke my heart. It affected the king as well, though in what way, I could not guess. *No man chosen by God to rule should display mere human emotions,* Archie Armstrong would have scoffed. His Majesty crossed his arms over his narrow chest as he watched Buckingham's women sweep forward to make their curtsies to the queen. Did they mean to demonstrate the queen's powerlessness by presenting themselves without the queen's permission? Ignoring the order protocol demanded? Such formalities had seemed unbreakable.

First, the countess of Buckingham put herself forward, any likeness to her son rasped off of her face by ambition. I had seen the old dragon browbeat duchesses and soldiers. I suspected she would have made any seventeen-year-old cringe. But my mistress looked down her Valois nose, making no secret of her contempt for a mother who had gained high station by pandering her son to a lecherous king.

Buckingham's sister came next, but even with chains of jewels draped upon her wrists and neck, Susan Feilding, the countess of Denbigh, seemed a paste imitation of her gemlike brother. The Villiers's triumph gave a smug primness to her mouth until the queen's spaniel grabbed the hem of her gown in its teeth. "Majesty," she said, trying to appear graceful while tugging the satin. Mitte would not release her hold and the woman had to drag the growling spaniel along the floor while the countess of Carlisle stepped to the fore.

Lucy Hay's skirts pooled into a satin rose on the floor as she curtsyed. Her body formed a stem of exquisite beauty as she tilted her body toward the king so her breasts showed to best advantage.

"Majesty, I've been enraptured, watching your masques," she said to Henrietta Maria. "We English do not like to admit it, but we know the French are true masters of the art form. I am eager to revel in the magic you have brought from the most glittering court in the world."

"Your interest in acting must explain why you paint your cheeks so dark." The queen's disapproval reassured me the countess would have little influence on her in the days to come. "Such tricks make you visible onstage but are too gaudy for everyday wear."

The countess's lashes lowered, but not before I glimpsed anger. "The restraint in the French court is known throughout the world."

The duchess of Buckingham curtsyed last, and I understood why the duke had presented the women in such an order: Placing his duchess after the other women should make her the most appealing confidante by contrast.

"Your Majesty, our husbands wish for us to become fast friends," the duchess said.

I could sense Henrietta Maria's contempt for the duchess's every word. "Yes. I have heard that the early days of your own marriage were tumultuous."

The king caught his breath, and I feared the queen had been unwise.

If the duchess felt any sting, she did not show it. "The great changes marriage brings can be difficult until you become accustomed. It does not mean your new life will not be sweet."

The queen glanced toward her husband, but she accidentally caught Lady Carlisle's eyes. Carlisle pressed a hand to her heart and rolled her gaze heavenward, openly scorning the woman whose husband was her lover.

I wondered who the countess was most determined to snare in her formidable web. The king Buckingham intended her to bed? Or the heart-sick French princess whose husband did not understand her?

The Freaks' Lair was shrouded in gloom when I trudged through the door sometime later.

Sara scrambled down from a stool, compassion softening her face. "Jeffrey!" she cried, waddling toward me. "We've been hearing such awful things! The king's guard marching on the queen. The surgeon running to Her Majesty's quarters. People are whispering that the queen was so desperate, she slashed her wrists! Suicide is a mortal sin. She would never . . ."

"Her Majesty's soul is safe," I replied. "She was pounding on a window and her fist shattered the pane. She did not cut herself on purpose."

Sara murmured a prayer of thanks.

"Do not rejoice too soon," Dulcinea said. "Suicide will look more inviting in the days to come."

"This is no jesting matter." Rattlebones scooped Scrap up, hugging him so hard, the spaniel whimpered. I hoped Mitte was nestled in the queen's arms.

"I'm not jesting." The rope dancer's mouth turned down. "Imagine our poor mistress—Buckingham's women stripping off her gown, bathing her, smoothing lotion on her skin. One of them will even sleep on a cot in her bedchamber. They will run to the duke when her moon blood flows, eavesdrop on the marriage bed and carry tales."

Tears spilled down Sara's cheeks.

Robin shot Dulcinea a quelling glare. "Stop rattling on. Can you not see how upset Sara is?"

"How did Her Majesty look when you left her, Jeffrey?" Rattlebones asked.

"Alone," I said, feeling hollow inside.

"Not while she still has us." Sara squeezed my hand. I gave a yelp as pain burned through the cut I had gotten while aiding the queen. Sara released me, dismayed. "You are hurt!"

"It is nothing." I tucked my throbbing hand against my middle. "Just a bit of glass."

"Gotten while helping the queen," Will said. "The tale is flying everywhere—how Jeffrey defied the duke of Buckingham, charged past him and into the chamber where the king was holding the queen. Jeffrey might have saved Her Majesty from bleeding to death."

"But I didn't. The veins in the wrist were not severed."

"Only by the grace of God," Will insisted.

"It was a brave thing you did, Jeffrey," Sara said. "One the king and queen will not forget."

"Nor the duke of Buckingham, I'll warrant," Robin said, his face grim. Was he warning me there would be reprisals? Or was he stinging over the fact that Sara had taken my hand?

"I do wonder who carried the tale." Will puzzled over this with his best sergeant porter frown. "The guards were escorting the French from the palace with me. There was no one save the king, the queen, and Buckingham to witness Jeffrey's actions. Someone else must have seen. . . ."

God knew, with all the intriguers about, it was possible. Far more likely Buckingham had scattered the tale. What better way to hide the fact that I was his spy? In one stroke, he had cast himself as my adversary and enshrined me as the dwarf who saved the queen from bleeding to death.

⁂

The next morning when I went to attend the queen, her eyes were as red as her gown. I wondered how she had managed to weep without Buckingham's women hearing her.

"I am dissatisfied with the work on this altar cloth," the queen told her new ladies. She gestured to the rumpled length of satin that had been spilled from her sewing basket in the scuffle the day before. "You will take it where the sunlight is strongest and pick the stitches out."

I stared at the pattern of lambs and lions I had watched the queen and her French ladies chatter over so gaily, their needles flashes of silver. Her willingness to destroy their exquisite work alarmed me.

Buckingham's sister looked dismayed at the behemoth task, his mother cross. The countess of Carlisle's lip curled in amusement over the queen's device for banishing her new attendants as far from her as possible. The duchess of Buckingham took up the rich cloth and traced a lion's mane with her finger.

"Majesty, are you certain you wish us to rip this pattern out?" she asked. "I have never seen more perfect stitches."

"The Carmelite nuns I stitched with in France held me to higher standards than you English ladies have. Be it in needlework or morality."

The duchess's eyelids narrowed as she carried the cloth to the window. Taking up a tiny pair of scissors, she began to pick out stitches. The other women followed her example, leaving me with the queen.

Henrietta Maria sighed, as if a stone had been lifted from her chest. She favored me with a smile, so drained of its liveliness that I wondered if joy would ever light her face again. "Jeffrey, I was afraid Buckingham would tear you away from me as he did my French household. He wants me to have no one who loves me nearby. They will not even allow me the solace of my confessor. I can wander anywhere in the castle at will, but I might as well be locked in a Tower cell."

It was true. Every waking moment, Buckingham's ladies held her hostage behind walls of English customs and determined cheerfulness. As the weeks passed, Buckingham's mother swelled with self-importance, until I imagined lancing her like the boil she was upon the queen's existence. The ravishing countess of Carlisle's sparkling wit made even Henrietta Maria's loveliness seem drab.

I had heard that some women welcomed a mistress who would relieve them of their husbands' attentions. I wondered if Henrietta Maria would care if Lucy Hay seduced the king now, broken as the queen's spirits seemed at her husband's hand.

At least Henrietta Maria knew enough of Carlisle's reputation to insist the countess was not a fit companion for a virtuous queen. Not that her protests had mattered. The king had dismissed the queen's concerns, insisting the rumors of the countess's indescretions were unfounded. Yet despite Henrietta Maria's determination to ignore her, the countess had a kind of merriment that drew light into the queen's chamber, whether Her Majesty willed it or not. I did not know if I should be grateful that she might spark life in the queen again, or if I should tamp down the least flicker to protect Henrietta Maria from the heartache that could ensue if the countess of Carlisle had her way.

※

The gardens rang with laughter as the king's courtiers and the queen's ladies drank in the sunshine as His Majesty attempted to bring color into the queen's wan cheeks. The pair had withdrawn from the rest of the company to sit beneath an arch of roses. From where I stood with some of the menagerie, I could see Her Majesty, still stiff with hurt but attempting an occasional smile. Yet the eyes of everyone else followed the lively game of shuttlecock being led by the countess of Carlisle.

"The countess is very beautiful," Sara said, tucking a tendril of hair beneath her wide-brimmed hat. "Look how everyone clusters around her."

"I wish to Heaven they would get out of my way." Goodfellow craned his neck to the left as his hand flew over the page. Half-formed figures seemed ready to dance off the page the moment he sketched in their legs. "Why can they not go hang about the Buckingham women under that lovely tree?"

"The countess of Buckingham scares *me*," Rattlebones said with a comic shudder. "Would you want to approach the duke's mother when she is looking like that?" He juggled three of the apples he had tucked into his doublet when we broke our fast that morning. He'd already eaten two others, as well as a wedge of cheese. I still could not believe how much the man ate. Perhaps he was right and some creature lived in his belly and gobbled the food before it could stick to his bones.

"Perhaps she is pondering some business her son is about," Robin suggested. "He has been gone for six days now, and it is not like His Grace to be out of the king's company so long."

I had been relieved at the respite Buckingham's absence afforded today—until Robin made me wonder what mischief the duke might be about.

"Never has a man had more power to bedazzle women," Simon said. "I think the duke could get those three ladies to leap from a parapet if he told them to fly." He nodded toward the Buckingham women and had the ill fortune to catch Archie Armstrong's eye. For a moment, even I wondered if Simon meant to summon over the querulous fool. But Rattlebones groaned as if he were as dismayed as the rest of us were when Archie left the king's other servants and strode toward us with what Goodfellow called his "angel of discord" expression on his face.

Armstrong bowed as Lucy Hay's clear laughter rang out, teasing the young swain who had missed the feathered shuttlecock. "I almost feel a trifle sorry for the fair Lucinda," Archie said. "She is cleverer than any of these men, yet she must hide it behind dimples and plump breasts and seductive smiles. I

live for the moments her pretense slips and the real Lucy cuts through—
sarcasm that leaves stupid people bewildered and frustration snapping into
temper." He laughed. "She is her father's daughter, then."

"Who was her father?"

"A Percy of Northumberland. Damned stiff-necked breed for centuries.
Her father, the earl, may have been the most unpleasant of the lot. Damned
useful, though, when it came to plying my trade."

"Useful?"

"When King Jamie and I came down from Scotland, I was looking for a
butt for my jests. God, how the English nobles hated Jamie's hangers-on—
Scots like James Hay, snatching royal appointments they thought should
have belonged to them. So easy to torment, the English were. Warms my
heart just to think of it."

A fly tried to land on Goodfellow's paper. Sara brushed it away before the
insect could interrupt the flow of Robin's drawing. Robin cast her a glance
filled with tenderness as Archie went on.

"Liked a bit of the bawdy, did the king, and Northumberland and his
wife got in such howling good fights, half the kingdom waited to hear about
their doings. Of course, preachers say God grants a man the tools he needs.
Gave Northumberland the gift of being deaf in one ear. Made His Lordship
impatient as the devil, especially when he was hard at his experiments or
chattering science with those mad friends of his. I think he was actually relieved to be locked up in the Tower once he knew his head wasn't going to
roll. He could drown himself in books and glass vials and heathenish tools
without interruption."

I frowned. "I cannot imagine being glad to be locked in one of those
dank cells, no matter how vexing my wife might be."

"Oh, the earl was not in the kind of cells we'd be shoved in. He and his
friend Raleigh lived fine as ever they did beyond the Tower walls. Just
couldn't pass beyond the gate. Northumberland had his wife send all his rich
furnishings and servants to wait upon him. He even built himself a stable on
Tower grounds because the regular accommodations weren't fancy enough
for his horses."

"Save your jests for someone easier to dupe." I nodded toward the nobles
who were playing shuttlecock on the lawn.

"What Archie says is true," Sara said, her tone earnest.

"Most of what I say is true, people find out to their woe." Archie chuckled.

"What are you laughing about?" I asked, wondering if he was mocking me.

"I was thinking that of all the luxuries allowed the earl, the one that amused me most was the shed the Lord Lieutenant had built for him out in the Tower yard."

"A shed?"

"Where Northumberland could do his mad experiments. That way, he would only blow himself to kingdom come."

"I had not considered that such trials might be dangerous."

"Why would court fools like us consider science at all?" Robin cursed when his charcoal snapped. He took up the stub and began carving a fresh point. "We're too busy trying to keep roofs over our heads to worry about the paths of the stars."

"Yet, with all the possible subjects here for you to choose from, you attempt to capture the incomparable Lucinda on your page," Archie said. "Is she not a star of sorts?"

"Robin is practicing drawing subjects while they are in motion, and the countess of Carlisle is flitting about everywhere," Sara said, defending Robin.

"And capturing hearts wherever she goes," Archie said. "No one in all the court has the power to charm like she does. Pity she rarely uses it on her husband anymore. I cannot think the earl of Carlisle expected such an outcome when he made his great love match."

"Love match?" I echoed.

"She spent two years in the Tower for love of James Hay, the earl of Carlisle," Archie said, then turned and walked away. The queen rose and shook out her skirts as the king called out, "Her Majesty is eager to feed the swans. Let us away to the pond!"

I heard Robin curse as he started to gather his scattered drawings, but Sara was already halfway through the task, her nimbleness born of practice.

I fell into step with the rest of the courtiers, questions tumbling through my mind. It was hard to imagine Lucy Hay suffering such a fate for anyone. If she *had* been imprisoned in the Tower I had to wonder—what had happened to kill the marriage she had bought at such a price?

⨂

I was going to visit Pug six weeks later when Robin Goodfellow overtook me, a bundle sprinkled with vermilion dust tucked under one arm. "How does it feel to bewitch the queen?" he asked.

I regarded him, wary. "I have done no such thing."

"You've worked some magic on her. Her Majesty is having craftsmen deliver a gift to you."

"Why would Her Majesty tell you?" I asked, surprised.

"She did not," he said, then walked away.

Yet nothing prepared me for the grand unveiling on the day that the secret was revealed. I had been much occupied entertaining the queen with jokes and tricks when she secreted a note in my hand and ordered me to my room. I raced through the corridors so fast, my legs ached, not daring to open the missive where anyone else might see, dreading what the page might contain. But when I opened my chamber door, the whole menagerie, including Archie, awaited me there, mouths sticky from some honey cakes Griggory was serving. "What is this about?" I demanded as I shoved the missive in my doublet.

"Evans herded us in here by the queen's command," Rattlebones said. "Except for Archie. He came to the Lair on his usual mission to stir up trouble and refused to be left behind."

"Her Majesty has sent you a gift." Robin gestured to the table where I attended my studies.

Atop its surface something rectangular lay hidden beneath a swath of black frieze—the stuff the queen had worn on her pilgrimage.

"Hurry and uncover it, Jeffrey," Dulcinea urged, sampling another honey cake.

"Not everyone wants to gobble pleasures up the way you do," Sara said. "Perhaps he wants to savor the surprise." Sara turned to me. "It was all Will could do to keep her from peeking."

I crossed to the table, their smiling faces pinching my conscience. I took hold of the coarse cloth and pulled. The frieze slid from my fingers.

Gasps rose all around me, and for a moment I forgot to breathe. It was a writing box, far plainer than the one that had fascinated me that first day in the queen's chamber, yet more beautiful than anything I had ever owned. A knight in armor was painted upon it, his sword frozen a heartbeat away from lopping the head off of a giant. The knight's helmet had been cast aside, his gold-brown hair and features so like my own, it astonished me. A captive princess looked on, hands clasped in prayer, her dark eyes unmistakably the queen's. But the giant was not Will Evans. The face half-revealed by the thrown-back visor had the look of Buckingham's.

"It is Sir Gawain and the Green Knight," Will Evans said. "Isn't that just like Her Majesty to have Goodfellow paint it for you?"

"Goodfellow?"

The artist tried to demur, but Will Evans gave a booming laugh. "I know your work, Robin. But you've made me look far too pretty as the Green Knight."

"You weren't my model, though I would have picked you had it been up to me. The queen gave specific instructions. Even the hound should remind you of someone."

Evans and I both squinted at it. I surrendered first. "I cannot see it."

"Good." Goodfellow looked a trifle grim. "I'd not get the queen in more trouble if I can prevent it, though I can't imagine why Buckingham or Bishop Laud would be hanging about the queen's dwarf, rummaging through your things, Jeffrey. Still, no reason to poke at them and make them any angrier than that foolish trip to Tyburn did. Hope the resemblance is close enough, though, to satisfy the queen."

"Laud and Buckingham!" Will exclaimed. "Bless me if it isn't so! I've seen just that expression on Laud's face when he's lecturing Her Majesty on the evils of the Catholic Church."

He smoothed one Goliath-size hand over the perfectly fitted drawers. "What do you think is inside this, Jeffrey?"

I pulled open one drawer, then the next, finding them filled with things like powders for ink, sand in a shaker to dash across a wet page to keep it from smudging, a pearl-handled penknife, and wax with a dipper to melt it in.

"You've even got your own seal," Evans said, eager. "Press it in the wax to see what it is."

I took the dipper and bits of wax, melted this over the candle, poured it onto a sheet of paper. Then I took up the heavy weight of the seal and pressed it deep into the pool of red.

I pulled it away, saw the embossed design the seal's ridges and curves had left behind.

"I cannot make out what it is," Will said with a frown. "A sea horse, perhaps?"

Robin Goodfellow broke in. "It is Latin. The lads who craft my brushes and such fitted out your box. They told me that the motto is to be your own now, Hudson."

"What does it say?" I regarded it with nervous fascination. Words had such power that to read them was magic. But these words—cast in brass, running backward—seemed even more potent.

"*Molto en Parvo,*" Goodfellow said. The phrase engraved itself in my mind.

"I wonder what it means," I said.

" 'Much in little.' "

"It suits you," Will said.

"We had best brace ourselves, friends," Rattlebones teased. "Jeffrey is becoming quite a gentleman of the queen's household instead of one of our menagerie. Before long, our Jeffrey will be far too important to socialize with people like us."

"Do not be ridiculous," I said, yet some of what Simon said was true. The queen clung to me now in a way she did not cling to the others: The way she had once clung to Madame Saint-Georges—her closest confidante, her most trusted friend. Had madame carried tales back to the French court when the king's men had packed them all back to their homeland?

I was grateful when the rest of the menagerie filed out. Will Evans lingered.

"Jeffrey," Will said softly. "I am glad the queen depends on you so. She needs a friend."

"She does."

"Might I share a secret?"

I felt a jab of alarm. What if Will confided something I must carry to Buckingham? I was still shaken by what had happened because I carried tales about the queen. Somehow, endangering Will Evans seemed even worse than those consequences. "Flocks of people greet you everywhere you go," I said. "You must have friends you would be better off confiding in than me."

"You are so clever. Cleverer than most of the courtiers are. I love to see you deal them a riposte with one of your jests. They dare not strike back at you because the queen loves you so much."

"I get so angry at the way they treat the rest of you, I wish I could challenge them to a duel. The queen has promised me lessons in weaponry."

Will frowned. "She would not allow you to touch a blade if she thought you might put it to such use."

"A pistol is the weapon for me. It does not matter how tall you are or how strong. It fires a bullet the same for me as for any other man."

"I suppose. But my secret . . ."

I smiled. "You might as well get the telling over with so I can get some peace."

Will chuckled, then looked away. A flush crept across his cheekbones. "I could tell you a hundred legends of Arthur and his knights from memory, but I cannot write my own name."

"There is no shame in that. Plenty of other folk cannot."

"But they are not giants," Will said. "Small men love to say I am as stupid as I am large."

A pistol ball, a sword thrust—I would have been happy to puncture those who tormented Will with either weapon. "Who cares what they say?"

"I do."

"Then why tell me such a thing?"

Will lifted his gaze to mine. I could see how much courage it took for him to answer. "I was hoping you might teach me."

ℱIFTEEN

•

It is not easy to snap a queen's spirit, I discovered to my joy. As winter's snow cast a coverlet over London's harsh edges, time similarly blunted the queen's heartache. Court ushered in 1627 and the New Year promised to be far different from the one we had left behind. I measured the months of spring by lessons learned.

I had hoped it would grow easier to pass my letters to Buckingham. But, though my hands grew deft at sliding missives into my saddle, it grew harder to write secrets down: tidbits I gleaned from half-finished letters begging for news from France, the queen's relief when the king permitted Father Philip to return and be her confessor, her feelings that her family had cast her aside. The silence in the months following the banishment of her household was more painful than that outrage had been.

"They might as well have cast me into the sea to drown," Henrietta Maria told me one night. "It is as if they have forgotten me."

Far more enjoyable were the lessons I taught Will about how to wield a pen. He spent hours in my chamber, grappling with the delicate process of forming his letters while I sat cross-legged on the table. Secretly, I was glad he continued strewing the pages with ink blots so I could badger him into returning to lessons so frustrating that most men would have quit. I had my own reputation to think about, I warned him. I would not be responsible for sending him out into the world with such clumsy penmanship. I pretended he did not know the motive behind my complaints: That I eagerly antici-pated Evans's heavy tread outside my door. I enjoyed his rumbling Welsh voice. Most of all, I craved the stories I wrung out of him when I complained how tedious it was to sit like a stump and make certain he did not spill the ink horn.

The queen tiptoed further beyond her bleak humors, as well. The king devised entertainments, disappointing the court by treating the queen with earnest tenderness, seeking to please her. Her new ladies added their own efforts, vying for the prime place in her affections. She would have to choose one of them. They were the only friends at hand and she was far too social a creature to remain isolated for long.

The first times the king availed himself of the marriage bed following her court's departure, the queen was hostile. The divide between Catholic French princess and Protestant king was still wide. But Charles's outburst comparing the Gunpowder Plot to the assassination of Henrietta Maria's father had penetrated the queen's outrage and eventually worked its way into her heart.

When she confided she had nightmares about devil-faced assassins murdering her father, I urged her to share those dreams with the king instead. During one twilight while they walked in the garden, I overheard them speaking in low voices not only of the assassins who haunted her dreams but of those who had stalked the king's childhood, as well. The Gunpowder Plot had plunged frail, shy four-year-old Charles into the horrific truth his father had experienced from the cradle. Traitors and assassins could wait around any corner. Survival depended upon the wheel of fortune, and it was forever turning.

I tried to control fortune's spin, contriving ways to smooth the damage my meddling had caused without betraying the divided allegiance that could be my downfall. I collected weapons I could use in the court's arena, discovering vulnerable spots in even the most invincible courtiers. I tweaked the countess of Carlisle, contrasting her worldly ways with the queen's youth and openness.

I reveled in the flickers of frustration in Lucy Hay's face when her wiles did not distract His Majesty's attentions from his wife. The king approached the queen's bedchamber with growing confidence, and the queen no longer seemed to dread his visits.

His attentions seemed to foster harmony between the queen and her new ladies, as well, and I began to relax a little more, able to let my mind wander, rather than being on constant alert.

One morning, a soft rain was falling, canceling the ride the queen had planned. The duchess of Buckingham was already in bed with a cold, and no one was willing to risk the queen getting damp.

To while away the time, the other ladies had gathered around the gaming tables, as they so often did. I sat upon a cushioned stool at the queen's side, all but forgotten as the queen gambled with the duke's mother and sister and the lively Lady Carlisle. For hours, they had played thus, the dice box rattling in rhythmic counterpoint to the women's voices. I let my mind wander, wondering what Samuel was doing, if he had visited the widow lately and taken the Virgin beneath the floor flowers, as he was wont to do.

Yet something in the queen's voice penetrated my musings. I discerned sadness, though I had not been listening to her words. The countess of Carlisle's reply I heard clearly.

"Majesty, I know you imagine what it would have been like if your father had lived. Maybe things would have been as idyllic as you dream. But there are daughters who might consider themselves better off if their fathers were plucked out of their lives. My father kept me in the Tower of London for two years."

"You cannot mean that."

"It was my mother's fault my sister and I turned out to be so headstrong, he insisted. We were raised by women, with no man about to guide us. He claimed it made us disobedient and full of strange ideas about our place in the world. I was only six and Dorothy seven when King James's court condemned Father for treason. It was Tom Percy's doing, but since that cousin visited my father just before the plot was to commence, the king believed my father was involved. So off to the Tower my father went for sixteen years. The only time we saw him was when our mother took us to visit him there."

"How awful for her, to have a husband locked away."

"The thing that confused me was why my mother worked so tirelessly to get him out."

"For shame, Lady Carlisle!" Buckingham's mother reprimanded. "To speak of your parents in so disrespectful a manner!"

"I am certain my parents would agree with me if they were here." Lady Carlisle plucked up the dice and cast them upon the table. "Things were much better at home without the two of them railing at each other, my mother dissolving into tears or burrowing into her room, too melancholy to care about Dorothy or me. I suppose our mother was considering her children's futures when she petitioned Queen Anne to pardon father. It is not easy to find husbands for the daughters of a condemned traitor. As it happens, Mother need not have exerted herself. Dorothy and I found husbands for ourselves."

The queen's mouth rounded in astonishment. "Is that allowed in England?"

"Not for an earl's daughters—unless they have an indulgent father. Our father definitely was not. In fact"—a crease formed between her elegant brows—"I do not think he cared for children at all—daughters in particular."

Her Majesty thrust forth another stack of coins to join the mountain of gold she'd already wagered. I could not help but wonder what simple folk would think if they saw such recklessness. She took up the dice. "I pray the king will be kind to our children when God grants them. He is kind to his horses and dogs."

I thought of my father, who would nurse his dogs with surprising tenderness. I did not have the heart to tell the queen that trait did not always carry over to a man's children.

"So tell us what happened, Lucy," Lady Denbigh urged.

"Armed with the proposals of our lords, Dorothy and I marched up to the Tower to inform our father of our decision. We were both quite terrified of his temper. The rows he had with my mother were almost the stuff of legend at court. But Dorothy and I were willing to face anything together. It helped to know that once our ordeal was over, we would be going to a banquet my betrothed had planned in my honor. No man at court entertained more lavishly than the earl of Carlisle. True, he was much older than I, but so elegant, so worldly—do you know he is the one who first invented the antebanquet?"

I had seen the wasteful practice several times since my arrival at court and it never failed to make me sick: an entire banquet of the finest delicacies laid out for display, then discarded and replaced with fresh wonders to eat.

"Father was not pleased with Dorothy's choice of Robert Sidney, but at least Lord Leicester was an Englishman of noble blood. When I told him I wished to marry James Hay . . ." Her eyes clouded. "I had never seen Father in such a rage. He ordered Dorothy to go home, have my things packed, then sent to the Tower. As long as I held to this lunacy of mingling Percy blood with that of a Scottish upstart, I would remain in the Tower with him."

"He housed you in a prison?" The queen gasped. "With men condemned of the worst crimes against the Crown?"

"I had committed my own treason, as far as he was concerned. He thought he would break my resolve. I am sure he believed I would relent by the time my belongings arrived. I did not. Trust me, being walled up in the Tower with him was torment beyond imagining. I went from being surrounded by the most jovial society at court to being captive by a deaf, ill-tempered tyrant who spent his time stirring up foul-smelling concoctions and attempting every kind of outlandish magic his half-mad friends could bring through the Tower doors. "

"It sounds dreadful. Two years is a very long time to be forbidden any kind of pleasure." Susan Feilding glanced at her mother, and I wondered if she was imagining being free of the old dragon for a while. "What did you do to fill your time?"

"Out of stark boredom, I read what books were at hand. Listened to father and his visitors drone on about whatever new theories travelers brought through the Tower gates. Sir Walter Raleigh was imprisoned at the same time. They had been fast friends my whole life, and kept each other amused. They merely quit having their discussions at Syon House and moved meetings with their band of scientists to the Tower." Lady Carlisle's voice softened. "I do not think Father has ever recovered from Raleigh's death."

Lady Carlisle's father was still alive?

"Raleigh was executed for piracy, was he not?" the queen asked. "He was meddling with Spanish ships?"

"He was executed for failing to bring back the gold he had promised. King James released him for one final voyage to Guyana with the understanding that they would bring back riches to equal the Spaniards' gleanings from the New World. It is still something to be hoped for—an English share in that wealth. If the king upholds the grant King James gave to my husband, including the Caribbean islands—"

"The king will dispose of the islands as he chooses, Lady Carlisle," Buckingham's mother said. "One of my son's servants is determined the house of Villiers will succeed where other men have failed. In my opinion, he has listened too much to those speculators in the new East India Company—merchants intent on grabbing more money than is decent. He is eager to have my son invest in his enterprise. But Master Ware is no more fitted for such independence than his father was. Or my late husband, for that matter. I knew it from the time Uriel was a lad."

It was hard to imagine Ware was ever a boy. I imagined him stumbling, fully formed, out of one of Will's cyclops caves.

Apparently, Lady Carlisle agreed. "Master Ware had a father?" Her face dimpled. "He must have been a grim fellow."

"I remember him being rather vague and ridiculous instead," Lady Denbigh said. "He was a clerk in the spicery and was always chattering with spice merchants and sailors. Kept his purse full of useless things he found—stones with dragon skeletons trapped in them and polished seashells. My Lady, remember how Uriel used to follow him? Father said you couldn't take a step around Edward Ware without treading on his son's toes."

"Or Genevieve Armistead's," the countess of Buckingham said drily.

"Was that Ware's mother?" Lucy asked.

"Hardly. She was the baseborn daughter of a seaman. She brought Edward Ware those heathenish rocks he was so fond of. He claimed she was as fascinated by them as he was."

Lady Carlisle's brow wrinkled. "Of course it is impossible to believe a woman might wish to explore something like that."

"His wife was too canny to swallow such nonsense. Her mistake was not ignoring the indiscretion like other wives do. Off she went to some prayer meeting in a wheat field, carrying back threat of hellfire to try to shame him."

"Remember the day Mistress Ware left?" Lady Denbigh said eagerly. "It was quite the scandal, Majesty. She stole the smithy's hammer and shattered the dragon stones to dust. When her husband tried to stop her, she struck him, as well. George saw her drag Uriel away, the lad sobbing."

I tried to imagine Ware thus. My imagination had grown to encompass green knights and marauding dragons, but Uriel Ware weeping was beyond its scope.

"The woman must have been mad to try to murder her husband!" the queen exclaimed.

"Her husband lived," Lady Denbigh said. "Mistress Ware must have been too weary from all that smashing to finish him. As soon as he was strong enough, he went in search of Uriel, but they'd vanished like the creatures in the stones."

"Yet you say this Master Ware now works for the duke?"

"He appeared at our door one day, asking for his father. Edward Ware was dead, but my brother took the son in. Master Ware has worked for the Villiers ever since. Now he hopes to follow in Raleigh's footsteps."

"But Raleigh's enterprise ended badly," Henrietta Maria said.

Lady Carlisle nodded. "When the mission failed, he could not resist taking a few fat Spanish galleons. One cannot blame Raleigh for attempting to salvage the voyage thus. Queen Elizabeth would have applauded such audacity."

"In secret." The countess of Buckingham pursed her lips, a wasteland of wrinkles appearing around them. "Gloriana was far too wily to let her sea hawks' prey know that she approved of such tactics. Yet too practical to turn away her portion of the loot they had stolen. The condition of the royal treasury is of utmost importance to anyone who wears a crown." The duke's mother regarded Henrietta Maria through narrowed eyes. "It vexes a king to be robbed of money that is rightfully his."

The queen swallowed hard and I heard the accusation unspoken between them. The French king still refused to deliver the remainder of the queen's dowry until the English honored the terms agreed upon for the marriage and lifted the persecution of Catholics. Part of that wealth had been meant to support the queen's household. The lack of it made Her Majesty dependent on the king's already-strained purse—a strain only the increasingly troublesome Parliament could ease.

"Perhaps Your Majesty would be wise to put an end to the day's wagers," the countess of Buckingham said.

It was good advice. Court buzzed with rumors of the queen's appalling gambling debts. Yet I knew better than to think the queen would yield to the old dragon's impudence.

"You forget yourself, Lady Buckingham." She drew off a necklace twinkling with diamonds and cast it on the growing pile. "Does anyone else dare match this?"

Lady Carlisle tossed an etched emerald brooch onto the table, then took up the dice and cast them. She clapped her hands. "I fear you have lost your stake again, Your Majesty," she said. She scooped the pile of jewels and coin into her hands.

⁂

In the weeks that followed, I congratulated myself that I was on a winning streak, as well. Every day I was becoming more accustomed to the court's quagmire, dancing across the danger as Dulcinea did her rope. I spent more time with the queen than any of my fellow curiosities. They prepared for thrice-weekly performances, while I was summoned as soon as Her Majesty was dressed and often not sent away until she retired. Those hours I did not attend her, I found plenty of other audiences grateful to applaud my capers. I collected information along with their coin.

Father Philip loaded my table with books. I would wrestle the heavy volumes to the table, always aware I could topple them over onto myself if I were not careful. Balance—that quality my very survival depended upon.

Yet just when I was growing smug, the devil yanked on my ordered life as if it were the string upon a huntsman's bow. Nothing could have prepared me for Will Evans's announcement when he bounded up the stairs and found me practicing dancing steps upon Dulcinea's rope. His broad face reflected delight. "Jeffrey, a surprise awaits you belowstairs! Family from Oakham!"

I tumbled from my perch. Luckily, Dulcinea had taught me how to fall, rolling myself up and letting the momentum carry me where it would.

"You broke his concentration!" Dulcinea scolded Evans.

Will turned the color of brick. "Forgive me. Jeffrey, are you hurt?"

"Is there ill news from home?" I asked.

"No!" Will exclaimed. "Fairly pop-eyed with awe, he is."

I scrambled to my feet, dizzy with excitement. No one fit that wide-eyed description better than Samuel. "My brother—has someone brought him to London?"

"No." Will shifted his shovel-size feet, reluctant to disappoint me. "It is your father who has come. Alone."

I could picture my father gawping up at Will. Imagined what cruel, ignorant things my father might say, this man who scorned the legends Will bur-
nished bright with honor. Strange, but I wanted to spring between Evans
and John Hudson as if I were Gawain shielding the Green Knight instead of
battling him.

"Your father said he had some business in London and stopped to see
you."

What business is that? I wondered. Does he want money? Perhaps hopes
I might bring him into this luxurious life he has thrust me into? My stomach
suddenly started to pitch from the fall.

There was nothing I wanted less than to see my father's blood-caked fingernails, smell that lingering stench of entrails and animal panic that clung
to his clothes even after my mother and sister had scrubbed them. It had
been bad enough in the shambles to be known as such a man's son. But the
thought of having people in the palace see where I had come from sickened
me. I imagined Lady Carlisle's sneer, the queen's abhorrence. I did not even
want the rest of the menagerie to see John Hudson. How was it possible that
in such a short time I had changed from the child he had starved to stunt my
growth? I was the favorite of the queen of England now. I ate my fill of the
finest victuals.

"Tell Master Hudson I cannot interrupt my practice."

Will frowned at the chill in my voice. "The man has traveled a long way.
You owe him a father's due."

"Nothing on God's earth could compel me to see him unless he has brought
others of my family along." I should have known better than to challenge God
with such a declaration.

Will had not been long gone when he returned, sheepish. "The king and
queen wish you to join them in the king's privy chamber."

I made my way to the chamber, wading through crowds of supplicants
and ambassadors until the gentleman usher announced me.

The king and queen sat together in the light of the window. Catherine
Villiers, Susan Feilding, and Lucy Hay clustered some distance away, worldly
beside the maids of honor perched on cushions. The giggling bevy of noblemen's unmarried daughters were ever ready to offer sips of wine or nips of

dried fruit to the royal couple or untangle the embroidery silks Mitte, the spaniel, was merrily stealing from the queen's sewing box.

Her Majesty outshone the other women in my eyes. Her head was bent over some needlework, her hair soft and dark, her gown billowing around her in shimmering folds. The king sat beside her, watching the picture she was making. He would have seemed stiff had he been any other man, but for Charles Stuart, he appeared almost at ease until I entered the room. Disappointment clouded his features as I made my bow.

"Majesty, you wished to see me."

"Jeffrey, is it true that your father has come to visit you and you have turned him away? Say you are not guilty of such disrespect."

I wanted to demand to know if Will Evans had been carrying tales, but I could hardly behave like a thwarted child in front of the king of England. Even so, His Majesty's mournful expression made me want to drop an anvil on Will Evans's foot to keep the giant from tramping into my private affairs in the future.

"Majesty, my life and my father's were separated at his wish, not by my choice. Your own actions with the queen's French household show that sometimes it is better to put one's past life behind one."

The king's brow furrowed. "This is a man who has worked to put bread in your mouth and clothes upon your back. When God grants me a son, I hope no minor quarrel will divide him from his father's love."

How could I explain to Charles Stuart the kind of love my father had shown me? The hungry nights, the tight bandages bound about my limbs to keep me small, the mercenary glint in my father's eyes when he sold me as a spy to the duke of Buckingham. I wondered what the king would think of John Hudson if he knew that.

"It is my wish that you and your father no longer be divided." The king turned to the duchess. "Do you have anything to add?" he asked her. "Jeffrey hailed from near your estate in Rutland, did he not?"

"His father trains His grace's bull-baiting dogs," she said.

"I imagine Jeffrey looks like a tender mouthful," Lady Carlisle smacked her lips in a way that would have enticed most men. "Did a bitch ever mistake you for a meal, little fool?"

I remembered my old terror of being eaten alive—the image of being clamped, helpless, in canine jaws and shaken until my neck snapped. But it would be a fool indeed who allowed Lady Carlisle a glimpse into his nightmare. I crushed my fear and latched onto my fool's trade, turning a series of cartwheels and flips. The last feat I executed on the seat of an empty chair and propelled myself atop a table as Dulcinea and Rattlebones had taught me. The room erupted in applause at my trick. I bowed with a flourish so I could catch my breath. "I am rather harder to catch than a bull tied to a stake by eight feet of chain," I quipped to the countess.

Her Majesty gave me a tender smile. "Thank God you are so nimble. I could not do without you, Jeffrey." The queen touched the red scar the glass had carved into her hand.

"I am certain Jeffrey will serve Your Majesty until the end of his days, you are so kind to him." The duchess of Buckingham turned to me. "Jeffrey, your father will be pleased to see what a gentleman and scholar you have become. I am certain he wishes all his children should have such advantages."

"So the father shall see the son's triumph!" the king said. "Jeffrey, you will entertain your father in your chambers in a style worthy of the queen's fool. Tell Her Majesty's page to have meat and drink sent to you there." I saw the page bow, then dart from the chamber on the king's errand. Then the pounding of running feet could be heard.

I wanted to plead for the king to call him back, explain that I did not want my father entering my refuge. I did not want his fingerprints on the table, his imprint on the seat of Will Evans's chair. But when the king gave orders, what could I do but obey and thank him for his kindness?

The moment I exited the royal presence, I ran down the gallery, past men at arms and disapproving hangers-on at court, startling servants busy at their tasks and setting dogs to barking in my efforts to reach my chambers. What should it matter if I arrive before my father? I asked myself as a stitch dug into my side. But I felt a need to sweep away anything he might pry into, especially the blotted pages of Will Evans's writing, which Father might jeer over, though it was the giant's own fault my father was to be in the chamber at all.

At length, I stumbled through the door, blessedly alone. I scooped the evidence of Will's lessons into a wooden chest, then paced the length of my room and fed more coal into the hearth than the harshest winter would demand. Somehow, the sight of shiny black chunks being devoured by fire gave me the assurance of power. Father had ever been miserly when parceling out fuel.

When I heard a rap on my door, I crossed my arms over my chest and bade my father enter.

Did he look a trifle fleshier in the face? Buckingham's gold had fed him well. I wondered if any of that bounty ever found its way into Samuel's stomach.

"Jeffrey, lad!" he exclaimed in a rustic accent that made me cringe. "You've done well for yourself. I'd wager you piss in golden pots!"

"Piss is still piss, whether you splash it in a gutter or a palace chamber pot. Why have you come, Father?"

"To see my boy in such fine lodgings. I did well by you, Jeffrey. No father could have done better."

I said nothing, only walked to the table. It took both hands to maneuver the ewer and pour myself a glass of wine. But my silver goblet had been cast in my size, a gift from the queen on New Year's Day. I caught the stem between my fingers as gracefully as any courtier and gulped down a mouthful, longing for that dulling of sharp edges I had experienced at banquets. But the pain my father awakened was still too keen to be dispatched thus.

"Is Mother well? My brothers and sister?"

"Aren't they just grand? And they're like to be grander. Do you remember your cousin Starkey? Came through Oakham five years ago on his way to sign on with a captain going to Virginia."

"The man with tattoos over his face?" Starkey claimed the natives he had encountered had showed him how to rub ash into tiny scratches in the skin. He had offered to make the same markings on me, so my parents could pass me off as a pygmy and make even more coin. Fortunately, my father had seen plenty of ugly creatures on display at fairs. Things of beauty were far fewer, and the more valuable for that scarcity.

"So you do remember him," father said. "He came traveling through the village on his way to the ports. He had spoken for a crate of ship's cargo but hadn't the money to pay now it was in harbor. He agreed to split his profits with me, since I staked him."

"Didn't such dealings with him fall through before?" I remembered it as one of the rare times my mother had fought back, trying to wrestle the bag of coin out of father's hands. He'd given it to Starkey anyway. Those had been hungry times, when even Father had grown thin.

"It wasn't Starkey's fault that ship was lost at sea! This time will be different."

"The duke's money was to take care of Ma and Ann and the boys!"

Father's face turned red as raw beefsteak. "It's not for you to say what I put my own money to! I'm the head of the household, by God and the law. You can't deny I made young John comfortable as any Oakham lad could hope for in his apprenticeship."

It was true my elder brother seemed satisfied following in my father's trade. John's broad shoulders and lack of imagination made him able to swing the cleaver without thinking it was living flesh. English tables needed men with that skill to provide them with meat.

"As for you, Jeffrey," Father continued. "B'God, you're turned out in luxury fine as any lord in England."

"You and everyone back home should have been kept comfortable with the money Buckingham paid for me. I doubt you will see Starkey again. What do you intend to do without the money you gave him?"

Father threw out his chest, in that way he had whenever he was about to say something the listener would dislike. "I've arranged an apprenticeship for Samuel with Beetle Garth, stirring up the blood pudding and chopping the scrap meat."

Beetle Garth? Twice, lads in his care had gone missing. The ones who had lost only fingers through careless chopping were the lucky ones. I thought of Samuel trapped in Garth's shop, digging through the worst of the butcher's gore, stirring the huge hot cauldron stinking of blood. My stomach bubbled the same way. "Samuel is not to work in the shambles."

"Pah!" Father spat into the fire, the gobbet of phlegm sizzling. "You are not master of the Hudson family, in spite of your high-and-mighty doings! Were Samuel stunted like you, I might have been able to place him in a noble household. Do better for him if you can, you with your court position! Surely there is a place here—in the stables or kitchens."

The idea of my gentle brother at court, under the eye of Buckingham and

Lady Carlisle, was more than I could bear. What wickedness might they force me to do if they realized how far I would go to protect my brother?

My father crossed to my writing table, tugging open the drawers in my writing box and rummaging in them the way a pig might root through a pail of slops. " 'Od's fish, where'd you get this fancy bit? What is it?"

"It is a writing box, a gift from the queen."

"What did you have to do to get it? Turn a few somersaults or dance on the table?"

I remembered the queen crumpled on the floor, sobbing. I was not about to reveal that ugly scene to my father. "Her Majesty cut herself on broken glass. I stopped the bleeding." Had I not done just that in the months since? Attempted to bind up her wounds, apparent and more hidden? Using whatever chance came my way to mend what I could between Henrietta Maria and her husband—without letting any of the Buckingham faction detect my efforts?

"Might want to perch some spectacles on that honking French nose of the queen's. Face on the knight looks like you sure enough, but had you painted a bit taller than life, didn't she? What do you think you could sell this lot for?"

I felt revolted by the avaricious bent of his smile, and yet for a moment I wondered. Surely I could raise enough to spare Samuel from hell at Beetle Garth's hands.

"Turn these trinkets to coin and put them to something useful for the family instead of hoarding it all for you," Father said. "Starkey told me of another venture—"

Father's words dashed any possibility I could spare my brother pain with coin—either raised from selling my possessions or by handing over the purse Buckingham had given me: my own Judas pieces of silver. Father would just pour fresh coin into the fool's ventures, doubling the size of the purse he had already wasted. "I wouldn't insult Her Majesty by selling her gift," I told him.

"The French goose wouldn't have to know. Isn't likely to come to your bedchamber, now is she?"

The sneer implied in his words pinched more than I wished. Had I imagined such a visit from Henrietta Maria? Her lively chatter filling the silence?

The quick movements of her hands like a sparrow in the air. I would give her the seat nearest the window, where she could look down and see the flowers. But such a visit would never happen. Queens did not visit their servants' chambers. Or if they did, it was to chambers of men like the earl of Leicester during Elizabeth Tudor's reign. Handsome, dashing, dangerous men those queens were half in love with. Men like Buckingham, not like me.

"I will not sell this box," I insisted. "There is no other painted like it. Someone else might discover it was gone, or tell her. Do you want me to risk losing her favor?"

"Doesn't seem your high position will be doing me much good if you can't even help me to seize the chance Starkey offers."

I swore under my breath. "Do you think the chance to join a royal household and better ourselves comes every day for folks like us? If I behave rashly, as you want me to, it will slip away. I will do my best for all of you back in Oakham as long as you do right by Samuel. Do not send him to Beetle."

My father shrugged. "The apprenticeship is all signed and sealed. Nothing either of us can do."

Sick panic gripped me and I knew it was true. I could no more pluck Samuel safely from this briar of contracts than I could wrest myself from Buckingham's grasp. But perhaps there was a way I might convince the duke or king or queen to champion Samuel's cause. They would be able to do the impossible and cut my brother free.

As soon as my father left, I went to my trunk and dug out the coin Buckingham had paid me for brewing the trouble at Tyburn. I pictured the queen's face as it had been at the banquet at York House, so fresh, as yet unmarked by the grief of losing Madame Saint-Georges and the others. I was the author of that grief. If I approached the duke now, would the price of Samuel's freedom mean conjuring more trouble between the queen and her husband? Injuring them both another time? There were moments I almost believed Henrietta Maria might be able to ease the sadness in Charles Stuart's eyes and that he might cherish her as she deserved. But not while the duke of Buckingham had his spies to poison the air between them.

"I am sorry for the wounds I cause," I said aloud. "But I cannot let that regret change what I must do."

Steeling myself against the memory of the queen's now-rare smiles, I tucked the purse in the front of my doublet, then set out in search of the duke. What would happen if someone noticed me on the way to his court lodgings? Would it stir suspicions? This time, I had to take the risk.

I could explain there was some business about my father if anyone asked. That much, God help me, was true.

It was astonishing how swiftly the duke admitted me to his presence. His gaze—greedy, calculating—echoed my father's.

"Jeffrey Hudson, I had not expected a visit from you. I heard you had a most unwelcome guest of your own at the palace." One corner of his mouth ticked up in amusement. "I hope there is no ill news from Oakham."

Why should his mockery bother me so much? Buckingham was the one who had plucked me out of the shambles gutter and set me up in this new life. I wondered what he saw when he looked at me now in my fine garments with the simple bits of jewelry the queen had added. Those marks of her favor provided a startling contrast to the guilty weight of Buckingham's cross-etched ring.

Did he still see the scrubbed raw, overwhelmed, half-starved boy he'd poked and prodded like a horse for sale? Or did he see the queen's most trusted servant—the one among all of Her Majesty's royal attendants whom courtiers must bribe in order to have access to Henrietta Maria? No, I realized, reading the expression on Buckingham's face. When Buckingham looked at me, he saw what he had always seen: a freak.

"Have you intelligence on the queen or her ladies?" Buckingham asked. "The beautiful countess does not fare well in her siege upon His Majesty's virtue. The king finds her lively, of course, but perhaps more so than he is comfortable with. After his father's lecherous misadventures, King Charles has a horror of scandal."

I tried to erase pictures that sprang into my mind—a far younger Buckingham being fondled by the coarse-mannered Scottish king who had exchanged a dukedom for such freedoms. Had Buckingham paid in full the sexual tribute James apparently had desired? I could not guess. I knew only that the man before me seemed ambitious enough to submit to anything.

"There are times I miss the old king." Buckingham seemed to guess the path of my thoughts. He did not seem to mind his place in them. "There is something to be said for a king who can be led about by his prick. But I have confidence Lady Carlisle will succeed in the end. She and her husband are putting the finishing touches on a most original idea to gain His Majesty's attention at the hawking party they have planned."

"Her husband is aiding her in casting lures for the king? Doesn't the earl object to his wife's playing courtesan? I heard theirs was a love match."

"Considering Lucy's boorish father, it is little wonder she was charmed by Lord Carlisle's impeccable manners. However, once they were married, she discovered that she was three times cleverer than her husband. He did not appreciate her more . . . unusual assets. Her beauty, however, well . . ."

Buckingham looked as if he'd tasted something sweet. "Carlisle knows he cannot keep such a beauty all to himself. He has most graciously shared his divine Lucy with me. It is an even bigger honor to share one's wife with the king. Of course, it all depends upon Lucy succeeding in ensnaring Charles. But the entertainment will be worthy of her: a temptation that might as well have been torn from one of her Wizard Earl father's books of sorcery."

For a moment, elation overcame the foreboding I always felt in the duke's presence. He had spoken of using dark magic upon the king! Even a duke must be executed for that—had not charges of witchcraft been one of the weapons that brought the downfall of Anne Boleyn?

Still, my excitement faded, reality crowding in. Buckingham was Charles Stuart's oldest, most trusted friend, the one the king depended on for love, support, advice. The king would cling to Buckingham more loyally than to his own wife.

Even back in Oakham, we had heard how Charles had spent his first four years in an iron brace upon wheels, the weak-legged prince unable to walk on his own. In the years that followed, Charles had learned to lean on the duke of Buckingham in the same way, reigning with the duke's support, not on his own strength. Rip away the duke of Buckingham and what would happen to the king? Would he fold into a heap on the floor, unable to rule?

The possibility alarmed me—for England, for myself, for the queen. But the fate of kings would have to wait until I found a way to secure my brother's safety. I shoved thoughts of Lady Carlisle's new plot away and turned my energies into wresting Samuel from a life that would drown him in blood.

"What passes between the king and countess is their concern. Mine is a personal matter. I wish to give you something." I reached through the slit in my doublet and withdrew Buckingham's richly tooled leather purse.

His brows arched. "Is the purse still full? I remember paying you well for serving my interests."

"I do not want your coin." I dropped it with a heavy clunk upon the table.

Buckingham made no move to pick the purse up. "A partnership like ours is impossible to sever."

I met his gaze dead-on. "I do not wish to sever our partnership, only to alter the terms."

"It is becoming an inconvenient pattern. First Ware wants to sail halfway across the world; now you wish to change things that are already working in my favor." Buckingham folded his hands. His rings glimmered. "I am satisfied with arrangements as they are."

"This amendment will be to your advantage."

"I am listening."

"My father apprenticed my younger brother to a master in the shambles. I prefer Samuel be tutored and given a clerk's job somewhere well clear of the place."

Boredom dulled Buckingham's eyes. "It is your father's right to dispose of his son however he chooses."

"As he disposed of me?"

"Just so." Buckingham licked his thumb and forefinger, using the moisture to perfect the point of his beard.

"Your Grace, my effectiveness as your spy depends on my goodwill, does it not?"

"More upon fear like the cane a tutor wields over a pupil."

"Samuel will not need a violent inducement. He is clever and eager to please. He is so honest, you could lock him in your bake house when he was starving and he'd not steal a bite of bread."

The duke plucked a loose pearl from his sleeve and tossed the gem onto the table. It clattered softly as it lodged beneath the cover of a book. "Destined for sainthood, is your brother?"

"No!" I said with a force that startled me. "We left such superstitious nonsense behind with the Pope. But an honest lad like Samuel would be a boon to any employer. Any man with a strong arm can butcher meat."

"I have no time for such trivialities. The king has finally gotten the lackwits at Parliament to finance a fleet so I can relieve the starving Huguenots holding out against Richelieu's guns. I mean to destroy the French with such panache that no one will ever mention the tangle at Cádiz again." A muscle in his jaw knotted. "Jeffrey, go back to your post."

He intended to turn me away. Why had I not stopped to consider? What did a purseful of coins mean to such a man? It was said he had instructed his seamstresses to stitch the jewels on his clothes loosely when he went to negotiate the king's marriage in France. He had shed gems wherever he went, setting servants and even gentlefolk scrambling to snatch the glittering stones from the ground as he passed. In the face of such excess, what could I offer?

Panic washed through me, and I imagined my brother trapped in Beetle Garth's world. I remembered what Dulcinea had told me before I did my first leap upon the high rope. *No linnet ever flew by imagining itself crushed from a fall.*

"Your Grace, you were wise to warn me about the queen's charms," I said, keeping my attention firmly on my goal. "It is not an easy thing to resist her."

Buckingham scowled. "What nonsense is this?"

"I could become so devoted to Henrietta Maria that even threat of death could not prevent it—especially if the Channel between England and La Rochelle divides you from me."

Buckingham shoved back his chair and rose to tower over me. How many times had I been treated to such a display by jeering apprentices back home, in the halls of three different palaces, even by my own father? But it was harder to intimidate me in such a way since I'd grown accustomed to Will Evans's height.

"Obviously I must add one more task to my preparations before I sail for La Rochelle. I must make you better aware of what my displeasure would cost you," the duke said.

"You may do so, of course. But there is a better way to assure I remain loyal only to you."

"You plan to extort more coin from me? Shall I tell you what happened to the last fool who tried it?"

"I have returned a purseful of coin I earned. Why would I do so only to demand another?"

He smoothed his mustache.

"Your Grace, I might be tempted to keep Her Majesty's secrets from a man I feared." I dared the sly smile I had mastered when teasing members of court. "After all, how would Your Grace ever know I had withheld something if it were a secret?"

"You find yourself amusing, fool?"

"It is a riddle, is it not? To pay one for exposing deep, dark secrets. By nature, such confidences are difficult to keep tally of. It is unlikely anyone else would be privy to them and race to you to expose my perfidy."

"My wife is in the queen's privy chambers, as are my mother and sister and the countess of Carlisle."

"They were thrust upon the queen when she did not want them—an indignity she will not soon forget. I braved royal wrath to staunch her bleeding when you and the king ripped her friends away. She trusts me as she would never trust anyone associated with your household. Besides which, I am not even human—is that not what people say? Not human and yet her most trusted friend."

Buckingham's face darkened. "You sound as if you are already the queen's man!"

"I am not. You wish to keep me loyal to you, bound by fear. I say that if my patron saved my brother from the horror of a future such as my father offers Samuel, well, then nothing could shake my loyalty."

"I was not aware it was in danger of being shaken until now," Buckingham said silkily.

"It isn't. From the moment my brother begins his studies."

"You have become quite devious in your short time at court. Exceeded even my expectations. I have yet to decide whether that is a good thing or a bad thing."

"A dog will fight if it fears its master, but when overmatched by a foe, that dog will be glad to succumb to the inevitable. But if a dog loves its master, it will never surrender until its last drop of blood is shed. Which kind of dog would you rather send into the court's bear pit?"

The duke paced around me, his gaze filled with a new and grudging respect. "I will consider your proposal."

I swept His Grace a bow.

"Go! You will have my answer presently."

I did.

Next morning as the queen's household returned from chapel, the duchess of Buckingham approached me. "Is it not strange to be compelled to attend Catholic Mass? For so many years it has been outlawed."

"No one can hold it against us," I said. "We are required to accompany the queen."

"Did you know that I was Catholic before I married His Grace? My converting to the reformed faith broke my father's heart, but I surrendered the old faith to win George Villiers as my husband. I can deny him nothing."

It did not surprise me that my soul was not the first His Grace had bartered for. What had it cost Catherine Manners to turn her back on her father and her faith?

"I confess I do not mind my prayers the way I should in chapel. I keep thinking that a secret Catholic would be grateful to be in my place, instead of fretting over kneeling on a lump in their gown. I look at the queen's other ladies and wonder if any of them are recusants. What do you think, Jeffrey? Is the countess of Carlisle a follower of the Virgin Mary?" Her humor surprised me.

"I don't believe Lady Carlisle believes in anything virgin, blessed or otherwise." The jest slipped out as one so often did now—so quickly, I did not have time to consider how it might wound. "Your Grace, I beg your pardon. I did not mean to . . ." Taunt you with your husband's mistress, I thought.

"Do not apologize. Court fools are allowed to tell the truth with impunity." The duchess frowned. "It is obvious Lady Carlisle seeks to ensnare any man powerful enough to advance her fortunes. The king has shown greater will to resist her than most men."

The duchess's tone told me what I had long wondered about. She did know Buckingham and the countess of Carlisle were lovers. That knowledge caused her pain. Yet she must speak civilly to Lady Carlisle every day; endure the woman's flirtation with Buckingham whenever the duke entered the room. Did Catherine Villiers watch her husband's gaze follow the countess's exquisite form? Did she imagine the pair of them together, yet have to smile into Lady Carlisle's smug face?

"My husband is trying to kindle something between the countess and king. He wishes me to encourage it." She chafed her wedding ring around her finger. "A conscience is a troublesome encumbrance at court. The duke insists one should shed it before one enters the palace—like a cloak with frayed edges." Her laugh was only a little forced. "You know, he was quite poor when first he came to Whitehall."

"I have heard the tale. I was told to learn from his example when I left home."

"Home! That is what I meant to speak to you about before I got distracted." She seemed relieved to change the subject. "Jeffrey, His Grace tells me you came to him, determined to better the lot of your brother. He says you will pay out of your own purse. It is very generous of you."

"Your Grace, you have never been in the shambles at night, heard the screams of the animals as they are slaughtered. They sound like children. As for the master my father would apprentice Samuel to, he is more beast than man."

The duchess averted her eyes.

"I do not mean to shock you, Your Grace, only explain why I must aid my brother. Samuel is a good lad. He is clever and far too tenderhearted to spend his life battered by a cruel master and deafened by animal screams."

The duchess's hand moved toward me. She stopped before she touched me, as if she realized it would be patronizing. She would not have touched a full-size man thus. "Your brother is lucky to have you on his side, Jeffrey. It happens that I know a learned man in need of a pupil. Master Benedict Quintin is the cousin of my childhood friend. He returned to London after years on the Continent spent leading young men on their grand tours. Master Quintin sought me out especially in hopes I would help him find a situation."

"But my brother is not in London. He remains in Oakham."

"Rutland will suit Master Quintin perfectly. He says there are plenty of places for people to pray in the city."

"Pray?"

The duchess laughed. "It seems I have religion on the mind since we left the chapel." The duchess caressed the miniature of her husband, its gold-filigreed setting pinned to her bodice. I almost felt Buckingham's painted eyes following me. "But my stumble over the word may not be so strange when considering tutoring. Are not church-bound places the centers where scholars often learn their letters?"

"I suppose."

The duchess seemed to consider. "Is your brother a Puritan? I understand they have distaste for anything smacking of the formalities of church."

"Samuel is no Puritan. He is a loyal subject to the king and goes to the parish church every Sunday." There was only one church in Oakham's parish—the Church of England, with the king in place of the Pope.

Did the duchess hear the defensiveness in my voice? I thought of Samuel, the holy medal, and the widow he visited who kept the statue of the Virgin Mary beneath her floorboards.

"In light of your description, I would say that Samuel and Master Quintin should suit each other. Do you trust me to settle this matter?"

Far sooner than I would trust your husband, I thought.

"I am sending some servants back to Burley-on-the-Hill to fetch a few trinkets my father could not bear to throw away. The priests at the Queen's Chapel might have use for them, and it seems a pity to have them moldering in storage. I will dispatch Master Quintin to join the servants' trek to the country."

"Is a kitchen page named Clemmy Watson one of those you are dispatching to Rutland?" I asked.

"I had not thought to send him." She must have seen my disappointment, for she asked, "Why?"

"He promised to carry a letter to Samuel for me if the chance presented itself."

The duchess was silent a long moment. "There is no reason Clemmy cannot be one of the party returning to Burley. In fact, I will send him whenever there is such a trip to be made, so that you might have word of Samuel's progress in these lessons you fought to secure for him."

"You are too good, Your Grace."

She thought it was flattery. It was not. It was the truth. She was far too good to be Buckingham's wife.

Hours later, I was too restless to retire to my room alone. Instead, I amused myself in the Freaks' Lair watching Pug try to eat the pomegranate Robin Goodfellow was painting on a panel for the queen's new masque. Sara watched every daub of color, leaning so close to Goodfellow that her hair brushed the artist's shoulder. Though she cast a shadow over the work, Goodfellow did not complain.

Simon was wrestling a muddy spaniel into a lead tub filled with warm, soapy water—he trusted no one else to bathe his charges since a servant had splashed water and given one of the dogs a putrid ear.

Will sat in a big chair beside the fire. He held his hands carefully apart to apply the perfect tension to a skein of blue silk Dulcinea had looped around them. She wound the thread into a ball along with Evans's soulful gaze.

It felt good to lose myself in the familiar—the bright colors and confusion, the tools of our trades scattered about. But for the first time, I craved more from this place, these people: a deepening too dangerous to pursue.

I had bought Samuel's future. Its price would have to be paid in some future betrayal of the queen. Had I not all but promised the duke some nugget he could use against her? Yet, even with that looming over me, I could not completely quell a sense of victory. I wanted to tell Robin and Will, Simon Rattlebones and Sara. I even thought Pug might take delight in the fact that for once one of Her Majesty's Freaks and Curiosities of Nature had bested the mighty duke of Buckingham. For once, His Grace is doing *my* will, I wanted to crow. I did not dare. I would have to be satisfied holding my secret close to my heart.

I had faced down the duke and Samuel would be safe, far from Beetle Garth and my father. The duchess of Buckingham—the kindest of the queen's ladies—had recommended his tutor. I might fear for the queen, for the king, and for myself. But even if I had sold all of our souls in this devil's bargain, at least when it came to Samuel, I had nothing left to fear.

SIXTEEN

•

Three days of strange weather circled the Carlisle hunting grounds on lazy wings, as if awaiting the flick of a sorcerer's silver stick to set it free. Harried servants scurried about, making preparations for entertainments indoors, should they be needed. Yet the morning the royal party set out, falcons at the ready, the world glittered with sun and expectation.

We rode into the morning fifty strong—plumes on wide-brimmed hats sifting the wind, curls bouncing on elegantly clad shoulders, skirts on ladies' riding habits rippling back and revealing flashes of ankle and leather shoe. Men preened like stallions, showing off their skills, trying to jostle closer— not to the queen but to Carlisle's countess, whose wit and beauty seemed more captivating than ever before.

The earl of Carlisle surveyed his wife's male conquests as if their eagerness to get the countess in bed was the greatest compliment they could pay him. The elegant Scotsman even embraced Buckingham with an air of indulgence that left no doubt he knew the duke had been intimate with his fair Lucy.

Watching Lady Carlisle flirt with her suitors, it was easy to see why any man would be fascinated by her. Even Charles Stuart's gaze pulled her way, the dark flush on his cheekbones showing he was not impervious to her charms. She'd even won from him an occasional shy smile.

I could not shake the ominous feeling that Buckingham's warning about this day had created in me—his promise that some trick would be wrought that might snare the king in Lady Carlisle's net.

I hated the fact that the countess had helped to breach the aloof shell about Charles Stuart, cracks evident eight days ago, when he'd demonstrated his concern for his wife by the mount he had given me: a willow wand of a mare, slender enough for a special saddle designed to hold me in place. It fit me far better than Buckingham's offering had. Nooks of hardened leather padded with velvet gave me a place to tuck my thighs; stirrups set in the perfect place gave me leverage when I needed it. Even the mare's reins were more slender than usual, so they could fit in my hand. Not that I needed the bridle. This mare had the softest mouth God ever put on a horse, responding to the slightest twitch of the reins.

When the earl of Carlisle had first spoken of the hunt to be held in a fortnight, Charles Stuart had drawn me aside, surprised me by saying, "I had meant this to be a first mount for a prince, but there is time to train another in its stead."

"Majesty . . . it is too generous." I had started to protest, and then stopped, knowing I must ignore my scruples and scoop whatever I was given into my private hoard. Archie was right. I would need something to fall back on when the royals discovered my perfidy. *If* they allowed me to escape Tyburn's scaffold. "I am honored, of course," I said.

"The horse comes with a royal charge. I command you to keep pace with my wife on the hunt, on rides, everywhere, Jeffrey. You showed courage the day she cut herself. It takes a brave man to challenge a king's orders. You did not let my anger keep you from coming to Her Majesty's aid. You will not let any man's." He hesitated for a moment. "You have heard I may send relief to the besieged Huguenots at La Rochelle?"

I shifted my feet, uneasy. I could hardly tell him the duke of Buckingham and I had discussed it while I bargained for my brother's future. "It is my task to make the queen laugh. A hard thing when the discord between Your Majesty and France breaks her heart."

"That grieves me, Jeffrey. But it is as the duke of Buckingham says. My kingdom's honor depends on striking back at those who betray our trust. He has offered to lead my fleet to open La Rochelle's port. Is that not noble of him?" He did not expect an answer. "I fear he suffers guilt over his ill-starred raid on Cádiz. Many beyond the palace walls still blame him for that failure.

But they hated him even when my father was still alive. It is nothing but jealousy, such hate. How can a mediocre man understand one as magnificent as Buckingham?"

"I am not even a mediocre man, Your Majesty. One small as I am can hardly be expected to judge. But I fear—" I stopped, not brave enough to finish.

"Fear what, Jeffrey?"

"I know simple folk, Majesty. They will not believe the queen is loyal to England once Your Majesty and France cross swords."

"I know." He looked away from me. "My wife may need someone to defend her in the days to come. I will depend upon you."

The knot in my belly had nothing to do with my old fear of horses. I had become used to them, and to the courtiers' laughter. But for the king to mock me was something new. "Majesty, look at me. My size. I am not one to protect the queen if trouble comes."

"You guard her spirit, Jeffrey." Charles Stuart gazed into the distance with sad, dark eyes. "I do not possess the gift of inspiring laughter in people even when I wish to." I had seen vulnerability in him for just an instant. I wondered if he was picturing his dead brother—that new Arthur who had bested all in tournaments wielding his mind or lance. For all the splendor of his crown, the divine fire that had made him king, I could feel a kinship with Charles Stuart, a man trying to fill spaces too large for him.

Now I shook myself out of my reverie, aware of the excitement all around me. We set out across the fields, hounds and large spaniels bounding ahead to flush game from the brush and send the falcon's prey into a frenzied race against death. My mount kept me near the queen as the falconer prepared to cast the king's gyrfalcon into the heavens. I watched the master remove the leather hood that blinded the mighty bird, then release jesses that tethered the creature. He cast the gyrfalcon skyward, and we watched it chase a dove. Fierce talons struck the terrified bird in flight, and the falcon carried it back, limp, dead.

Rabbits were next, the dogs flushing a fat one from the brush. But as the gyrfalcon took off yet again, it spotted a different prey. That moment, I saw it also—chestnut and white, a small blur of silky ears, the joyous yap of greeting. Mitte, the queen's toy spaniel.

How had she gotten so far from the manor? Had we doubled back some-how in our travels? It did not matter. The gyrfalcon abandoned the rabbit, seeking more interesting prey. I could sense those golden eyes, feel the talons stretch, eager to sink into flesh. The great shadow of the falcon's wing-span sped toward the little dog.

I shouted warning to the falconer, knowing it was hopeless no matter how he whistled or swung a bit of raw meat on a leather thong above his head. The queen cried out, and I spurred my horse in a futile effort to startle the hawk, fearing it might mistake me for prey, and wheel about to fly into my face. Mitte yelped as the falcon struck, sinking its claws into her shoul-ders, lifting her off of the ground. The spaniel's paws flailed the air, a keen-ing bark rising above the shouts of horror. For a moment, I feared the bird might drop Mitte to her death.

The falconer held out his gauntlet, doing all he could to summon the bird back to its perch, but the gyrfalcon glimpsed the turmoil below and its own instincts kicked in, making it wheel away from what it sensed was danger.

The queen pleaded, distress causing her to jumble words into a mixture of French and English. The king cantered a few paces after the bird. But not even royal decree could order it from the sky.

Charles Stuart turned to a lad with a bow slung across his back and a quiver of arrows in case they were needed to finish a kill. "You, there, boy. Are you a good archer?"

"I am."

"Shoot the gyrfalcon if you must to save the queen's dog."

The queen gasped as the lad slung his bow down off his shoulder, the other courtiers voicing their shock. He drew an arrow and knocked it.

"Majesty," Buckingham exclaimed, wheeling his mount next to the king's. "The falcon is worth a fortune, while the court is overrun with toy spaniels."

"My wife loves this one," Charles said stoically, but I could see how much the choice pained him. His gaze followed the magnificent bird with regret.

Suddenly, above the furor, something sounded—a pipe of some sort, is-suing strange music. At the crest of the nearby hill, a black eagle seemed to form out of air—wings spreading wide, feathers shimmering, a body the size of a man.

The queen crossed herself, and servants made signs against the evil eye.

Something about the figure whispered of other worlds. "Who is that? What . . ." someone began to question. But another hissed, "Do not startle him."

Startle whom? I wondered. The falcon we had set out to hunt with that morning, or the earthbound creature who seemed more imposing every moment?

A hush fell as courtiers and servants alike shifted their gaze from falcon in the sky to the figure summoning it. Even Mitte ceased her struggles, and I feared the spaniel might be dead. The king's gyrfalcon veered farther away from its keeper and glided in a slow spiral downward. An arm's length from the ground, the talons withdrew from flesh, dropping the spaniel at the strange figure's feet. I spurred my horse forward, determined to scoop up the dog and return her to the queen's arms if Mitte should be alive, or else sweep her away to shield Henrietta Maria if the bird had made a kill. As if concealing death could somehow ease the sting. But even as I drew near, the sight before me grew stranger.

It was as if the piping had melted the wings of the creature who had played it. What had seemed wings fluttered down to pool upon Mitte, protecting the little dog, her rescuer transforming into a man whose skin was darker than black velvet.

The gyrfalcon, that fiercest of birds, hopped onto the man's arm. The falcon ascended to his shoulder in razor-clawed steps, then pecked at a ruby that glowed in the man's ear.

Was the man mad? The bird seemed likely to pluck out his eye. Instead, the gyrfalcon made a low throaty sound and settled more quietly than when hooded on its master's arm.

Even my arrival did not jar it from its perch. I loosed my feet from their stirrups and slid from the mare, thudding onto the ground so hard, I was knocked to my knees. I did not care.

"Is it safe to uncover Mitte?" I asked.

The black man nodded. He was humming, the gyrfalcon seeming to hang upon every sound.

Not fully trusting the man or the bird, I scooped Mitte up in the cloak. I could hear the other courtiers thundering toward us as I carried Mitte behind a tree. Once hidden from the gyrfalcon's sight, I uncovered the little dog. Blood stained the white patches of her coat where the talons had gripped, but she was still breathing. She opened her liquid brown eyes and whimpered. Unsteadily, she pushed up on her paws. I was too involved in checking her for other wounds to see the rest of the party ride up, only heard them pooling around me.

"Majesty, Mitte lives," I reassured the queen, "thanks to this man."

The king wheeled his horse to face the stranger. "We owe you a debt. Who are you?"

"They call me Boku."

"What witchery is this?" someone murmured.

The king frowned, suddenly suspicious. I wondered if the falcon tamer knew what danger he was in. "How did you achieve this feat? You lured the gyrfalcon out of the sky when even his keeper could not."

"Majesty, forgive me," Lady Carlisle burst out. "It was no witchery, but a fortunate coincidence that Boku was able to intervene. He was to entertain us once we reached the pavilions. After we supped, Boku was to work his illusions. One was to involve your gyrfalcon. He had been working with the bird in secret to achieve it."

The king scowled. "An outsider was meddling in the royal mews?"

"Boku was not to be an outsider after today. He is my gift to you, Majesty: A master of the art of illusion. Though I regret he cannot be introduced to you in the way I had planned."

She did indeed look vexed. Yet the queen was all gratitude. A groom caught hold of her reins as one of the keepers of the hounds took Mitte from me and held the dog up for inspection.

"The little bitch should be fine after a bit of rest," the bucktoothed fellow said. "It's a good thing as well, for if I'm not mistaken, she'll be having a litter of pups to be telling her adventures to."

The queen reached out her arms for the spaniel. The horse scented blood and attempted to dance sideways, but the queen was far too fine a horsewoman to be rattled. She gathered Mitte close. "Thanks to our Lucy."

The new intimacy that flared between the queen and Lady Carlisle undermined the relief I felt at Mitte's escape. I was certain "our Lucy" would have happily dropped Mitte—and the queen—down a well if it meant her "entertainment" could have gone forward as planned. Besides, it was not the fine lady who had risked the gyrfalcon's talons—or who doubtless had deep punctures in the arm upon which the predator had landed. I glanced at the conjurer; saw those unreadable eyes on me.

"Lady Carlisle has done me an immense service today," the queen announced. "From this moment on, I will cherish her friendship, as she deserves."

"Lady Carlisle, wherever did you find such a wizard?" Buckingham drawled. "He is most remarkable."

"I acquired him from a captain recently returned from rounding Cape Horn."

"Did the Spaniards challenge him?" someone in the crowd asked.

"Spaniards are no match for English sailors!" Lady Carlisle exclaimed, her cheeks dimpling. "Since the days of Sir Walter Raleigh, foreign claims have not barred stout seamen from plucking the choicest fruits from the New World and bringing them to our ports."

The queen addressed the magician. "Monsieur Boku. I am sorry to have spoilt this entertainment Lady Carlisle planned. But I am grateful you will be in His Majesty's household." She withdrew a ring from her little finger and extended it to Boku. "Take this as a token of my gratitude."

He reached for it, and I noticed the queen dropped the ring before she could touch his skin. His palm was a startling pink, and quilted cloth bracelets as wide as my forearm spanned from his wrist halfway up his arm. The pearl in the ring's center glowed as Boku nudged it with his thumb. "A tear wept by the sea."

"What a beautiful thing to call a pearl," Henrietta Maria said. "Did you conjure that phrase yourself?"

"Someone else called it that," he said in a strange accent.

"In the place where you are from?" the king asked.

"There is only here, Majesty. Only now—where I am to lighten the king's weariness and show you illusions such as England has never seen."

"We shall be the judge of that," Charles said in the patronizing tone that often made those around him work to hide their irritation. "Savage peoples cannot fathom what amuses England's royal court. You must bow to the discernment of your betters, our intellect and cultured tastes."

Boku hid his hands in the draping cups of his sleeves. "Majesty, I have made it my passion to understand your English amusements very well."

I was not certain why the words of this man from tropic climes made me cold. Even after he excused himself to prepare for his coming performance, I could not shake the strange chill. It was absurd. He had rescued the queen's dog, not sent the gyrfalcon to hunt it.

At that moment, a red-faced footman ran up to Boku, his livery askew. "The little wretch! Someone said you had found . . ." He slammed to a halt, gaping at the queen. He bowed so hastily and low, it was a miracle he did not clunk his brow on the ground. "Majesty, forgive me! The little dog must have climbed into the cart carrying the pastries before we left the kitchens. We did not find her until we were already here. I tied her to one of the tent posts, but she chewed through the ribbon."

"So that was how you got here, Mitte!" the queen exclaimed.

"Majesty, I swear I did not know it was your dog. I would have taken it straight back to the manor house if I had."

The king frowned. "You are fortunate all ended well. Be more diligent in your duty from now on."

The servant fled, looking afraid he still might be clapped in the Tower. Carlisle's other servants seemed to be attempting to make up for their fellow's blunder as they performed their assigned tasks with even more alacrity than usual—grooms taking charge of the guests' horses and helping the ladies alight in clouds of blue and crimson, green and gold. Serving girls hastened forward to take riding gloves as they were stripped from ladies' hands, and helped adjust hats the wind had blown askew. Fresh-faced pages offered cups of spiced wine to soothe throats strained in attempts to converse over the sound of hooves on turf.

The earl linked arms with his radiant wife and made a pretty speech to welcome the king to the lovely picnic spot the Carlisle servants had arranged for us. We descended to flower-decked tents of green and blue beside a silver lake the shape of a shield. What looked like a mist-draped island stood in the middle of the pool. Had it been crafted by men or by nature? I could not tell. I had seen many displays of scenery since my first court masque and wondered what delights the gauzy shroud might conceal.

For now, there was a feast to be had. Beneath fluttering pennons affixed to the tent poles, tables had been assembled and lined with chairs and cushions. Mountains of honey-dipped cakes and meat pies that had been carted from the manor house kitchens tempted our palates from silver plate. Most impressive of all was a creation that would have made Will Evans look small: sugar spun into falcons that soared above cliffs made of gingerbread. Some device sent a waterfall tumbling down a metal chute through the crags to a pool lined with silver.

Grabbing several cushions to boost myself to table level, I slung them into my chair, then clambered up to the seat, taking a moment to be sure of my balance. The queen would not let Mitte out of her arms as festivities commenced with a dozen maidens dressed as water nymphs piping melodies near the shore.

As the hours sped by, even entertainments as magnificent as any I had ever seen could not draw any but the most cursory of the queen's attention from the small creature in her arms. She wrapped the spaniel in her riding cloak, feeding the little animal bites of meat, sips of wine from the goblet meant for her. Her passionate tenderness and gratitude spilled over upon the king. I could not keep from watching her, nor could he.

I knew the prime performance was in the offing when music such as I had never heard began to rumble from the center of the mechanical waterfall—drums with rhythms like the heartbeat of some great beast, a dry rattling sound shaken in accompaniment, the scent of cinnamon and pepper and other spices I could not name suddenly in the air. Almost against my will, I leaned forward, nearly slipping off my cushion perch. My pulse pounded an answer to the drums, one I could feel echoing in every person present, from Buckingham to the lowliest page. Even Mitte's small pink tongue bobbed in rhythm. Just when I thought I could not bear the building suspense another moment, the drums stopped. Crags of gingerbread exploded in a burst of scarlet-and-green smoke, a dozen doves dyed bright colors taking wing.

As the smoke cleared, a figure took shape where the waterfall had been. There stood Boku, his robes spattered with the blue stones that had sparkled at the bottom of the gem-strewn pool. Most startling of all, the king's gyrfalcon perched on his arm.

I felt a jerking sensation as people snapped free from whatever bonds the drums had held them in. Exclamations of amazement filled the tent. No jesses bound the falcon's leg, its noble head and powerful hooked beak bare of the leather hood designed to blind the high-strung creature to its surroundings and prevent it from going wild at the slightest noise or unexpected movement. The kind of chaos this crowded tent contained must have seemed a hell for the huge, fierce predator: crowds of chattering people, the cloth roof overhead, blocking out escape to the sky, the heavy smells of food mixed with courtiers' perfume and sweat from the ride.

The doves were certainly panicking, fluttering frantically to escape. Their black-bead eyes glistened with terror as they bumped the top of the tent and swooped over the shrieking guests.

In the midst of the uproar, Boku stretched out his hand to a dove the color of primroses.

"Come." The man's deep voice held more power than the drums. "Come, flower of the sky, to the warrior who would pluck you."

Was the dove beset by some lingering madness from the drums? The wings slowed and it swung toward Boku and certain death. No hoodless gyrfalcon would tolerate prey drawing so close. The gyrfalcon would explode in a rush of powerful wings and crush the dove with its talons.

I did not want to witness the dove's death. I started to make excuse that I must answer a call of nature, but as I rose, Boku's dark gaze locked on me.

"Master Hudson," he called, and I wondered how he had learned my name. "Have you the courage to snatch the dove from death?"

"Merely leave off your strange summons and let her fly away," I said. "I have a pressing errand of nature to attend, so you might choose another guest to aid you."

"It is not as if any guest will do. Are you afraid of being struck by these talons?"

I looked at the razor-sharp hooks digging into Boku's strange bracelets. "I prefer to keep my eyeballs in my head."

"Do you not trust me?"

"I do not know you well enough to have an opinion."

I could tell from Boku's steady look that he knew I had lied. The foreigner

cast me off balance, filled my head with black magic and quicksand path-
ways and mysteries I dared not unveil. "Jeffrey, do as he asks," the queen
insisted. "Mitte wants you to help the man who saved her."

"Perhaps I should not have been so hasty to go to Mitte's aid," I muttered
under my breath. I could almost hear Archie's cynical voice: *It might cost you
an eye, Jeffrey, but you would not want to disappoint Her Majesty's dog.*

Still, I could not disobey a direct command from the queen. My feet
dragged as I made my way to Boku. He placed his hand above me, then lowered it to cover the top of my head with his palm. I felt something strange
prickle against my scalp.

"Close your eyes and whistle," he said as he drew his hand away. "Call
our winged friend."

I did as he bid me. Wind and feathers brushed my cheek. The dove
landed atop my head, and I heard its soft coo. Every muscle in my body went
stiff. I opened my eyes and saw yellow raptor eyes glaring into mine, the
gyrfalcon's bloodlust evident in the restless shift of her talons on Boku's
wrist.

"I am told your Christian God says to love one another," Boku said. "Let
us test his philosophy by allowing the falcon to give your dove the kiss of
brotherly love."

"I have brothers," I said thinking of John's bouts of temper. "I would not
count on a happy resolution when one brother has talons and the other does
not." I heard the audience laugh, but Boku's expression did not alter.

He brought the falcon so close, I could see a spot of blood on its beak.
"Do not move, little man," Boku said so only I could hear. My knees started
to tremble. Why was the dove not thrashing to get away? The gyrfalcon
stretched its neck toward me as if trying to decide whether the dove or I
would make a tastier meal. But as Boku gave an almost inaudible whistle, the
great bird tapped the dove's beak with his own.

"Thank Master Hudson, my sharp-taloned friend," Boku said.

"No need for that," I protested, but the falcon pecked the top of my head.
The crowd exclaimed in wonder and I prayed they would not startle the falcon into sampling my eye.

"Fool Jeffrey!" Buckingham's jovial voice rang out. "Do you still need to
answer nature's call, or has the falcon made you soil your breeches?"

The earl of Carlisle laughed. "Your Grace would not have risked your pretty face." Not when Buckingham's "pretty face" pleased the countess of Carlisle so much, I thought as I left the tent, the dove still frozen on my shoulder. Had it died of fear? I wondered. When I was far enough away from the tent, I plucked the bird off of me. I examined its eyes, now strange and glazed. I gave it a shake, hoping to rouse it, but it showed no sign of waking from its stupor.

One of Carlisle's servants approached. "I keep the earl's dovecote," he explained. "I will take charge of the bird." I handed the dove to its keeper and wondered if its drowsiness was contagious. I might have stolen a nap myself, but I was burning with curiosity to see what the magician would do next.

I returned to the tent in time to see him split a pomegranate. He tucked some ruby-colored seeds in his hand. When he unfurled his fingers, the whole assemblage exclaimed as eight perfect butterflies rose on deep red wings and alighted upon the queen's sleeve.

Next, Boku chose a pitch-soaked stick and set it afire. Murmuring words we could not understand, he raised the torch high, then jammed the blazing end down his throat. Ladies screeched in horror; gentlemen shouted. When he drew the torch back out, we stared, stunned. Somehow the end of the charred stick had transformed into a red flower that filled the tent with its scent.

The excitement had scarce died down when the magician swept up before the duke of Buckingham. "Your Grace, are you familiar with the workings of locks? Some gentlemen use them to protect their treasures—or their womenfolk's virtue." A spate of nervous laughter died almost before it began. I glanced over and saw the priggish king's smile falter.

"I am familiar with locks," Buckingham said.

"Could you test these, Your Grace? For if they are sturdy enough to withstand your efforts, no man can question the marvel I am about to perform." Boku handed him the implement in question.

Iron rattled as Buckingham strained to open the hasps. At length, he surrendered. "I defy any man to open these," he said. Boku offered the duke a strange set of keys. Buckingham applied them, turning the keys in the lock with great effort. The lock sprang open.

Boku took the lock and handed it to the page beside him. The illusionist crossed to stand before the queen. "Majesty, you have loaned me your valiant fool; now I ask to borrow something else precious to you. Madame Silken Ears."

For a moment, Henrietta Maria's eyes widened in panic. Her arms tightened around her dog. "Mitte has already had a most trying day. She would rather remain on my lap, and I have not the heart to dislodge her."

"Shall we let Mitte decide?" the magician asked. I could not imagine the spaniel would want anything to do with a man who smelled of the falcon that had nearly killed her. Boku extended his hand. Mitte wriggled free and ran to him, her tail waving like a white plume.

The queen started to protest again, but despite the rough treatment Mitte had received in the falcon's talons, the spaniel trusted Boku—or had succumbed to the same spell her attacker had.

"You must trust me," Boku said. "I mean no animal harm." Boku glided down to the lake's edge, the page shadowing his every step. Three grooms stood ready to launch a small boat.

Boku climbed into the vessel, Mitte in his arms and the page at his feet as they rowed across the water to the gauze-obscured island. Once they had disembarked, Boku waved his hand, and the gauze dropped to the ground, revealing an apparatus that drew whispers from the crowd.

It reminded me of the scaffold at Tyburn. Was this some clever jibe the Carlisles had planned, alluding to the queen's ill-fated pilgrimage? Whatever the case, the magician was already far beyond anyone's reach. My heart started to pound in my ears. No, I realized with a jolt, it was the drums again, throbbing, inexorable.

Boku grasped something bloodred and shook it out—a sack of some kind. He placed the all-too-willing dog inside it, then clasped the bundle against his chest as three sturdy grooms crossed chains about the man's arms and legs and body, manacling him to the tallest wooden post and locking the bonds in place.

I could hear Henrietta Maria's nervous voice as she talked to the king, and I saw Charles reach out to pat her hand. She grabbed hold of his and would not let it go.

The men rowed back, leaving Boku and the wriggling sack containing

Mitte upon the island alone. When the oarsmen alighted, the page went to the countess of Carlisle. I could see how nervous the boy was. "He's chained up tight, my lady. We all of us pulled on the locks, trying to open them. We were all to tell you that." He handed her the strange set of keys.

The countess took care not to touch his fingers, but once in possession of the keys, she offered them to the king. I could tell the queen was almost faint with alarm, but the king soothed her, and she watched the proceedings with wide eyes. Suddenly, the island began to sink slowly into the water.

The guests gasped and the queen shrieked, but not before I heard the low rasp of some sort of mechanism, a sound I recognized from the menagerie's tricks. I knew those uninitiated in the ways of such "magic" would never detect it.

I did not realize I was holding my breath as Boku's bright turban vanished under the lapping waves. Then—an explosion; fire and sparks and the island surfacing like Atlantis reborn. The stake—empty. The chains lay coiled upon the ground, the sack a flat puddle of silk.

"Mitte!" the queen cried. "Where is Mitte?"

At that instant, we heard a frantic yapping, and the merry little dog leapt from the platform where Boku had first performed. Around Mitte's neck, in lieu of a collar, was a bright blue ruffle the hue of Boku's turban, pinned in place with the ruby that had pierced the man's ear.

"How is it possible?" the king and queen marveled, the whole company stunned. By the time Boku reappeared, his clothes dry, his bald head gleaming and bare, Her Majesty was laughing in wonder.

"What do you think of your gift, Your Majesty?" the countess asked the king with a triumphant smile.

King Charles beamed. "It is marvelous indeed, although my wife suffered some perilous moments when Mitte disappeared. It would have been dreadful enough had my falcon torn up Jeffrey's face, but to lose Mitte—that, she would never have forgiven any of us."

The rest of the company laughed. I found his humor less amusing.

"In reparation for the strain the queen suffered, I will not keep your gift for myself. Let your conjuror serve a mistress his skill has already saved from grief. Boku will join Her Majesty's Menagerie of Freaks and Curiosities of Nature."

"Majesty, no!" I protested, the idea of this strange man joining our troupe ill news indeed.

Buckingham objected, as well. "Fool Jeffrey looks to your interests, Your Majesty—though he should be reprimanded for impertinence. The queen has a host of rarities to entertain her. It is admirable you have retained your father's fool, but you are owed better diversions than Archie Armstrong can provide. Keep this illusionist for yourself."

"As always, you look to my comfort, my friend, but I have made my decision. Jeffrey may pay for his impudence by serving as the conjuror's guide among Her Majesty's Curiosities. What better home could there be for a magician who can charm falcons from the sky?"

I saw Lady Carlisle suppress a frown and Buckingham's nostrils flare in frustration. But the queen beamed at her husband, their gazes intimate in a way I had never seen before. Only one expression in the company did not change. Boku's elegant features remained emotionless as onyx.

By the time the royal party returned to Whitehall, the moon was a curved knife blade culling unwary clouds. The king and queen had reined their horses so close together, the skirts of Her Majesty's riding habit lifted on the wind as if to caress her husband's thigh.

He would visit her bed tonight. I envied him, and took some small comfort that King Charles—another shy, small, awkward man—would woo Henrietta Maria and win her smiles.

Whitehall blazed with candles as we entered the queen's side of the palace. I expected some reaction from Boku as we walked through the magnificent halls. If I, an English village lad, had been overwhelmed by my first sight of royal wealth, surely this man from a land of godless natives would be even more stunned.

I could not rein in my questions another moment. "How did you do it? Charm the falcon? Get loose from the chains?"

"Next time, I could put you in the sack instead of the queen's dog, if you wish to find out."

"No, thank you. I'm not an animal." Did he understand the edge beneath my reply? Realize that I had caught the strange undertone to his statement? I could not tell.

Boku did not shift his gaze to me any more than to the majestic vistas around him. He stared straight ahead. Neither awe nor curiosity insinuated itself into Boku's features as I performed the office Will Evans had done for me, taking him to the menagerie's lodgings. A hush fell over the troupe as each dropped whatever pastime they'd been involved in—Sara, the headdress she was embroidering; Goodfellow, the sketch he was working on; Simon, the trick he was teaching Pug; and Dulcinea, the rope she was examining under Will's watchful eye. No one bothered to hide their stares. Even Simon Rattlebones's constant chatter was dulled.

Only Pug, the monkey, seemed eager to welcome Boku. The creature scampered over to him, deserting Rattlebones. Deserting *me*. The magician and the monkey drew apart from the rest of us as if to share memories of hot climes and the loss of sweet fruits England would never taste. It made me wonder how the conjuror and the animal had been captured, what cages they had been imprisoned in, and whom they had left behind.

It grew late, the clock on the mantel chiming. None of us seemed to have gotten far in our chores since the stranger had entered our lodgings, upsetting the balance among us.

I remembered my first night in the queen's household back at Denmark House: Will Evans giving me his bed, helping me out of my armor, fashioning a nightshirt for me out of his stocking. But I was not Will Evans. Besides, this native nearly got my eyes clawed out and threatened to put me in a sack underwater. For all I knew, Archie Armstrong was right about Boku. He could be a cannibal and eat me in my sleep.

I strung out conversation as long as I could, determined to delay the moment of reckoning, but even curiosities of nature had to sleep sometime.

Sara and Rattlebones surrendered first, stealing a last nervous glance at the silent newcomer before they wandered off to their separate beds. Robin Goodfellow snapped another stick of charcoal he was sketching with and tossed the pieces onto the table in frustration. He scooped the scattered charcoal, the paper, and other tools into a paint-smeared casket and prepared to shove them on a shelf.

For the first time, Boku spoke. "You wish to capture souls upon that page? Take three shavings and stand with your back to the fire. Cast the shavings over your right shoulder and the souls you seek will surrender."

"Heathen nonsense," Goodfellow blustered.

"I've seen *heathen nonsense* wake the dead," Boku said. "To capture a soul on paper is small magic indeed. If you are satisfied to be a commonplace artist, you need not try it."

After a moment, Robin took down his paint box. He plucked what must have been bits of wood and charcoal from the casket's confines, then walked over to the fire, carrying out the little ritual. Boku nodded in approval as Goodfellow scurried from the room. Dulcinea smiled. "Have you any advice to help me when I dance upon my rope?"

"Do not fall," Boku said. I would have laughed had I not been so worried about where to dispose of him for the night. Dulcinea was not so amused. She flounced out. Only Will and I were left with Boku.

I feigned a headache—the skill acting the queen's masques had stood me in good stead. I knew it was a cowardly thing to do, but I could not think of any other way to shift the burden of our new "curiosity" into Will Evans's hands—much larger, more capable hands when it came to these matters than mine would ever be. Even as I slipped away, I felt I had taken advantage of Will.

I did not expect to hear the scratch of someone at my door an hour later. I crept to the door in the dark, opened it, half-afraid it would be Boku. It was Will. He stood there rolling the brim of his hat in his hands, a nervous habit Dulcinea hated.

"I'll buy you a dozen goose quills to make up for deserting you down there, Will," I said. "I did not want to get stuck with him overnight. I kept thinking of tales of Raleigh and savage natives and figured that if Boku tried to take a bite of *you,* at least there would still be enough of you left to object to being made his main course."

I expected to be rewarded by one of Will's chuckles, but he only shrugged. "I offered to take the man to my lodgings, but he would not sleep in a bed. He rolled himself in his cloak and slept by the window. I told him it would be warmer by the fire, and tried to offer him cushions, but he would have none of it."

"He's probably searching for ways to poison us," I grumbled, longing for our accustomed banter. Will remained silent. "You have missed your cue, sergeant porter," I complained. "It is time for you to scold me for being cynical and warn me not to be like Archie."

"There are more pressing worries than Archie or Boku to bedevil me at the moment."

"That's because you did not see what that conjuror can do! Will, he—"

"Jeffrey!" Will cut me off more sharply than he ever had before. "When I was passing Dulcinea's chambers, I saw a page leave a bouquet of flowers beside her door."

"This is what you're worried about when we have a cannibal in our midst? I'm certain most of the serving men in the queen's household would be Dulcinea's gallants if she let them."

"This was not the gift of some moonstruck lad. It was one of Buckingham's pages and the stems were tied with Buckingham's colors."

"It would be better if he showed his appreciation in something useful, like coin."

Will started to speak, then stopped. His jaw clenched. "I do not trust His Grace. He and the countess of Carlisle mean mischief. This Boku has been placed in the queen's household for some purpose."

I concealed my own twinge of guilt by saying, "Boku was not supposed to be placed in the queen's household. The countess intended him for the king. She and Buckingham were most unhappy when His Majesty insisted such a skilled magician was better suited to the queen's menagerie."

Evans looked a little chagrined. "Hmm. I might have welcomed him more warmly, then."

"You can leave him some flowers." I meant to tease, but he spun and stomped away. "Will, it was just a jest," I called after him. He did not answer. I crossed to the door, locked it. Against what? I wondered. The kind of menace that stalked me was of a breed that seeped between the cracks in walls and windows, down chimney flues, and under the skin.

I lay awake pondering Will's anxious words. What danger would Boku carry into the menagerie's lodgings at Lady Carlisle's bidding? More troubling still: What had the countess and Buckingham planned for this day that Mitte's misadventure had foiled?

SEVENTEEN

•

In the weeks that followed, Boku's presence permeated the menagerie's lodgings like the scent of strange spices that wafted from his skin. His clothes, despite exotic touches stitched by costume makers, were stout English wool.

I caught myself watching him a dozen times a day and wondered if this was how people who gawked at me felt—fascinated, a little repulsed, unanswerable questions whirling in their minds. Had I the power His Grace had, I knew I would have stripped the velvet gauntlets off of Boku to see what was beneath them—whether the conjuror wanted me to or not.

At least he was no longer sleeping by the window in the menagerie's lodgings. He'd been given a bed in a room with Robin Goodfellow and Simon Rattlebones, though Rattlebones complained the queen might as well have given the bed to his dogs. Boku still slept by a window, nothing but a threadbare black robe to shield him from the cold stone.

I might have made jest of his behavior had it been anyone else in the menagerie. But there was something unassailable in Boku, a dignity that reminded me of the gyrfalcon he had charmed. Sharp eyes seemed to see everything, and dismiss us all—a world of scurrying mice not tasty enough to rouse him from his branch.

I wondered if the countess of Carlisle and Buckingham intended him for a spy, as well. Would a magician that powerful be manipulated as easily as I was? For once, I agreed with Will Evans's judgment of character: "The rest of us in the menagerie are creatures of hearth and wall, tamed to the queen's hand. Boku is wild."

The queen also had tried to cling to dignity as war with France and Spain loomed. Not even her "curiosities" or the masque Inigo Jones was designing afforded her pleasure. She fretted over the deepening rift between the king and Parliament. The Commons was outraged at the measures the king was taking to finance the war. Soldiers must be fed and munitions bought, ships mustered together and fitted out, if there was to be a war. Where was the funding for this great enterprise to come from when a bunch of moneygrubbing merchants and farmers in the House of Commons refused to vote the king the money he needed unless he met their upstart demands?

Buckingham's shameless manipulation of the king was making the duke's enemies more vocal than ever. The queen would not have objected had Buckingham been besieged thus. But royal subjects questioning the divine right of kings was unthinkable.

She picked at the tangled threads of loyalties and love, knowing it was impossible to make them smooth again. Her stitching often lay idle in her lap, her mood so close to tears that the sound of a lute could make her dab her eyes with her kerchief. Everyone hoped that the birth of Mitte's puppies would ease Her Majesty's bleak humors. Instead, the litter of furry rogues made the queen more withdrawn than ever.

Her Majesty had even sent her ladies of the bedchamber away when I arrived on a rain-washed morning two months after the hunting party at the Carlisles'. I found Henrietta Maria in a position unsuitable for a queen, sitting on a thick rug, three chestnut-and-white pups playing hide-and-seek with one another under the folds of her skirt. The barrier our stations built between us thinned, until she seemed almost within my reach. I would have stood there silently and watched her much longer if I could have found a way to excuse such behavior. But the king himself had asked me to discover what grieved the queen. It touched me that in spite of Charles's ongoing battle to wrest his due from Parliament, he showed such concern for his wife.

"Majesty, are you well?" I asked as I drew near her.

"Am I not allowed time alone to read letters from home?" She tucked a folded paper deeper into her sleeve. I wondered what was in it. News of the war? Complaints about the English? Demands that she put an end to the hostilities any way she was able? As if one young woman could hold back men's hunger for wealth and power and glory and the war such lust unleashed.

God knew she could not receive a letter from France without the whole court believing they had a right to snatch it from her hands and learn what was inside it. I merely invaded her writing box—though not as often as Buckingham would have wished. For the moment, I had set intrigue aside. I was more concerned with the fact that she seemed to be pining away.

"Forgive me, my queen. I know you grieve the enmity between your husband and your homeland. I do not mean to vex you. But you grow pale and only pick at your food."

"I've been lost in musings." She gave me a tremulous smile. "Jeffrey, are not babes the most wonderful creatures—be they pups like these or chubby babes like the ones the garden lass brings with her to nurse while she is dead-heading the roses?"

I had not realized the queen had noticed the servant and child, and I feared the young mother might be reproved. Yet there was wistfulness in the queen that made me hope otherwise. "You will have a babe in time. The king visits you more often than ever." In spite of Lady Carlisle's continued efforts to distract him, I added to myself. "Although I could not help but notice the past few weeks you have retired for the night alone. I know it is forward of me to pry, but I have been hoping you had found more happiness here in England."

"I am becoming used to the changes. I miss home, especially Mamie. She is as much family as my mother is. More, in truth. I rarely saw my mother even before my brother Louis exiled her to Blois. Gaston, the brother closest to me in age, tried to comfort me at the time. But the tales people told—how Louis watched through a window as his guards murdered Concino. And Concino's poor wife. They burned her as a witch after . . ." She shuddered.

"Concino? Was that one of your brothers?" I asked, horrified.

"No. He was my mother's most trusted adviser. She brought Concino from Florence when she wed my father. The fact that he was Italian was reason enough for my brother's courtiers to hate him. Concino's wife had been my mother's childhood friend—her Mamie. I remember thinking that if the Concinos could die so horribly, if my lady mother could be imprisoned by her own son, if my father could fall to a madman's dagger, then how could I ever be safe?"

I wanted to reassure her, but how could I? I made her world more dangerous with every secret she confided in me.

"I had such nightmares," she continued. "Gaston insisted all would be well in time." She plucked a bit of straw from one puppy's ear. "But we were never a family again as we were before that breach." A faint line appeared on her forehead. "Perhaps we were not a real family even before it. I was only six months old when my father was murdered."

"All Europe has heard stories of Henri le Grande's tolerance and wisdom and courage." I imagined what it would be like to have a father I could admire.

"I was so envious of Mamie," the queen confessed. "I loved the way her mother would scoop the little ones up to dry their tears. My mother was too busy trying to make us a credit to France and to herself. I suppose she had little opportunity to do anything else—an Italian de Medici far from her native land, surrounded by enemies. I understand her better now."

Her forgiveness said more about her time here in England than anger could have.

"But it was Mamie's father who fascinated me. The way he would toss his children high in the air and always catch them before they fell."

I wished that I could give her that feeling of safety—not because she was my queen, but because she was crumpling her gown while playing with the puppies on the floor. Because she allowed the sadness of her fatherless childhood to creep into her voice. I was tempted to tell her my own truth—that fathers sometimes throw you into dangerous worlds on purpose, with no intention of catching you if you fall. Instead, I said nothing. I merely let one of the puppies gnaw on my finger. The queen filled the sudden silence.

"Why does God not grant me a babe, Jeffrey? Am I failing Him somehow?"

"Majesty, I am certain in time—"

"Time is running out. The duke of Buckingham is determined to spur the king into war with France. My brother refuses to negotiate, in spite of my pleas. I write him and try to explain. . . . to beg. . . . Do you remember when His Majesty sent Mamie and the rest away? I begged him to send me back to France."

A reckless plea, some might even say a treasonous one. I loathed the fact that I should pass it on to Buckingham. "How could I ever forget your pain?" I asked. Especially since I was the one who had caused it.

"Now, with war brewing between our countries, I fear that His Majesty's advisers will convince the king to dump me at the gates of Versailles, barren, damaged, a failure in every part of being a wife, a queen, daughter of Henri le Grande."

"Whatever the Privy Council thinks, I know the king does not see you that way."

"You have not seen his face when he hears other ladies are breeding. Lady Carlisle tells me he counts the weeks between my courses, hoping."

It surprised me, her sharing womanly secrets with me. But why should she not speak of moon cycles to her pet Jeffrey? To her, I was no man. "I hardly think His Majesty confides such concerns in Lady Carlisle," I said. "He is particular about propriety."

She considered this for a moment. "My husband is very fond of Lady Carlisle. He was right to advise me that English ladies could teach me the ways of his court. The countess has even given me paint to redden my cheeks after I have sleepless nights—though His Majesty and his more somber advisers are not pleased when I wear it." Her mouth set in misery. "It is not my fault if I must resort to such measures. I am distressed by the trouble with my homeland, fear what might happen when the king locks swords with the combined might of Spain and France. Here in England, His Majesty's own subjects refuse to grant the king the funds he needs. It is humiliating! The king having to borrow against the Crown Jewels because gentlemen are choosing to go to jail rather than grant him the loans the law requires of them."

"His Majesty would use those funds to make war on your brother," I said softly.

"I know. But to see my husband—the king of England—treated like a beggar is unbearable. Even Parliament's attacks on Buckingham are an attempt to undermine the king's authority. You know how I loathe the duke, but what does Parliament expect His Majesty to do? Fling his favorite into their hands knowing that—if they have their will—it is a mere step from impeachment to a headsman's block on Tower Hill?"

For a moment, the downfall of Buckingham glimmered in my imagination, a possibility to free myself from his toils. But had not the duke warned that such falls from grace often dragged servants to hell with their masters? All it would take was one of the notes I had passed to the duke to surface and

I would fall with him. "The king shows great loyalty," I said. "But it is probably best His Majesty sent Buckingham off somewhere."

"To Plymouth to take charge of the king's ships," the queen said. "I confess I am relieved. It is harder for the duke to chasten me about my gambling debts from there. Before Buckingham left, he took the king and me to see his new yacht. It was cunning and light and swift as the wind, but His Grace made such unpleasantness over my debts that the man giving us a tour of the vessel intervened. He sent me a most gallant letter, saying he would be honored if I would accept a loan. He had made some fortune investing in East India cargo. He wrote that if he ever succeeded in mounting a venture to the Americas and it proved fruitful, Maryland might be a fine name for a tract of land."

I took a fool's liberty. "Doubtless this gallant hopes his generosity will be repaid in something more valuable than coin: Your Majesty influencing the king to regard this enterprise with favor."

"Everyone at court seeks some sort of boon. Master Ware is no worse than any other."

Thank God one of the puppies decided to set up a yapping, hiding my reaction. Uriel Ware had volunteered to loan the queen money? Was he working for Buckingham, or had he seen an opportunity to circumvent the duke and seize some control of his fate by securing the goodwill of the queen? If Buckingham had still not granted Ware permission to attend to his oceangoing vessels and mount the explorations Ware hoped would fill the ship holds with spices and precious metals, the man must be frustrated beyond bearing.

The queen gathered the agitated pup to her breast. He chewed the lace at her collar. "It does Master Ware credit that he did not even mention my predicament to a friend as intimate as you."

"Friend . . ." I could not think of a way to explain my relationship with the man. Another frustrated captive of the duke's power?

"Do not be distressed, Jeffrey. I know you are sensitive about your connection to the duke of Buckingham. Sometimes when His Grace is about, you look quite fierce. I suppose it is because you love me." The word jolted me. She seemed so certain of that love. As if it was expected. Her statement drove deep.

"You dislike Buckingham because of his behavior toward me. Is it not so?"

"I loathe him, Your Majesty." That much was true.

"Master Ware told me how wretched you were under the duke's roof. I am glad Master Ware took such kind care of you. One would not have expected it of such a grim man upon first meeting him. But perhaps the distressing incidents Lady Denbigh told about Master Ware's childhood explain his demeanor. Of course, you broke through his reserve. You are such a winning little fellow. Who can blame him for being as charmed by you as all the rest of us have been?"

"I am a charming fellow." It helps deflect suspicion when I'm dredging out people's secrets.

"I felt quite safe confiding the woes of my purse to him once I knew of your connection."

Except that Ware—and Buckingham—had already known of the queen's debts. I looked down at the puppies, but instead of white-and-russet fur, I saw the note I had scrawled to Buckingham just over a week ago. Had the duke supplied Ware with funds to be loaned? Or was Ware really acting on his own?

"Normally, I would shy away from speaking so freely to someone outside my circle, Jeffrey. But you are the best judge of character that I know. Perhaps it is because you see people from the boots up." She loosened the pup's teeth from the exquisite threads woven by a convent in France for her trousseau.

"I tend to register a favorable impression of people if they do not tread on me," I said. I did not add that I had the prints of His Grace's boots over every inch of my body.

"Ah Jeffrey, you do make me laugh. How would I fare without you and dear Lucy to guard me and guide me when things seem so bleak?"

Oh, yes, we would guide her between us. Right off the nearest precipice Lady Carlisle and Buckingham could find.

But Buckingham would be sailing for Ile d Ré any day now. Perhaps he was even now on the prow of a ship that was cutting through the waves of the English Channel. I could only hope the French would do the queen and me a favor and blast the duke to hell, where he belonged.

Is it too much to ask for the accursed monkey to come to me when I enter the Freaks' Lair? I wondered. Especially when I had whiled away many a sleepless night letting Pug off his chain. Freedom that afforded him the fiendish glee of ripping stuffing out of the life-size poppet Rattlebones had been constructing for one of his tricks. But Pug was far too busy trying to peel away the gauntlets that covered Boku's wrists to be bothered with me. The magician did not even seem to notice Pug's intrusion. Boku's hooded eyes fixed upon the scene being played across the room.

Dulcinea had drawn as far away as possible from the table where Simon and Robin were gambling for mismatched stakes—a penknife with a broken point, an ivory toothpick, and three mended handkerchiefs. Sara sat atop the table, combing out one of the spaniel's ears. Sara's own rich locks gleamed as she and the other occupants of the table directed their attention anywhere other than the pair locked in heated conversation half a chamber away.

Dulcinea applied her needle with irritated vigor, stitching tiny silver bells onto a gossamer veil the color of lapis lazuli. Even from where I stood, I could see the veil's quality was far finer than any she had used before, silver unicorns embroidered around the border.

I had never known Will Evans to take exception to any legendary creature, but at the moment he wore a scowl that would do credit to the fiercest Welsh dragon. I could not count the times I had heard Will Evans offering fatherly advice to whoever happened to have the good fortune to attract his notice—from Jenny, the scullery maid we had met that first night, to the queen herself. But there was none of that long-suffering patience in the giant now.

What parts of his face weren't covered with his bushy beard were red, his fists like boulders as he flexed them. I could not hear all he was saying, his rumbling voice kept low, but Dulcinea's retorts rang clear. I was not the only person wandering off at night, it seemed, though I had only been sneaking to the Freaks' Lair to free Pug.

"It is not your affair where I go or when!" Dulcinea exclaimed. "You are supposed to guard the queen's door, not mine!"

"The king will turn you away if he finds out! He'll not allow anyone of questionable morals around his wife."

"Then why does he favor Lady Carlisle? The duke of Buckingham?"

Dulcinea tossed her head, bells on her veil jingling. "If I choose to take the risk, why should you care?"

I winced at the pain Evans attempted to hide. "Because you have no one else to guard you from the palace's snares." He tugged the linen collar around his barrel-thick neck. "We are family here in the menagerie, Dulcinea. We must stand together."

"The lords and ladies do not. They snatch what they can from royal favor and hoard it for themselves. I would be happy to have just a few of the pretty things they possess. And I mean to have them. Archie says—"

"Archie?" Will blustered. "Tell me you are not heeding that old fool."

"I have a strange way of heeding the truth! I will not have this face and this form much longer. There is a short time I can seize the fine things in life before my chance is gone."

"Dulcinea—"

"Don't say my name in that tone, Will Evans!"

"What tone?"

"As if you were my husband and I was making a cuckold of you! If I want a man who smells of perfumes, a man with soft hands and smooth skin, then why should I not have one? Am I not good enough for your precious noblemen?"

"You are too good for the likes of *him*."

Him? I wondered if Dulcinea's admirer was Buckingham, as Will feared.

"He will use you and discard you. He has done so with half the ladies at court. Virtuous ladies! Oh, I have heard of his methods. He has his fine friends lure women he desires off to see his mother. But she is not there. Once the lady he desires arrives, he debauches her while his cohorts stand guard."

"If he treats fine ladies that way, how long do you think the maidenly protests of a rope dancer will hold back him back? A man used to seizing whatever he wanted from the time he could reach out his hand?"

It was true. I could see in Will's expression that he knew it as well as she did. Still, he asserted stubbornly, "There are six of us in the menagerie. We can make certain that you are never alone."

Dulcinea gave a scornful laugh. "You've grown daft with your fool stories of honor and chivalry, Will. What business has any of us to attempt such virtues in this life we lead? I see things as they are. What choice do I have in this affair? I can go willingly and gather a few baubles along the way or I will be forced to submit and be left with nothing but a sore cunny."

Will's breath hissed through his teeth at the ugly word and the uglier truth. "Dulcinea, I beg you, do not hold yourself so cheaply." Pain contorted Will's face. I hoped Dulcinea did not see it for what it was—the jealousy of a man who fancied himself in love with her, an ugly man who knew he could never hope to win the kisses of one as beautiful as the rope dancer. I could not bear his vulnerability, and rushed to deflect everyone's attention from him as best I could.

"Look at the lot of you—dawdling about when the queen is fairly drowning in misery." Six pairs of startled eyes turned to me. "I won't have it, I tell you. We've only two hours before Her Majesty dines to come up with a way to make her laugh."

Rattlebones grimaced. "What do you think we've been trying to do for weeks now? I've run out of tricks."

"Design new ones." I would have to do the same, especially if I were to find a way to outwit Buckingham.

I turned to Boku. "Surely you must have some way to dazzle the queen? Teach the king's lion to dance or ride the elephant His Majesty keeps in the St. James's Menagerie?"

"He will need bigger chains to keep a lion under control," Rattlebones jested, pointing to the slender gold thread about the monkey's neck.

"It is not a lion's destiny to be tamed," Boku said. "Your God would call it a sin."

"A lion is an animal. Just another animal."

Captive in a menagerie, Boku's voice whispered in my ear, though his lips did not move. *Like we are.*

───※───

My head ached by the time I trudged up to my chamber. The last thing I expected to see when I opened the door was Clemmy's wide grin.

"Surprised you, did I?" He capered, jerky as a puppet on strings. "Thought about hiding and jumping out at you like a bogey, the way I used to do when I went back to see my mam and da, but couldn't hold still long enough. I was that excited to see you! The duchess o' Buckingham said I must bring you such good news myself. Isn't your Samuel as fine a lad as I've ever seen?"

My heart leaped. "You saw Samuel?"

"Right there at his lessons at the Ball and Claw, didn't I? Bright as a new penny is your brother, from what his tutor says. Didn't Master Quintin send a letter with me reporting to Her Grace about Samuel's progress? Did not expect such a fine lady—a duchess, no less!—to set such store by a lad like your brother, but she does. Should have seen her face shine while she read what the tutor had to say."

"Is Samuel well? He always looked too thin and pale."

"Learning must agree with the lad. He's plumping right up. Eyes looked a little red—too much studying by firelight, I'd imagine. When I walked in the room, he closed up the book so quick, he nearly dropped it! Master Quintin said he'd had to teach the boy to do so as a matter of manners when guests dropped by. It was the only way the lad could show me the attention I deserved. The tutor told me that if it was up to Samuel, he'd not stop even to sleep. Latin, if you can believe it! A boy from the shambles of Oakham learning Latin."

"What I would not give to see it!" I turned away so Clemmy would not see my eyes fill with tears. For the first time since I had made my bargain with Buckingham, I felt real joy—a moment only—then Samuel's earnest features shifted in my imagination to the sorrowful countenance of the queen.

"Here is the best news of all! Her Grace is so pleased with Samuel's progress—and, I do believe, is so much your friend, Jeffrey—that she is having Master Quintin come to London to buy whatever books your brother might need. As a kindness to you, she has commanded Samuel to accompany him!"

"Samuel? In London?" My heart nearly leapt out of my chest at the prospect. "When?"

"Two months. Maybe three, by the time the arrangements can be made."

I swiped my hand across my eyes and scowled. "Accursed fleas," I said by way of explanation. "I must've gotten them from the infernal monkey."

"You needn't make excuses to me, Jeffrey," Clemmy said. "When I heard the treat in store for you, my eyes got leaky, too."

August 1627

Strange how long it took me to thank the duchess of Buckingham in the weeks the anticipation of Samuel's impending visit rooted and grew in my heart. I quieted my unease regarding Ware's connection with the queen as much as I could. What were a few gaming debts to Her Majesty? There was no real danger. Her husband had the wealth of the royal treasury at his disposal. What if Buckingham intended to use this monetary connection to the queen somehow? Between my deceit and the countess of Carlisle's increasing intimacy with Henrietta Maria, how much more damage could this new plot do to the queen? As for Ware's claim that he was my friend—that was something I objected to. But I could not think it would do any good to confront him.

Better to turn my mind to delights to come. Samuel. What would my quiet brother think of the cacophony of London? The crush of people, buildings piled atop one another, their upper stories thrusting out across the narrow streets, blotting out the sky. There were so many wonders to show a lad who had never stepped beyond the borders of his home county.

I thought of the store of coins I had collected, tribute tossed to me by courtiers I had amused more than the rest of the crowd. Coins earned by my own wit, less tainted by Buckingham. What delights could my money buy for Samuel? A new suit of clothes made out of whatever color of cloth he chose. A doublet boasting real buttons to fasten down the front instead of the pins village folk used. I could show him through the palace, where we could crawl into the bed the queen gave me as we once shared the tiny cot in the loft back home. But this time, we could talk all night if we wanted to and no one could stop us.

I could take him riding upon my horse in St. James's Park. We could wander through St. Paul's Cathedral and the Exchange, where a man could buy almost anything he imagined. I would treat Samuel to the theater and feed him his first taste of an orange. I grinned like the fool I was, imagining my brother's too-solemn face puckering at the sourness, then savoring the sweetness, juice running down his chin. Samuel had always been wary of trying new things, waiting and watching until John or Ann or I did so first, fearful of making the slightest mistake.

But that would change. A whole new world would unfold to Samuel because of the lessons he was learning. Because of me. Was I merely groping for a way to make what I had done less reprehensible? I could not be sure. But I stitched hopes and expectations along the length of Samuel's upcoming visit the way Dulcinea sewed bells on her costume—adding more and more until the gauze threatened to tear beneath their weight.

Wait and see how perfect his visit is, I told the part of me that could not escape guilt and shame. Seeing Samuel happy would make my tribulations under Buckingham seem worth the price. Samuel would be so proud when he saw how I moved among the greatest nobles in the land, ambassadors from foreign countries greeting me by name. I would show Samuel the coins they slipped into my pocket, a fee for helping people get past Will Evans's vigilant guard so the statesmen could make petitions to the queen in person.

At some point during Samuel's stay in the city, I would even take him to the menagerie's lodgings. What might Samuel think of the "curiosities"? Our tricks would astonish him—the members of the menagerie were brilliant at fascinating people when they wished to. I would make certain my fellow performers wished to please Samuel when the time came. But not yet. For now, Samuel's visit was a delicious secret. Mine alone.

I found myself setting up extra japes before those courtiers disposed to be generous. With the dissension in Parliament, more people were seeking royal audiences than ever before. I began to ask about the finest entertainments to be found in the city. But I was wary of showing too much interest in securing private conversation with the duchess of Buckingham, for fear it might raise questions of my loyalty to the queen.

One sunny day in August when I was on my way to join some of Her Majesty's household on the bowling green, I stumbled upon the duchess sitting alone.

She was perched on a bench beneath a willow in the garden of St. James's Palace, where court had moved three weeks past. The waterfall of leaves all but concealed her.

Far ahead, the queen and Lady Carlisle were gliding down the garden path, Mitte and her puppies a yapping, scampering train of delight following after.

I swerved out of my way and went to the ring of willow fronds that cloistered the duchess from the world of court. I cleared my throat to warn her of my presence. When the duchess looked up from the letter in her hand, I spoke.

"Your Grace, I do not wish to intrude on your solitude, but I wanted to thank you for your kindness to my brother." I could not guess how much of her husband's schemes the duchess was privy to. Did she know Buckingham at all? "I owe you a great debt." My throat felt tight. "The chance to see my brother is more than I had hoped for."

She turned her face more fully into the light filtering through the leaves, and I saw that the duchess was weeping.

"I pray there is no bad news from France?"

"My husband has taken Ile de Ré. He must still lay siege to the citadel there—but with the blockade he has set up, it is only a matter of time before it falls. Once His Grace forces those loyal to the French king to surrender, the Huguenots at La Rochelle will see how much support England is ready to give their rebellion. They will rise against the French government and join my husband. Buckingham will have a port for English ships on French soil, and from there, God alone knows how far he might go. It will be such a triumph, people will forget what happened at Cádiz."

She pressed the note against her breasts, her eyes burning with adoration. "Think what a blow that will be to those who oppose His Grace. The people of England will see him as a hero, tested in battle, winner of a great victory over His Majesty's enemies."

From gossip Rattlebones brought from his performances in the city, there were many in Parliament and in the rest of the citizenry who could stomach the loss of a few ships as long as Buckingham joined the sailors he had squandered at the bottom of the sea.

I wondered if she knew how far Buckingham's list of adversaries now stretched. I felt the duchess must know of their enmity, and yet it was hard to imagine she could be duplicitous enough to care for the queen so tenderly while seeking to undermine Henrietta Maria's position. But the fervor in the duchess disturbed me. She had surrendered her faith, scorned her duty as a daughter in welcoming Buckingham as a husband when he had destroyed her honor. Had she known Buckingham's plan beforehand? Aided the scheme said to have broken her father's heart?

I remembered Simon once saying that men are taught to see women as either wicked or angelic. Most men were disgruntled to discover women merely human, with all the flaws and graces mixed together. Did women see men the same way, cads or heroes? If the duchess loved her husband so fervently, could she bear the truth? What would happen if she saw the ugliness Buckingham hid beneath that glittering exterior? The duchess gave me a wobbly smile. "Jeffrey, you need not linger here while I grow morose over things I have no power to change. I am worried my husband will grow even more reckless in order to prove his enemies wrong. I yearn for my little ones back at Burley-on-the-Hill. Moll's and Georgie's nurses write they are doing well, but I cannot guess when I will see them next. The city is too full of contagion to risk bringing them here, and I must protect my husband's interests at court while he is away. Court is filled with jealous men who would go to despicable lengths to damage the king's affection for my lord if they could. You see? I am dismal company. You should follow Her Majesty's example and seek more amiable friends. The countess of Carlisle is always amusing."

"You are of a finer cast. You have shown it in your kindness to my brother."

"It was His Grace who asked me to find your brother a tutor. People do not give him credit for the generosity he shows." She fingered the miniature pinned at her breast, an exquisite disk of ivory painted with Buckingham's face. "I cannot bear to see him so foully misjudged."

She seemed to be waiting for me to say something in the duke's defense. I thought of how Buckingham had made her father beg him to wed her honorably. I thought of the women Buckingham and his friends lured out so he could debauch them. I thought of His Grace sending Uriel Ware to entice the queen deeper into debt. And there was my own unholy alliance with the duke.

"His Grace is fortunate to have so loyal a wife."

"Someone should be loyal to him," she said with heat. "When I am holding my own little Georgie . . . a boy's mother should guard him, not thrust him into . . ." Her voice trailed off, but I guessed what she was thinking—

of King James's passion for pretty young men. I had no doubt Buckingham's mother was ambitious enough to put her son in the king's path. My stomach curled at the thought. "My husband wants to be a good man, Jeffrey," the duchess insisted. "A wise adviser to the king. But who will take him seriously after . . ."

She might have been speaking of the rout he suffered at Cádiz, a third of England's great fleet limping home in defeat. But I sensed it was something far more personal, shameful clouds cast when beautiful, young George Villiers was being kissed and fondled by the old king.

"It is not my place to judge anyone, Your Grace." Especially after the things I had been coerced into doing.

"I would do anything in my power to see him honored as he deserves," she said fiercely.

Did she see my reaction? She rushed on. "I see that look upon your face—even you sit in judgment on him. There is nothing I would change about my husband. Nothing. Except perhaps—his only fault is that he loves women too well."

She stopped, collected herself. She smoothed the passion from her face, seeming the gentle duchess again. "Now, here, I have chattered on about things in a most inappropriate way. I fear I cannot speak of such things among the queen's ladies, and certainly not with His Grace's mother. I have no excuse except that I am so worried and you . . . Jeffrey, you are a good listener."

I quelled my sudden bitterness, concentrating on her kindness to Samuel instead.

"Your Grace, I would do whatever I could to lighten your worries. The duke might have agreed Samuel might have a tutor, but you found a kind master, one, I have heard, Samuel is most attached to."

"Master Quintin is the kindest man I have ever known and one of the bravest." It was a strange word to describe a tutor.

"I can think of few things more dangerous than disciplining an unruly scholar. I would far sooner join your husband in storming French citadels."

She rewarded me with a laugh. "I can understand your view if your brother has anything close to your sharp wit."

"Samuel is nothing like me, Your Grace." Just as you are nothing like the man you married, I added silently.

EIGHTEEN

•

It seemed a hundred years had passed since Father marched me out the door of our cottage in Oakham, stopping to warn Samuel that he'd not endure any son of John Hudson giving way to womanish weeping. My brother had swallowed his tears as he followed us as far as the stone step. But when I glanced back over my shoulder some ways down the street, I saw the terrible silent weight of his grief. I carried it with me, like a beggar's bundle, to Burley House and every step I took beyond.

Now, at last, I would have a chance to paint over that image of my brother the way Robin Goodfellow fixed a miniature portrait that did not please him. I clutched the top edge of the coach door, bracing myself as the equipage the queen had ordered me to take jolted over the streets. The spire of St. Paul's Cathedral pricked the September sky. Somewhere near the imposing building, lanes rimmed with booksellers could be found, and the shop where I was to rendezvous with my brother lay somewhere in their midst. Samuel's tutor was staying with a school friend who had married a printer's daughter, and Samuel had not been able to work himself free of the arrangement. My brother was always loath to injure someone's feelings, even when it was in his best interest.

But I would remedy that bit of foolishness. Master Quintin could be made to understand that the chance to lodge at the palace was too great an opportunity to miss.

I could hear the coachman swearing at the hackney driver who had squeezed too close in the crushing traffic. The coach jolted, flinging me against the door, the blow cushioned by the oranges I carried in a bag tied to my waist. I checked the fruit I intended as a treat for Samuel, consoling myself that even a crushed orange would be more delicious than anything my brother had ever tasted.

If I ever reach Samuel at all, I thought. I begrudged every minute this tangle was eating away from the three-day span the queen had granted me to enjoy my brother's company. Archie Armstrong had managed to cast a shadow over Her Majesty's generosity, saying I'd better squeeze as much diversion into the first afternoon as possible. Her Majesty was likely to decide she needed me to lighten her mood after all. With a wave of her hand, she could order a page to fetch me, and that would be the end of my time with Samuel. I hated Archie for clouding my excitement with dread. I hated him more for being right. It was possible the queen would change her mind. Her Majesty had much to worry about these days.

The seventy-six gentlemen imprisoned for refusing to lend the king money had insisted they could not be held without a trial. Parliament supported their assertion and refused to grant the king moneys no king had ever been denied before. It was easy to whip up public anger in citizens forced to billet soldiers in their homes for a war they did not want, military law laid down in troublesome swaths of the country, taxes seized without Parliament's consent.

Once the king had realized he could neither win the funds needed nor protect Buckingham from impeachment if Parliament continued to meet, His Majesty had solved the impossible deadlock the only way left to him: He disbanded Parliament a second time.

The members had returned to their shires furious over the king's abrupt reprisals and had left a trail of discontent in their wake. What had the fools expected for their pains? I wondered. That this king, so jealous of his dignity, would thank them for their impudence?

"I cannot deny you the pleasure of seeing your brother, no matter what it costs my peace of mind," the queen had said when she learned of Samuel's visit. "But you must travel by coach. There are disturbances in the street since the king dismissed the Commons. I cannot fathom what these English merchants hope to achieve."

I shook off the memory and glared out the coach window. "They are succeeding in frustrating me," I muttered. Just down the street, Samuel was waiting. I could have reached the address hours ago if I'd been allowed to ride my horse.

I considered making a dash for it, but once on the ground I would not be able to see my destination. Getting lost meant reaching Samuel even later.

The equipage rattled forward, then slammed to a halt. The hackney driver had overturned a cart, its load of cabbages rolling about the street. Thrifty housewives chased after the bounty, filling their aprons. Heaven knew how long it would be before they got out of the way.

I viewed the path to my destination: Seven doors in the direction of the basket and broom seller who was hawking his wares, a tower of straw hats stacked on his head. If I could spring across the street and make it to the first door without getting turned around, the rest would be simple.

I took a deep breath and pushed the door open. "I'm going on foot!" I warned the driver. Despite his protests, I made a leap Dulcinea would have been proud of. Trying not to be knocked over by rolling cabbages like a pin in a game of bowls, I scrambled to the first door. With a triumphant grin and a few jostles, I reached the open front of the shop, not much worse for the wear.

A boy of about thirteen with pimples on his nose gaped at me. "You must be here for Master Quintin. They said you'd be coming by coach. I didn't see one."

I'd been in the company of Boku and Inigo Jones for too long. People want to believe illusions. That's why they see what a conjuror tells them to see, I thought. "I decided to travel by magic instead," an imp of mischief made me say.

The boy made a sign to ward off the evil eye. Several other lads who'd been hovering near the shop—doubtless to get a glimpse of me—whispered among themselves. A hard-eyed lad with bald patches on his scalp and a nose squashed flat as the oranges in my bag said, "We don't hold with devils here."

I did not want to get the bookseller in trouble, in spite of my frustration over Samuel's reluctance to refuse his invitation. "Look down the street," I said. "You'll see the coach Her Majesty sent me in."

"Might as well be sorcery," Patch Scalp said. "The queen is just another Catholic chanting spells. Turning bread into flesh and eating it." He spat on the floor.

Outrage swelled in my chest. "You dare speak against the queen?"

"She is French and a Catholic, is she not?"

"Stop it, Scabbers!" the pimpled youth said. "Should've left you at your own shop and never told you the queen's dwarf was coming. Master will give me no supper if he hears you blathering."

"You need not fear going hungry, Fred," a cultured voice said from deep among the tables full of books for sale. Everyone turned to look in that direction. A man stood on the stairs that lead to the upper floors, where the bookseller and his family no doubt lived. Was this man the owner of the shop? If so, he had been working too hard. His face was paler than good health would allow. The smile he gave me was patient, grave. "The queen is indeed a Catholic, though there are more gentlemanly ways of saying so. Perhaps we may all agree on that and return to our duties."

"Scabbers" and his friends scattered as the man came toward me. If my brother John had seen the newcomer, he would have wanted to hang him from a hook in the butchery's ceiling to straighten the fellow out. The stranger would have been a fine, tall fellow if John had succeeded, but as of now his right shoulder crumpled inward toward his chest, giving him a hunched appearance as he limped toward me. He wore a scholar's gown of brown frieze with frayed cuffs that ended halfway down his forearms. The doublet and hose visible where the robe hung open were of sturdy wool the color of moss. Those garments seemed as large for his lean body as the robe seemed small, as if no one could agree what size the man was.

"You must be the famous Jeffrey Hudson," he said, addressing me.

"Are you the master of this shop?" I asked.

"He is occupied setting type in the back. I am Benedict Quintin, the tutor fortunate enough to have your brother for a scholar. Samuel cannot say enough wonderful things about you."

I was not sure what I had expected in a tutor secured by the duchess of Buckingham, but it was not this man with his red-gold hair.

"I fell off a mountain," he said quite amiably.

"What?" I asked, startled.

"I was accompanying the grandson of a baronet around Europe and I was contemplating Socrates instead of watching where I was going. Pardon my abruptness, but I find it easier to satisfy people's natural curiosity about

my appearance at once. That way, they don't have to exert themselves probing around the subject to discover how I was injured. I am not offended by
their prurient interest and they can concentrate on more important things—
for example, going upstairs to see your brother. I expected him to have his
nose pressed to the window, watching for you."

"So did I." I felt a sudden twinge. I followed the tutor up the steep flight
of stairs into a dark, cramped room. Wattle and daub plaster was lime-
washed white, cut into diamonds by dark wooden slats. Against walls soot-
stained by three generations of coal fires, one bright spot shone: Samuel. My
brother sat at a table so rickety, it seemed in danger of pitching the articles
arrayed atop it onto the scrubbed floor: an ink pot with a chipped rim, a penknife that had been sharpened so often that the blade curved inward instead
of out, books and blotting paper and a vial for sprinkling sand to dry the ink.
The few rays of sun that dared to filter through the grimy windowpanes were
tangled in my brother's dandelion-fluff hair.

I swallowed hard, remembering. It had never mattered how often our
mother had combed it to make it stick down straight. Before half an hour
had passed, it would spring back, wild as it had been before she started.

He did not even look up, so engrossed was he in whatever task was at
hand. His brow rumpled in concentration as he copied something in what
looked to be Latin. I tried not to feel hurt that Master Quintin had to speak
three times to get my brother's attention.

"Samuel, did I not tell you to rest so you might enjoy your brother's visit?"

"Jeffrey will not be here for hours yet. I just hope I have time to finish this
before—"

"Your brother is here now."

I sensed that Master Quintin interrupted to spare my feelings. Samuel
dropped his pen, his head snapping around to see me. I expected him to rush
over and embrace me, horrified at his blunder. He did not even seem to realize his words might have wounded me. *Had* wounded me.

"Jeff!" he cried, but it was as if someone had stitched his breeches to the
seat as a jest. He shifted, as if wanting to answer the call of brotherly affection, yet could not pull free of his task. "I am so glad to see you! Don't think
that I'm not! It is just that I am not quite finished—"

"Yes, you are," the tutor said, limping over to take the pen from Samuel's hand. Quintin clamped the quill in the vee between his thumb and first knuckle, and I noticed his fingers were as rigid as the hooks in the butcher shop's ceiling.

Samuel cast me an apologetic glance as he braced one hand on the table to push himself to his feet. The entire surface wriggled, slopping ink over the edge of the pot. He groped for a cloth to wipe the spilled ink from his hands. "I am so sorry I was not ready to welcome you. Now, here I am, so clumsy, and you, dressed so fine. I don't dare greet you properly or I will ruin your clothes."

I wanted to close the space between us and tell him I had a chestful of clothes. I had only one Samuel. But something seemed askew with my brother, and his tutor was looking on. Some affection was too precious to expose to a stranger.

"Your brother is the most diligent student I have ever come across," Master Quintin said. "It is my dearest wish that you take this lad out into the sunshine and convince him to enjoy himself, Master Hudson. The one lesson I cannot squeeze into that busy mind of his is that a scholar must stretch his body as he does his wit. Cramp either of them overlong and it will atrophy from disuse." He dropped the quill some distance from my brother.

Samuel grinned at him—the wide grin that had once been saved just for me. "I never imagined there was so much to learn, Jeff! Master Quintin is the wisest man I've ever known."

The tutor's brow arched. "That is not so great a tribute as it seems, since you never set foot outside your country village until we came to London. Your brother, however, has moved in the court's highest circles." Had the tutor known what I was thinking? If so, his words translated it as deftly as Tobie Mathews translated for the queen that first night at York House. "I am certain Master Hudson will tell you of truly remarkable men."

Was the tutor jesting about the menagerie when he used the word *remarkable*? It was hard to tell. There was something guarded about the man, yet he had humor in him, as well. His next words seemed utterly serious, almost wistful. "I have heard the king is as fine a collector of art as any man in the world."

"That is why I wished Samuel to lodge with me at the palace. So he could see it with his own eyes." Samuel dropped the ink-splotched rag on the cluttered table as Quintin leveled him with a puzzled stare. "You did not tell me that you had been invited to the palace."

Samuel fished the quill out of the muddle of writing tools. He flattened the feathers as if to smooth ruffled feelings. Mine? Or Quintin's? I could not guess. "Plans were already set to stay here. I did not want to upset them. Much as I love my brother, Master, I don't belong in such a grand place. Not when I can be of use to you."

I tensed. Was I being overly sensitive? Why did it seem as though we had been apart for more than a year?

"The chance to see the royal collection is a rare privilege. Not one any student should miss." Quintin said it tenderly, without real reproach. No wonder Samuel seemed to be blossoming under his care. "I have heard that the queen has built a most amazing chapel designed by Inigo Jones, the finest architect in all England. He has carried countless ideas from Italy, the classic designs of Palladio. I would give much to see Jones's work myself."

"Then come with us!" Samuel urged. "Jeffrey would not mind, would you, Jeff?" My brother turned to me, so eager and sure of my approval. Perhaps it was no wonder John got the urge to punch him sometimes. Could Samuel not tell how much I had counted on seeing him alone?

I hesitated just long enough that his tutor understood without words. "I fear I have only gotten permission for you to visit the queen's side of the palace."

The tutor shuffled the papers together on Samuel's desktop. I could tell my brother wanted to grab them back. "Samuel, I have managed to get along without you somehow these forty years." Quintin smiled. "Granted, I do not know how, but it is not good to grow too dependent on you."

Quintin sniffed the air, his eyes drifting shut. "I vow, I might be in Valencia again, the scent of oranges is so strong. Your Samuel delights in oranges."

I had not known he had ever tasted them, let alone developed a fondness for them. I would not get to see him take that first sweet-sour taste of them after all. Disappointed, I untied the bag I had brought with me, my offering seeming inadequate. "They were crushed on the way here."

Quintin sighed. "It is a hazardous path between our station and the palace. There are countless pitfalls on the way."

Pitfalls indeed. What had Quintin called him? "Your Samuel"? He did not feel like my Samuel anymore. He'd sprouted so, he'd soon be taller than John. A satisfying prospect if it meant Samuel would be harder to bully, but with Samuel's nature, the best I could hope for was that people who did not know him would be more likely to leave him alone. His face was fuller in the cheeks. His cowlick even obeyed him now. But there was still a hungry expression about him, something in his face that seemed to yearn outward. It startled me to realize I did not know toward what.

"Go on, lads. Off with you. When you return, Master Hudson, there is someone anxious to see you: a friend of yours."

"I cannot imagine who." I did not have any friends save Samuel and those in the menagerie.

Samuel seemed to sense his tutor's resolve. He grabbed the sack of oranges and thrust them into his teacher's hands. "I wish you would eat these while I am gone," Samuel said.

"They are for you," I wanted to protest, stung, but Quintin was quicker to reply.

"Your brother intends them for you. But if you decide to share them with our guest when you return, that would show Master Hudson the good manners I am intent on teaching you."

I heard the thud of footsteps on the stairs. A portly man appeared so intent on wiping ink-blackened hands on his apron, he didn't see me. Tufts of white hair thrust out above each ear, the top of his head bald and gleaming. "Has Samuel's brother arrived? Never heard such a clamor from the street vendors down below."

Master Quintin chuckled. "They are hoping to flush out a customer with ties to the palace. This is Samuel's brother, Jeffrey Hudson. Master Hudson, this is my boyhood friend, Bartholomew Rowland."

Rowland looked down at me. He tried not to gape. "W—welcome to the Saracen's Bane. My girls are anxious to meet you." Rowland shouted down the stairs. "Maggie! Gwendolyn! Alice!"

What sounded like a trio of bullocks thundered up the stairs. I was stunned when three delicate girls between the ages of five and ten peeked out from behind their father.

"Girls, say good morrow to Samuel's brother," Rowland bade them.

The middle child buried her face against her big sister's shoulder, while the younger one looked as if she thought I might eat her. She obviously thought her thumb was the tastiest morsel, for she popped it in her mouth. The eldest girl tried to curtsy, no easy task, since her sisters were both clinging to her. "Good morrow, sir," she said.

A door at the back of the chamber opened and a thin woman bustled out. The two younger girls bolted over to her, the thumb-sucker scaling the woman like Pug climbed Inigo Jones's scaffolds.

"Forgive them their breech of manners, Master Hudson," the woman said, cuddling her daughters close. "The girls have grown quite shy of visitors."

"My wife, Margery," Rowland said, introducing the woman with a wave. "No woman in London is finer at stitching together a book's pages or etching copper plates for illustrations. She learned at her father's knee."

"I am honored to meet you, Master Hudson," she said. "The girls and I are off to my aunt's for the night. I regret we will not be here when you return."

"I plan to retire early as well," the printer said in obvious discomfort.

I could only be grateful. That would be one less batch of intruders when it came to time with my brother. Yet what was driving Rowland from his own hearth?

The monkey child piped up from her mother's arms, "I'm going to be taller than Gwenny someday, so mama says she'd best not pull my hair. Are you going to be taller than Samuel?"

"I will never be taller than Samuel." I had known that truth for a very long time, but saying it to this small girl made the truth ache.

Quintin cleared his throat. "Master Hudson, you really should hurry. It's unkind to get the peddlers' hopes so high when you have no intention of buying anything."

He wished to help me escape the discomfort. I could tell in the tone of his voice. I seized the chance and made my way down to the coach with Samuel.

A footman waited to open the door. Samuel's eyes widened at the liveried servant. My brother hesitated a moment before he climbed into the equipage. He ran his fingertips across the velvet seat, never able to resist feeling something soft.

For as long as I could remember, Samuel had comforted himself by twirling his silky curls. John had often grabbed the curl out of Samuel's grasp, giving it a stiff yank. I often thought John would have to shave Samuel bald if he wanted to put an end to the hair twirling. What no one but Samuel knew was that I was the one who'd started the habit. At night when I'd been anxious or scared, I would run one of my brother's curls between my fingers so I could sleep. I had almost asked him to snip one off so I could take it with me to Buckingham's.

The thick silence in the coach's interior left too much space for painful imagining. I filled it with mindless chatter as best I could.

"You are so tall, I almost would not have recognized you. I hoped you would get more to eat without me around."

"I did. For a while. Until . . ." Samuel reached for a strand of his hair and wound it around one ink-stained finger. "I don't blame them. You would have been as mad as Father and Mother and John if you'd caught me."

"Doing what?"

"Everything would have been fine if that meddling baker's wife hadn't praised mother for her 'Christian charity' in feeding the widow."

"Oh, Samuel. Doesn't the widow have her own son to do that?"

"He turned lunatic from his time at sea. When she got sick with the pox, he took all the food that was to last the whole winter, took the widow's coins and even the Virgin statue from under the floorboards, then ran away. 'Saved the widow's life, you Hudsons have,' Mrs. Baker told Mother. 'So careful of the widow's pride, as well, sending food all secret with your lad.'"

"I meant Buckingham's coin to make things better for you!"

"I couldn't break the habit of sneaking food away from the table, and it would have been a sin to waste it once I'd already taken it."

"That argument lacks a certain logic."

"It is up to Master Quintin to help me sort it out. You have only yourself to worry about now." Samuel looked me up and down. "You've grown as well in the time you've been gone."

Was it possible? A child's excitement surged through me, the hope I'd felt after one of John's attempts to stretch my inadequate body. But that child had watched his brothers and sister grow—seen hems let down and breeches grow so short that they had to be passed down to the next child in line. My shirtsleeves reached my wrists, hose plenty long enough to tie to my breeches. Irritation at my gullibility pricked at me. I hadn't expected such tricks from Samuel. "I have not grown at all."

"Not in size, Jeffrey. But there are other ways to grow. I do not know how to explain it except that since you left Oakham, you've grown large in . . . *knowing*."

I lowered my eyelids for dread Samuel would see the ugliness I had learned of. How strange, to protect a lad who had grown up in the shambles from the luxury-filled life where I now belonged.

"May I tell you something? I half-dreaded your coming to see me. I was afraid you would be ashamed of me," Samuel confessed in that shy way of his.

I started to protest, but Master Quintin's lessons had infused some new confidence in my brother. "I knew you would not want to feel embarrassed by me and you would try not to show it. But Father told us you turned him away when he first came to the palace."

I remembered the sense of violation I had felt when Father had touched things in my room. How mercenary Father had been, wanting to sell the writing box the queen had given me. Did my abhorrence of the man who had sired me make me as ungrateful as the king had claimed? Samuel, of all people, should understand my wanting to keep Father out of my new life. But Samuel couldn't. He was fool enough to go chasing into the cottage of a lunatic and a widow with pox. He would never bar the door to his own parent. There was no way to make Samuel understand, but I did the best I could.

"You are not Father," I said.

"I know that. But it is not so hard to imagine I could shame you. You were always so much cleverer than I was. I could never think what to say. But now—everything is changed!" His eyes sparkled. "Jeffrey, I cannot believe my good fortune."

Warmth filled me. I had never seen Samuel this happy.

"And I owe it all to the duke of Buckingham's kindness!"

The warmth whooshed out of me as if I'd taken a fist to the belly. "Buckingham?"

"I hear what people say about him. Sometimes Father would take me with him to the public house—the master there won't take his coin anymore.

Gives him free ale because he's father of the queen's famous dwarf. But folks there spew hate along with their spittle. Especially the widow's son. Told tales of Cádiz that spread like fire. People say such evil things of the duke of Buckingham, you'd think him a devil instead of a man. It is absurd. I tell them what good he has done you—and now me. They refused to believe it."

I wanted to leap in, yet what could I say? The last thing I wanted was to ruin Samuel's happiness, betray my own sins. Still, touting Buckingham as a hero was dangerous.

"It is better not to spread it around that Buckingham is responsible for your tutor," I warned. "England loathes the duke—so much so that the Commons tried to impeach him for treason. They failed, yet people like Scabbers and the other apprentices would love to take their wrath out on someone connected with Buckingham. They would not care who."

"If someone is wrongly accused, isn't it important to defend him?"

"Even men who do terrible wrong are capable of some acts of . . ." I could not squeeze out the blasphemy of using the word *kindness* and the name Buckingham in the same phrase. "Acts that benefit someone who deserves . . ." I fumbled to a stop again. "Just be careful."

Quiet fell, and I wondered what Samuel was thinking. Instead, I filled the silence with a question I knew he would jabber on about long enough to give me time to gather my thoughts.

"How are things at home?"

"Little has changed since I wrote you last."

"You sent me a letter?"

"Eight of them. Clemmy said you would marvel at how my penmanship has improved. It was so kind of him to carry them."

"But . . . I never got . . ." My stomach knotted. My time at court had taught me well—I needed time to sort things out before I spoke. I had to think what the missing letters might mean.

One letter might be misplaced, even two. Clemmy might have been embarrassed to confess his carelessness. But eight letters over months? That was no accident. Samuel was staring at me, strange in the silence. "Did you not like the letters? I am sure you are used to far more exciting news than I could share."

"Even the best letters are not the same as hearing about family from your lips. Tell me the news again."

Samuel looked at me strangely. "I'd not expected to waste time—"

"Indulge me in this. Please."

He let go of his curl and began. "Mother is fretful, taking care of Father. He's not been himself since John was taken by the press gangs."

I fought to hide my shock. "Press gangs?" I echoed, as if to prod him forward.

"He'd taken to drinking like Father, telling everyone about his fine brother at court. After the way he used to try to stretch you, I thought it was a change for the better. It might have been, if the innkeeper hadn't given him all the ale he could swallow. One night, John left with some strangers and never came back. Turned out, they were a press gang grabbing sailors up the coast. Father walked through a rainstorm to Portsmouth, searching, but it was too late. The fleet had already sailed for France."

I tried to imagine John sailing to war that hot June day, laying siege under Buckingham's command. Was there any chance the duke would guess John was my brother? Unlikely in that crush of men, but if he did, would Buckingham's attention serve John good or ill?

Samuel was looking at me, puzzled again. I could not think, pressured under the searching in his eyes.

I rapped on the coach top. The coachman stopped. I leaned out the window. "To the Rose and Crown Theatre," I said. I would be able to think more clearly amid the familiar furor of a performance, and the play would keep Samuel's attention directed away from me. Could there be a more apt place to unravel this knot than in a theater full of actors?

I could not even enjoy Samuel's excitement as the play began. I had seen enthusiasm before. Clemmy had all but quaked with delight at Samuel's impending visit. Could Clemmy be such a fine actor as to fool me into seeming my friend? Who had Samuel's letters? Buckingham? The queen's enemies, or the king's? Was it possible I had an even more intimate foe myself? What of Archie Armstrong and his fall from popularity since I had come to court?

More important, why would this adversary keep the letters once he had read them? He had to know the theft would be discovered the moment I saw Samuel. Everyone at court knew the reason for my absence. Somewhere, someone was leafing through the confidences Samuel had written for my eyes only. That person knew I was aware of his mischief. Did he only want to unnerve me? Or was there a more sinister purpose behind his actions?

I watched the comic villain of the piece inch his way across a narrow ledge toward the window of the maiden he planned to seduce. The man gripped a lantern in one hand, unaware the girl's scruffy dog was creeping along the ledge behind him.

Suddenly, the dog clamped his teeth in the villain's breeches, shaking him until he dropped the torch into a box left as a trap by the hero. Shrieks and applause filled the theater as fireworks exploded, raining down on the audience. It was a miracle the theatrical effect meant to surprise and delight did not set the place afire.

Samuel flung his arms around me, shielding me from the sparks as he laughed. That was what I had missed most of all, wasn't it? The closeness we'd always shared? The way we had both tried to shelter each other? Despite Samuel's efforts, a glowing fleck landed on my hand. I clung to Samuel all the tighter as it burned me, knowing that a single stray spark from a foe I could not see might burn Samuel's whole world—and mine—down to ash.

Night had fallen by the time the coach lumbered up to the Saracen's Bane, heavier by the weight of as many packages as Samuel and I could carry. The smell of the new leather shoes I had insisted Samuel wear as we left the boot maker's stall mingled with the satisfying rustle of clothes getting their very first creases.

He had spent much of the trip fastening and unfastening the lower three buttons on his tawny wool doublet, as if practicing to get the new process right. Handsome green stockings without a single snag warmed legs that still seemed astonishingly long to me. A warm brown cloak draped Samuel's shoulders and a felt hat with a pheasant feather pinned to the side brought out the gold in his hair. But of all the things we had bought, the one that pleased him most was the simple russet robe he had fingered so longingly at the secondhand clothing stall near the shop where we'd bought his own suit ready-made.

I still was not certain what made me buy it when Samuel had said it would fit his tutor. Or maybe I did so to protect the purchases I'd already made. It would be just like Samuel to trade his new hat for the robe once I was gone.

Yet it was hard to remain disgruntled as I watched my brother bound up the stairs, his eyes shining in that absurd way they did when he was sneaking food to someone he thought was hungry. What was to become of him without me or John or our parents around to make sure he was warm enough or fed enough? Could the tutor be trusted to guard him?

I was wondering how I might steal a word with Master Quintin as we entered the chamber above the shop. For an instant, alarm gripped me as a small dog yapped. I crushed the irrational fear. Even if the queen had ordered someone to fetch me, they would not have brought one of her dogs. A small bat-eared bulldog trotted toward me, wagging its stump of a tail. But every thought in my head vanished as its master stood and I saw the guest that had made the Rowland daughters shy.

There, framed against a crackling fire, was a face that might have escaped from hell. The top half was ordinary enough, with its green eyes and delicately drawn arched brows. But beneath those regular features, the tip of his nose curved like a scythe, reminding all who saw it of the blade used to carve a ghastly smile that stretched from the knob hinging one side of his jaw to the knob hinging the other. We had both been ten years old when I had last seen that face at the Oakham Fair, but who could forget it?

"Jeffrey, my old friend!" he cried, hastening to embrace me. "I know you have not forgotten the Gargoyle!"

"Phineas! Of course I have not forgotten you! Where have you been these many years? How have you fared?"

"Not as well as you! But I roved all over the world with traveling players. Even spent some time in Valencia, where Master Quintin's quick action saved me from a most unfortunate encounter with some Spaniards intent on burning me for a demon."

I suddenly wished I'd bought a hat to go with Quintin's russet robe.

"The good master took me in and taught me as much as I could hold, but the knife that carved my smile must've nicked a hole in my brain, for I fear the learning tumbled out as fast as Master Quintin tried to stuff it in. Imagine my surprise when I visited my old tutor and found my favorite Fairy Piper was his new student. How kind of Master Quintin to share news of your visit and invite me to see Oakham's Fairy King."

It took some getting used to, that grin that never changed. Yet if one could look past it to the Gargoyle's eyes, there was pain and sorrow, patience and humor. Bitterness and gentleness all tangled together unrecognized, still waiting for people to see. "I am glad you are safe," I told him.

"No more ranging across the globe, where I can get my hinder parts singed. That encounter in Spain was too close a call. I've a mask and hood good Master Quintin gave me to wear when I go among the vulgar herd, and he finds me enough work here and there to keep body and soul together."

I saw past the toothy grin to a wistfulness Phineas didn't bother to hide. "I miss performing, but there is not as much need for a horror like me— once the ladies and gents shriek, they scurry away. It is angels like you people can gaze at forever."

"That depends upon what use we're put to. We've a whole troupe under the queen's protection. They call us the Royal Menagerie of Curiosities and Freaks of Nature."

The Gargoyle touched the scarred edge of his grin. "Nature had nothing to do with this, but I am a freak now, by anyone's opinion."

"There are countless roles in Her Majesty's masques. I will have to wait for the right time to ask, but there might be a place for you."

The Gargoyle tipped his head. "You would do that for me?"

"It would be good to have an old friend nearby." Especially since I could no longer trust Clemmy.

Samuel was falling asleep in his chair by the time I walked the Gargoyle to the door. I watched him place the full mask over his mutilated face, noticed it was the type the plague doctors wore, with a long, hooked beak they could fill with herbs to ward off disease. When he pulled his hood up over his head, he chuckled. "Never have to worry about any ruffians bothering me when I'm decked out this way. The nastiest brute runs the moment he thinks I've come from a plague house."

"You know how to take care of yourself," I said.

"No choice. I'm not beautiful like you, nor do I have a kind brother to watch out for me. I always envied you and your Samuel the piper."

"Phineas, I . . . I cannot explain, but something is troubling my brother. I fear for him."

The green eyes between the slits in the Gargoyle's mask turned away from me. At first I thought he was searching for the door latch. But then I realized that he had not rushed to reassure me. Was that a matter for concern? Or had he just seen so much cruelty that he was never surprised by a sinking sense of dread?

"Master Quintin will guard him as he did me. Would God that the good man would take as much care of himself."

"Is there something I should know?"

"Nothing certain. If there was, then I would tell you."

"Will you keep watch on my brother? I know it is much to ask."

"Refuse a request from the Fairy King? Never!" He clapped me on the shoulder, and I was reminded of Will Evans's warmth. The Gargoyle sobered. "I do not forget a friend, Jeffrey. In my life I have had too few of them."

I watched him disappear into the shadows. I knew the coach was parked behind the bookseller's now. The coachman had doubtless found someplace with a warm fire and a flagon of something bracing.

I could rouse him and return to the palace, and yet I trekked back up to the shop, where Samuel was still dozing. Master Quintin sat opposite him, regarding my brother over folded hands.

"It is a rare thing to see the sleep of innocents," Quintin murmured.

"Not so innocent. He's a thief, you know. Used to steal food for me, then bedevil his conscience until he could confess it."

"So he told me. Shall I carry Samuel down to the coach so you might take him to the palace?" He must have seen my doubt, for he said, "Despite appearances, I am stronger than I look."

I imagined him lifting my lanky brother, limping to the stairs. I imagined them both pitching down the risers. But, strangely enough, I doubted the tutor would fall. In spite of that, I shook my head.

"Who am I to disturb the sleep of innocents? Can you get him to his bed?"

"I've done it often when Samuel fell asleep over his books. Will you stay the night, as well? It would be a fine surprise for the lad to find you here when he awakes."

I nodded. The tutor went to Samuel and lifted the youth with a gentleness no one save me or our mother had ever shown my brother. I followed them to a nook behind a curtain, where a small bed was tucked under an eave.

"You will have to crowd in with your brother. But then, he has never gotten used to sleeping the night without you."

"Hasn't he?" I looked at the tutor in surprise.

"I gave him an extra bolster, which he tucks against his side. But tonight he'll have his brother instead."

"I had to learn to sleep alone." An unexpected knot formed in my throat.

"I fear you've had to learn a great many things you did not choose to at court."

I stripped down to my shirt as Quintin helped Samuel out of the unfamiliar garb, the tutor's hands awkward, yet careful as a mother's.

He settled us both beneath the covers, and in the light of a flickering candle, I saw him smile.

"Tonight may our blessed Mother guard your sleep," he said. "Our Lady had a special tenderness for lads, I think."

It seemed so natural—Samuel's love of Christ's mother, the medal he had given me blending with the quiet benediction of this man. I had lived long enough in the queen's Catholic household that I did not question devotions that harkened to the old faith.

Quintin took the candle from the room, leaving us in darkness. I could smell the familiar scent of Samuel's hair, mingled with new smells of ink and musty books, oranges and the faint, acrid bite of gunpowder from the fireworks at the theater.

For a long moment I lay, awkward and apart from him, so tense, my body began to ache. Or was it my heart? We were beyond boyhood's realm now. At least I was. I doubted Samuel would ever leave innocence behind. My eye stung with loss. Then moonlight struck one of my brother's curls.

I reached out and slipped the strand between my fingers, seeking the familiar comfort as I closed my eyes. I had not quite drifted to sleep when Samuel shifted closer, his arm groping for where the bolster usually was. Instead, my brother flung his arm around me.

I had not slept so well since I had left the cottage loft in Oakham. I doubted I would ever sleep so well again.

Nineteen

·

November 1627

I had wanted the duke dead, prayed for it—a fiend's prayer that Samuel would have been ashamed of. No concern for the duchess of Buckingham and her children or grudging sympathy for what Buckingham had suffered as a youth had been able to change the course of that prayer.

Only after I knew that the nobleman who controlled my fate also had John's life clutched in his glory-hungry hands did I hope for the scheming duke to win the victory he craved.

Victorious armies brought more soldiers back to home shores alive.

I gleaned whatever scraps of news fell from the royal table, waiting to hear that the citadel had buckled under the pressure of Buckingham's blockade. I pictured John keeping vigil on moonless nights. I imagined him fighting sleep as the ship rocked, the soothing lap of waves filling the monotonous hours of his watch. He would be listening for the muffled splash of oars or snap of canvas that meant a French boatman was attempting to slip past the English blockade to carry food to those starving Catholics trapped behind the fortress walls. Frenchmen were still blocking the English path to the Protestants Buckingham hoped to make our allies.

From what I'd heard, John would need food nearly as much as the French did. Neither the king's fury nor the soldiers' distress had moved Parliament to allot the funds needed for an invasion. The Commons and Lords had weighed their hatred of Buckingham against the need to provision simple soldiers. Thwarting Buckingham had won.

For months, the king had scraped together what funds he could and poured those resources into Buckingham's hands. But in the end, even God stood against the duke. The Scots' fleet Charles raised to go to the aid of the beleaguered forces sailed into a storm. Buckingham's salvation had scattered to the winds.

Worse still was the news Will brought me one November afternoon. "Jeff, lad, a messenger just rode in from Portsmouth. The French slipped past Buckingham's blockade. While our poor bastards starve, those French in the citadel are eating their fill."

"It is hopeless then," I said. "Buckingham has to abandon the campaign. John may already be sailing home."

"I pray God it is so, but . . . there is one more thing you must know. Buckingham refused to admit defeat. He flung his forces against the citadel walls."

"Even Buckingham cannot be such a fool. The citadel walls were too strong to breach when the army's bellies and guns were full! How did he expect starving men to break them down?"

"The duke is guilty of the worst kind of arrogance. His pride—his accursed pride. He cast them all—whatever men they had left—on a suicide mission. Even those who reached the walls under that terrible cannon fire were doomed. When the lads went to scale the walls, the ladders they flung up were too short."

I closed my eyes, picturing it—the clawing hunger in John's belly, his arms weighed down with the ladder he prayed his weakened legs would have the strength to climb. I could smell the choking gunpowder, see the bright flare of weapons firing, and hear the screams of dying men. I could feel the rough wood of the siege ladder pushing splinters into John's hands as he and his comrades swung the ladder up against the fortress's rough stone. Had John climbed first? He had always insisted on shoving ahead of Samuel and me. Had the smoke been so thick he could not see far enough to realize the ladder that was supposed to get him over the wall never would? It would only strand him in a hail of musket fire, with nowhere to hide.

Samuel was the Hudson who had always prayed. John had never bothered much about religion, trusting God did not need a lad from Oakham telling Him His business. I prayed enough to keep Samuel from fretting, but I couldn't imagine God would heed someone He'd fashioned from birth to make others think of demons and devils and witches and such.

But as I looked into Will's worried face, I said, "God help John. God help them all."

"They say what's left of them are straggling into Portsmouth."

I gripped the table, to steady myself. "How many?"

Will hunkered down, curving his hand over my arm. "The messenger thinks two thousand."

"Two thousand died? Out of a force of seven thousand?"

"Two thousand are left."

I tried to take in the scope of this disaster. "John survived," I said, more to myself than to Will. "You do not know how strong he is. I've seen him fight three lads at a time and win." I did not say he had been defending me.

"There will be no way to tell for some time. I think half the families in England will be waiting for news."

"I know that John survived."

"Buckingham cannot. Even the king will see him for the villain he is now. The duke is to wait upon the king at Whitehall. Buckingham will get what he deserves at last."

It was true. Fierce joy warred with my fear for John and my sick horror at the thought of those skeletal corpses littering French ground.

Buckingham would fall. As the days slid by, all of England cried for his blood. What would happen to me when the duke faced justice? Would he expose me as his spy to spite the queen? Make certain Her Majesty would send me away? That would be the best I could hope for. An image of the old bloodstains on the scaffold at Tyburn flashed in my memory. No, I dared not think about suffering that fate.

Instead, I imagined my life beyond the palace gates. It would not be easy to go back to cottage living—scarce food, winter's cold numbing fingers and toes. But it was another kind of hunger that would be most painful to endure. I would not have books or tutors, beautiful art to fill my hours. Nevertheless, I could surrender all with scarcely a pang if it meant Buckingham's downfall. It was the thought of losing the people inside these walls that made my heart ache: Henrietta Maria, with her quick delight and fierce temper. Will Evans, the bedrock so many depended upon. I would miss Robin's paint-speckled scowls and the way Sara hummed while she combed out Scrap's ears. I'd miss seeing young pages grow wide-eyed as Simon told them the story of how he'd grown so thin—claiming he'd swallowed a minnow whole as a boy and it was still swimming around in his stomach, gobbling everything he swallowed before it could stick to his rattly bones. I wouldn't be there if Boku ever told us where he had come from, where he had been. I would miss watching Dulcinea float above the crowd like a bright-plumed bird.

But I would not be able to harm them anymore. I would never have to betray the queen again or see disillusionment fill Will's eyes. Most important of all, Samuel would be safe.

I had seen Quintin's love for my brother, knew the tutor meant it when he said he would care for Samuel no matter what. Even if I could not pay for Samuel's lessons, Quintin would keep him to assist as a scribe. Once Buckingham was in disgrace and I was exiled from court, Samuel would cease being a pawn in the duke's hand. My brother could sink into obscurity and so would I. It would be worth the cost, and yet, as court and king waited for Buckingham to ride from Plymouth, I tried to imprint in my memory the sound of the queen's laugh when she danced with the king or played with her puppies in the garden, the feel of her hand those rare times she touched me. I studied the great furrows concentration carved into Will's brow when he practiced his writing and the wistful way he smiled when he watched Dulcinea dance upon the rope he'd secured himself.

As I committed my friends to memory, I caught Boku watching me with his own kind of intensity. I would never get to know the man concealed beneath those inscrutable eyes. Why did I sense he knew me? The ugliness, the betrayal, the lies? Perhaps this dark man had some secret beneath the velvet gauntlets he wore, secrets dark as those I kept myself.

Late November 1627

It was no small feat to sneak past the guards and hide in the chamber at Whitehall on the day the duke of Buckingham came to face the king. His

Majesty had required all the most powerful men in London to attend, leaving no room for insignificant playthings like me. Yet I would have risked more than the guards' anger to see my enemy's downfall.

From my place behind an arras, I could see the dais where the throne sat beneath its cloth of estate. By the time the king mounted it, the chamber was thronged with lords, the nobles slavering like Father's dogs, hot with the scent of blood.

It was a miracle Buckingham had reached Whitehall alive, some claimed. Most of England wanted him dead, and assassins were said to lurk around every corner. I wished them luck—but only after this day I had waited for so long.

I stood on tiptoe, trying to see, as a booming voice from the back of the chamber announced, "George Villiers, the duke of Buckingham."

Snarls of outrage raced through the crowd as a figure strode toward the throne. I could see the sheen of Buckingham's hair—he stood taller than most in the room. His head high, shoulders flung back, he seemed more conquering hero than the man who had decimated the fleet and lost five thousand men. His sapphire velvet doublet gleamed with silver braid. A chain of rubies encircled his neck just beneath his collarbone. Had he worn the stones as a kind of defiance. Mocking the blood the headsman's ax had drawn from the neck of Edward Strafford, last of the ancient line of Buckingham dukes King Henry the Eighth had executed a century before?

If Buckingham mounted the scaffold, would I go to witness the execution? The question popped into my head unbidden. I had never developed a taste for blood sport, but before I had my first pair of breeches, I had learned the danger of turning my back on a wounded bull. Better to see his throat slit than be gored in the back by a creature who had managed to live.

I held my breath, trying not to think of the duchess of Buckingham, the one person in the kingdom I cared for who must be glad of his return. Buckingham reached the foot of the throne and knelt. "Your Majesty," the duke said, his voice filling the chamber. "I have come to beg forgiveness for the loss of so many brave men. My officers were the finest any commander could ask for. My soldiers fought with such courage as to break a commander's heart. I alone am responsible for the defeat they suffered at the hands of the

Catholics guarding the port to La Rochelle. It is my fault that we did not get past the island to free the Protestant stronghold beyond."

I looked to the king, hungry as the rest of the crowd to see the duke savaged by royal wrath.

Charles Stuart rose and closed the space between them. The king's unlovely face looked all the worse beside Buckingham's beauty. "It is I who should beg you for forgiveness," the king said. "I have failed you and your brave officers. Your king and these lords who would judge you have slept safe in soft beds while you suffered hunger and danger. No man—not in the House of Lords or the Commons—shall ever question your bravery in my hearing. This defeat is the fault of those who clutched at their purse strings while your army shed blood for king and country."

The king's voice cut through the murmur of the crowd's disbelief. "Your Grace, I command you to rise." I could see the gleam of tears in the king's eyes as he drew Buckingham to his feet. "You are and will always be my most beloved, valiant friend. We will gather another fleet for you to command. You will sail to the aid of La Rochelle on a brighter day and I dare any man to tell you nay."

Bile rose in my throat as the king embraced my nemesis. I sagged against the wall. My legs gave way and I slid down to the floor, but I did not need to fear anyone would see me. The lords were beyond caring about one stowaway eavesdropping behind an arras. They knew now, as I did, that nothing on God's earth could break Buckingham's hold on the king but the duke's death.

I could not forget a tale my tutor once told me: how blind King John of Bohemia had been so eager to fight in a battle that he tied a guide rope between his horse and six of his knights, then rode into the fray swinging his sword. When the fight was over, people found the lot of them all slain—six knights and their king still tied together—tangled, with no way to cut free of one another.

Would King Charles end the same way? So bound to Buckingham that His Majesty would be destroyed in the chaos of Buckingham's downfall? If one as powerful as the king might vanish beneath fate's trampling hooves, what chance did Samuel and I have?

TWENTY

The court still reeled at the news of Buckingham's pardon as the queen's household moved once again to St. James's Palace. As the weeks after Buckingham's return passed, descriptions of the king's welcome of England's most hated villain flew through the streets of London, then onward along every road to the far reaches of the kingdom. Hatred of the duke grew—a force so dangerous, a proclamation went out forbidding any man to speak of the duke of Buckingham, for fear it would incite an uprising.

It should have been such a simple thing for one of those furious people to kill a man so widely hated. Yet as the duke raced back and forth between London and Portsmouth, dealing with his shattered army, planning the fresh assault the king had promised he would lead, I began to wonder if His Grace had drunk some devil's potion so that no poison or dagger or lead musket ball could pierce him. I began to fear whatever weapon aimed at Buckingham's heart would always be turned aside by fortune's hand to lodge in someone else's chest.

How had I ever believed I could remain separate from it all? Tell my jests, make my bow, and then sail, untouched upon tumultuous seas—a miniature Noah safe upon my ark of grotesques.

Who would be struck down next in his stead? Samuel? The queen? Me? I had seen the handbills nailed on church doors and passed from hand to hand.

Who rules England? The king?
Who rules the king?
The duke of Buckingham.

Who rules the duke?

The devil.

Would people think me part of the duke's demonic plans if they discovered I was in his employ? What vengeance might they take, lashing out in the pain of grief?

Beyond the palace gates, mothers and wives waited, hoping their men might still come home. I imagined my own mother squirreling bits of salted beef away, hidden from the rest of the hungry family, imagining the feast she would lay out with her meager stores when John marched through the cottage door.

Five thousand soldiers would never sit at their mothers' tables again or return to their wives' embraces. I fretted over the question so many across the island were tormented with, wondering if my mother would have to wipe John's pewter plate one last time, then place it upon the shelf to gather dust forever.

Imagining the emptiness John's loss would leave drove me to shun my own chambers. Instead, I retreated to the menagerie's lodgings to practice a new trick with Pug while the queen was with her newly acquired music master, learning to play the lute.

I could hear Dulcinea's voice, high and sharp, as I rounded the corner to the room and was surprised to see her flouncing out with her arms full of costumes, her face flushed, defiant. But startled as I was by her swift exit, I was more surprised by the only other person I found within the menagerie's lodgings: Uriel Ware.

I had not seen Buckingham's hireling since the duke's sister had gossiped about Ware's childhood. The man's visits to replenish the queen's purse had been surreptitious meetings I was not party to. Yet there he stood, beside the locked cupboard Boku had brought with him from Carlisle House.

Light snagged on the objects Boku had removed from the mysterious cupboard and scattered on the table nearby—copper bowls, vials of liquid, half-assembled mechanisms, and oddly shaped rocks. Ware trailed his fingertips across them, and for a moment I wondered if he was searching among them for a dragon stone like the ones his father had loved. Then I banished such musings, filling my head with suspicion.

"What are you doing here?" I demanded, tense at seeing him within the menagerie's walls. I made a quick turn around the chamber, checking to make sure no other member of our troupe had darted for cover when the intimidating man entered the room.

"The queen was in need of coin."

"From your own purse or from Buckingham's?"

"Even you are not certain who initiated the loan? How illuminating."

"You want support for voyages to the new world. Buckingham refuses to move forward on the matter."

"Add that the queen believes any reasonable person can see that she is being treated unjustly and it is little wonder the ruse worked. Buckingham fills the purse I offer to tempt Her Majesty deeper into debt. The duke hopes her continued excesses will anger the king, since he is in such dire financial straits. A forlorn hope, I fear. The king has a dangerous tenderness for those who fail him—as long as they profess undying love."

I could not deny Ware was right.

"After I finished my business with the queen, I decided to see if that illusion master I have heard so much about might provide a charm to change my master's fortune. My own fate is tied to Buckingham's, as you say, and his luck has gone quite sour. When the government issues a proclamation forbidding the general populace even to mention a nobleman's name, it is time to take stock of one's options."

"What has Dulcinea to do with such matters?"

"I try to guard the duke's reputation where I can. It is a thankless task, and one he makes quite difficult. Some women behave in an overly familiar fashion at inappropriate times."

"I have heard the same accusation leveled at His Grace and friends. A woman goes to a household she believes is completely respectable, only to discover it is not. What kind of man uses a lady's visit with his mother to bait his quarry?"

"The duke's mother is familiar with His Grace's rather unorthodox methods and lodges no objections. Especially since just such a ploy snared the Villiers family England's richest heiress. Of course, I would never admit such a thing to anyone but you."

"Buckingham's wife, mother, and sister may be the only people in England who do not object to the duke at present."

"Do not forget the king," Ware said. "Yet since the fleet's return from France, His Grace has fewer friends than ever. It is not a favorable situation for a Lord Admiral bent on restoring his honor. Armies must be fed and re-supplied, a costly and complicated business—something the citizenry preferred to ignore. Not that I wish to underplay Buckingham's own stupidity."

Ware's tone startled me. "A dangerous way to describe your master," I observed. "God forbid he hears of it."

Ware's expression shifted, suddenly more unguarded than ever before. "I would be frank with you, Jeffrey. The man fancies himself the English Richelieu, a brilliant statesman and military strategist. But put Buckingham into the fray—be it in a council chamber or upon a beachhead—and he becomes as ineffectual as he is pretty to look at."

Did Ware sense my reaction? He regarded me a long moment. "Have you something clever to say about that, Jeffrey? You look as if you do."

"I am trained to look clever as often as possible: a court fool's way of building his audience's expectations before he makes a jest. I was only thinking I have never heard you talk in such a way about Buckingham."

"His Grace keeps me running his errands like a half-wit page instead of provisioning ships to Guyana. Someday soon an Englishman will break the Spanish and French stranglehold on the Spice Islands. If Buckingham continues to use me in this way, I will have to watch some other man realize that dream." Ware grimaced. "It is not always easy for servants to keep their superiors on the right path. I am sure you understand. It can be a frustrating endeavor for those of us who are so much more intelligent than they are."

I opened my mouth, shut it. Even I did not dare voice what had sprung into my mind. Everyone knew wolves at a distance were watching Buckingham, waiting for a chance to close in for the kill. But the hand close by might well be the one to take Buckingham down.

"I am attempting to use the queen's new music master to distract those who would destroy the duke," Ware explained. "Stirring suspicions in English minds is easy when it comes to foreigners. A few words in this tavern or among that group of apprentices and soon the whole city will believe the queen has been smuggling information to the French by slipping notes into the hole in the lute's belly."

I forced my hands not to curl into fists, thereby betraying my fury at this new danger to the queen. "You know such a notion is absurd."

"I assure you people will believe it. Household servants make the most calculating spies."

I could see the lute master, his forelock tumbling over his white brow, his eyes squinting as he placed the queen's slender fingers on the lute strings. Musicians were never the hardiest lot when exposed to a torturer's art. Had not musician Mark Smeaton cracked under torture in the reign of Henry the Eighth, forced to confess to committing adultery with Anne Boleyn? A chill trickled down my spine.

"The musician forgets his music half the time," I scoffed. "He would be the most disorganized spy ever seen."

"The better to conceal his true purpose."

I saw my opening, addressed it. "There are no secret missives from the queen, but I do want my own letters back."

Ware's eyelid did not even flicker. "His Grace chooses to keep letters his hirelings write him in case he should need to use them as leverage later."

"These letters were not meant for the duke, unless he has taken a sudden interest in my brother Samuel's schoolboy's scribbling that was meant for me."

"Unless your brother is involved with treachery against the king, I cannot imagine why anyone would annoy themselves with such letters. Perhaps they were lost somewhere on the way to you."

"Eight of them? It makes me wonder if letters I sent to His Grace have gone astray."

Ware's jaw hardened. "Surely you could not have been so careless."

"I slip my letters into the nook in my saddle. They are gone the next time I go riding. I never see the person who retrieves them. It could be anybody."

Ware drove his fingers through his hair, snagging the ribbon that bound his eye patch. It pulled askew, showing the puckered scar. "How many have you written? What is in them?"

"Around fourteen, I think. How can I remember how many I wrote? I'm not even sure they are missing."

"It would be unfortunate if evidence against His Grace slipped into the wrong hands. Buckingham escaped impeachment once, but there are plenty in the country who would behead him as a traitor now without the bother of a trial."

"Would you tell me if you were the one who took Samuel's letters?"

"I do not make accountings of myself to servants. How did you discover the letters were missing? You must have some idea how they were to be delivered."

I thought of Clemmy's saw-toothed grin. Was it possible Clemmy was working for one of Buckingham's enemies? It was more likely the missing letters were a trap set for me, to see if I would reveal my suspicions to Ware or conceal them. There was no point in dissembling. One question to the duchess would lead Ware straight to Clemmy.

"Her Grace was generous enough to arrange for a servant named Clemmy Watson to carry news between Samuel and me. He was to carry the letters."

It was eerie how unreadable Ware could keep that single eye. "Clemmy Watson," Ware said. "I know something of him. He would be easy for the right person to manipulate. A country boy, kind by nature. Overly fond of his family."

"Are you telling me that the duke threatened Clemmy's family to get his hands on my letters?"

"I told you, I know nothing about your letters. Though I do know a trifle about Clemmy. He has gone missing."

"Missing?" I was not sure what to feel. Anger at his betrayal, or fear about what might have happened to him. Had he fled Buckingham's household or been dragged away? Disposed of somehow? "What happened?" I asked.

"Some incident involving his sister, though I cannot recollect the details. There are many weapons decent fellows put in their foe's hands. Beloved family members can be wielded with the effectiveness of a torture master's rack."

"Is that why you never married?"

He looked at me a long moment, then hooked his finger beneath the black ribbon holding his patch in place. He lifted the velvet wing that hid his empty socket. The jagged scar puckered the skin; the lids sucked inward, outlining the bony orbit as if in a death's-head, waiting to break free. "Jeffrey, tell me. What do you see?"

"An ugly mess."

"Shall I tell you how many women have asked me to see the wreck of my eye? The gaping hole frightens some of them; others, it excites. They disgust me equally."

He frowned. "Strange, people always are suspicious of the ugly. They needn't be. Temptation is beautiful. If I was bent on some witchery, I would use creatures like your rope dancer or the dwarf with the face of an angel."

"Or someone like Clemmy?" I hoped to see some reaction that would tell me how deeply my former friend was embroiled in Buckingham's mire. Nothing. My hands knotted into fists. "What has Buckingham done with him?"

"It is difficult when someone you care for disappears." He sounded almost regretful, and I wondered if he was thinking about his father. "But I must leave you to fret over the mystery yourself. Filling people's minds with suspicion can be useful. That way, there is not as much room for them to hatch plots of their own. The menagerie should provide plenty of upheaval soon."

Ware's talk of witchery haunted me. Familiar mismatched faces filled my mind, the easy, everyday fellowship that often filled these walls. Protectiveness flooded through me, potent and unexpected. "Buckingham has no power here."

Ware started to turn away, then paused at the door. "I almost forgot. There was a bit of business I was to conduct in regards to you. The queen herself has intervened in your behalf, compelling His Grace—or should I say me?—to make exhaustive inquiries as to the fate of a particular soldier: John Hudson."

My pulse leapt. "You have news of my brother?"

"You will be gratified to learn he fought bravely. He saved the life of one John Felton, though Felton came away grievously wounded. His hand was rendered useless, yet he has the temerity to request a commission as an officer. It is true that other officers have continued to serve after such a wound. You only need one hand to wield a sword. But Buckingham did not wish to be reminded of the debacle at the citadel. When the duke denied Felton, the man spread it about that the duke had not paid his men."

"I have enough coin to spare some for John."

"You would have to cast the coin into the ocean. Your brother John is dead, tossed in some French ditch with five thousand other poor souls."

My lungs burned. John? Dead? Ware had known it the whole time he had baited me. Had I already known it as well, deep down in places beyond reason? "I must speak to the queen," I said. "Get permission to ride to Oakham. Someone must tell my mother and father."

Ware arched the brow over his good eye. "I had not known you were so devoted to Master and Mistress Hudson of the shambles. Everyone at court spoke of your ungrateful behavior when your father came to visit."

I clenched my jaw. "My father and I do not agree on much, but he has been in ill health ever since the press gangs took my brother. This news of John's death will be a terrible blow."

"To lose the one son among three who is neither a freak nor a bookish coward must be devastating. Your eldest brother was meant to inherit the shop John Hudson has worked to bring to fruition these thirty years. The coward would rather do anything except wield your father's good cleaver."

"Samuel is no coward."

"Only time will tell. Your brother is proof that one cannot always predict how hardy a seedling will grow when one thrusts it into the right soil," he said.

It chilled me, Ware speaking as if he had seen my brother recently.

Ware walked to the table, flicking one of the hoops Rattlebones held for dogs to jump through. "I would not count on Her Majesty's allowing you to travel to Oakham, despite your family's loss."

"Why would she not?"

"It is uglier beyond the palace gates than you might imagine. I travel the roads every day in my labors for the duke. Do you know how many people would love to kill Buckingham? Even the survivors he brought back from France are wrecks of men, starved, maimed, humiliated by their defeat. Every man who died has a family and a street where they were well known, a village they belonged to. Every man has parents, brothers, and sisters or uncles who would see it as a badge of honor to assassinate Buckingham for using their loved ones as fodder for his military vainglory. The queen is hated as much as the duke because her brother is the king who outwitted our forces. Rumors have wings, as you know. They roost in the brain and such trivialities as truth have no power to root them out. They say the French knew how to evade Buckingham's blockade of the harbor because Henrietta Maria passed intelligence on to her brother."

For a moment, I wondered if it could be true; then I dashed the disloyal thought aside. I said, "You do not believe that."

"Don't I? You would be astonished at people who can be convinced to take part in intrigues: some for coin, some for excitement, and some for a sense of power. Many for a cause they believe in. Of course, there are less congenial reasons. Coercion is sometimes a regrettable necessity. But then, those who resort to such measures believe that the end justifies the means."

Ware smoothed a wrinkle from his sleeve. "Whichever the case, there is none other like you in ten kingdoms. Everyone who saw you would know Jeffrey Hudson, the queen's famed Lord Minimus. No. Her Majesty would not be wise to permit you to wander outside your gilded cage. Better to send word through your brother Samuel. He seems the sort one might wish to find on the doorstep if one must receive ill news. A court fool might be tempted to make someone laugh."

"I do not find my brother's death the stuff of jests."

"I could carry a letter to Samuel if you like," Ware offered with a thin smile. "I take a tender interest in educating the lower order and am intrigued by what I hear of his tutor. I would like a chance to ask Master Quintin where he learned the tutor's art. Such a gifted man should be cultivated."

I thought of Samuel's master, his kindness not only to my brother but to Phineas, as well. *Our Lady has a special fondness for lads, I think.* Quintin's dangerous words rose in my memory. The last person I wished to visit the booksellers' was Uriel Ware.

"I will get word to Samuel myself."

Ware gave a slight bow. "As you wish. My condolences on your brother's death. Yet, I can't help but be grateful he saved Felton. Felton and I spent several summers together when we were boys. We sat together at Bible meetings until our arses went numb. Our mothers were distant cousins, you see, and after my mother left the Villiers's service, she naturally sought family."

Ware turned his face away, something almost wistful in the cast of his mouth. "Goodwife Felton tried to do right. At night, I could hear her reading parts of the Bible to my mother—the bits about God's love and having one without sin cast the first stone. But my mother liked those stones in her hands. The power a vicious God gave."

Ware adjusted his eye patch. "Ah, well, at least having my sins laid bare to the other Puritans on the village green was more comfortable than Tyburn was."

"Tyburn?"

"My mother liked to take me to public executions there to show me what happened to the wicked. She took the Bible very seriously. 'If your hand offends thee, cut it off.'"

"Not very far-thinking of God," I said. "Most of the world would have no fingers if people followed it."

Ware arched the brow over his good eye. "One does often puzzle over what compels men to become heroes. I would imagine your brother grew reckless because of you."

The words stung like the lash of a whip. "Because of *me?*"

"Your brother would have had to find a way to prove himself worthy somehow, with the famous Lord Minimus in his family. Must have been a blow to his pride. It is the kind of thing that pushes a man into heroics."

"Why should John have had to prove himself against me? I have risen to this station through no merit of my own. I was born this way. I was forced into the queen's service."

"But you have made the best use of the opportunity. You are a very clever man."

"If I were, I would have found a way—" I stopped at the last moment. But Ware knew what I was going to say. That I would have thought of a way to escape Buckingham's toils.

I turned, stalked to the fire. I felt Ware watching me.

"I prefer to deal with my brother's death alone," I told him.

"Death must be dealt with, as must the shame of a defeat like Buckingham's. Much of England is half-mad with grief and outrage. The tiniest wellplaced nudge can push someone over the edge of reason." He looked away, and I wondered if he was picturing his mother smashing the dragon stones. The empathy I felt for that boy was drowned by the thoughts Ware had planted in my head about my brother.

"You'd know just how to apply that nudge," I said. Had he not managed to push me into places I did not wish to go? Dark places where I wandered now, accompanied by John's ghost.

I heard noise outside the door, a babble of voices, each person trying to talk over the others. Little Sara and Robin, Boku and Rattlebones tumbled into the room in wild disorder, a reluctant Dulcinea herded before them.

"Go sit and I will put a salve on your blistered foot," Sara was saying. When they saw Ware and me, they seemed ready to sweep me out of the man's company, as well.

Dulcinea gave Ware a defiant glare, then crossed to the chair as far away as possible from where Buckingham's man and I stood.

"I can see that my presence here is causing Mistress Rope Dancer some distress, so I will take my leave." Ware made a slight bow. "I hope I have been of service to you, friend Jeffrey. It was no easy feat, unearthing the fate of one butcher's son from a list of five thousand casualties"

"You are not my friend." Why did I say it for the menagerie to hear, undercutting the excuse Ware had given for his visits to me? Was it worth taking such a risk to warn them Ware was not to be trusted? The man adjusted the ribbon of his eye patch with long white fingers.

"It is an old tradition, this impulse to kill the messenger who brought bad tidings. I do not take offense, but, rather, offer my condolences and trust that our friendship will prove strong enough to survive this momentary breach. My offer stands. I am still willing to take a letter to Master Samuel Hudson, informing him of the death of your brother."

I heard Simon's gasp, Sara's muffled cry of sympathy. It made the cutting edge of John's death keen. I fought to keep my voice steady.

"I do not want your help."

"As you wish. Good day, Jeffrey. Until later, my fine freaks." He bowed one last time, then exited the chamber.

"Jeffrey," Goodfellow said. "I am so sorry. To lose a brother . . ."

"To find out about it from that dreadful man!" Sara exclaimed. "I wish there were something we could do to soften your loss."

Only Boku and Dulcinea were silent—the magician impassive, the beauty's eyes swollen.

I stood, rigid as my gaze skimmed each face. Ware's words about upheaval to come haunted me. Hatred needed someone to blame. The outcasts this chamber sheltered would be easy for the ignorant to demonize, a perfect place to strike at the queen. Or what better way to distract ill attention from Buckingham than to make the menagerie into devils? Boku slipped a bundle of dry herbs from his sleeve and set it alight with the nearest candle. A sweet, haunting smoke curled into the air. He began to chant, throbbing words from his distant land.

"Snuff out those herbs!" I snapped. "You must not do such things where men like Ware might see."

Boku's hand stilled, the blue smoke coiling like a snake around his arm. "I call your brother from the dark to help his spirit find its way home."

What could I say? It did feel darker now that John's life had been snuffed out. It was so strange. Before I learned that John had gone to fight in France, I could have told you every act of brotherly injustice he had perpetrated against me. After I learned that John had sailed, I remembered kindnesses: the way he would shoulder his way through a crowd, feigning impatience as he strode in front of Samuel and me. John's broad shoulders sliced through the press of people like the prow of a ship, cutting a path for us to follow in his wake. With all those memories in my head, all I could think was that I had never thanked him.

My chest ached as I wondered what it must've been like for him—the proud, swaggering youth who had been leader of our pack of brothers for so long. Had it hurt him to see shy Samuel going off with his tutor, the world of books and philosophy and science opening before him? Had it bothered John to listen to the village world he had once ruled marvel over my going to serve the queen? For the first time since Father announced he was selling me to the duke of Buckingham, I wondered what it had been like for John to be left behind.

Boku's voice drifted to silence, the smoke still curling its sweet, forgetful magic through the air, calming me, even if I did not wish it to.

"Jeffrey, you are not the only one that man distressed," Sara scolded under her breath. "Ware upset Dulcinea, as well. Look at her! She's whiter than ice. She didn't need anyone to put strain on her. She's already missing her marks when she performs."

Dulcinea did look haggard as she stared into space, seeming not to hear a word we said. She had appeared wan and miserable for months—when her mood was not soaring so high above everyone else's that she might as well have been an ocean away.

"How has Ware upset her?" I asked, but Sara only shook her head.

"No one knows. She's scarce had two words to say to me of late."

"About that letter to your brother," Simon said, "Robin and I have business in the city tomorrow. Goodfellow has secured a commission for a miniature some smitten gent wants to pass to his lady love, while I must make a trip to the docks. Boku claims if I can provide him with the appropriate herbs and stones from the Indies, he will be able to dose Mitte with some medicine that will keep her from going into fits. The poor bitch has not been right since the falcon struck her at the Carlisles' hunt. It will be simple enough to deliver a letter to your brother on our way."

Sara drew near, pressing a cup of wine into my hands. "Drink this," she urged.

I took a long swallow. "I am going to my chamber," I said. "Ask Will to join me there when he is able."

"He'll have to finish his duties," Sara said, "but I know he will hurry as fast as he can. He'll be as sorry as we are. If you want to talk before he gets here, any of us would be happy to hear about your brother."

"Sometime later," I replied, managing to squeeze the words from a throat suddenly raw.

I forced myself to my feet, started toward the door. Pug shrieked like a mewling infant, outraged that I had forgotten to give him a treat.

Dulcinea poked her head up from where she was lying on a divan, her beautiful face contorted. She flung a slipper at the creature. "Quiet that monkey or I will suffocate it myself! I cannot bear such wailing!"

Simon hurried over to scoop up the frantic monkey before Pug strangled himself with his tangled gold chain. "Pug behaves this way all the time," he grumbled. "Why get upset now?"

I did not stop to find out Dulcinea's reason, but I passed her on my way to the door, saw her head bowed, hands clapped over her ears. The rope dancer was crying. I wanted to do the same. Cry for John and all the things he would never do. Cry for my mother, who did not know she would never serve John the welcome-home meal I'd imagined her planning for so long. Cry for my father, who would lose the one son who had not disappointed him.

TWENTY-ONE

.

I did not know how long I slept, only that I awakened to the warm span of Will's hand draped across my shoulders, a heartening cloak of friendship. I dragged my head up from where I had pillowed it on the table, the letter to Samuel half-finished, the ink now dry in the nib of my quill, ruining that pen. I had been too weary to take up the penknife and sharpen another.

"Jeff, lad, Sara told me the fate of your brother. I am that sorry I never got to meet him."

"I'm glad you did not."

I saw Will start at the edge to my voice. I tried to explain. "I would have filled your ears with all sorts of tales of the wrongs he had done me, every trick or slight. I kept a hoard of brotherly wrongs stored up over all these years. Samuel was my good brother, my kind brother. The one I shared everything with. The pair of us against the world from the time our parents shoved us into the little bed in the loft. While John—John got his plate filled first. Got his own bed, near the fire. John got clothes made of whole cloth woven new just for him. Samuel and I—we got breeches patched together from whatever our mother could snip from around the places he wore through the clothes."

"I suppose the eldest is a marvel because he is the first. But your parents have other sons. My mother saved most of her love for the babe of the family, the child of her autumn years."

"Who loves a child who is a freak of nature? What mother loved any of us best? They feared us, recoiled from us."

"Sara's mother loved her so much, the miniature Goodfellow painted of her is like a talisman. Sara touches it whenever she is grieved or frightened or lonely. Robin Goodfellow's mother saw his talent and sat with him on the doorstep of a great artist until the man took Robin in to paint his backgrounds. Robin surpassed the master and came to the attention of the queen. My mother loved me best of all my brothers, no matter how tall I grew. She told me if my head pierced the clouds and my legs grew taller than any tree, I would still be her babe."

"My mother feared she would be burned as a witch because of me. It could have happened. It still might. If I'd been a weakling pup, my father would have drowned me."

"Did he ever say so?"

"He did not have to. He would trade my life for John's without a moment's thought. Especially if he knew . . ."

"Knew what?"

"Ware said John rushed in to save that man's life to make himself a hero, to match me in importance. It is my fault John is dead."

I wanted Will to leap in with hot denial. Will folded his giant paws. He stared down at his knuckles, his voice low.

"Men do what they do for their own reasons, Jeff. What do we know about the workings of your brother's mind? What little Samuel told you? That John walked into the public house on his own legs. That he drank more than his wits could handle. Once he set foot on French shores, well—perhaps he was driven by some imp of envy at your fame. Or perhaps he was driven by friendship. There are brothers born from the same womb. There are brothers we choose as I chose you."

"Will . . ."

"Only John knows why he charged in when he might have held back. John and perhaps the man whose life he saved. You must make peace with what *is* and not tear yourself apart over what *might* be. God does not blame you for things you cannot help."

I sucked in a breath so deep, it hurt my chest. "I did not love John. Not as I love Samuel. I did not love John because he was tall and strong and brave."

"You are brave. I saw your courage at Tyburn. I saw it the day the queen shattered the glass with her hand. You faced the wrath of a mob that might have trampled you and, later, a king who could have cast you into prison for going to the queen's defense. Any father—any brother would have been proud of you. I was."

My throat ached.

"Tell me about John."

I did. I told Will everything. I told him how John lifted me into the branches of trees so I could climb. I told of the day some neighbor lads dared me to walk the fence rail penning the dogs that were to fight that night. I had fallen into the pen, but John had yanked me out. He'd cuffed me himself, but he carried the scar from a bite meant for me on his left hand when he'd sailed to France.

"I never told him thank you for saving me that day."

"Hard to thank someone after they hit you."

"I needed hitting. It was a stupid thing to do, walking on that fence. I knew before I began."

"There are times we cannot help ourselves. We do things even when we know better." Will gave a wry chuckle. "Jeffrey, I know I am not a clever man."

"You are doing well with your writing. With more practice—"

"Time is coming you'll hear plenty of people call me fool."

My hackles raised quick as one of father's dogs. "I'll make them regret it if they do."

"You'll think me one yourself. As for Archie Armstrong—well, I cannot imagine what he will have to say."

"Tell me, Will. What is this about?"

"I am to be congratulated. You see, I am getting married."

"Don't tell me one of those sweet serving maids you cluck over like a mother hen is going to take you to the altar."

A red tide rose up Will's throat, coloring his face clear to his bushy brows. "I am marrying Dulcinea."

"What the blazes? Why would she—" I bit off the hurtful words. "Damn it, Will, you know I do not mean to wound you, but I cannot help but—"

"Act as though I'm the Kraken and she's Andromeda? If my best friend behaves thus, what is the rest of the world to think?"

"I just . . ." What could I say that Will Evans did not already know? That he was an ugly man and she an exquisite beauty. That he was grave and kind and serious, and she had no more weight of soul than the gauze she wore. That he was rooted as a mountain to the ground, while she was insubstantial as light, drawn to all that glittered. I remembered the night I had overheard Dulcinea and Will arguing, his worries over the nosegay left at her door by some other man's servant. Dulcinea, defiant, demanding to know why she should not have a rich man and all the pretty things he would give her—even if it were just for a little while.

There could be only one reason for this unexpected announcement. "Dulcinea is with child," I said.

"She says she has only to ask and the father will give her a house and coin. But even if that is so, the king would turn her away for loose morals. She would never perform in the palace again. How could she endure that? All the comfort in the world could not make up for losing the finest audience in the land. If I claim I am the father and make her my wife, I believe I can convince Their Majesties to overlook her indiscretion."

"That may be so, Will, but this is not some practical bargain you are striking. Do not pretend it is. You are in love with her."

"Is it that obvious?"

"Only to anyone who is not blind. Has she claimed she will give up this great lord who fathered her child?"

"I did not ask her to."

"What are you going to do? Watch her flit hither and yon to his bed? It will make you miserable."

"I know I am not the kind of man to inspire a beautiful woman's passion. But I will love the child. Perhaps the mother's love will follow."

"If it does not?"

"It is a risk I am willing to take."

I wanted to shake sense into him. I wanted to shield him from the hurt I could see barreling toward him. But no one—especially not one small as I—could move Will Evans once he took a stand.

"Say something, Jeff," he urged.

"She does not deserve you," I grumbled under my breath, figuring Will's ears were too far above me to hear. I should have known better.

"I will not allow even you to speak ill of my wife." He looked so solemn, I could not resist tweaking him.

"What are you going to do? Challenge me to a duel?"

"You know I would never."

"I can aim a pistol as well as many at court, and astride a horse, I am tall as most."

Will surrendered to humor. "You could blindfold me to even the odds," he said.

"To be fair, you should blindfold *me*. I'm the smaller target. You're broad as a house. I could just wave the pistol in your general direction and I'd be bound to hit you somewhere."

Will chuckled. "With all those fancy lessons you've been taking—horsemanship, shooting, sword fighting—you could best me in about anything."

"Except honor."

Will started to protest, but I waved it away. Instead, he asked, "Will you stand up as witness for me?"

It might give me one last chance to talk him out of this rash action. Perhaps I could understand John's recklessness in France the better for Will's plea.

"Fine," I said. "I'll stand up for you. If you wanted me to, I'd follow you to hell."

"Is that how you think of marriage?" Will asked.

"I do not think of marriage at all," I said with a stab of bitterness.

Evans grinned. "I believe Sara would like to change your mind—much to Robin's frustration."

"She will find me a very stubborn man."

Will grew quiet, and we sat in companionable silence for long moments, listening to the crackling of the fire. Will was the one who broke the hush at last. "If the babe is a boy, perhaps we can name him John, after your brother," he said. "Would you like that, Jeffrey?"

"I would rather you name him William." My voice caught. "For the most honorable fool I've ever known."

TWENTY-TWO

•

I did not bother going to bed after Will left to begin his duties. Instead, I wandered past the sleepy night watch and slipped my letter to Samuel under Simon's door. Who could say what time Rattlebones, Goodfellow, and Boku would set out on their errands? I wanted to be certain word of John's death reached the rest of my family as swiftly as possible. Put an end to their agonized waiting. I hoped the tale of his heroism in saving John Felton would soften Father's grief. Courage in battle—be it with dogs or with men—was what the elder John Hudson valued most of all.

I thought of life in Oakham as it had once been. Four stools for us children drawn up by the cottage hearth. Ann darning the holes John was forever wearing in his stockings, Samuel practicing tunes on his whistle, Mother stirring something in the kettle.

I pictured John rubbing grease into the new boots he was so proud of. Even Father, lounging in his chair, was in an expansive mood. His dogs had acquitted themselves well in the ring the night before. The duke and his guests had shown their delight by being generous with their coin. Father was promising to buy my mother a new apron, Ann a ribbon for her hair. He never would make good on such presents. We all knew it. The coin he'd meant to use would be sucked away by some necessity or spent on some risky scheme like the one that had eaten up the funds he'd gotten for selling me. But in the warm glow of the fire, the *possibility* of ribbons seemed enough.

It was good to remember life had not *all* been ugliness at home. Now, though, the cottage in Oakham could never be whole. John's stool would always be empty.

I swallowed hard. Was there a stool in Heaven? Boots to keep out the rain? I wondered if Samuel's tutor could tell me.

Thoughts of Heaven drew me to the Queen's Chapel. I knew Samuel would want me to pray for John's soul. I could add a prayer for Clemmy, whereever he was, as well.

Not so much as a trickle of rose in the sky hinted the sun would rise as I entered the chamber that inspired such outrage among the king's Puritan subjects. They wanted to strip the priests of vestments, the altar of chalices and crosses, the windows of stained-glass pictures that glowed like jewels when sun slanted through the leaden panes.

No music to help spirits take wing. No candles to drive back darkness. I did not grudge them their own choice to live that way, though I did not understand it. But it was beauty that comforted my grief now—that and the memory of a woman whose loveliness reached even deeper.

I had accompanied the queen to Mass every day since I had come to serve her. But I had spent the time I should be praying staring at the triangle of skin where the queen's curls parted to bare her nape. I would imagine how that skin would feel under my mouth if I were tall enough to lean over and kiss her. While John suffered, I knelt here in comfort, wondering if the queen's hair smelled of roses. Had John ever smelled anything so sweet? Had he ever done what I had only dreamed of? Taken a woman off to some secret place and bared her breasts?

Fornication was a sin. Yet ominous as hell might be, there was something desert-bare in never making love to a woman. Not a quick animal coupling, the way I imagined Dulcinea's fine man with soft hands had bedded her. But the way Will Evans would make love to his wife, if Dulcinea ever had the wit to appreciate his worth. A beloved one driving back dark so you could never again be alone.

Was that what I had come here to pray for? Will's marriage? John's stolen caresses with a village lass? Some end to my own loneliness? I could not touch the queen. Better to pray that Charles Stuart might realize fortune had given him something far more precious than a throne. He was the man who had the right to win Henrietta Maria's love.

I crossed to an arch at the right of the altar. Inside the niche, Samuel's beloved Virgin stood in a golden pool. Her bare feet trod upon a snake and a crescent moon. Her blue veil framed a face that seemed to hold all the sorrow in the world. She was a far more artfully carved image than the Virgin hidden beneath the floorboards in Oakham, yet in the strange, shifting shadows, it was the widow's Virgin I saw.

As I folded my hands, I heard a quiet rustle at the rear of the chapel. My fingers tightened in irritation. The last thing I wanted now was platitudes from a priest. I closed my eyes, fiercely determined to put such a wall of concentration around myself that the intruder would not dare disturb my prayers—prayers that had degenerated into bitter orders that God make this person leave me alone.

But the click of heels drew nearer. The scent of roses wafted to me. A lake of satin pooled around my right side, enveloping me in a woman's skirts. I opened my eyes and saw the pale outline of a Valois nose, teeth pushing the red curve of a top lip out just a trifle too far for conventional beauty. The curls, which I knew took hours to position in perfect ringlets upon the brow, had rebelled and tumbled this way and that in beautiful disarray.

"Majesty," I said in surprise. "I did not expect to find you here. It is still so dark."

"The chapel is usually empty at this time. The duchess of Buckingham and I often steal away from the other ladies before our day begins—with Sergeant Evans to guard us. But when I saw you, I commanded Kate and Sergeant Evans to wait outside. I wished a few moments alone to speak to you. Perhaps we could withdraw?"

Wistfulness filled me, knowing that she would hesitate being alone with any other man save her priests. But to Henrietta Maria and the rest of the world, I was even less of a man than the priests. A sexless toy to be petted, fretted over, and ignored by turns.

She rose and so did I, leaving the chapel to enter a small chamber where Will Evans and the duchess of Buckingham flanked the door, near enough to hear should Her Majesty need them. Will had shown me even more consideration, managing to engage the duchess in conversation so that she was turned away from the queen and me.

"Jeffrey," Henrietta Maria began, fiddling with the cross at her throat. "This war between my brother and husband has cost so many lives. Now, Will Evans tells me that your brother died in the siege."

"So Master Ware tells me. It is ill news, but at least now I know what happened to John. I would still be waiting to hear his fate were it not for Your Majesty. I'm grateful for your kindness."

"Do not be." She wrapped her arms tight around her middle. Her shoulders slumped. "None of those soldiers—French or English—should have died. I should have been able to prevent the war."

"Wars are not the provenance of queens. Kings are born to conquer; commanders like His Grace thirst for glory. You cannot stop them."

She crossed to the window, traced a diamond pane in the leaded glass. I remembered the day Buckingham had driven her French ladies away, how Henrietta Maria had pounded on the glass until it shattered, how her hand had bled. "I cannot tell you how many times I wrote to my brother, pleaded with him to end hostilities. My husband, as well. But His Grace is right. I failed them both."

I bristled in her defense. "The duke dared say that to you?"

"The duke, my lady mother, my French family. People all over this kingdom are saying it in public houses, in cottages, outside their churches. I am a barren queen. A hated Catholic. A traitor who smuggled letters from the palace to Richelieu and the king of France."

I masked my shock at the confession, knowing what such letters would cost her if they fell into Buckingham's hands.

"There are many who would like the king to cast me off," she said.

"His Majesty never would. He has proven most loyal."

She did not look comforted. "They say that the king embraced Buckingham upon his return to court after the defeat at Ile de Ré. Before all the lords, as if to dare them to attempt to punish Buckingham for the men he'd lost. I wonder if my husband would be so loyal to me, especially if he discovered what my enemies say is true."

"True?" My pulse faltered.

"I did not betray military secrets, but I did promise my brother that I would try to win some concessions if France made peace. The Pope himself advises me now." She rubbed her hands on her arms as if she were suddenly cold. "If I fail this time, I will fail God. My lute master says—"

"Say no more," I blurted out, so frightened, I dared to interrupt the queen. "It is dangerous to speak of such things with anyone. Even me. There are ways. . . . Your enemies might try to make even your most devoted servants betray your secrets."

Her eyes widened, and I wondered if a commoner had ever spoken to her thus.

"Forgive my impertinence, Your Majesty," I said. "I am so deep in grief for my brother that I have forgotten my manners. But I could not bear it should any harm come to you."

"There is only one way I can be truly safe. That is what they all tell me—Father Philip, the Holy Father in Rome, my family in France. But it is not safety I think of when I come to the chapel and light candles, asking our Holy Mother to fill my womb. I pray to have one part of my husband that the duke of Buckingham cannot touch."

I thought of the rumors of sexual liaisons between King James and Buckingham, rumors never proved. Surely the queen did not suspect that kind of impropriety between the duke and her husband. I had to be careful, though, how I reassured her. "His Majesty's fidelity to you is a thing all other wives envy."

"The king can be the kind of husband that brides dream of winning: so attentive and generous and passionate. When the duke was fighting at La Rochelle, things between His Majesty and I grew so much better. Now that Buckingham has returned, everything in the king's life seems to revolve around the duke—more than ever now that Buckingham is so hated by everyone else."

She gave a ragged laugh. "His Grace has even overtaken this time I meant to spend with you. I have spoken far more of him than of your brother. I did not wish to laden you with more troubles."

The hint of shame in her face made my heart ache. "I would take all your troubles on my own shoulders if I had the power."

"I know that you would. I would spare you pain, as well. Just know that I grieve your loss."

She was small in stature. It took far less for her to lean down than it had taken Will to make the same gesture. I had seen her lavish her affection on her spaniels, scooping them into her arms, burying her face in their fur. I had seen her frolic with her maids of honor, giving the girls embraces, as well. I held my breath, scarce daring to hope. She wrapped slender arms around me as she had in my most secret dreams. With infinite sweetness, she kissed my cheek.

I had not really cried for my brother. I wept as she held me and stroked my hair.

My queen.

My love.

The betrayal that would damn me.

TWENTY-THREE

•

Christmas came and went in a welter of confusion—quicksilver emotions sweeping me from dark to light each day. John's death haunted me. Clemmy's disappearance frightened me. The queen's embrace filled my dreams, while Will's betrothal reminded me of all the attentions I would never have the chance to show the woman I loved. I should have known a Welshman schooled in legends of Arthur's court would want to woo his ladywith the courtliness of Sir Gawain. It moved me to see the changes Will made in his chamber for when they were married—how he ordered softer linens so the bed wouldn't chafe Dulcinea's skin, how he got Sara to find a looking glass for the wall—this ugly man who had never looked at his own reflection if he could help it.

He'd neatened his beard and trimmed his wild mane as best he could, but no matter what care he took, he could never compare to the great court gentlemen who still paid attention to Dulcinea every day.

Yet in spite of that, Dulcinea seemed to notice Will's efforts. I was glad to see her smile at him more often, touch him whenever she passed near. Eat with gratitude the fruits and sweetmeats he tucked about our lodgings for her, hoping to tempt her appetite. Only Will and I knew she was still recovering from the sick mornings of those weeks last summer when the babe began to grow. She thought the child would be born in late March. By my calculations, the child had been conceived the month before Buckingham had sailed to France. But Will seemed to have put such thoughts from his mind. Even Dulcinea's belly did not remind him, thickening so little that no one else had guessed her secret.

It felt bittersweet, watching my friend woo his lady while the rest of the palace looked on. It seemed the giant could not go two hours without somebody, from the most pimply-faced scullery maid to the most elegant courtier, offering him congratulations. Even the queen took interest in the wedding plans, one of the few subjects that drove the concern from her eyes. All of England had noted that Buckingham was soaring in the king's favor more than ever.

The queen insisted that her sergeant porter be fitted for a new suit of clothes, and Dulcinea be garbed in something new. It seemed a losing proposition—Her Majesty's efforts to turn poor Will into a handsome bridegroom. Dulcinea would look beautiful alongside my friend if she stood before the priest in a swath of sacking with her hair uncombed.

There were moments when old women embraced Will, their chapped hands cracked and ugly as he was, that made my heart feel too big for my chest. Their rheumy eyes filled with gratitude for his many kindnesses, with hope that he might be happy, with fear that once he wed flirtatious, luxury-craving Dulcinea he never would be.

They must have suspected the truth. But it made me think how let down some people would feel if they believed Will had put a babe in Dulcinea's belly, then married her because the king's strict code left him no choice. I could not decide which reaction was more painful—pity or disillusionment.

But as Twelfth Night came, it was a far different emotion I saw darkening Buckingham's eyes. His recklessness danced along the brink of sanity as he raced back and forth between Plymouth and the court, mustering the fleet that would make another assault on La Rochelle. Buckingham was untouchable now.

As we gathered for our performance, I wondered how many goblets of wine the duke had drained as he waited for the entertainment to begin. What bitter muttering had he overhead? Tales of soldiers billeted in houses on the coast, Buckingham's shattered army spreading contagion wherever they went. Irish troops and Scots were all but naked, enraged by lack of pay. Men who had stormed the citadel ran wild through the towns, many dropping dead in the streets. When people spoke of the horrors those brutish soldiers wrought, they laid that lawlessness at Buckingham's door.

The queen feared the duke's return, as well, her voice trembling as she confessed, "I know Charles loves His Grace more than me. I try not to grieve or feel envy, yet every time Buckingham is near, I can feel Charles's love slip a little more beyond my grasp. Do you think I am a very silly woman?" I could not look her in the eye.

Tonight, I could see the queen's uncertainty. Her gaze, so watchful, so wary as it traveled between Buckingham and the king.

I was grateful when the time came to excuse myself from her side and slip behind the curtain that hid the space where the menagerie would soon perform. Simon held a hoop he would soon set aflame and soothed the dog that would leap through it. Will climbed down the piece of scenery where he'd just checked Dulcinea's rope. Boku sat, cross-legged on the floor, murmuring words, which Pug listened to and seemed to understand.

Dulcinea, garbed in green and blue, swept over to Will and gave him a distracted smile. Will touched her belly ever so gently with the tips of his fingers. I had never seen such pleasure in my friend's eyes.

"Ah, at last I find the happy couple!"

I started at the sound of an aristocratic voice. Dulcinea stiffened and Will seemed to grow larger as Buckingham drew near, his moves a little less graceful than usual, his words a trifle slurred from too much wine. What in the name of God is he doing back here? I wondered.

"I believe I am the only one in the whole court who has not had a chance to wish the lovers well. At least my wife tells me so. She claims that everyone from the queen to the spit boy is overjoyed to see the loyal sergeant porter win such a beauty for his bride."

I could imagine how much it cost Will to be civil. "The duchess is very kind." Will placed his hand on the small of Dulcinea's back ever so lightly. I knew he wished to draw her into the crook of his arm, to shield her from the nobleman, but he did not dare so much familiarity in a duke's presence. "I am fortunate in my bride and in my friends, Your Grace."

"I confess I have encountered one small difficulty mustering the same enthusiasm as the rest of the court. But I am much involved in practical details, fitting out the fleet that is to sail to La Rochelle."

Any other jester would find more opportunities for satire embedded in that single comment than I could count. I could not think of anything funny in this situation at all.

Buckingham smoothed the lace at his cuff. "I cannot help but imagine your bridal night, good sergeant. As men—be they highborn or low— always do. How the . . . ah, mechanism will fit, if you will."

Will's face darkened. "His Majesty would hardly consider such a subject an appropriate discussion for a bride's ears."

"Yet King Charles tells me his own *relations* with the queen grow more satisfying. He may play the prig, but we men are alike—we've a great interest in where we place our cocks, whether it is a king's or a duke's or a giant's. That is my concern, you see. You must not rend our sweet Dulcinea in two. She is not without friends of her own who would take any damage most personally."

Is Buckingham mad? I wondered. Tweaking a giant this way? Or does he think himself invincible? Why shouldn't he, protected as he is by the king and by Will's lesser station?

I could not stop myself from leaping in. "Your Grace need not be concerned with Dulcinea. She has found a far more deserving husband than many a fine lady."

Buckingham looked down at me, his eyes narrowed the way my father's had when he'd come home from the public house after one of his dogs had run from the bull. "You sound as if you have a particular 'fine lady' in mind," Buckingham observed.

"I cannot think of any man in Christendom worthy of Her Grace or Her Majesty."

I wanted the reproach to have teeth, to drive Buckingham back to his place beside his wife. I wanted him to think, for a moment, what that lady was owed. I wanted to drive him as far away from Will and Dulcinea as I could.

"My dear Lord Minimus," Buckingham drawled. "I did not know you were a romantic. A true Sir Lancelot sprung from the Oakham gutter."

I met the duke's gaze, held it. "You were the one who dressed me as the queen of England's knight."

The first notes of music sounded from the loft above us. Buckingham took his leave, and for the first time since he'd approached Will, I was able to draw a deep breath.

Dulcinea raised a hand to her hair, straightening the silk butterfly pinned in the coppery strands. Did her fingers tremble, or was it my imagination?

"I must go," she told Will.

He bent down, brushed her lips with his. "Dance well," he said, his brow furrowed with concern. "Take c—"

Dulcinea interrupted. "Don't say it! It's bad luck."

"I love you," Will said.

She gave him a preoccupied smile, then climbed the ladder and mounted the soaring platform that held one end of her rope aloft.

Ever so graceful, she stepped onto that impossibly small strand that crossed the audience and was fastened above the queen.

A basket hung upon a hook at the far end of the rope, just as Dulcinea had asked when she'd laid out her performance. I had helped Sara fill the basket's cup with the rest of the butterflies Goodfellow had painted when he had fashioned the ornament for Dulcinea's hair. We had cast the silk butterflies into the air time and again in the lodgings, testing to make certain the effect would work as planned. Butterflies would flutter down upon the queen, life-like as if they'd been gathered from a meadow.

I stood beside Will as we watched his future bride dip and sway, her arms like willow fronds, her legs long and graceful, and her bare feet seeming too fragile to hold her.

No wonder Will was besotted. She did not look human, as if one touch would go right through her. A woman no man could catch or hold. Was he afraid that Buckingham might try to?

"You know I've had concerns about you and Dulcinea," I said. "But I'm beginning to think that Sara knows better. Dulcinea cannot help warming to you when you love her so much."

"She smiles at me more often." He grimaced. "Unless His Grace is around."

"Buckingham is a pompous arse," I said. "Do not heed his nonsense."

"It is not *all* nonsense," Will said. "Sometimes even His Grace is right."

"The devil he is!" I cuffed Will in the shin, trying to jar some of that infuriating reasonableness out of him. "I vow, you'd say Judas Iscariot had a point or two worth defending."

"Actually, if Christ's death was ordained by God Himself, someone had to betray—" He stopped. Doubtless for fear I'd hit harder. His voice softened. "I must be careful not to hurt her when I take her to bed, Jeff. I am such a hulking, clumsy thing, while she is made of fairy wings."

I grumbled under my breath, knowing the truth. Fairy wings like Dulcinea's were far stronger than they looked—far less likely to be torn than Will Evan's wide-open heart.

Boku slid silently up beside us. Was the next act his? Buckingham had unsettled my mind so, I could not remember. I set my mouth, determined. I was not sure how I was going to do it, but I was going to find a way to make Buckingham turn his attentions elsewhere. The palace was full of women ripe for his philandering. There was only one lady who had captured Will Evans's heart.

The music quickened, drawing my attention back to the performance. The rope gave just a little, absorbing Dulcinea's weight. Was Sara right? Dulcinea had been missing steps, wavering just a little more than I had ever seen before. The babe in her womb was bound to change her point of balance, her breasts growing heavier, pulling her shoulders forward. I could not imagine any other woman performing as she did six months gone with child.

How long will she still be able to dance upon her rope? I wondered. Will she have the wit to know when it grows too dangerous? She craves an audience's admiration. What will it take to stop her from seeking it out?

I heard a creaking noise, a strange twanging as Dulcinea's right foot bounced upon the rope, her hand catching the basket handle. She dipped one hand into the silken butterflies, skipped one step nearer the queen. My irritation flared as one of the maids of honor caught Her Majesty's attention, drawing the queen from beneath the rope just in time to ruin the effect.

"Will Evans, you must stop this," Boku said. "Something is not right."

"What would you have him do?" I asked in irritation. "Go haul the queen and her lady back to their seats?"

"Now!" Boku said, his voice suddenly strident. "Get Will's lady down."

I saw Will hesitate—a player's instinct not to disrupt the performance. But he sensed something amiss, as well. He barked an order to Simon, then plowed through the courtiers, drawing cries of protest as he tried to reach the far side of the room.

I started after him—to do what, I could not say. The scaffolding above the queen's seat was listing now, Dulcinea struggling to gain her balance. Her arms flailed, turning my blood ice-cold. She screamed. I heard Will bellow in alarm, lunging beneath her as a hideous crack split the air. The structure smashed down, Dulcinea plunging earthward, as if the king's falcon had struck her from the sky.

TWENTY-FOUR

.

I will never know how I was not trampled in that chaos of panicked people, shattered scenery, and tangled rope. I clambered over the maze of up-ended tables and chairs, clawed past whoever stood between me and the far end of the room.

"The queen!" I heard King Charles shout. "Where is my wife?"

"Safe, Majesty!" Buckingham yelled. Relief she had escaped surged through me. I could see Boku and Rattlebones with Dulcinea. No one save me rushed to the pile of planks and rigging that buried Will.

I could see him through the wreckage, his green shirt torn, blood smearing the frayed edge. Slivers of wood could pierce right through a man. I had heard the commanders returned from France say those shards killed more men than the cannonballs that sank the ships.

I clawed off the first plank, calling Will's name. "Help me!" I screamed. "For God's sake, somebody!" Splinters drove into my palm, but I barely felt them.

The pile of wood shifted, and I saw his craggy face, his deep-set eye. "Dulcinea . . ."

"Boku and Simon are with her. She's moving." He seemed to sag, his eye drifting closed. "Goddamn it, Will, for once think of yourself!"

"Jeffrey, leave off."

"The devil I will! You great blockhead! I'm going to get you out of there."

"Not . . . enough time . . ."

I felt as if my heart was ripping from my chest. "Don't you dare die! Try it and I vow, I'll—I'll torment every serving girl I meet! I'll tip over their buckets and . . . and Archie will seem the soul of kindness."

The pile of wreckage shifted. "Not dying. Need to get to Dulcinea. Not time to have you dig me out." The wood shifted beneath me as if an earthquake were hitting the palace. Will—shoving himself up onto his hands and knees with a groan.

"You're bleeding," I said, scrambling out of his way. "You should not move."

"It would take more than this to crack a head as hard as mine. Just the wind knocked out of me and a few scratches."

He pushed to his feet. The rest of the broken scaffolding clattered to the ground. He swayed, dizzy. I grabbed hold of his leg and braced myself in an effort to steady him. He was already staggering toward Dulcinea, dragging me along.

By the time we reached her, he'd gotten his balance. She moaned, her eyes at half-mast, her hands clutching her belly. "Fetch a surgeon!" Will bellowed, wild-eyed. But what medical man would bother with a rope dancer when aristocrats were in need of assessment?

Boku knelt beside Dulcinea, lifted her eyelids, and peered intently into the green depths. "I will tend her. In Spain, they burned books filled with more methods for healing than you can imagine."

"Heathen places!" Rattlebones objected.

"Allow me to work on this girl that she may live. Let these barbarians with their unclean ways care for Dulcinea and she will be dead before she can be your bride."

"Will, this is madness." Rattlebones said. "Why should you trust this man?"

"The Spaniards did burn medical books not written by Catholics," I said. "Called them works of the devil. People say the same thing about us."

Will stared into Boku's black eyes, his mouth curved into a frown.

"If you care for Dulcinea, will she be all right?" he asked.

"*She* will be." Boku gestured to the dark stain spreading upon the gauzy fabric between her legs. "Some things are not meant to be."

Will sucked in a shuddery breath, tears filling his eyes. "Can I move her?"

"Away from here, where I can help her."

"Easy now, love," Will soothed as he scooped her up. "I've got you safe."

Dulcinea twisted against him, cried out in pain, and went still. For a moment I feared she had stopped breathing, but her chest still rose and fell as he carried her through the halls to his chamber. He laid her on the big bed with its bridal linens.

No one spoke of propriety as he undressed her to her shift, slipping one of his big shirts over her head as a nightgown. Boku glided in and out like a shadow, applying poultices, pouring physics down her throat. Will kept vigil, changing the rags Sara brought him to catch the flow of blood.

"How could the accident have happened, Jeffrey?" he asked as he sat beside the bed, holding the unconscious Dulcinea's hand. "I checked the rigging three times this morning to make sure it was secure. I had Inigo Jones and Robin check it, as well. Dulcinea even practiced upon it. You know how particular she is if there is even the slightest question about the rope."

I stole out a little later to see what remained of the scaffolding myself. I was not the only one. Inigo Jones was examining the broken wood, grumbling under his breath as he showed the piece to a cluster of people beside him.

"Master Hudson!" the surveyor of the king's works called when he saw me.

I gave a light bow of greeting. "Master Jones. Did you find what made the tower fall?"

"Some flaw in the wood. I might have missed it had Master Ware not discovered the evidence."

Two of the onlookers turned, Buckingham smiling while Ware observed me with his single eye. "I am glad Ware's years of examining my ships for seaworthiness could be of use to the palace," Buckingham said, all traces of drunkenness gone.

"How is Sergeant Evans?" Ware asked.

"He claims not to be hurt. He wouldn't tell us if he was. He'd rather sit by Dulcinea's bedside."

"Ah, the rope dancer," Buckingham said. "How is Evans's lovely bride?"

I gave the duke a cold stare. "She suffered a grippe in her belly. It is over now, but there is still much bleeding."

Did the duke actually look grieved? "I am sorry for it. It would have been a beautiful . . ." His voice tracked off. "Performance," he finally said.

"That performance might have cost the queen her life if that little maid had not drawn Her Majesty off to one side," Ware said. He nudged the basket that had held Dulcinea's butterflies with the toe of his boot.

Jones frowned. "What I am trying to understand is how this wood split so cleanly. Across the grain."

"I've heard you talk to Will about the wood you choose for support beams," I said. "It does not split against the grain unless the design is flawed. Could you have put too much weight on it?"

"There was nothing wrong with my design!" Jones roared, and I saw real fear in his face. "Do you think I'm fool enough to make such a mistake with the queen sitting beneath the frame?"

My stomach knotted at the stark truth. But if Jones had designed it and Will had inspected it, what could have caused the disaster? Unless someone had sabotaged the structure on purpose. If so, who was the target? Dulcinea? Or the queen?

"I beg pardon for Jeffrey's ill manners, Master Jones," Buckingham said. "He was briefly a member in my household and should know better. Master Ware, could you escort him back to the Freaks' Lair and remind him of lessons you attempted to teach him when first he came to Burley House?" The patronizing bastard laid a hand on my head. I jerked away.

"Oh, I've learned many lessons at your hand!" Rage blinded me. But at the last instant, Samuel's face flashed in my mind.

Ware stepped between the duke and me. He gave me a shove toward the door. "Friend Jeffrey, let us start refreshing our lessons by recounting the respect due a peer of the realm." I started to balk, but Ware said beneath his breath. "You will not like it if I grab you by the collar and heave you out of here like one of your father's dogs."

I swore under my breath and strode out of the room. Ware thrust me into the nearest empty chamber. He grabbed me by the arms, lifting me up to eye level. He thumped me against the wall. "What do you think you were doing in there? Stirring up mischief where there is none!"

"The queen could have been killed! Will Evans almost was! And Dulcinea—"

"It sounds like the little bird is lighter by the weight of a bastard."

"You knew about the child?"

"Of course I did. She's lucky she fell!"

"You mean Buckingham is lucky! Did he want to get rid of the child? Is that what this was all about? Or did you sabotage the beam for him and get carried away? Did he mean for the whole structure to fall, or was that part accidental?"

Ware slapped me so hard, I saw stars. "Buckingham could have you killed for spouting such rot, and I would not blame him. What does Buckingham care about fathering one more bastard?"

"He's plotted against the queen from the moment he placed me in Her Majesty's service."

"Intrigue is one thing, regicide another! The queen is Buckingham's greatest ally at present, the only thing standing between the duke and disaster!"

"That's ridiculous!"

"It is the truth!" Ware said. "At least with her around, people can divide their hatred between the French queen and the duke who squandered the fleet!" I clutched my aching jaw, hating that Ware was right.

"You want to do something useful? Discover who would benefit most from an accident befalling the queen."

"Lady Carlisle wishes to become the king's mistress," I said. That much was true. But could the countess be involved in this debacle? I could see her employing love potions, or plotting masked seductions. But toppling a scaffold seemed more a scheme that a man would think of.

"Whatever her role, no woman would know how to sabotage that scaffold," Ware said, and I squirmed at the feeling he could read my thoughts. "It was too complex an undertaking to keep it standing, seeming safe. Everyone knows that Will Evans scrutinizes any structure you curiosities perform on."

I sorted through the guests at the performance, those closest to Lucy Hay. Sir Tobie Matthews, the toady who adored her, countless other men dazzled by her beauty and charm. James Hay, the upstart Scotsman she had suffered two years in the Tower for and had defied her terrifying father to wed.

"What about the earl of Carlisle?" I said. "If he was willing to ally himself with his wife's lover to gain power, would it not be even more valuable to pander her to the king?"

"Even if Carlisle was subtle enough to conceive of such a plan—which I doubt—he is too indolent to carry it out. He has friends who might help him, but they are inept, as well. No. This plot nearly succeeded. We are seeking a more cunning foe. You were behind the stage. Is it true that black devil knew something was going to happen?"

A chill ran down my spine. They needed someone to blame. Who could be more convenient than Boku? The mysteries of the "black devil's" cupboard had given rise to wild imaginings even in the menagerie. I thought of Boku's care of Dulcinea, the falcon's trust in him, the way he had saved Mitte. Most of all, how Pug had clung to the illusionist the first night I had taken Boku to the menagerie's lodgings.

"We all knew something was wrong," I said, lying. "The rope was wobbling."

"I see. No member of your band of freaks would play assassin, but the most powerful noble in the land would murder the queen in such a crude fashion? Buckingham could have the queen aboard a ship to France before nightfall if he wished it. You want to help the queen? Get back to your Freaks' Lair and do what you do best. Creep about listening behind arrases and pry through people's letters. I'll find you when the duke has need of your services." Ware strode from the room, sure I would obey.

I stalked out of the palace to the master of arms the queen had secured for me. I did not wait for a servant to open the door. I burst in to where he had just finished a lesson with one of the earl of Carlisle's pages.

I saluted my master. "En garde." The page sniggered as the master turned to fight me. I flung myself into the battle more fiercely than ever before.

No one was laughing by the time I put down my sword.

⌘

Exhausted, drenched in sweat, I made my way to Will's chamber, intending to tell him my suspicions. He sat at Dulcinea's bedside, his great paw engulfing her hand as Boku fed her sips of some foul brew.

I slipped up beside them. "How is she?" I asked.

"She will be fine in time," Will said, his smile a broken thing. "She must rest and do as Boku tells her."

I thought of Ware's suspicion of Boku. "Has she seen a surgeon?"

"Butcher, more like!" Will snarled. "Poking at her until she screamed! But Boku put a stop to it. Dulcinea's resting now. All will be well."

"It will be, Jeffrey." Dulcinea let her head fall back to the pillow and gave me a wan smile.

My throat felt raw. "I am sorry about the baby."

"She is better off this way. Will promised he would see my baby girl buried in consecrated ground even if he's damned for it."

"Will would have made a fine father," I said.

Her beautiful eyes drifted closed. "But I would have made an abominable mother. Maybe worse than mine was—and she was a witch indeed. That is why I am glad about what happened. The one thing the surgeon and Boku agree on is that I will never be able to have children."

"Will won't care about that," I said. "He loves you."

"I know." Tears ran down her cheeks, dampening the pillow. "But you see he does not need to marry me now. I can stay free like the butterflies."

I looked at Will's face. Had he looked so stricken when I had entered?

"Is that not right, Will?" she asked.

"Yes. A butterfly should be free. But I will be here if you need someplace to land." Will let go of her hand.

I stood there, uncertain what to do. He had burdens enough to bear without me adding my suspicions. I had no solid proof, nothing except the hard knot of instinct beneath my ribs. But he was the queen's sergeant porter— the shield that stood between Henrietta Maria's private quarters and the outside world, a world that had become far more dangerous.

I could keep my secret for a few days while he dealt with Dulcinea's rejection, but if something happened to the queen, I would never forgive myself. Worse still, Will Evans would never forgive me.

I tapped him on the arm, nodded my head in the direction of the door. Will followed me into the dimly lit corridor.

I looked the passage up and down. When I was satisfied no one was listening, I drew him into a nearby alcove. A marble bench built into the wall looked out a window over the garden. I patted the seat and Will sat down. I climbed up onto the surface and stood, thinking how easily the pair of us had made adjustments to our difference in size. This would be a harder gap to bridge.

"What is it, Jeff? I need to get back to Dulcinea."

What would be the point of reminding him Dulcinea had just jilted him? I sucked in a deep breath. "Will, I've been down in the hall where they're clearing away the wreckage. The timbers splintering might not have been an accident. Master Jones and Uriel Ware are attempting to find out what happened."

I could see Will's temper smolder. "You think Buckingham did it to rid himself of the child?"

"Dulcinea told you Buckingham fathered the babe?"

"She did not have to after that outburst of his just before she performed. She was shaking before she even stepped onto the rope! I'll kill him with my own hands if he hurt her."

I imagined Buckingham's throat crushed in Will's grip, Will squeezing while the duke's face turned a satisfying purple. How would His Grace like the sensation of being totally helpless in someone else's grasp?

No, even the pleasure of seeing my nemesis thus would not be worth the price of involving Will. Retribution would be terrible if a commoner—one of Her Majesty's freaks—murdered a peer of the realm. What payment would the king demand in forfeit for his favorite's life? Just imagining the repercussions made me cringe. No wonder the most hated man in England was still alive.

"I know you would do whatever it might take to punish a coward who endangered Dulcinea, Will. But Buckingham? Why should the duke want to kill her?"

"To get rid of the child."

"There are easier ways. Every cunning woman has a potion hidden away for just that purpose."

"Who else would want to harm a rope dancer?"

"If this wasn't an accident, whoever is guilty of this thing did not care whether Dulcinea lived or died. Her weight on the rope was just the trigger that set their trap in motion. The target the villain meant to kill was the queen."

⁂

The fire on the hearth drew orange fingers into a pile of embers and sighed its dying breath as I crept into the menagerie's deserted lodgings. The room was cluttered with the reminders of the performance that had gone so wrong:

snippets of ribbon Sara had woven around the handle of Dulcinea's basket, peacock feathers Boku had refused to wear in his headdress. Rattlebones had thrust the plumes into the ear of a cyclops mask left from some other masque, making Will laugh. I wondered when my friend would laugh again.

The glow from my lone candle snagged on the blue-green of a discarded butterfly. The beautiful creature Robin had painted lay crumpled on the floor, its wing wrenched off by Pug in the hours before the performance— before the disaster that had likely been designed to kill the queen. Was it possible that the plot had originated here, as Uriel Ware feared? Had Boku shared wine and warmth and companionship with Will and Dulcinea all this time, then sent her up onto that rope to fall?

I had been placed in the menagerie to cause trouble for the king and queen. How much more trouble could an illusionist like Boku stir up if some shadowy master or mistress commanded him to? What secrets might be hidden—not only beneath the velvet gauntlets but in the strange patched-together cupboard he had brought with him from the Carlisles'?

I made my way to the corner Boku had made his own. Shelves and cases for the accoutrements of his illusions ranged up the wall. Some of the small doors in the structure were locked. But among the skills I had practiced with Ware was the ability to pick locks. I drew what looked like a bent toothpick from a tiny sheath inside my boot and began the tedious process of tripping the lock's tumblers.

My upper lip grew moist before I heard the click of the mechanism opening. I grasped the knob that opened the door, pulled. A book copied by hand was in the first cupboard, a swooping heathen script written on pages made of some sort of animal hide. Five pointed stars and beasts were drawn in the sky. A crude rattle of some kind was painted with a man-bird with gold-rimmed feathers, wings spread like those on the king's gyrfalcon. A small alabaster urn was capped with the face of a dog. Small bones were laid out as if to form a living creature, and for an instant I wondered if Boku were attempting to bring back the dead.

As I moved to search the next cupboard, a voice behind me nearly made me piss myself.

"You must search more carefully than that if you hope to find what you seek."

I wheeled around, to find Boku just behind me. My throat went dry and I wondered if he had been hidden in the shadows the whole time. Still, I tried to lie. "It was open when I came in and I could not quell my curiosity. Perhaps Pug is cleverer than we knew. He must know where you hide the key."

"There is no key. The locks are there so I will know if someone has been prying in my things. The bird engraved on the bottom of the lock reverses itself if anyone tampers with my case. There are many such precautions built into the chest. It is based on a puzzle box stolen from an ancient grave. The thief died three days later, a tiny insect bite turning putrid. They claim the box was cursed."

"You're not dead."

"I spoke to the spirit who cursed it, promised that if it gave up its secrets to me, I would return the box to its rightful place. Perhaps the old one understood that sometimes we are forced to desecrate things we do not wish to. Or perhaps there was no curse at all." Boku reached over my head and plucked up a chain hidden between the book's cover. He tugged, and a flat disk set with crystals thinner than glass slid free, swaying gently as I watched it drink in my candle's light. "I shall tell you an illusionist's greatest secret: People see what they are told to see. Instead of a grief-mad old woman muttering to her long-dead child, they see a hag coupling with your Christian devil. Instead of a gyrfalcon trained to seek a morsel doused in an elixir that strips it of its will, they see a gyrfalcon tamed to a stranger's hand. And you—a court fool so tiny, he is thought to be no more powerful than Pug upon a chain."

"What are you?"

"One who travels paths my masters set my feet upon. As you do."

"Why did the countess of Carlisle place you in the royal household? To harm the queen?"

"What do you believe?"

"No." The herb scent grew stronger, and I wondered if Boku was drugging me as he had the falcon.

"The countess is, perhaps, the greatest illusion I have ever encountered." He reached over my head and pressed something I could not see. A drawer slid out and he plucked up a blown-glass vial with letters painted upon it. I recognized that they were Hebrew, like the page Samuel had shown me in his lesson books at the Saracen's Bane. "Now, I have retrieved what I came for, I must return to Dulcinea and use it to ease her pain. We will not speak of this again." He gently shut the cupboard door. It was not until he was gone that I realized I had never heard the magician speak so much. Yet he had never asked what I had been looking for.

～～

I tilted with phantoms long into the night, trying to unearth motives and strip away disguises that might conceal whoever had meant to harm the queen. Did Henrietta Maria realize that the nightmare that had terrified her since childhood had come true? A shadowy assassin stalking her, rigging the scaffolding to crash down upon her?

I could not shake the image from my mind—some faceless predator milling around during our rehearsals, listening as we pieced together our dances and acrobatics, timing them to the music. Had the villain talked to Rattlebones about the spaniels or examined one of Goodfellow's painted butterflies? Or had the malignant force stood beneath Dulcinea's dancing rope to help Sara retrieve the butterflies as Dulcinea scattered them time and again in an effort to perfect the effect Jones had designed.

It chilled me to imagine calculating eyes attempting to gauge where best to weaken either the wood or the performers. I wondered if the queen's attacker knew that in some ways a botched assassination attempt would be a more effective torture for the queen than its success. A swift, crushing death would put an end to this horrendous speculation, be in many ways more merciful than the terror of looking into every face that came your way, wondering if it was possible that the next person you saw was plotting your murder.

How do you protect a queen from an assassin? I wondered, feeling helpless. I could not even decide what reaction I *hoped* to see in her or what I could do to make her safe. On one hand, I wanted her walled inside a tower, where no malevolent force could reach her. I wanted her fearful enough to put an end to her secret trips to the chapel while the rest of the palace slept. Even with stalwart Will guarding her, it was not safe. An enemy who got wind of her ritual need only hide behind an arras or statue, then cause some sort of commotion Will would have to investigate. When his back was turned, it would be easy enough to strike.

I wanted Henrietta Maria to regard every member of her household as if that person might be a spy. Trusting no one would be wisest. After all, she could not trust me—a man who would gladly die to save her, if Samuel's future had not hung in the balance.

Yet to see that relentless dread in Henrietta Maria's eyes—to have her grow suspicious of those who loved her most . . . it would be like denying her sun and air. She had been luminous from the first moment I saw her. To extinguish that light was more than I could bear.

It was not as if Henrietta Maria was new to the dangers of court intrigue. She'd cut her milk teeth upon it. The struggle for power between her brother the king, before he was of age, and her mother, whose regency was struck down—that battle had marked her childhood. She'd witnessed Richelieu's Machiavellian plotting, the de Guise family grasping whatever power they could steal. She was far more learned in the ways of this deadly political game than I could ever be. As I entered her chamber, it was obvious she refused to allow the accident to shake her courage.

The queen had dressed in a gown of defiant crimson. She was determinedly going about the business of her day, yet there were dark circles beneath her eyes and a tiny cut on her brow.

I pulled my gaze away from it and made my formal bow. "Majesty, forgive me for my tardiness. Are you well?" I asked. "Does your wound hurt?"

She touched her fingertips to the scab. Her wedding ring glinted. "I did not even realize I had been cut until dear Lucy dabbed her handkerchief upon it and I saw blood. I was too horrified at what befell the rest of you. I have never seen such a thing happen before—scenery crashing down! If I had been in my seat at the time—" Her voice hitched in unease. "His Majesty said I might have been killed!"

"I will never be able to thank your maid enough for drawing you away. It is the first time I have ever been grateful for someone in an audience ignoring a performance the menagerie worked so hard on."

"Little Jane had just received a marriage proposal and was all aflutter. His Majesty may knight her suitor. Their eagerness to share their joy likely saved my life." The queen managed to smile. "King Charles was most attentive to me after the accident. He came to my chamber to make certain I had not suffered from shock. His Majesty said His Grace had his man Ware inspect the wreckage. They insist the accident was not Master Jones's fault. The mistake must have originated with one of his workmen. Such a fine architect as Master Jones could not possibly have botched such an insignificant construction."

"I believe the duke has used Inigo Jones often on his own projects. Some might call his interest selfish, but I agree with His Grace on this point. I do not think Master Jones is at fault."

"Someone must be held accountable! I might have been killed. How many others were injured?"

"I do not know."

"You were not hurt, Jeffrey?"

"A sliver jammed into my palm, but that was after the collapse of the scaffold, while I was pulling timbers off Will."

"How is Sergeant Evans? And Dulcinea? She fell so far. It quite chilled my blood to hear him cry out to her. When the scaffolding landed upon Sergeant Evans, I feared the worst."

"Will says his head is too hard for a few blocks of wood to damage him. Dulcinea is resting. She has lost—" I stopped, remembering the babe's existence had been a secret. "She has lost a lot of blood. She will need to rest. But the surgeons are taking good care of her."

"Tell her she must get well. I expect her to be beautiful by her wedding day."

I wondered if it was my place to tell the queen that there would be no wedding now. Was it not up to Will to do so? Yet something about the way the queen had spoken made me want to spare Will the pain and embarrassment of explaining the situation.

"There is not going to be any wedding."

"Of course there is! The gown is all but finished, the feast planned. I even convinced the king to give the bride away."

I drew in a steadying breath, trying to remember this behavior was not her fault. From the moment of her birth, she had had countless servants racing about to satisfy her every whim. Yet this was one time Her Majesty must be disappointed. "You have been kind to take such an interest in the menagerie's affairs," I began. "None of your curiosities deserves your generosity more than Sergeant Evans does."

"I admit that when I first heard of the attachment, I was startled. Yet I've grown very fond of the idea. Now it is a matter of necessity. After what happened last night, the whole court needs some pleasure to distract them. What better than a menagerie wedding?"

"Majesty, there are so many wonders at your fingertips—the finest performers in the world clamor to entertain you. Will and Dulcinea have chosen not to wed. I beg you to accept their decision and seek your diversion somewhere else."

"You seem most eager to see this wedding canceled. Is it possible that the Countess Carlisle is right? She claims you have a *grande passion* for some lady."

My cheeks burned.

"Even Kate Villiers believes it. By the look upon your face, I think it must be so. Who is this woman who has won the heart of my Lord Minimus?"

"Did not the greatest knights in Arthur legends serve their lady in secret? I would do the same."

"Is it Dulcinea you love? Is that why you wish me to let this inconvenient breach in the betrothal stand?"

She was such a mass of contradictions: tender and kind, imperious and selfish. Childlike when she romped with her spaniels and played with her maids of honor. A woman, praying for babes to fill her arms and secure her husband's love. Did she have any idea how fragile this world of hers was?

What would she do if I told her the truth? Said that I did not love Dulcinea but that Will Evans did. That Dulcinea would break his heart if she wed him.

"You do love her!" the queen exclaimed. "I can tell by the anguish in your face."

I did not deny it, only whispered, "Please, Majesty, do not let her marry him."

I thought the queen would keep my supposed love secret and the whole wedding nonsense could fade without any more upset. I should have known better. Three nights later, while I sat in the menagerie's lodgings Will stormed in, his eyes burning under his shaggy brows.

"Jeffrey, what the devil have you been up to? Telling the queen you are in love with Dulcinea?"

"Her Majesty said it. I just didn't contradict her."

"Is it true?" He looked so stricken. I could feel his sense of betrayal, feel his horror at the thought of all the times he had spoken of his love for her, how that might have wounded me.

"No."

"Then why would you let her believe such a thing? The queen's ladies have spread it far and wide. They claim that is the reason the wedding has been canceled. Because the queen will not allow her precious Lord Minimus to suffer seeing a beast like me wed to his lady."

"Does it matter what they say?"

"The truth always matters."

"The queen intended to force you to go through with the wedding—as if it were a game to entertain the court. I could not let that happen."

"Do you think I would have minded? Game or no, Dulcinea would have ended up as my wife. I could have protected her. Even Buckingham would not have the courage to torment my wife."

"I do not think there was any 'tormenting' going on at all where Buckingham and Dulcinea were concerned. I do not want to wound you, Will. But it is the truth. She would have gone right on chasing after her fine gentlemen. Three years from now, when you met a woman who could make you a decent wife and take care of you for a change, that woman would have been beyond your reach. Dulcinea would have made you miserable, and you know it."

"It was my life! My choice! I did not ask you to meddle in it!"

"Dulcinea did not want to marry you! You heard her, Will. She's a fool for not realizing what a fine man she'd have as husband, but then anyone who climbs up on a rope that high in the air and dances on the thing is not the smartest woman God ever put on earth!"

"Damn you, Jeffrey!"

"I did this for your own good," I said. "You are my best friend. You said yourself—'the brothers we choose.'"

"Not anymore."

"You don't mean that."

"I do. For once, Archie Armstrong is right. At some point you stopped being one of the queen's pets and began to be one of *them*."

"That's ridiculous."

"As ridiculous as a hideous giant marrying the most beautiful woman he ever saw?"

"You're not hideous!"

"Did you stop to think what it will be like for me? Not only having the wedding called off but knowing that everyone in the castle believes that it was because my best friend used his influence with the queen? Got her to cancel the wedding so he could have a chance with the woman I love?"

I kneaded my temples, my head aching. "Is that worse than having people think you put a babe in her belly? You with all your fine honor? Or, more humiliating still, that she got pregnant by some nobleman and married you because she had to if she ever wanted to perform at court again? Will, whatever those fools think or say, it doesn't matter! We know it's a lie."

"You say that as if the truth doesn't matter at all."

"It doesn't. Not here. They do not even know what the truth is anymore. The king would paint Buckingham as a hero—hand him another fleet to squander. Let him make officers of fools with no more military experience than Pug while good soldiers rot. The court will kiss Buckingham's arse while waiting for a chance to stab him in the back. I wish they'd get on with it! Stab away!"

Will's eyes narrowed, his voice suddenly quiet, cold in a way I'd never thought to hear. Not when he spoke to me. "Why don't you kill him yourself? You're grand at stabbing men in the back."

Will turned and stalked away.

He will see reason, I told myself later as I scribbled a report to Buckingham, documenting the loss of Dulcinea's babe, the medical skills Boku employed, and my role in getting the queen to cancel the wedding. In time, Will's temper will cool, I thought. I went out to the stable and slipped to the place where my saddle was kept. I slid the message into its accustomed place.

It was gone when the queen went riding the next day. Will Evans's anger was not.

TWENTY-FIVE

•

June 1628

I thought I had known all there was about being an outcast, but it wasn't until the menagerie quietly froze me out that I realized how comfortable I had become in their company, how enveloped in the daily warmth of friendship, of family.

I should have expected some reaction as the rumors spread. No one could help but notice the rift between Will and me. We had always been together when not at our duties. A footman claimed there was even a public house that had called itself the Dwarf and Giant in our honor.

The whole court seemed divided: Archie jubilant at the triumph of our darker angels, Sara wounded, Simon reproachful, Goodfellow chill and distant. Boku said nothing, only watched with his fathomless dark eyes.

Dulcinea frustrated me most of all, accepting my supposed adulation as her due, as if she found it easy to believe best friends would betray one another and go to war over her favors.

The courtiers found the triangle of giant, dwarf, and beauty titillating—the stuff of legends and romances. Of course, they cast the beautiful and witty Lord Minimus in the hero's role.

Scorn for the courtiers built up inside me, honing new edges into my jests. Sometimes when I dealt one, I could see the wounds I left, and for the first time I understood Archie's satisfaction in seeing all that aristocratic pride bleed. What did the courtiers know of true worth?

Only the queen seemed to understand my loss. Her affectionate caresses rained down on me more often than ever before—each feather-light touch of my lady's hand Heaven and hell.

As May gave way to June, the king wrestled with his own challenges, summoning Parliament in a bid to raise funds for Buckingham's return to La Rochelle. On the seventh, the whole court was afire with ill tidings for the king.

Archie stormed into the lodgings, furious. "Have you heard the news? A crew of malcontents—Eliot and Pym, Thomas Wentworth and Prynne—they've forced the king to sign something called the Petition of Right."

For days, the Commons and the king had been locked in a battle of wills, the queen distraught over their impudence to the king. I had heard her disbelief, her outrage, her longing to defend her husband.

"What does this petition say?" Sara asked.

"It is not so terrible," Rattlebones reasoned. "The petition just assures we keep the rights won in the Magna Carta. Look at what Buckingham has had the king doing—forcing loans from the wealthy, imprisoning men like Wentworth if they refused to pay."

I ventured out of my self-appointed exile in the chimney corner. "Parliament denied the king money for ships," I said. "Funds no king has ever been denied before. I know Wentworth and the rest denied the funds to spite Buckingham, but once they did so, the king had to find another way to fill his purse." It was the queen's argument, one she'd laid forth with tears of frustration.

Though Rattlebones deigned to speak to me, his tone was chill. "The king will not make the Commons more amenable to his requests by imprisoning its members and denying them habeas corpus. He will not make people love him by declaring martial law in areas that disagree with him or billeting soldiers in their houses whether they are willing or no. The petition sets forth in law that His Majesty can do none of those things."

"Let the great ones tussel over such matters," Sara said, disliking the conflict. "It has no effect on us." As the others turned back to their ale, shutting me out once again, I wondered if she was right.

When July came, the court split, the queen's household leaving for Wellingborough, the king and Buckingham for Portsmouth to ready the fleet.

No one in England wanted to go back to war. Not that the king heard the protests or heeded his wife's loneliness. He stayed with the duke at Portsmouth, overseeing ships and supplies, demanding more coin from subjects who struggled as crops failed.

While the two men played at war, the queen was left on her own, breaking my heart as she waited for His Majesty to ride from Portsmouth to visit her bedchamber.

The holy site at Wellingborough was said to give aid to barren wives desperate to conceive. I accompanied the queen to the site and held her hand as healers applied ointments that burned and fed her tisanes and foul-tasting concoctions to stimulate the womb. She was so brave, so hopeful, my Henrietta Maria. She was drawn to every babe she saw, be it one of the village folks', lambs in the fields, or the puppies Mitte brought forth again with so much ease.

One night, I found her weeping in the garden, having sent all her ladies some distance away. I went to her, dared lay my hand upon her hunched shoulders. "My dearest lady, what grieves you so? I cannot bear your tears."

"What if I can never have children?" she cried. "I pray and pray, and yet perhaps the people who say Charles should send me back to France are right. I am useless if I cannot give him a prince."

"Never say that, Majesty."

"It is true! But I had rather die than be sent away. I love Charles, Jeffrey. So much."

"The fleet will sail," I said, trying to soothe her. "Then His Majesty will return to your side. With Buckingham gone, all will be well. Boku says that discord can clench the womb shut like a fist. Once Buckingham has sailed, you and the king will be able to relax in each other's company."

"Do you think so?"

"I am sure of it."

I was not the only one. In mid-August, Uriel Ware arrived at Wellingborough, bringing news of the king. I stood at the queen's side as Ware bowed before her.

She read the missive, then raised her eyes to him. "Master Ware, we have heard grim tales even here. The Protestants in La Rochelle are living skeletons. Buckingham must sail if he is to save them."

"His Grace and the king are reluctant to have the fleet embark until it is provisioned with more supplies than they could need. But after what happened on the duke's last foray, the sailors are mutinous devils, refusing to risk boarding Buckingham's ships even with such generous provisions. They stalk the streets of Portsmouth, some of the curs even daring to chant 'death to the duke.'"

"A French king would never suffer his subjects to do such a thing. His Majesty is too forgiving."

"He sends out guards to nab the ringleaders, but the crowd protects them. I've never seen the like of it. Even the most staid housewife would shield one of the duke's detractors in her flour bin and give him her egg money to aid his escape."

Why would they not? I thought. Many women in the port town must have lost loved ones in the failed assault. Sending more of their men with the same commander must seem the height of idiocy.

The duchess of Buckingham grew even more drawn at Ware's words. "Master Ware, how does my husband fare under such strain?"

"His Grace does not let rabble interfere with his endeavors."

"Would that I could do something to shield him. I beg you tell him I love him. Tell him I commend him to God's care."

Lady Carlisle muttered wryly, "Kate prays so often, I begin to fear that God might obliterate His Grace just to get some peace."

The queen and the rest of the ladies gave Lady Carlisle quelling looks. "Lucy, I know you do not mean to be unkind," Henrietta Maria said.

"Oh, I do, Majesty, though I am sorry afterward. It is because I do not get enough sleep. It makes me grow so surly, my husband will not even approach me."

"If only other women's husbands would follow his example," I muttered.

Lady Carlisle's sneer grew more pronounced. "This from the paragon of virtue who attempted to steal his best friend's betrothed."

My cheeks stung. "They were not married, Your Ladyship. Unlike—"

"Jeffrey! Lucy!" The queen clapped her hands to silence us. "I cannot bear this bickering. Can you not see how upset the duchess is? How worried I am? If you wish to snip at each other, withdraw to the far side of the room, where no one can hear you. The duchess and I get news of our husbands without such trivial blather!"

I moved to where Pug, the monkey, sat, pulling crystal prisms off of a candlestick. Lady Carlisle stood her ground. "Majesty, I consider it my duty to tell you that Kate scarce sleeps anymore. She keeps us all awake with her pacing in the middle of the night."

The duchess looked away. She swallowed hard. "I do not dare sleep, for fear what might happen to my husband. I have dreams. . . ." She stopped. Shuddered.

"I know what it is to miss a beloved husband." The queen's mouth softened. "You must go to His Grace, Kate. Join him for whatever time is left before the fleet sets sail." Her eyes grew sorrowful. "I do think there are times that the king would like to sail with him. Have an adventure as he and His Grace did when he was still a prince. Do you know, the first time I saw my husband, they were returning from Spain. Charles fancied himself in love with the Infanta Maria. When diplomatic negotiations stalled, he and the duke raced off to woo her without King James's permission."

"The escapade did not end well," Ware said.

"I danced for them—one of the entertainments my brother planned for their visit. I remember stealing peeks at the English prince, thinking what sad eyes he had. He never had gotten over losing his brother. I remember wondering what it would be like to have such a prince do something so reckless and romantic for love of me. Perhaps that is what every woman wishes for."

"His Majesty is an English Protestant who married a French Catholic. That was judged a gamble by all of Europe at the time."

It was becoming more obvious all the time that both factions thought they had lost the roll of the dice. The alliances the royal marriage had been meant to forge had shattered in French eyes and in English. The Pope's desire for England's return to the fold had proved a futile one. France and Spain had combined their might, and not even the hint of a child had appeared to root in the queen's womb. Yes, there were plenty who claimed the king had made a bad bargain. I would not be counted as one of them.

"Wedding Her Majesty makes the king the most fortunate of men," I snapped.

Ware straightened his cuff. "I only speak frankly because I know of Her Majesty's propensity for playing cards beyond the limits of her purse. Gambling for coins and trinkets is one thing. A generous friend can cover Your Majesty's excesses. Overreaching the limits of a kingdom's patience is another. It is important the queen know of the discord her husband faces in his kingdom. There are rumors Your Majesty has enticed the king to attend Mass."

"Her Majesty has done no such thing," the duchess of Buckingham protested.

Henrietta Maria touched a gold cross at her throat. "No. But I wish that I could. If I could make the Church whole again, it would unite the opposing sides. The fleet would not have to sail, the Huguenots would not have to starve, and my brother's troops would not have to fight. I cannot understand why people find that a wicked hope. Perhaps our children—His Majesty's and mine—will not have to face this divide. If . . . *when* God grants us babes."

"I have heard that God grants worthy prayers," Ware said with a bow. "Now, if Your Majesty will excuse me, I will not waste any more of your time. I have vital business to attend to for the good of England."

"I have a charge for you, as well," the queen said. "Master Ware, you and your men will deliver Her Grace safe to her husband."

"I am certain the rest of His Grace's men will be happy to escort the duchess. I am not returning to Portsmouth. My lord has charged me with some other business to see to in his absence. The duke's other interests do not cease needing attention because he has gone off to war."

"I hope you may spare a little time for Jeffrey before you leave. The misunderstanding between Jeffrey and Sergeant Evans has caused them both pain. It helps to talk such matters over with a sympathetic friend."

I tried not to let Her Majesty see me wince. "Master Ware is far too busy for such confidences," I said, my vulnerabilities stripped bare.

Ware tugged at his neck cloth, his mask of calm seeming to slip a fraction. "Jeffrey, you are mistaken. Tonight, nothing could be more important than private conversation with you."

The queen smiled at both of us, pleased with herself. Resentment filled me. Could she not sense my reluctance to speak to Ware? "Go with him now, Jeffrey. I wish to reread my husband's letter and write back to him. Tell him how fervently I pray for a child. Kate," she said to the duchess, "you will want to set your servants to packing. You may have my silver-lace hat with the green feather. It would look well on you." The duchess curtsyed, then all but tripped on her way out the door, feverish eagerness in her eyes.

Ware bent down to place a hand on my shoulder, almost empathetic. "Shall we go to your private chamber?" he said as we exited the room. "I have heard you are not welcome in the menagerie's lodgings anymore."

"There is no point in avoiding my fellow curiosities. We perform together nearly every day."

Besides, I could always find work to seem absorbed in, while staying close enough to listen to the other members of the menagerie talk. I knew that Sara had a toothache but that Robin's kindnesses were making her smile anyway. Boku was working on a new illusion. Rattlebones was having trouble training the fluffy white dog he had gotten from Phineas when he'd delivered the letter regarding John's death to Samuel at the Saracen's Bane. I knew that Will Evans still watched Dulcinea, love heavy in his eyes.

"You will not wish your fellow curiosities to hear what I have to say."

I took him to my chamber. Griggory struggled up, sleepy, from his seat by the fire. "Master Hudson, may I serve you and your guest some wine?"

"The gentleman will not be staying that long," I said. "Leave us."

Griggory gave Ware that shrinking look so many did when faced with ugliness or a scar. He bowed, then did as I bid him.

I crossed my arms over my chest. "Well? What fresh misery does your master hope to stir up? Shouldn't he be concentrating on how to get all those mutinous soldiers onto ships bound for France? It's like herding animals into the shambles to be slaughtered. Doomed creatures are smarter than one thinks. They get a whiff of blood and terror and they panic."

"You say that with some satisfaction."

"It would not grieve me overmuch if His Grace met with a few well-aimed hooves. From your tone in our earlier discussion, you would not be overly sorry yourself."

"What His Grace lacks in wit and subtlety he makes up for in boldness. He loves England."

"England does not return the duke's affection."

"There are those who would if they knew the perilous stand His Grace is willing to take."

"What, pray tell, is that?"

"The king is eager to return to his wife's bed."

"Her Majesty is beautiful, spirited, and she loves the king very much. It is an intoxicating brew few men would be able to resist."

"Do you imagine yourself drinking that brew in His Majesty's place? I've seen the look in your eyes when Her Majesty touches you—and she touches you a great deal. I wonder what commoners would think if they saw it."

"They would wish to fondle me also, as if I were her monkey or dog. The queen does not see me as a man, and you know it."

"She does feel quite passionate about the king, however. Absence, combined with that unfortunate accident with the scaffold, has made the queen dearer in the king's eyes, as well. His Grace says that her letters to the king are quite moving."

"You are prying into the king's letters?"

"His Majesty shares them willingly with his beloved 'Steenie.' Charles Stuart is quite in love with his wife. Of course, he will always love Buckingham more: the nobleman who took 'baby Charles' under his worldly wing when Charles was a callow youth."

I thought what Will Evans's friendship had meant to me when I arrived at the palace, clumsy and uncertain in a world I did not understand. Buckingham had helped Charles through a similar ordeal. It forged a bond that Charles would never break, a tie with his father, his brother, his coming of age. Each time Charles had leapt to Buckingham's defense, he had built a higher wall around the two of them. To surrender Buckingham now would mean those battles he had fought on his favorite's behalf were meaningless, that the king had been a fool.

Ware broke into my dark musings. "His Grace no longer hopes His Majesty will be swayed by even the most accomplished of Lady Carlisle's charms."

"His Majesty prefers gold to dross."

"The countess would not appreciate such an unflattering appraisal. The duke fears that if this newfound closeness between Their Majesties results in a child, it will be disastrous for the kingdom. You must prevent that from happening."

"What do you want me to do? Leap into bed with them and kidnap the king's cock?"

He drew out a packet and forced it into my hand. "His Grace has found a more subtle method. You will place this powder into the queen's wine. That will prevent anything from taking root in her womb."

I recoiled from Ware's suggestion. "Your master might have used this preventative with Dulcinea."

"He did not consider her important enough to waste such a mixture on. This particular blend will make the womb wither like an old woman's." I felt sick as Ware continued. "His Grace wishes to make certain that Henrietta Maria will never have a child."

I paced the chamber, wishing to get as far from Ware and the ugliness Buckingham proposed as possible. "Do you realize what the queen has been enduring here at Wellingborough? The hours she has spent praying for a child? The cures she has attempted? She is breaking her heart over the fact that she has not been able to give her husband a prince. She is afraid if she does not, they will send her back to France."

"Buckingham is counting on it. Once the duke is rid of the queen, he can slip Lady Carlisle into place as the king's mistress. When another queen is found to replace the French disaster, His Grace will make certain she is a plain, biddable creature who will pose no danger to Lady Carlisle's influence over His Majesty."

I braced myself, Henrietta Maria's face and Samuel's swimming before my eyes. It will never end. The truth struck me. There will always be some new deviltry to do, the price of Samuel's safety growing greater until I can be of no more use. And once that happened? Would Buckingham allow one who knew such dangerous secrets to wander about the court free? It would be easy enough to drop a scaffold on me. There were a hundred ways to kill a man so small. God only knew what these villains had done to Clemmy.

I clung to the memory of Samuel's goodness, the feel of Henrietta Maria's kiss on my cheek. It gave me strength. "No," I said. "I will not do it."

"What?"

"Tell His Grace I am finished."

"That would be a reckless course to take."

"And feeding a queen of England poison that would shrivel her womb is not?"

"You are mired too deep in plots to resist the duke now. He will have you flung into a dungeon where the rats are bigger than you. They gnaw on the flesh of full-grown men when they are sleeping. They would have no fear of you."

"I can only hope I would turn their stomachs."

"Your brother would provide sweeter fare. It is far easier to face such a fate yourself. Harder to see such a fate befall someone you love. It drove my lady mother mad."

"Prison?"

"The Church fathers sent her there after she sliced out my eye."

"Jesus, Mary, and Joseph . . . your mother did that to you?"

The story Buckinghams's women had told echoed in my mind, and I thought of the boy, being dragged away by the mother who had struck his father down, left him for dead. How had she come to turn a knife on her son? I did not want to feel sympathy for Ware, but I could not help it. The knife had left far more hideous scars that his eye, in places where no one could see them. "I pity you."

"Don't. My mother's madness honed me into a tool worthy of the duke. She made me skillful at reading people's tempers, able to guess what action they might take. She made me understand consequences should I fail, which is why I took steps to guarantee that you would do His Grace's bidding." Was there a touch of regret in his voice?

"What steps?"

"Your brother and his schoolmaster are languishing in Fleet Prison."

Bile rose in my throat. "They cannot be! They've done no wrong!"

"Everyone knows the Jesuits tried to blow up King Charles's family. They've spread insurrection throughout England, sneaking onto our shores, infecting everyone they meet."

"Samuel is no Jesuit!"

"His tutor is one of the most dangerous in England."

"I do not believe it! The duchess of Buckingham arranged for Quintin to be Samuel's tutor! Buckingham ordered her to do it."

"When you marched in with your demands that day, it was obvious you were going to prove more troublesome than the duke first expected. This was the only solution to assure that His Grace would have your continued cooperation."

"You bastard! I will go to the king. Tell him everything. The duchess of Buckingham has as much to lose as I do, since she was consorting with Jesuits!"

"Even if you could bring yourself to betray the good duchess, the king would believe she was duped. Jesuits are notoriously cunning. What chance would a woman like her have, matched against a force of such evil?"

Unease prickled my nape as I remembered the duchess's feverish expression the day I thanked her for her kindness to Samuel. I had never seen her so fierce, as when she condemned Buckingham's detractors. She claimed she would do whatever she could to prove Buckingham's worth to those who scorned him. I had pitied her, dismissing the outburst as words spoken in the heat of the moment, never to be acted upon. But what if I was wrong? Was it possible the duchess had knowingly placed Samuel with a Jesuit to provide her husband with leverage to force my hand? Make me sprinkle whatever this hellish concoction was into the queen's goblet?

If that was true, perhaps the kind duchess was more dangerous than the countess of Carlisle.

Master Quintin's image rose up in my mind—his painful hip, his useless hand. The way he had carried Samuel to bed, the courage he had shown saving Phineas from a murderous mob.

"Buckingham has taught me what evil is," I said. "So have you."

"Are your father's dogs evil when they tear out a bull's throat? Or are they just trying to save their own lives? Doing what greater powers force them to do? We are dogs, fool Jeffrey. You and I. Sometimes we even regret the lengths we must go to in the name of our masters. God knows, I do now. It grieves me to tell you that His Grace has taken one step more to assure you will poison the queen's womb. There is a guard at Fleet Prison who awaits a missive from the duke. The minute it is in the guard's hand, the man will go to your brother's cell and cut Samuel's throat."

In that instant, I was flung back into Oakham, saw my father's big hand yank back a lamb's head, bare its white throat. I saw the flash of my father's knife, the gush of blood. Smelled the metallic scent of terror and death. But it was Samuel's throat in danger this time, Samuel's eyes filled with horror. Samuel, knowing, as an animal could not, what was to come. I staggered to the chamber pot and retched.

"You must give me a few days. Even if I decide to do as Buckingham asks, I have to collect myself first. Look how my hand is shaking." I held up the hand, the cross on the ring Buckingham had forced me to wear reflecting the candle's flame.

"Your predicament grieves me sorely, Jeffrey. I have come to have affection for Samuel as I have observed him these past months. He reminds me a little of my father. That is why . . ." Ware looked away, his cheekbones darkening. "I experienced some difficulty over Samuel's letters."

"You stole Samuel's letters?"

"At first I intercepted them under Buckingham's orders so he could gather more ways to blackmail you. Once I had gleaned whatever was of use, I was supposed to return them to Clemmy so that he could deliver the letters to you."

"Then Clemmy was your creature all along?"

"Jeffrey, we both know that His Grace can make decent men do the unthinkable to protect those they love. In the end, Clemmy could not endure the guilt. He took the sister His Grace had threatened, and the pair of them ran off. I traced them as far as Liverpool, but they had already sailed on a ship bound for Ireland. I was not as vigorous in my efforts to hunt them down as Buckingham believes. The Irish are half-mad savages. Let Watson and his sister take their chances there."

Even in light of Clemmy's betrayal, part of me hoped he was safe.

"Why didn't you return Samuel's letters?" I asked.

A pink flush spread across Ware's cheekbones. "Sometimes even the most solitary man longs for some sort of connection. Human warmth. Samuel's faith is so different from the one my mother raised me in."

"If you know what a bright soul Samuel is, do something to help him!"

"I cannot. You see, at the bottom of it all—Protestant, Catholic, Puritan—most churchmen are scrabbling for mortal power, not God. Goodwife Felton, your brother Samuel, and, yes, even the king may strive for goodness. The rest of the world will trample them to gain control."

"Ware, I beg you—"

"I cannot help you. I know things look ill for you now, Jeffrey. But still, I envy you. I do not have your gift for inspiring friendship." Ware cleared his throat. "I will return for your answer once I finish my business. A fortnight should give you time to consider the consequences to Samuel if you should fail to follow the duke's command." He placed his twisted paper full of poison atop the writing box the queen had given me. "This respite is only delaying the inevitable. I am sorry, Jeffrey. But it is time for you to choose between your brother and the queen."

Ware turned and walked from the room.

I paced, half-mad with terror and fury and helplessness. Clemmy was fleeing, God knew where, because of me. Samuel might soon be dead. And Ware? Was he the cold manipulator who implemented Buckingham's schemes, or was he a victim, as tangled in Buckingham's toils and his parents' wreckage as I was?

God, what I would not have given for Will's counsel. I wanted to race to his chamber, beg him to aid me. I knew in my gut that he would. But I could not draw anyone else into Buckingham's trap. The duke was too powerful, the king too blind with love of him, the queen too vulnerable.

I tore through ideas, trying to find some way to cut free of these coils. I crossed to the writing desk, took up the paper cone filled with powder. I wanted to throw it into the fire, but I would need it in the future. I hid the deadly package beneath Will's blotted attempts at the alphabet, pages I had not been able to bring myself to throw away: ghosts of the friendship that had changed my life.

I could not go to my death without telling Will Evans what he had meant to me.

I scribbled a note, folded it before the ink was dry, and dripped hot wax to seal it. I drew off the ring Buckingham had given me and pressed it into the seal.

To Sergeant Porter William Evans, I wrote beneath the wax gobbet that glistened in the candlelight like blood.

I slipped down to the deserted menagerie's lodgings. Pug chattered from the cage Rattlebones had been forced to confine him in so he would not rend Wellingborough's tapestries. Pug stretched his hairy fingers out, tugging at the latch. I had no time to release him now. I crossed to the mismatched cupboard where Boku kept the makings of his illusions. Drawing the lock pick from inside my boot, I tripped the lock's tumblers as I had once before. Opening the doors, I took the supplies I might need: five paper tubes filled with a blend of gunpowder and some other substance that filled a room with smoke; a bundle of herbs he'd used to make his audience drowsy; a tinderbox to light them. From a peg on the wall I grabbed a gray drape softened with gauze. I had seen Boku vanish using such implements, distracting his audience so effectively, he managed to cross the stage without anyone knowing where he had gone. I prayed that when the time came, I could vanish, as well.

I stuffed my contraband into a leather saddlebag, then pulled the letter I had written to Will out of my doublet. I set it at his place at the table. The chair, despite how heavy its timbers, was listing to one side from evenings spent leaning toward Dulcinea. His whittling knife lay beside a wooden horse he had been carving for the child now buried under the rose shrub. He had not been able to stop himself from working on the toy even so many months later.

Grief washed through me as I tucked my letter beneath the knife so Will would be certain to find it.

Forgive me, my friend.

The last lines I'd written pounded in my head like the drums Boku sometimes beat when the moon was full. I strapped on the sword the queen had given me. I stuffed my pistol in my belt and threw a dark cloak over my shoulders. There was only one way to stop the duke of Buckingham from poisoning the queen or ordering his minion to take Samuel's life.

The duke of Buckingham must die.

Twenty-Six

•

I had never ridden through unfamiliar country alone and I had little notion of where I was going. Time and again, I took the wrong road and often I had to hide in the woods to keep someone from stealing my horse when I heard voices before or behind me.

My childlike size, the horse, and trappings, richer than any highway robber was likely to find elsewhere, made me appear an easy target, but I could not reach Portsmouth in time without a horse. I could not assassinate Buckingham without the weapons forged in my size. I could not fail, or Samuel would die.

Yet I had not slept for so long that I did not see the crabbed soldier make a lunge for my horse's bridle until it was too late.

The horse reared, and I might have fallen were it not for the harness built into the saddle. It bruised my thighs as I fumbled for my pistol, my attacker's grizzled countenance a blur before me. I swore as the man knocked the weapon from my grasp.

I thought of Samuel, struggled harder as the man knotted his hand in my cloak and dragged me from my saddle. I struck the ground so hard, black dots swirled before my eyes.

"Release him," a calm voice ordered.

The robber did so with the instinctive obedience of one used to following commands, then cursed under his breath. "Who are you to tell me so?" he snarled.

"Do it, Riggs." There was something in his tone I could not quite understand. "I don't want to have to hurt you." The brigand must have let go of my horse. I could hear hoofbeats pounding away. How would I ever catch the beast now?

"What are you doing here, sir?" Riggs asked. "I thought you'd be with the fleet!"

"The duke of Buckingham decided to pass over me for promotion in order to raise up some son of a nobleman or one of his cousins or such. God forbid an able officer be given command of able soldiers like you," my savior said. "Riggs, I know you are in dire straits. The duke owes me eighty pounds back pay. I can only imagine what plain soldiers are owed. But I cannot let you make war on children."

"I am no child," I said, struggling to my feet.

Both men gaped down at me as I shoved back the tangle of cloak and shook my hair out of my face. "What deviltry is this?" The grizzled man made a sign to ward off the evil eye.

"No devil. I am Jeffrey Hudson, Queen Henrietta Maria's fool."

"Hudson?" my savior echoed. "You cannot be . . . John Hudson's brother?"

I staggered a step, knocked more off balance by my brother's name than by my fall. "You knew my brother?"

"I fought with your brother in France. John Hudson died saving my life." The man extended one arm. His cuff fell back. I could see the ruin of his hand. Something glinted in the sleeve—the blade of a knife.

He followed my gaze. "It is a dangerous road we travel. My hand cannot grip a weapon, but it is strong enough to drive a blade home once I get close enough. I am Lieutenant John Felton."

"I know. The queen made inquiries into my brother's fate."

"You are fortunate. Most families will never know. Your horse must be a league away by now. You can hire men at the next public house to go in search of the animal. That is the only way you will catch your mount. It is a fine one."

"It was a gift from the king." I rubbed my bruised elbow, remembering how the horse had been trained to be first mount to the prince or princess the king and Henrietta Maria so longed for. If I did not put an end to Buckingham, those children would never be. The duke would find someone else to dump the powder into the queen's cup. Someone like the countess of Carlisle?

The whole plan hinged on my having that horse and the special saddle to ride him. I knew I must not only reach Buckingham and kill him, I would also have to race back to the queen, confess everything, and beg her to intercede on Samuel's behalf before I was arrested. I would be a murderer the next time I looked into Henrietta Maria's beloved face. I would never see her smile at me again. Desolation swept through me, mingling with resolve. She would know what vipers had surrounded her, though. It would be worth it. Even if the betrayer she hated most was me.

"Where are you headed, Jeffrey Hudson?" Felton asked.

I considered telling him but decided it was better not to. The fewer people who knew I'd been to Portsmouth, the better. "I have never seen the sea," I said. "Now that John lies across it, it seems the only way I can bid him farewell."

Felton looked away, and I could see the weight of my brother's death upon his shoulders. "You are right to honor him. A soldier who bleeds for his country deserves to be paid the respect he is owed."

We walked together until we reached the nearest inn, Felton telling me of John's exploits in France, and of his own return home: The weary, painful days at his mother's home, trying to regain some use of his hand. It reminded me of what Ware had said.

"Since you have served Buckingham, I wondered if you ever met one of his servants. A man named Uriel Ware."

"Uriel in the duke's employ!" Felton exclaimed with honest astonishment. "It is hard to picture the boy I knew working for a libertine like Buckingham. Especially after what Uriel's mother did."

"What did she do?"

"Made my mother sick for three months afterward. She'd wake up, sobbing. Ware's mother saw him staring at a girl at meeting. Cut out his eye for it. Meant to cut off his prick as well, but my father took the knife before she could finish it."

Horror flooded through me. What had the boy felt? Seeing that knife coming at him? Blinded, bleeding, his maddened mother fumbling at his crotch to butcher him even more? Had she damaged him somehow despite Felton's father's interference? Was that why he loathed women so much?

We walked in silence until we reached the inn.

"Where are you going?" I asked him as we said good-bye.

"To visit my cousin's boy." He adjusted his sleeve. "Lad has an itch to go to sea. I intend to make certain he never will."

☙❧

I hired some men to search for my horse, then watched from the inn's highest window, willing the beast—and my special saddle—to appear over the hillside. When at long last they did so—the horse lathered, the saddle askew—I had to wait for grooms to rub her down with straw to keep the beast from foundering, have the blacksmith repair a thrown shoe, and then wait while a storm drenched the earth.

It was dawn on August twenty-third by the time I rode into Portsmouth, damning myself for the time I had lost. The misfortune with my horse had prevented me from concluding my grisly mission before the duchess arrived at her husband's side. From my hiding place behind a tangle of gorse, I had watched the ducal envoys ride past three days before, the duchess's face just visible inside the coach that jounced in the procession's midst. It seemed cold-blooded to cut down a husband in front of a wife. Yet was she not responsible for linking my brother with the Jesuit who could get him killed? Would she recognize me? I was an easy figure to pick out if one knew me—unless I passed at first glance as a child.

I would just have to hope I could make Boku's illusion work when the time came. It seemed easy enough. I would appear to be some unpaid soldier's child, wandering near to the great ones to beg. I would have the length of fuse lit, hidden in the small metal box affixed to my waist, the smoke makers in pockets in the cloak. When I was near enough to the duke, I would pull the fuse out, light the paper tubes, and fling them under the feet of the duke's retinue. When they exploded, I would dart through their legs, run the duke through with my sword, and then shove my way through the maze of legs.

With just a little luck, I would be able to escape in the confusion.

I dirtied my cheeks, put dust in my hair, and stripped off any fine trappings that might betray that I was not the urchin I seemed. I did the same for my horse, though it was harder to hide his breeding. He was aristocratic by blood. I was a butcher's son.

I found a natural idiot to guard him for me—a hulking fellow with the wit of a lad of seven, accompanied by a terrier with one ear torn off. Only fate had not added these two to the menagerie or to some other noble's stock of fools. Much as I hated to take advantage of his simplicity, I had no choice but to threaten him. Who would believe him when he told them a Fairy King had charged him to guard his magical steed or be turned into a rat?

I left the horse in his hands, then made my way to Buckingham's head-quarters at the Greyhound Inn.

Morning sunlight baked the mud on my face into a tight shell. I looked at the sky, memorized the particular blue, the smell of the salt air blowing in from the sea John had once sailed.

Perhaps someone else's brother would live because of what I was about to do. Surely, with Buckingham dead, the king would put someone more skilled in command.

I had to believe it was so.

I sucked in a steadying breath, picturing what I must do. My weapons master had shown me where to aim to kill an opponent, painted targets on the straw dummy he had hung from a beam in the ceiling. I had driven my sword through those fatal spots marking the heart dozens of times. Would it feel so different thrusting steel through sinew and bone?

Guards stood at the door, deep in conversation. I skipped up to them and feigned an urchin's accent. "Somebody's scritching up the coach the duchess lady come in with they knife." I dug my finger into my left nostril.

The guards looked revolted as I popped my finger into my mouth. They turned, one hurrying off to the stable, the other avoiding looking at me. I darted past him into the inn.

I had barely gotten inside the door when I heard Buckingham's voice and glimpsed his arrogant form, head held high as he barked an order. My hand shook as I slid it beneath the cloak and drew out the fuse. I felt its slow burn, like wicking in a candle. Drawing out one of the cylinders, I judged the distance I would have to travel, the obstacles in my way, the place on Bucking-ham's body I must aim for.

If only that one man would get out of the way. He was moving toward the duke, calling Buckingham's name. What was it about the man that seemed familiar? The drooping hat, the patched jacket . . .

He was right in front of Buckingham now.

I felt the fuse singe my fingertips, fumbled as I tried to touch it to the paper cone.

A scream of agony pierced the air. Blood poured down Buckingham's doublet as he fought to stay on his feet. "Villain!" the duke cried, grasping the hilt of a tenpenny knife and pulling it from his chest.

"Murder!" Someone in the crowd screamed. "His Grace is struck down!"

The assassin turned toward me: John Felton—his useless hand crimson.

My head swam, my body bruised as Buckingham's men rushed to their dying master. I dropped the fuse and crushed it out with my heel.

A woman's shriek from the balcony overhead made the hairs at the back of my neck stand on end. I looked up through the chaos and saw the duchess of Buckingham, who was watching her husband die.

Twenty-Seven

•

I do not know how I got back to my horse, but as I raced back to Welling-borough, scenes kept swirling in my mind: the duchess stumbling down the stairs, gathering her dying husband in her arms. Keening . . . I had never heard such a hellish noise, even in the shambles, where dying animals sounded like screaming children.

Blood had soaked her hands, her breast; a smear of it was visible on her cheek. She had rocked him like one of the babes they had created, fatherless now in a world that devoured the unprotected. "You will pay for this!" she'd cried. "I swear I will make you pay!"

He had not deserved her devotion. He had humiliated her with his mistresses, worried her with his recklessness and his penchant for plotting.

I could not forget her words to Henrietta Maria at Wellingborough. Chilling dreams she'd had. Could those nightmares have been any worse than what had happened in the Greyhound Inn? Sitting in that pool of her husband's blood?

More inconceivable still: John Felton just standing there with hideous calm, announcing to the crowd that he was Buckingham's assassin.

As news spread beyond the inn yard, a sound far different from the duchess's anguish could be heard. Shock, yes, but then jubilation: shouts of triumph, flagons of ale toasting John Felton as hero, not murderer.

What had it been like for the duchess to hear the celebration of her husband's death? Why was it that I could not forget the image of Buckingham she had etched for me in the garden that day an eternity ago—a beautiful, all but penniless youth, thrust by his mother into the arms of a lustful king.

No. I must not think of Buckingham that way. I was glad he was dead. He could not hurt Samuel, could not hurt the queen anymore. They were safe at last. And Uriel Ware? Was it possible he would be released now that Buckingham was dead? Would he finally be able to seek some human warmth beyond stolen letters?

We were free, for the first time since Buckingham had plucked me from the shambles. Samuel's Virgin had granted me my own gift of mercy. Hope built inside me with each beat of the horse's hooves taking me nearer my destination. I did not have to bare my sins to the queen anymore. There was no need to tell her what evil I had done her. I could just say that my brother had been arrested by mistake, then ask Henrietta Maria to intercede for him. She would do it out of love for me, my generous lady.

This nightmare of betrayal and fear and helplessness was over. God help Felton—he would need it to endure the horrors he would face in retribution for Buckingham's death. But the man whose life my brother saved had rescued everything I loved. John had been my unwitting champion—and Samuel's—one last time.

Was it possible that Will might even forgive me? I had poured my heart into the letter I had written, begged his pardon for interfering, for the humiliation he'd suffered, the anguish. Healing took time. I had wished to mend things between us. Maybe now I could.

The queen's chambers at Wellingborough were so quiet, I knew that news of the duke's assassination had not reached her yet. I knew I must make my plea for Samuel before a messenger from Portsmouth could arrive.

Everyone whose path I crossed exclaimed in relief that I had come. The queen had been frantic, they claimed. I would banish that worry now.

I stopped in my chamber, hastily changed, then scrubbed my face free of the dirt I had smeared on it. I did not even stop to cram a chunk of bread in my mouth, though I had not eaten since I'd been at the inn where I'd lost my horse.

Light-headed from hunger, I rushed to the place Her Highness designated as a presence chamber. Will Evans was standing guard, his brow more furrowed than ever, dark circles under his eyes. The moment he saw me, his face lit up.

"God's blood, Jeffrey! Where have you been? Half out of my mind with worry, I was, and so was Her Majesty. Lady Carlisle has been closeted with her for hours, the queen sobbing. Heartbroken, I'm sure, imagining what might be happening to you out there. Mobs murdered Dr. Lamb—a quack Buckingham had dealings with. They're shouting that they'll kill Buckingham next."

"Someone did," I said, so low that only Will could hear.

"Buckingham? Dead?"

"Quiet!"

"How do you know? Rumors spread like fire. You cannot trust them."

"I saw Buckingham die with my own eyes."

"But he is in Portsmouth! What were you doing there?"

"I rode there to kill Buckingham myself."

Color bled out of Will's face. "Jeffrey, tell me you did not. . . ."

"He tried to poison the queen. He nearly killed Dulcinea, and he shattered our friendship. I wanted to kill him. I would have. I had the weapons, made the plan. But just as I walked into the Greyhound Inn, a soldier named John Felton thrust a knife into the duke's breast."

Will looked away. "I imagined myself killing him. Wanted to. Not just for what he'd done—turning a simple girl's head, planting a babe in Dulcinea's womb—but because he acted as if she didn't matter at all."

"He will never hurt another girl again."

"Or his poor duchess."

"The duchess was there, Will. She ran out onto a balcony, saw him bleeding. She ran down the stairs and held him in her arms. The sounds she made—the grief . . ."

"Do you think that is what is causing the turmoil in the queen's chamber? The queen was already distraught over your disappearance. Might the countess of Carlisle have discovered Buckingham's fate somehow before anyone else?"

"She was the duke's mistress, the pair of them locked in intrigues. It's no secret that Buckingham meant her to fill the king's bed." Had Lady Carlisle loved Buckingham? It was impossible to tell. Whom would the exquisite countess ally with now? What would happen to all of the duke's followers? Would Uriel Ware fade back into obscurity, glad to be free?

I pitied Ware now—a man as much a grotesque as those in the menagerie.

The scar where his eye should have been had been carved into Ware's flesh by the hand of someone who should have shielded him, just like the Gargoyle's ghastly smile had been.

Afterward, Ware had stumbled back to the only other home he had known. He'd been twisted, beaten down by the mother who had been supposed to protect him. What loyalty would he feel toward the man who took him in despite the horror of his face? Had he pictured the wrathful God of his mother with each step he took into Buckingham's darkness? Was it possible he'd been as trapped by the duke as I'd become? Not plunging into evil all at once, but inching into hellfire one tiny step at a time.

Maybe I would ask him when next I saw him. We could make peace now that there was no reason for us to clash anymore.

"Jeff, I'm that grateful to see you again. When I think what would have happened to you if you'd killed the duke—"

"The strangest thing is that the man who killed Buckingham knew my brother John."

Will shoved a lock of shaggy hair off of his brow. "Did he now?"

"John died saving Lieutenant Felton's life." I couldn't suppress a shiver.

"Your brother might have saved himself the trouble. Felton will die for sure now."

"John saved Felton's life. Felton saved mine by killing Buckingham before I could reach him. Now I have to find some way to save Samuel."

"Samuel?"

"Arrested and put into Fleet Prison. Uriel Ware gave me the news when he was here."

"What kind of trouble can a bookish lad like that have gotten into?"

"His tutor was taken by the king's pursuivants. Master Quintin is a Jesuit."

"Any fool can see that Samuel isn't one! Jesuits study for years. Have to go to Spain or France or some other Catholic place. That boy never left Oakham until a few months ago. Fleet is a terrible prison—full of contagion and the worst sort of criminals. We've got to get the boy out! The queen will help him, much as she loves you. I'm certain she'll convince the king that Samuel's arrest was a mistake. Wait here. I'll go tell her you've returned. I think she'll be so relieved to see you, she'll send the order to release Samuel herself."

Will gave me an encouraging smile, then went into the privy quarters. I tried to imagine what Samuel must be suffering. He would be so scared. Was he cold? Hungry? Of all the children in my father's cottage, he was the one most likely to get the grippe or ague. He was the one sensitive to shouting, wilting at brutality. Could there be any crueler place than prison for him?

My elbow ached from where I'd struck the ground when the brigand dragged me from my horse. I kneaded the bruise, composing what I would say to the queen as I waited for Will to return. I would fall on my knees before her. Beg.

I closed my eyes. "Please, God. You have to protect him until I can wrest him from his cell. He can't take care of himself."

I heard the heavy tread of Will's boots approaching, their pace slower than usual. I turned to him. What I saw on his face made my stomach drop.

"Her Majesty will see you," he said. "But Jeffrey, something is wrong. I've not seen her so distressed since the king exiled her French ladies. Maybe not even then."

"She's distressed. I left the palace without her permission and gave her a fright. She'll understand why I had to take such action when I explain." She had to. I wound through to the chamber, Samuel's pale features filling my mind. He must be so afraid.

An usher opened the door, announced me. I stepped into the room filled with familiar things: comforts Her Majesty's household carried with it from palace to palace, tapestries upon the walls, tables and chairs, books and chests, bright cushions and romping spaniels. Today, however, Mitte was cowering under a table.

Henrietta Maria paced the chamber, her gown of gilt satin crumpled, straggling wisps of hair sticking to her tear-reddened cheeks. Her eyes blazed with pain and something more—fury. Lady Carlisle stood at a wary distance, twisting her fingers together. Grief smudged the tender skin beneath her eyes. I was certain then that the countess knew that the duke of Buckingham was dead.

Of course the assassination was a shock. But shouldn't the death of the queen's greatest enemy be as much a relief to Her Majesty as it was to me? I waited, certain Henrietta Maria's eyes would communicate what her lips could not. Why was she glaring as if she hated me? A hook twisted in my chest.

"Lucy," the queen said with a fervent devotion that shook me to the core. "Leave us. But do not go far. I cannot be without my truest friend."

The countess moved past me on her way out of the room. She gave me a curious look as she passed, one I couldn't read.

"Majesty," I said bowing deeply to the queen. "Forgive me for leaving court without your permission. Master Ware brought alarming news that my brother Samuel had been cast into Fleet Prison."

"Perhaps I can find a dungeon to cast you into. One befitting a traitor." Her voice hitched, bleeding heartbreak.

My blood turned to ice. "Majesty, you are the most important person in my life. The love I bear you—"

"Do not make me retch! Since the day you came into my service, you have been conspiring with my greatest enemy. You have wheedled my deepest secrets from me, rung out my heartaches, preyed upon my homesickness, all the while reporting them to the duke of Buckingham. You even wrote to His Grace of my uncertainty in the marriage bed."

My legs started to quiver. My letters. How had she gotten hold of them just when I thought I was safe?

She flattened her hand upon her breast as if to shield her heart. "Did you and the duke laugh about my struggles, Jeffrey? Make some of your rapier-sharp jests?"

"I would never." Images flashed through my memory—the day I had found her with the litter of puppies in the stable, so vulnerable yet brave as she confided in me.

The queen dashed curls away from her cheek. "If it were not for Lucy's loyalty, I would still not know I had taken a snake to my bosom."

"She is the duke's mistress herself."

"Women have tender hearts, which can be won by unscrupulous courtiers. But when Lucy saw these letters between you and the duke, she chose to be loyal to me. God knows how His Grace will react once he discovers what she has done."

I almost blurted out that Buckingham would have difficulty arousing any reaction at all, since I had left him in a pool of blood, but Will's voice sounded warning in my ear. No one must discover I had been in the vicinity.

The queen gripped her stomach and paced toward the window. "It is just as the surgeons say about such ill-formed freaks. Your spirit is as unnatural as your form. You are a monstrous creature unable to love or give loyalty even to those who have shown you kindness."

I felt monstrous, my acts of betrayal seeming to boil up like pustules of some pox. I averted my gaze. "You have been the most generous of mistresses."

"I am your queen!" she shrieked. "You owed me fealty unto death!"

Would she demand my life as forfeit? Would I blame her if she did? I had been ready to sacrifice everything when I had ridden out to kill Buckingham, my only object that she and Samuel would be safe. Buckingham could no longer hurt Henrietta Maria. He could no longer sign the order that would spur the guard to kill my brother.

Yet, if Samuel remained in Fleet Prison, he might die a slower, more torturous death. The kind that made a quick blade to the throat seem a gift from God. Only through the queen's influence with the king could I hope to free my brother. I groped for the right words to plead my case, more afraid than I had ever been in my life.

"Majesty, I owe you more than I can ever repay. But there is one I owed loyalty even before I met you: my brother, whom I love as you love your brother Gaston."

The queen drew herself up, seeming far taller than her small stature allowed. "Loyalty to king and country must be stronger than family ties. Did I not come to England because of what I owed France? Did I not marry a man I had never met? Did I not lose everyone I loved when Buckingham convinced the king to rid me of my childhood attendants?"

A sudden awareness spread across her face. "That ripping away was your doing as well, was it not, Jeffrey? *You* were the one who gave me the medallion from an execution, who spoke of Tyburn. *You* convinced me that making a pilgrimage was the best way to show English recusants that I was their ally."

"You spoke of going to Tyburn first. I did not come up with the idea out of thin air."

"But I did not understand how the English people would react to such a pilgrimage on my part. I did not stop to think how heinous honoring those executed for the Gunpowder Plot would be to my husband. You understood all that, and more."

I tried to swallow. "There are things powerful men can do to coerce people into doing what they would never do willingly. Buckingham threatened harm to my brother and made good on it when he had Samuel arrested. Samuel is barely fifteen, and he has never hurt anyone." My voice cracked, hopelessness welling up as I looked into her face. "Ware says Samuel's tutor is a Jesuit. Majesty, Samuel is true to the old religion in his heart, but he is loyal to the Crown."

"A trait you do not share."

Please, God, I prayed. Give me words to convince her to aid Samuel. "I would die for you, Your Majesty. But I could not sacrifice my brother, let him suffer. I deserve whatever punishment you deem worthy of my trespass. But Samuel should not have to pay for my sins. Intercede on Samuel's behalf with the king." I sank down onto my knees. "I beg you, Your Majesty."

"You want me to alienate my English subjects further? Champion outlawed Jesuits in direct defiance against the king and laws of the land? That would give the Puritans fodder for their handbills."

"You would be saving an innocent lad from unjust punishment. If you honor your faith, surely you must—"

"Don't you dare fling my faith at me! As if a creature like you knows anything about God or—or piety or honor!"

I could see her nostrils flare, her breath coming quick and sharp.

"Do you know that I cannot even banish you from my household?" the queen raged. "I would have to explain my actions to the king. What could I say? That I gabbled on to you about our marital relations? Told you what happened when my husband and I went to bed? Could I tell the king that I was fool enough to let you lead me into making the biggest mistake of my life? I had not the wit to understand you were manipulating me into making my English subjects hate me—all to the duke's benefit, of course? What kind of fool would my husband think me? How worthy a consort? No. I must suffer having your betrayal paraded before my face every day."

Was it possible that she would not have me brought up on charges? I knotted my hands together. "Majesty, I will leave court of my own accord.

Just release my brother and I will make up some excuse—ill health or responsibilities at home or some immoral act. Tell the king anything you wish." I thought of how Will had attempted to save Dulcinea from being banished from court. "Tell the king I defiled a serving girl and refused to wed her. Just make some name up. It will hurt no one."

"You think the king would believe a woman would have anything to do with a freak like you?" Something seemed to crack in the queen. Horror at what she had said bleached her face, and I thought she might be sick. Yet she refused to take the words back. Why should she? Most would say her statement was true.

"Majesty, throw me to whatever lions you wish. I will confess to any crime—for Samuel's sake and to spare you the sight of me."

"So you will go back to whatever dirty hovel Buckingham dragged you out of, willing to sacrifice yourself for your brother?"

"I would."

"Once you were back in such a lowly setting, how long would you keep silent about the happenings at court? You have come to live for an audience. How long before you would go to the public house, drink too much ale, and start telling the inn patrons that the queen of England could not satisfy her husband, the king, in bed?"

"I swear upon my soul I would never do such a thing."

"I intend to make certain of it. You will not leave my service. You will be within my reach every moment, where the slightest whisper of scandal can be stamped out at once."

"But Samuel—you must at least let me go to see him. Even if it is only to make arrangements with the jailer, pay to provide food for my brother, a blanket to ward off the cold."

"I *must*? How dare you! A queen does not take orders from her subjects. A queen gives her subjects commands. I command you not to leave the menagerie's lodgings, or you will join your brother, and you both may starve."

Desperation clawed at me.

"I do not want to see your face. Do you understand?" the queen demanded. "You are forbidden to take part in the masques, the court feasts. I wish to God I never had to see you again."

"What of Samuel?" I dared ask one last time.

"Pray to God to save him and his Jesuit master," the queen said. "After the discord you caused at Tyburn, I cannot."

A commotion sounded outside the door. The countess of Carlisle burst in, allowing the flood of tears finally to break free.

"Majesty—a rider has just come with ill news from Portsmouth!"

"Please, God, tell me the king is all right!" Henrietta Maria exclaimed.

"His Majesty is well. But the duke of Buckingham is dead."

The queen braced her hand against the nearest table. "Dead?" she echoed. "Was there an accident in the shipyard?"

"The duke was stabbed by an assassin at the Greyhound Inn."

I could see the queen's instinctive horror, the echo of her father's death. She wheeled away from us. I could tell she was crossing herself.

She was shaking. She must be feeling relief, I thought. Buckingham can harm her no more. But when she turned back to us, her face creased with concern. "This will be devastating to my husband. Lucy, have the household packed up at once. I must go offer His Majesty what comfort I can." She all but trod on me as she hastened away.

Will was waiting for me when I walked out the door. He gave me a grin he meant to be bracing. "How soon will Samuel be free? Is the queen writing to the king even now?"

"No. She believes it is too dangerous to interfere in an arrest involving an accused Jesuit."

"She's been doing battle over religious matters since the moment she set foot on England's shore. Why would she not help an innocent lad—your brother, no less—be freed when he's been imprisoned unjustly?"

"She no longer trusts me. She will not risk displeasing the king."

"You were willing to do murder to keep her safe!"

"Oh, and can you not hear the laughter if I were ever so foolhardy as to tell her that? Look at me, Will. A dwarf riding off to slay the most powerful nobleman in England? It would make me look ridiculous."

"But she holds you in affection more than anyone else in the menagerie."

"Not anymore."

"Jeffrey, I don't believe that. What could have changed things between you so abruptly?"

"Look at the friendship you and I shared. The right force applied snapped it."

"Our friendship mended, given time."

"Has it?" I looked at him, feeling a trifle hopeful.

"You know it has." Will patted me on the back. "The queen's affection for you will heal in time. Wait and see."

I looked out the window, imagining the confines of Fleet Prison, the darkness, the stench, the fevers that raged through the cells. The queen had rendered me helpless to send Samuel aid. "Time," I said, listening to the clock chime in the distance. "Time may be the one thing my brother does not have."

"We will work for Samuel's relief as much as we can, Jeff. You are not alone in this, my friend."

I pictured Will's face if he should ever see the letters I had written to the duke. Honorable Will's horror, the loathing that would envelop his homely face.

I covered my eyes with my hand, exhausted beyond imagining, feeling smaller than I ever had in my life.

TWENTY-EIGHT

.

Never had the queen's household flung itself into packing with more haste, Her Majesty determined to rush to her husband's side. I wondered if she longed for comfort herself after my betrayal. She, too, had lost her oldest friend in England.

I would have given almost anything to see her happy. But in the months that followed Buckingham's death, I saw her not at all. Only heard Will Evans and the other menagerie figures marvel over how tender she was to the king. How Charles Stuart clung to her now that his beloved Buckingham was dead.

Felton was hanged, the king's retribution no surprise. But the reaction of the rest of the country must have seared the king's heart. Bonfires filled the streets, people from Dover to Edinburgh hailing Felton as a hero, rejoicing that the duke would never again hold the king in his thrall.

The only people who truly mourned Buckingham's death were Buckingham's mother, his sister, his wife, and the king. The countess of Buckingham turned her dragon fire on Buckingham's enemies, accusing French spies of plotting against her son to stop his fleet from sailing. She cast about wild tales of Frenchmen enlisting Felton's help to keep Buckingham from returning to French shores to rescue stranded Huguenots. Her daughter Susan, Lady Denbigh, wept over her brother's death, yet she was forced to put on a brave face as her husband took Buckingham's place as Lord Admiral. The earl of Denbigh was less suited for the post than his brother-in-law had been.

When the new dowager duchess of Buckingham returned to court, she brought her fatherless children with her, Moll, Georgie, and little Francis, beautiful as the duke had been.

One of the first things the duchess did upon her arrival was to send for me. I was ushered to the gallery, where she sat in an alcove, watching her children play with the king's gift to them, a pair of spaniel puppies determined to make them smile.

The duchess's eyes were the most haunted I had ever seen. I could not forget the last time I had seen her, daubed with blood, vowing to make someone pay for her beloved husband's death. "Jeffrey," she greeted me, her voice so unlike the frenzied one I had heard in Portsmouth, I could scarce believe her half-mad cries had been real. "The world has turned upside down since Master Ware came to Wellingborough. Who would have guessed that the next time we met you would have fallen out of the queen's favor and I would have seen my lord murdered before my eyes?"

I could not say I was sorry for her loss. My only regret was that I had not killed him before he had cast my brother into Fleet Prison. "Your Grace, you loved your husband well. No wife could have loved a man better."

"So many people hated him." She twisted a mourning ring around her finger. "No one understood why he was driven to do the things he did. Now he is dead. Sometimes I pretend he is off in the countess of Carlisle's arms, or in France with Queen Anne of Austria, or in bed with that beautiful rope dancer. That he is losing a fleet in Cádiz or in the harbor at La Rochelle— anywhere as long as he might still come back to the children and me." She blinked away tears.

"Love does strange things to us all," I said.

"I am sorry for your rift with the queen. I worry my husband may have had something to do with it."

"You are not responsible for what someone else has done."

"I am the one who has done you harm in this case, I fear: placing your brother Samuel with Father Quintin."

"Father," I echoed. "Then he is a priest."

"One very dear to me. I was attending a secret Mass at the house of a childhood friend when someone betrayed us to the king's pursuivants. He had been captured once already and sent to the cane fields to work. One of the other Jesuits said he had asked to take the punishment meant for a child there, had his hand crushed."

I remembered Samuel's determination to save his tutor the labor of scribing things on paper. Had Samuel known how Quintin had crippled his hand? If so, little wonder my brother was devoted to the man.

"We all knew that if Father Quintin were captured by English authorities again, he would be executed and that the property of anyone who had helped him would be confiscated. We barely had time to hide him in the priest hole the family was in the midst of building. The joiner had left his tools behind. We had to shove them all—mallet and ax, wedge and saw—in with Father Quintin lest the pursuivants grow suspicious. Quintin is a tall man—not compared to Sergeant Evans, but not easy to fit into a small space, either. This was the smallest place imaginable, crammed behind one of the support beams. It was the only way they could design the hiding place without disturbing plaster, so the priest hole would not be easy to detect."

I remembered what I had felt like when I'd been crammed into the pie the night Buckingham had given me to the queen. I had not even spent an hour thus and my body had ached and burned. What would I have suffered if I had been forced to stay still in that tiny space while men who hoped to arrest me and the flock I had come to minister to were trying to hunt me down?

"For two weeks, the priest-hunters milled around the house, sure if they watched closely enough, they could flush him out. Father Quintin was jammed in so tightly, it stopped the flow of blood to his leg. I cannot imagine the agony he was in, but he never made a sound. If he had, we would all have gone to prison."

"That is why you called him brave."

"He never regained the full use of his leg. After the priest-hunters left, my friend's uncle and I bundled Father Quintin onto a ship bound for Spain. He was so weak, we did not expect him to survive the voyage. He must have had angels on his side. He could have stayed in Spain, safe, or gone to Italy or France. He had suffered enough for his faith. I cannot tell you how it terrified me when I saw him in London. I grew desperate to provide a shield to hide his true calling. When your brother needed a tutor, it seemed God had answered my prayer."

"God wanted you to put an innocent youth in harm's way?" Hard words, yet I could not stop thinking of Samuel's suffering. This woman had played at dice with my brother's life to gain a friend's safety. How far into darkness might she have gone to support her beloved husband's schemes? Could she have had any part in arranging to topple a scaffold on the queen?

Her chin tipped up in aristocratic pride. "I did your brother a service, giving him the chance to be educated by a fine scholar who has been in the great courts of Europe. More than that, Father Quintin has fed a hunger in Samuel for the true Church. Even I had heard how often your brother visited the widow who hides the carving of a Madonna under her floor."

"You know of the statue?" I asked, my nerves clenching even tighter.

"I have packed away treasures of the old Church myself, in hopes I might bring them into the light one day. Now that my faith cannot damage my husband's position at court, I can be true to my conscience, like Samuel may choose to be. Perhaps I will even have saved your brother's soul."

"My brother's soul is not your concern! You nobles play with people's lives as my father plays with the lives of his dogs. Regretting when we are killed, but then shrugging it off and turning to the next diversion."

"Is faith a game? Sending people to Heaven or hell? Baptizing babies? Giving the dying Extreme Unction? Offering them confession and the comforts of Mass? Your brother would not say so."

"Do not presume to tell me what my brother would say. You do not even know him."

"Perhaps I understand him better than you do. Father Quintin wrote me often about his progress. Samuel's faith is a thing of beauty, his devotion to Father Quintin—"

"If God and Father Quintin are so great, they could have managed Heaven and hell without dragging my brother into the fray. And so, Your Grace, could you. Moreover, the duke himself threatened to have Samuel killed unless I complied with his wishes."

"My husband wished to rival Richelieu in intrigues and battle, to burn Cádiz like Sir Frances Drake." She wrapped her arms around her stomach. "Great men do not climb to heights on the backs of butcher's sons, Jeffrey Hudson."

I wanted to assert that Buckingham had used *this* butcher's son, threatening

my whole family unless I became his pawn. Yet, the court teemed with nobles eager to take Buckingham's place. Was it possible one might be conniv-
ing to rise to the highest position in the kingdom? If so, those who had hated
Buckingham's influence on the king now had another person's influence to
fear—that of the Catholic queen who had taken the duke's place in King
Charles's heart.

"I did not summon you here to defend my late husband. I only wanted
you to know that I am seeing to your brother's needs and those of Father
Quintin. Everything possible is being done for their comfort."

"I suppose I should thank you."

"I do not expect you to," she said.

Yet she gave me a surprising gift months later, when Christmas holly was
being garlanded about the palace. She approached me as I hovered about the
outskirts of celebrations I would not get to see.

"I wanted to be the first to tell you something about the queen," the
duchess of Buckingham said.

"Her Majesty no longer wishes me to be privy to her affairs."

"Jeffrey, when one loves as I have loved His Grace, one sees feelings
other people wish to hide." She looked at me, so sympathetic, I could almost
forget my suspicions about her. Almost. "There are tidings about Her Majesty that you will be most happy to hear."

"My companions in the menagerie keep me apprised of court doings."

"Not even the king knows this yet. The queen is with child."

My chest swelled with joy for Henrietta Maria. I should not have cared so
much. The queen had refused to help Samuel, forbade me to see my brother.
Yet I had betrayed her, not the other way around. Perhaps now my homesick
French princess would be tied to England in a way that would make her subjects love her at last. Was it possible that, in her happiness, she might be willing to forgive me—at least enough to help my innocent brother?

Tears filled my eyes at the thought of Henrietta Maria bending over a
cradle. Henrietta Maria with a babe to her breast. Henrietta Maria with a husband and child on whom she could lavish all the love in her passionate heart.

Perhaps it was just as well that she had cast me aside. She would not need
her fool Jeffrey at all now.

"I am glad to know that Her Majesty will be happy," I said.

"Jeffrey, I confess, I am a trifle uneasy. Not everyone will be happy at this news. The other day, one of the pages knocked over the queen's goblet in the grass. There were strange flecks that clung to the leaves. When I walked in the garden the next day, I noticed something strange. The Christmas rose the cup spilled on had withered."

She seemed to shake herself. "Of course, it's more likely one of the spaniels has dubbed that plant its favorite place to make water. But the world can be a treacherous place, especially for a woman with child."

I heard one of the maids of honor call out for the dowager duchess—some part in the Christmas decking of halls to play. But long after she had gone about her tasks, I was haunted.

Was it possible the queen had another enemy?

I thought of the powder I had secreted in my writing box the night I rode off to kill Buckingham: the dose that was supposed to wither the queen's womb. Is that what had been in the cup the page had spilled? If so, the attempt had failed. The queen would bear a child, and that would put an end to those who wished Henrietta Maria to be sent back to France. She would be mother to a prince or princess. Untouchable.

Her enemies would claim she was now more dangerous than ever.

⌘

I guarded her from a distance in the months that followed, urging the king to make certain someone tasted anything that touched her lips. His Majesty, already vigilant, did everything he could to protect her, make her happy. Bonfires blazed in celebration of the coming prince; ambassadors came to congratulate the royal couple. Prayers were lifted up in churches across England, beseeching God to grant the queen a safe delivery and that He would make her a joyful mother of many children.

Sara shared news of the queen's gratitude when the king paid off her mounting debts, banishing the tradesmen who had been clamoring at the queen's door. It was no small feat to come up with the vast sum. His Majesty was again low on funds. When he called another session of Parliament in hopes of refilling his purse, members were hopeful, saying that things between them and the king seemed to be going well. Yet, after a night in the queen's bed, the king sent the MPs home.

Archie visited the lodgings with the delight of one of the horsemen bringing down the Apocalypse. "Your mistress is doing a fine job spreading dissension throughout the land. The streets are full of chatter regarding her 'crimes.'"

"Some poor servant girl was thrown into prison for saying she wished the queen be ducked in the sea with a millstone round her neck," Rattlebones said. "While boatloads of captive French fishermen were allowed to go free at her request."

"She has even convinced the king to begin talks with the Venetian ambassadors about making a treaty with France," Archie grumbled. "It is rumored the queen got a condemned Jesuit priest not only reprieved but pardoned."

My heart had all but leapt out of my chest with hope. "The priest . . . do you know his name?"

"It was not Master Quintin," Will said quietly. "I am sorry, Jeff."

Sorrow clouded court the day we learned the French Huguenots had surrendered at La Rochelle, despite the English fleet in their harbor. The king had been determined not to desert them. But now, that last bar to peace had been removed. We grieved at the news that the French king had ordered the starving Huguenots be fed, but their stomachs had been so far gone, they had died with the meat in their mouths.

But it was Sara who brought the most surprising news of all. The French wanted the queen's French household restored to her as part of the treaty. It was Henrietta Maria herself who put an end to that hope. "She fears it might shatter the harmony she now has with the king," Sara said. "I am so glad she was wise enough to see that danger."

It seemed as if the fates wished to reward the queen, for on Sunday, May 10, 1629, the king and queen stood at the window of the gallery at Greenwich Palace as peace with France was proclaimed.

I could see Her Majesty place a hand on her swollen belly, tears in her eyes as a trumpet blared and four heralds announced we were no longer at war with her homeland.

She grew ever more luminous with joy and confidence as she took her barge to Somerset House to have the Te Deum chanted in thanksgiving for peace. I rejoiced that my love now had everything she could want within the palace walls. But in the world beyond, unrest simmered.

I tried to ignore the grumbling growing ever louder at the notion of a Catholic queen giving birth to England's heir. Robin Goodfellow had brought word just the week before that some on the streets were claiming that Henrietta Maria had convinced her doting husband to let the heir to the throne attend Catholic Mass.

But despite the discord such rumors created, I did not guess anyone might try to strike her down in the palace. Not even after Will Evans burst into the menagerie's lodgings at Greenwich to tell me three dogs had attacked her in the gallery. Dulcinea had seen the whole thing.

"What the devil bull-baiting dogs were doing running free, I have no idea!" Will complained. "Should've seen them—all torn up and scarred from the fight. If the earl of Carlisle had not been nearby, the beasts might have rent the queen from stem to stern."

"The birth pangs have seized Her Majesty," Will told me.

"It is too early," I said, sick at heart.

Will nodded. "The king has summoned the queen's doctor and His Majesty has done what no king has done before. He has defied them all—the midwives, the ladies-in-waiting—every scrap of protocol for royal births. He refuses to leave his lady's side."

I knew Henrietta Maria did not want me near her. But she would not have to see my face. I would wait outside her chamber and pray. I'd pray as I had rarely prayed before.

May 12, 1629

The queen's screams pounded in my skull like those of a madwoman desperate to escape Bedlam. Hours upon hours, I paced outside her chamber, watching servants dash in and out, exhausted, fearful, and—in the case of Lady Carlisle—with a kind of expectant aura. Did the countess really hope her mistress would die? Ripped apart in the act of trying to give the king a son?

I plied anyone who left the room for news of how the queen fared. What scraps I got cinched my fear so tight, I could not breathe. The queen was tiring. The babe was turned crosswise. The king would not stir from his wife's side, Henrietta Maria clutching at his hands so hard, they were swollen and bruised.

From the cluster of chairs nearby, I could hear Charles's advisers mumbling. Were they raking through lists of princesses they hoped would replace her? I winced as I saw Archie Armstrong peel himself away from a cluster of the king's servants, the old fool slouching toward me with a wicked curl to his mouth.

"Quite a spectacle baby Charles is making of himself," Archie used the pet name Buckingham and King James had once used to describe the stammering prince. "A confinement chamber is no place for any husband, let alone for a king of England. Ha! When Henrietta Maria was born, her father was playing cards and plotting how he was going to retrieve a runaway mistress—the kinds of pursuits a king was meant to engage in."

"I am certain His Majesty's advisers would be eager for your opinion," I said. "I am not."

"Come, now, Jeffrey. I would not want to interfere with their happy musings about which Protestant princess would make the most advantageous royal bride if we are so lucky as to rid ourselves of the French beggar girl."

"I'll not hear such talk."

"What else do you call a wife was brings no dowry?"

"Can you not hear how the queen is suffering?"

"I think everyone within a league of Greenwich can hear it—which is why I brought wool to stuff in my ears." Archie made a sour face. "What is King Charles doing in there anyway? All his life, the man has had a horror of fierce emotion. Not a speck of passion in him, or he'd have taken Lady Carlisle up on her offer of a tumble in bed, as Buckingham had. Besides, the king and queen have spent most of their marriage fighting. Why the great change?"

Because they have fallen in love, I wanted to say as the earl of Carlisle and the earl of Denbigh summoned Archie with a wave of their hand. The king and queen loved deeply, completely, in a way that made me happy for them, yet which tormented me, as well.

As Archie sauntered away, I imagined Charles in the next room, bending over his wife as I wished I could do, stroking her hair back with man-size hands. In my mind, I could hear his voice—marred by the stammer he had worked so hard to eradicate, worn down with worry and exhaustion, but murmuring words of encouragement. Was he kissing her brow? Regretting that his lovemaking had caused her this pain? Did he feel as afraid and helpless against the alchemy of womb and birth as I did?

When Will Evans was not on duty, he brought me food and stayed to make certain I ate it. Simon, Robin, Boku, and Sara hovered nearby, as well, while Dulcinea floated restlessly here and there, as if she could not find a flower pleasing enough to light upon.

She even wandered into the queen's wardrobe, but a servant shooed her from that forbidden room. If I'd had the king's power, I would have swept every soul out into the gardens—anywhere I could not hear their macabre accounts of the most horrific birth tales anyone had ever told them.

I was half out of my mind by the time Charles Stuart and the queen's physician stepped outside of the birthing chamber, the duchess of Buckingham and the countess of Carlisle following in their wake. The king's advisers flocked over to hear the news. I doubted any of them noticed me drawing near, as well. The doctor look haggard and was spattered with blood; the king's hands were trembling.

"Your Majesty, this cannot go on any longer," the doctor said. "I can remove the child from your wife's womb two ways. I can open her belly to save the babe. If I do, Her Majesty will bleed to death. The other method is to pull the babe out its normal passage with a hook, killing the child to save the mother."

Bloody images from my days in the shambles made me dizzy. The notion of the queen's soft flesh under a knife nearly drove me to my knees.

"How do you wish me to proceed, Your Majesty?"

"There must be some way to save them both," Charles said, his voice breaking.

"If the queen were able to speak, I know what she would tell you." The duchess of Buckingham pressed her hand to her stomach. Was she thinking of the other children she and the duke would never have? "Given a choice, any mother would rather you spare her babe."

"There are greater considerations than a woman's opinion," the earl of

Carlisle insisted. "Majesty, you must think of your kingdom. It is the queen's duty—and yours—to give England an heir."

The king wheeled on him, his face contorted with helpless rage. "Do you think I do not know what my duty is?"

"It is hard to make such a sacrifice," Lady Carlisle said soothingly. "But the queen has been raised from the cradle to understand the one purpose of a princess is to bear heirs to the throne. To be barren would be worse than death."

She looked away, and I wondered why she was childless.

"There is one more thing to consider if you do choose to spare the queen." The surgeon pushed back his blood-speckled cuff. "If I use the hook to pull the babe out, the womb will be damaged. It is possible—even likely—the queen may never be able to bear another child."

The king gave an anguished moan, wheeling away from the cluster of people. He stalked my way. Suddenly, those sad royal eyes met mine.

"Jeffrey." He did not sound surprised to see me standing vigil, despite the fact that I had not waited on the queen these many months. "Do you hear them? The doctor? My advisers? Even the queen's own ladies-in-waiting?"

"I hear them, Your Majesty."

"They say I must murder my wife or my child. I would rather cut out my own heart."

I could imagine the hell Charles Stuart must be suffering. "There may be other children," I said softly. "There is only one Henrietta Maria."

The king bent down to clasp my hands. I could feel the anguish the royal couple had shared in the weary hours of the queen's labor, holding on to each other, trapped in a world they could not command. "Of all the court, only you understand," Charles said. "I cannot live without her in the world."

"Neither can I," I told him. He nodded, and I could see him square his shoulders.

I watched the king return to the cluster of people, give his command. "Save the queen."

He did not linger to hear the protests his advisers clamored to voice. He did not pause to notice the impatience sharpening the countess of Carlisle's pretty face and the disapproval even the dowager duchess of Buckingham showed. He returned to his wife's bedside, refused to leave it even as the surgeon did his work.

Sharper screams, more agonized. I had not thought it possible. I haunted the queen's door until the king emerged with his tiny son in his arms, rushing the struggling mite to be baptized before he died. The moment the little prince breathed his last, Charles returned to his wife's chamber, her screams having given way to grief-stricken sobs, the loss of their child a burden shared. When he emerged later, I was still waiting.

"She is out of danger," the king said, drifting his hand down on my hair as the queen used to do when I was her best beloved pet. "Tell the menagerie to prepare a special entertainment to help the queen learn how to laugh again."

"I am certain Simon and Goodfellow can plan something that will please the queen."

"Not as much as you did." The king frowned. "I wish that you and the queen would make up your quarrel. Will you not tell me what has driven this wedge? I can fix it."

I wanted to pour out the tale to the king, rid my soul of its ugly burden. But to do so would mean exposing the queen's secrets and Buckingham's villainy. It would make things worse for the royals I loved, not better.

"Even a king cannot order affections to be mended." My voice thickened with regret. "Her Majesty has a truer confidant in you, Your Highness. Your love and trust was what the queen longed for. I am grateful she has it."

I dragged myself down to the lodgings. Everyone sat in their accustomed places around the table, not even bothering to pretend to work at the tasks that they had been using to keep busy. What had they been thinking as their hands slowed, then grew idle? I wondered as I looked at those faces I had come to care about so much. Had they been wondering what would happen to us if the queen died? Would our troupe be preserved intact by the king or divided up and scattered to other noble houses? Her Majesty's Curiosities and Freaks of Nature a menagerie no more?

I shut the door louder than necessary. They spun toward me.

"The queen will live," I reassured quietly.

"God be praised!" Sara exclaimed. Simon scooped up his fluffy white dog and buried his face in the fur. Robin Goodfellow closed his eyes as if in silent prayer to his God of ceruleans and crimsons. Boku glided to the window on feet that made no sound. He whispered some unknown language to the moon.

I had sagged onto a stool, when I heard a hiss, saw Archie spit into the fire. No doubt he'd come to stir up strife in the lodgings, since his own master was at the queen's bedside. "Trust baby Charles to shy away from doing a king's duty," the old fool said. "Kill a Protestant prince to save a Catholic queen who's been nothing but trouble from the day she landed in Dover. King James would never have made such a mistake, nor would Charles's brother Prince Henry."

"Your queen is alive!" I snapped. "You should be grateful!"

"There are plenty in this kingdom who will not be," Archie sneered. "They've broken Buckingham's hold on the Crown, only to have the queen take his place in the king's esteem. Do you want England to be the chattel of a French woman? A Catholic? Better fling the country to the Irish savages and let them rend it to bits!"

He stalked from the room. Dulcinea stood up, as well.

"I had best try to caution him before he goes spouting his nonsense to someone who might tell the king," she said.

"Do you wish me to go with you?" Will started to rise from his chair.

"No!" Dulcinea said with startling vigor. "I'll do better myself. I have a talent for cozening men." Were her eyes overly bright? Her hands more restless than usual? Something about her set my nerves on edge.

Tension gripped Will's shoulders, and I wondered if she knew how badly such talk still hurt him. I wondered if she ever thought about the wedding that wasn't or the man who had longed to be her husband.

As she went in search of Archie, the rest of the menagerie trailed off to bed, leaving Will and me alone with nothing but the soft chattering of Pug from the corner.

Will sighed with such force, the candles on the table guttered. He laid his hand across my back. "So, the queen is going to be well, Jeffrey. I am glad. I only hope someday she knows what a loving servant she has in you."

"All that matters is that she is safe and the king loves her. She can never doubt that now. He went against the advice of all of his councillors to save her. She may never be able to bear another child."

"Did the king know that when he made his decision?"

"I heard the doctor warn him."

"Then His Majesty does love her." Will gave a thoughtful nod.

"More than the future of his crown."

"I am glad for the queen," Will said. "I think there is nothing she needs more than her husband's love. "

I looked at Will, unable to shake the memory of his face as Dulcinea disappeared. "At least the queen will have the wit to know she is rich beyond imagining." I fetched a bottle of Rhenish wine some courtier had given me when people still sought my favor. "Rich, not because of crowns or jewels or palaces, but because she has earned a good man's love."

"But not the country's love." Will mourned. "I have heard there were some reckless enough to raise toasts at the possibility the queen might die. Perhaps they would not have dared light bonfires in the streets as they did when Buckingham was assassinated, but that does not change the fact that they wished her dead. How will that change if the queen cannot bear a prince? Will the king have the strength to set her aside if the country demands it?"

"He never will forsake her." I poured the wine into flagons. We drank to the queen's health, to the king's love. We drank until I drifted to sleep at the table. From some misty world of half dream, I felt Will lift me, carry me, lay me upon my bed.

I woke a little as Griggory undressed me. At last, I slept.

I watched from a distance as she took her first steps from the confinement chamber, her arms empty of the child she had nurtured in her body, yearned for so much during her lonely, heartsick times. She was too pale, her eyes dark with grief. Even the finest delicacies the kitchens could prepare could not tempt her appetite. None of Simon's dog tricks or Pug's capering or the wiles of the rest of the menagerie could hold her attention.

Cocooned by my fear for her and my isolation from the everyday world of the court, I did not realize that the menagerie had gained the attention of a new and dangerous audience until the countess of Carlisle sought me out in the stables.

I had not really spoken to the countess since the day she left my life in ruins. I let my hatred of her show in my face. "Is there a piece of my correspondence to His Grace you are unable to decipher for the queen?" I asked. "Intrigue demanded that I dash those missives off in great haste."

"I took no pleasure in giving the queen your letters. But I had to protect someone I love. With Buckingham dead, it was the only way I could maintain enough power to do so."

"Your *power*?" I scoffed.

"Power is nothing to sneer at. What would you sacrifice right now to open your brother's cell door? Do not tell me you wouldn't hand the queen someone else's letters. We both know it would be a lie."

"Someone you loved was in danger?"

"Yes. The person I love most in the world." A self-deprecating smirk curled her lips. "Me."

"You?"

"I am not a great believer in the unselfish gesture. I leave that to women like the queen and Kate Villiers. I decided long ago that no one—not my father or mother, certainly not my husband or any man—would ever take care of me as well as I could. It is unwomanly, I know. But it is the truth."

"Honesty is a refreshing change. Are you considering making it a habit?"

"Only if it serves my purpose—as this gift will." She extended the packet. I took it, wary, and opened it.

"Dog collars?" I touched the unique pattern of metal studs I had seen my father drive through leather straps so he could identify his dogs.

"I have seen identical collars at Buckingham's bull-baiting contests," the countess said.

"Did you take them off of the gored dogs as souvenirs?" I asked.

"I took them off of the beasts that attacked the queen."

"How could my father's collars—" I stopped cold with horror.

"Do not look so ghastly. No one else saw them. No one ever will."

"Why—why would you bring them to me?"

"Anyone who linked them to your father would believe you arranged the attack to punish the queen."

"You do not believe it?"

"I know you would not harm her."

"Do you know who did?"

"They took a man to prison. Some underling so bewildered by it all, it was useless to question him. I did not see him, hooded as he was. The guards said it was just as well. Dogs had torn up his face."

"I suppose that I should thank you."

"Buckingham would tell you not to bother. Someday I will collect payment for the service I have done you."

I wondered just how much she thought my life was worth.

"There is one more matter I must bring to your attention," she said.

"What is that?"

"It involves what some friends of yours are printing. I believe their shop is called something knightly, like the Saracen's Bane."

Wariness flooded through me as I remembered the portly printer, his thin wife and three little daughters. In my fear for Samuel, I had not stopped to wonder what their fate had been.

"Is that not the place where your brother and his Jesuit were arrested?"

"My brother had a tutor who deceived him. It is rumored the man was a Jesuit."

"Strange that the printer was not jailed with them."

"I am glad."

"I would not be if I were you. Since the pursuivants' visit, the bookseller has become fierce in condemning the queen and her Church, though the king has not yet traced these broadsheets to their source." She indicated the crumpled wrapper in which I had found the collars.

I smoothed the broadsheet—slightly smeared ink images on paper made of the cheapest rags. I stared, horrified, at the woodcut someone had stamped upon the page: an orgy of twisted limbs and malformed bodies, leering faces, and court ladies swiving with creatures barely even human. Nuns and priests, French bishops, all fornicating merrily right under the king's nose. I could recognize us all—the queen's curiosities—engaging in the worst sort of vice. Most repulsive of all was the image of me in my devil-imp costume, suckling on the queen's bared breast while pieces of the child the queen miscarried hung from meat hooks above us.

The true purpose of the Royal Menagerie . . . the broadsheet proclaimed. *Blood alone can save our king.* . . .

TWENTY-NINE

•

D awn was creeping across the floor three weeks later when I was awakened by an insistent rap. I sprang out of bed, panicked that childbed fever stalked the queen, the contagion that killed more mothers than any other malady.

I flung the door open, expecting to find a servant in the king's livery. Instead, I was staring at Will's hairy shin above boot tops with no stockings.

"What is it?" I asked, more frightened than ever. "The queen?"

"Dulcinea." His voice broke. "Good God, Jeff. Boku claims someone poisoned her."

"There are people at court a dose of poison might improve, but a dancing girl?" I scoffed. "Why would anyone seek to harm Dulcinea now that Buckingham is gone?"

"That is what I said! The quail she was eating must have been spoiled, or she caught some ague that is twisting her reason. I would not have left her side except that she's thrashing about, asking for you, Jeff."

I flung on breeches and boots, threaded my arms through a doublet. Leaving the garments open, I started after him. "She's young and strong," Will insisted more to himself than to me. "I know she will not die." He paused, searching my face. "We just have to put her at ease. If she will let Boku do his work . . . watch. She will get well. She will get well."

For once, he did not spare my dignity. He scooped me up and set me on his shoulder. Anguish rippled from him in waves as he loped back toward the women's quarters in his awkward, knock-kneed gait. I grabbed handfuls of his bristly hair to keep from falling off.

"We must hurry," Will said as we passed wide-eyed servants and gape-mouthed guards. I knew some part of Will still hoped one day Dulcinea might change her mind and love him.

My teeth were near jarred out of my head by the time we reached the chamber Dulcinea shared with Sara. I had never been inside it before. Dulcinea had obviously taken all that was prettiest, softest, and best in their small store. Her bed might have belonged in a sultan's harem, draped with sheer loops of gauze and luxurious embroidered linens. A pewter plate scattered with tiny bones of a quail sat on the seat of a chair. A table by the window was piled with vials and small casks of creams and lotions and unguents that smelled of musk and jasmine. But not even those rich scents could disguise a creeping odor of death I knew from the shambles. Dulcinea will never dance upon her rope again, will never learn to love my friend, I thought with sick certainty.

She lay on a pile of cushions, thrusting her long legs against the mattress. My heart twisted to see that sometime in the past weeks Will had given her the wedding linens he had gathered for her so tenderly. The alabaster flesh that had won her the attentions of a duke was beginning to mottle. Slender fingers gripped handfuls of coverlet. Her gaze darted from dark corner to dancing shadow, as if seeing devils no one else could see.

"Dulcinea, love, I have brought Jeffrey," Will said as he set me on my feet. I wobbled a little, the absence of his jouncing gate oddly more jarring than his running had been.

"Jeffrey. I need to confess before I die."

"You are not going to die!" Will growled. But he was the only one in the chamber who believed that.

"I'm no confessor," I said as gently as I could. "Better to summon Father Philip."

"I do not want Father Philip! You are the one I have done a great wrong. To you. To the queen." A haunted expression crossed Dulcinea's face, as if she had been shaken out of her pretty dream world to find she really lived in the gutter.

"Do you believe in hell?" she asked.

"My brother is in Fleet Prison. That is close enough for me."

Terror flickered at the backs of her eyes, and I wanted to give her ease. "How can anyone really know what Heaven or hell are?"

"I do. Wanting what you can never have. Scorning what you should be grateful for. Getting so greedy that you gorge on pleasure until your soul splits open and everything good in you seeps out. Believing someone loves you when that person tramples over you without even noticing. You know how that feels, don't you, Jeffrey?"

Was she thinking of the falsehood I had told so the queen would cancel the wedding? "If you have been listening to the rumors regarding my feelings for you, you need to understand. I was lying in a meddling attempt to save Will from breaking his heart over you. I let the queen believe I loved you. I don't."

"Neither did Buckingham. But I loved him."

I felt Will flinch.

"We were beautiful to look at. If you could have seen us, tangled in the duke's fine sheets, you would have been amazed. He had mirrors hung so we could watch ourselves. We didn't see that we were empty inside."

"Dulcinea," Will soothed her said soothingly, "that was in the past. Do not fret about things you cannot change. Just get well."

"I never can, Will. Someone so pretty was born to be a whore. That is what my mother said. She handed me to one of her customers when I was barely eight. I learned to cross laundry ropes, strung between houses, to get away. Buckingham . . . couldn't get away from King James. No rope in the kingdom was high enough or long enough. The king could always reach him."

Had not Buckingham's wife said the same thing with different words?

"Buckingham wanted to be so much more than a body people wanted to grope. So did I. We wanted to dazzle the world with such . . . brilliance that we'd never be forgotten. Now Buckingham will be remembered as a reckless fool. And I . . . I will be known as the woman in league with the man who tried to murder the queen."

"You?" Will exclaimed. "I don't believe it."

"I would have done his bidding forever, stirring up trouble when he wished it, loving Buckingham when I was able. Then Buckingham died. I threatened to tell everything."

Who would want to silence her—to protect Buckingham's reputation? The mother who had idolized Buckingham and turned panderer to a king?

Lady Carlisle, his mistress? I thought of Buckingham's duchess—her fierceness. *Would that I could do something to shield him.*

Even poison a young woman? Who else could care so much about Buckingham's reputation?

"You threatened whom?" I asked. "The duchess? The king?"

"No. I had stolen letters. Listened at keyholes. Betrayed all of you; the queen, the menagerie. He told me it didn't matter, that freaks do not have feelings."

Every flaw in Will's body and mine seemed to swell larger, twist uglier with the label she had given us. It was as if the monsters depicted in that grotesque broadsheet were trying to break free.

Will looked as if he were going to be sick. "You were spying on us?"

"He needed a way to get to the queen. What better way than through the menagerie she loved? But once I knew he was trying to kill the queen—"

"Buckingham is the one who sabotaged the scaffolding the night you lost the babe?" I asked.

Dulcinea gave a ragged laugh. "Buckingham was not clever enough to plan such a thing. The duke became as much a tool in evil hands as I was."

"If not the duke, then who?" I prodded, knowing from the rattle in Dulcinea's chest that the poison was doing its work. "Was the Wizard Earl's daughter the one behind the plot?"

"Recognized who it was the day . . . set the dogs on the queen. Meant dogs to rip out the queen's throat."

"Dulcinea's not making any sense," Will said, but she plunged on.

"Could scarce believe my eyes. Dogs knocked mask askew. A devil's grin carved . . ." She touched the hinge of her jaw, revulsion flooding her face.

Simon Rattlebones shuddered. "The dog trainer I met at the Saracen's Bane when I took your letter to Samuel," he said. "He had a hideous grin."

"Phineas," I whispered, disbelieving. "I've known him since I was a child. He would never use dogs to kill."

"Stopped savage dogs before they could do the dark angel's will. Frightened me at first, but the Gargoyle . . . his eyes were the kindest I've ever seen. He was searching for you, Jeffrey."

"He never reached me."

"Guards dragged him off. Poor Gargoyle kept telling them he didn't do it. Not easy to train a pack to attack a specific person. Didn't try to bite the queen's other ladies. How could someone do that?"

"My father could make his dogs fight lions if he wanted them to," I said. "Get a piece of clothing—something that smelled of the person. Savage the dog with a pike wrapped in cloth with the person's scent on it."

"Other ways, as well. Stitched something on queen's petticoat. Oil made dogs go mad. When the queen was sick, I sneaked into her chamber. Found the clothes she'd been wearing when she was attacked."

"That's what you were doing in the queen's chamber the day she lost her babe."

"Waited for a chance to sneak away. Take the clothes to the . . . angel that Dr. Dee summoned."

"Dr. Dee?" Rattlebones frowned. "Is she talking about the alchemist?"

"The poison must be spinning visions in her head," Sara said, looking to Boku. "Is there nothing you can do to ease her?"

The conjuror shook his head. "It is too late. As for this master of angels, John Dee, I learned of him in the years when I first knew the countess of Carlisle. I studied about Queen Elizabeth's sorcerer. Some think he went mad trying to speak to an archangel: the one who holds the key to hell at the End of Days."

"What was the archangel's name?" I asked, hoping it might give us some clue.

"Uriel."

The name hung in the air, realization dawning in me. "There is a man named Uriel," I said. "Buckingham's servant, Uriel Ware."

Dulcinea's head and shoulders came up off of the pillow. She strained, hoarse, her eyes red as vessels burst beneath the white film. "Yes. Angel Uriel would not let me into the Garden of Eden, no matter what secrets I sold him."

"You sold the secrets of people who trusted you?" Will said. I had never known my friend to refuse forgiveness. But something in his face had turned immovable as stone. If I had ever wondered how he would react if he discovered my secret, I did not wonder any longer.

"The archangel Uriel checked doors for lamb's blood the night the first-born were slaughtered in Egypt," Sara said softly.

Dulcinea nodded. "Your brother, Jeffrey. The sacrificial lamb awaiting the knife in a Fleet Prison cell."

"Ware was only a hireling," I insisted. "Buckingham was the one who cast Samuel in prison. Buckingham had a guard ready to kill Samuel if I did not do as he wished."

Dulcinea shook her head. "Buckingham didn't even know your brother was in jail. The blind angel was the one determined to keep Samuel in his power."

I felt dizzy, remembering Ware's face as he spoke of my brother's letters, how Samuel reminded him of his father. If Ware was behind my brother's imprisonment, Buckingham's assassination had not made Samuel safer at all. Even now, the order could be winging its way to the guard's hand. Ware's assassin could be turning the key in Samuel's cell door, knotting his hand in Samuel's golden curls, yanking Samuel's head back to expose his throat to the sharp bite of a blade.

"Ware needs Samuel to make you destroy the queen, Jeffrey."

"Jeffrey never would!" Will raged.

"Ware determined to show the whole world how unholy the queen's household is. Angel set up so the people will not stop razing palace until all the unholy are dead," Dulcinea said.

"Ware is no Puritan. His mother was a madwoman, cut out his eye. He turned his back on the Church. Buckingham told me. Felton . . . Ware told me himself."

"Buckingham told me everything about Ware. How Ware blamed a Catholic woman for bewitching his father. Magic dragon stones. Curiosities collected from voyages. How Ware believed a Jesuit gave her some . . . some saint's blood to drive Ware's mother mad. Make his father forget his son."

"There was a woman involved with Ware's father," I said. "Genevieve Armistead. I heard Buckingham's mother and sister speak of her."

"Ware vowed he would rid England of Catholics, starting with the queen. He would grab the seas from the Pope's minions; put the power in the hands of honest, hardworking Englishmen. Only way to save from becoming slaves to the Pope was to purge England of every Catholic, every freak of nature. Wants to turn us against one another like dogs . . . tear one another apart trying to save ourselves."

My hands knotted into fists and I prayed she would not reveal my part. Was it selfish of me to care if she did? What did it matter? If Buckingham was not behind Samuel's arrest—if Buckingham's signature wasn't necessary to make the guard murder my brother in jail, then that meant Samuel was in more danger than ever.

Was that why Ware had disappeared after Buckingham's death? When I was imagining him, free to do what he wished at last, free to find a berth on some ship, join the East India men exploring the world, was Ware putting other pieces of his plan into motion? Using other cogs to turn the wheels of his machinations? Wheels like Dulcinea? Maybe even Phineas? Or was he merely waiting to put the right pressure on me?

"Where can we find Uriel Ware, Dulcinea? Do you know where this accursed angel is?"

"Went to see him tonight. Took evidence of how he got the dogs to attack the queen to the Saracen's Bane."

The hair at the nape of my neck stood on end. "Saracen's Bane? The bookseller's? There are rumors he's printed lascivious broadsheets accusing the queen of fornication with us."

"Was that not where Samuel was staying when he came to London?" Will asked. "I thought your brother's tutor was friends with the bookseller. Why would he spread such slander?"

"Owner trapped since Ware had the Jesuit arrested there. Must do whatever Ware tells him to or daughters killed. Meetings there, inciting apprentices, people's rage. Saying Jeffrey told of orgies at the palace. Ware promises that once the queen is dead, a witness would rise to testify that is what the queen keeps the menagerie for."

My stomach pitched, and I guessed who Ware's witness would be. My testimony, my final betrayal would be the price of Samuel's life.

"Many will *want* to believe it's true." Sara's voice—small and soft— came from behind us. "People far gone in superstition are already afraid when they see us. My mother always said not to mind them, to feel sorry for their ignorance. But I don't. I think they like to hate us."

"It's all a lie—Ware's salacious tales," Robin insisted.

Dulcinea groaned. "The army Ware is gathering thinks it is their duty to 'save' the king from the devils that surround him."

"But where will they strike?" I asked.

"Six weeks from now. At St. James's Park. There is to be a children's pageant to celebrate the queen's recovery."

"I've heard of no such pageant," I said. "Who would think such a gathering of children would cheer a woman who just lost her babe?"

"I think Archie proposed it just to vex everyone else," Sara said. "Buckingham's little daughter was there and he promised her the main part. Neither the king nor the queen could bear to disappoint the fatherless little girl."

"It's made a good deal of trouble for the rest of us." Robin Goodfellow frowned. "The king told Moll Buckingham she could have any scenery or props she wished. I am designing a dragon for her to ride. A servant is to be hidden inside it to make it gambol up to the queen so Moll can present Her Majesty with a toy sword to slay the 'demon.' "

"Ware is counting on the queen's sorrow to distract those around her during the play. The king, her ladies, and even her guard trying to shield Her Majesty's feelings. That way, Ware can strike more easily."

"Strike how?"

"He would not say, only that once the queen is dead, he will claim before all that he is cleansing England of enemies—foreign powers that consort with the devil's spawn and plot to make us the slaves to the Pope. That is when Jeffrey is to mount the stage and say the broadsheets' claims are true."

Will raged. "There is no power on earth that would make Jeffrey lie like you have!"

"Ware has . . . some kind of secret signal arranged. Let his allies know if Jeffrey has obeyed. If he doesn't, a mob will be waiting outside Fleet Prison's gates. The guards will fling Jeffrey's brother into their midst to be torn apart."

"God in Heaven," Sara whispered, and I could see her clasp her hand around her mother's miniature. "Why didn't you come to us earlier? Tell us instead of going to face Ware alone? We could have found a way to fight him together."

"Haven't I paid for that mistake?" A spasm gripped her, and she tossed her head on the pillow, her red hair damp with sweat. "Ware forced poison down my throat. Locked me in a room so high, he didn't believe I could escape. But I found a ledge, a piece of rope." She shivered. "I was so . . . afraid, but kept conjuring Will's voice in my head, the words he always says before I step onto my rope. I danced well, didn't I, Will?"

She reached out one hand to him, looking so hopeful, for a moment the butterfly the giant had not wanted to crush in their bridal bed.

"Tell her she danced well," I urged him, those familiar words holding the keys to forgiveness. Will glared at me.

He nearly choked on the words. "You danced well."

"Don't . . . hate me," Dulcinea moaned. "I didn't mean any harm."

I watched, helpless, as Dulcinea's hand fluttered gracefully through the air one last time and came to rest upon the pillow she and Will had never shared.

"She is gone," Boku said. "It is over."

Silence fell, shadows seeming to freeze upon the walls—monster forms of dwarfs and giants, sorcerers and fatal beauties. Masks and dragons to be built of wire and papier-mâché, cloth of silver scales, a glittering world of imagination with a thousand places an assassin could hide.

"We must alert the king. Stop the pageant," Simon insisted at last.

"No," I said, startled by the sound of my own voice. "We will put an end to this blind angel ourselves."

"Jeffrey, I know you are desperate," Simon said, "but we deal in illusion, entertainments. The queen has guards trained to protect her. Let them handle this peril."

"Are you certain none of those guards belong to this army of Ware's? It only takes one hand to wield a knife, shoot an arrow, or aim a pistol. Dulcinea had access to Her Majesty every day and no one suspected her for a moment. You cannot doubt Ware has other minions seeded within the queen's household. Any person we pass might be waiting for a chance to strike."

I saw Simon and Robin look at each other, sensed their unease.

"You are wondering if Ware has agents in our own menagerie," I said. "You know he has my brother Samuel. Ware believes he has me at his mercy. He would, except for one weapon I have left: all of you. The tricks we master together, the trust we have to have in one another if we are to leap from mock towers, pretend to slay one another with swords, fly in midair attached to pulleys and wires and cogs that could plunge us to our deaths."

"But our tricks are just for show, Jeffrey," Goodfellow said. "Mock battles, not real ones. Ware and his men will be trying to kill us in earnest. Even if we can cut Ware down, we will never find all the others."

"We may, if we are canny. Kill Uriel Ware and the pack turns on itself, fighting to define the new leader. We just have to be vigilant—alert. We can pick out Ware's dogs in the chaos."

Simon rubbed the back of his neck. "What Jeffrey says is true. There's not one of us who has escaped without some scars from the world beyond. Our very survival depended on gauging the temper for violence in a crowd."

"There is one problem with your plan, Jeffrey," Sara said. "The queen has banished you from her presence. You'll not be allowed anywhere near the pageant."

"That might be an advantage in this case. The rest of you will have parts to play. I will have no other task except to watch out for Ware." I raked my hand back through my hair. "Robin, can you work a place for me to hide into your design: a place where I can conceal myself from the audience but see as much of the surrounding area as possible?"

"What do you want me to do? Put a crow's nest on the dragon?"

"Tell Moll dragons are far too commonplace for her play. A ship with a sea serpent figurehead—that is something no one has ever seen before. It's sure to dazzle the queen."

Robin frowned. "It will mean a good deal of work. There is not much time."

"Then you had best get to it."

Robin plucked a stick of charcoal from behind his ear. He went to the hearth and started sketching something on the stones. "I'll need help," he said, casting a glance at Will.

I went to my friend. He stood there, so stoic, I did not know what to do to rouse him.

"Are you going to stand there while Uriel Ware uses children as a shield so he can murder the queen and kill my brother? Or doesn't it matter anymore? Freaks don't feel things like the beautiful do? Maybe Ware is right, since he killed the woman you love and you would barely even tell her good-bye."

Will rounded on me, and for a moment I thought he would strike me. I clambered up onto the nearest table, determined he would have to look me in the eye—or at least as close as I could get to it.

"They want to paint us as monsters?" I put my hands on my hips. "I say it is time to hunt down the real monster who is trying to destroy everything we love. Are you going to ride with me, Will Evans?"

I could hear a clock's muffled ticking, counting down minutes Dulcinea could never spend. The whole menagerie seemed to hold its breath.

Will gritted his teeth. "I ride."

I heard an exotic murmur, words from lands I would never see. Boku reached down and gently closed Dulcinea's eyelids. His dark, deft fingers unlaced his left gauntlet, the velvet parting and revealing ghastly scars. Upon the pale ridges were markings—each a different shape. "When slavers came to my village and took my mother and father, I could not stop them. When they took my sisters, I could not defend them. The slavers had my wrists bound so tight. One of the white men dropped his knife. I cut the ropes. I wanted to kill myself. The gods cursed me, and made me live. I tattooed these marks so I would not forget. Wherever masters sold me, sent me, I sought out magicians, sorcerers, thieves who could teach me their secrets, tricks to make certain no rope would ever hold me again. Tonight, I fight back for this new family I found."

Resolve surged through me, a sense of belonging such as I had never known before. "We will fight Ware together," I said. "Boku, prepare anything that might be of use to us during the pageant. Ways to distract, to climb unseen, ways to hide blades or make them appear when they're not expected. Ware is clever. He'll be watching."

"What should I do?" Sara asked.

"Ware's spies will have told him Dulcinea reached the palace. We must cloak how much we know of Ware's scheme. Find servants you know will gossip, tell them Dulcinea has been stricken with some strange apoplexy and cannot speak. Say Boku is trying to gather strange herbs to brew some antidote but has had no success."

"Why not let him know she is dead?" Robin asked. "Ware would act more boldly."

"If Ware fears she has survived, it will put him off balance. We want to pluck at his rope, shake him as much as we can. Nervous people make mistakes."

"I'm nervous," Sara whispered. She leaned against Robin. I saw him take her hand.

"You must try not to show it," I said. "Stay near the queen. Watch and listen. Have you a knife of some sort?"

"I do."

"Find a way to conceal it in your costume."

"What of Samuel?" Simon asked. "He is locked up, beyond our power to help."

"Ware needs my brother alive if he wants to force me to defame the queen. Samuel will be safe until things at the pageant go awry. We need to find some trustworthy guards at the prison who could move to protect Samuel on the day of the pageant. Will, you know half of London. I don't suppose you have some acquaintance in Fleet Prison? A secret Catholic? Do any of you know such a person?"

"There is a man I have seen collect coin from the dowager duchess of Buckingham. He carries food and such to Master Quintin for her. I saw him sneak into the Queen's Chapel once and light a candle at the Virgin Mary's feet."

"When next you see him, tell him I wish to send something to my brother."

"What will you do? Tell him about Ware's plan?" Robin frowned. "It is a great risk."

"It is a risk to sneak into the Queen's Chapel. I have seen the gift Master Quintin has for inspiring loyalty. We will have to hope that this guard will be brave enough to protect Samuel and his priest."

Sara nodded. "I will send him to you. Is there anything else I can do?"

I touched the miniature of Sara's mother. In a voice only she could hear, I said, "Next time you see Robin alone, ask him to paint an ivory image of Dulcinea as she was: before our butterfly flew into the flame. Pray that Will might forgive her enough to ask for the miniature one day."

Sara nodded, and I could see something wistful in her eyes. I hastened from the room, not wanting to wonder whom she was thinking of. There was no time for anything but trying to save the queen. The woman I loved. The woman who had cause to hate me.

The menagerie and I would fight the evil that threatened to consume her. Perhaps Henrietta Maria's curiosities did not know whether we sprang from God or from the devil. We only knew that we must rise or fall together.

THIRTY

·

July 1629
St. James's Palace

O nly Archie Armstrong was fiendish enough to maneuver the king into putting the royal theatrical stores at the disposal of a seven-year-old child. In the mayhem that followed, the crabbed court fool fairly burst with pride as he watched Moll Buckingham drive everyone else involved in the performance insane.

After a whole life petted and adored, then set aside and neglected until someone scooped her up to indulge her again, Moll seized power like I had seized the food Samuel had sneaked up to the loft when I was at my hungriest. Still reeling from the murder of the godlike father she adored, the child tried to cram every bit of delight into whatever time the adults would grant her.

Not that a sense of confusion was unexpected in the menagerie's course of work. There was always a mad roil when a pageant was being staged— scenery, crew to move the pieces about, mechanisms to try out, costumes to change, musical cues to match to actions, visual tricks to insert where needed. We had even worked with a few children in our performances in the past.

But this chaos permeated more deeply than any I had experienced before. As I peered out at the shifting maze of children, the surveyors and designers, the cast and the workmen, the foreboding in my belly grew cold as stone.

Moll had embraced my idea of a sea serpent ship with an enthusiasm that made everyone involved in the performance want to throttle her, the child intent on turning dry land into a fantastical realm beneath the sea. She had Master Jones's apprentice drape tree limbs with ropes that looked like seaweed. Platforms shaped like giant shells perched in forks in the branches. Scalloped edges glittered silver. False pearls large enough for a woman to sit on had been balanced in the shells' cups, providing a perfect place to conceal an assassin who was skilled with a pistol. Ship's rigging scaled trees, making it possible to scramble up the thick trunks, despite the fact that they were wound with gauze—Moll's attempt to transform them into the pillars of Triton's castle.

This whole area of the park was a veritable wonderland of climbing and leaping and swinging about for Moll, the girl determined to revel in the hazardous entertainments her nurse and her lady mother usually forbid her to enjoy.

"Such pursuits must be allowed this once in the interest of the queen's pleasure," the king had said, apologizing to the worried ladies, gifting them with one of his rare smiles. Just as the queen must loan her menagerie to Buckingham's daughter for these few days—the performers one more piece of scenery in Moll and the king's view.

That is how Will Evans became Moll's favorite toy.

I might have found the sight of the pretty child in her ribbons and curls enthroned upon Will's shoulders as enchanting as everyone else as I skulked about in the background, but Moll's fascination with "her nice giant" curtailed my ability to ask his advice while setting up our defense of the queen.

I had planned to station Will as close as possible to Her Majesty, but Moll would not have it. Will was to stay at her side with the "pretty Moon Lady"—the role in which Moll had cast Lady Carlisle. I could imagine the pain it would cause the dowager duchess of Buckingham to see Moll with Buckingham's exquisite mistress, listen to the child marvel at how beautiful the courtier was. I had even dared to come out of hiding and waylay the child myself. But my attempt to dissuade Moll met with an obdurate glare that would have done her father proud.

I was fairly certain Buckingham's daughter would have happily fed me to the sea serpent Goodfellow had transformed her dragon into: a project that had kept him up all night, even with the help of Will Evans and Boku. It was an amazing piece of work—newly set wooden planks here and there giving form and substance, billowy sails caught up on masts Robin cautioned could snap if too much pressure was put on them, the correct supports not having been built into the design. The dragon's mobile face had been altered into the ship's figurehead—a sea serpent upon the bow.

Boku was to be wedged into the cramped space in the serpent to make it come alive when it was time to devour the Mermaid Princess. Every time Robin fastened the sorcerer into the compartment, there was a feverish tension in Boku that I had never seen before. I wondered if it reminded him of his captivity.

If Moll had been working hand in hand with Uriel Ware, she could not have crippled our efforts any better. It made me wonder if Ware was moving Buckingham's daughter about like Inigo Jones shifted scenes.

I tried to quell my mounting frustration as I attempted to find the best places to conceal other sentinels we needed to watch for any unusual actions in the play's midst or about the perimeter.

If Ware does suspect we hope to foil his plan, the bastard must feel smug, I thought. Whatever plan we laid out, Moll dashed with her next command, changing her mind so often that no one—not even Moll, I was convinced— knew where anyone or anything was to appear at any set time.

In desperation, I even sent Sara to the king. But when she suggested that the performance might be more pleasing to the audience if Moll did not have quite so much control, Charles had grown so sorrowful, Sara said, his countenance brought tears to her eyes.

"Letting the poor poppet have her way in this is small recompense for the papa she has lost. Just last week, I found her weeping because some lads were tormenting her, saying what a villain her father was. I told her His Grace had been my dearest friend. He loved me when no one else did—when I was still an awkward, stammering boy. I told Moll that I could not give her father back to her, but that I would stand in her father's place, love her and protect her," Charles had told Sara.

"The king would have been such a good father," Sara said. "I cannot understand why God would take their child but saddle parents who can't feed one babe with so many children, they have no choice but to sell them."

I thought of the desperation simple people must feel and the actions such emotions might drive them to. Felton had murdered the duke, who had cheated him of his livelihood and sent countless troops to their death. Would it not be easy to imagine that I was lashing out at the queen in the same way—because of the rift between us? If our plan went awry, wouldn't people think I was involved in the plot against her, willing to revenge myself for the rejection I'd suffered at her hands?

If I failed, what would it matter? The queen would be dead. I could not close my eyes now without seeing that horrific scene play out in my head.

The only victory I won over our beribboned tyrant was in convincing Moll to create a costume for Her Majesty to wear—a steel breastplate and pretty feathered helmet that might at least be some small defense against arrow or blade. It was too small a victory.

I stole out to take my post before the royal party passed through the gates of St. James's Palace. I felt as if I could not breathe as I wound through the park. This path was stalked by ghosts of the youth I had been, a butcher's son, trapped by intriguing courtiers and so bewildered in this strange world that he'd not even attempted to stand against them. I could see Henrietta Maria as she had been—spoiled and headstrong, homesick and so unhappy, pressed on all sides to be a Joan of Arc who would save England for the Pope. I could not forget her bare feet in the muck as she walked to Tyburn, her earnest face as she murmured prayers. I could not forget the crowd pressing along the sides of the road, how exposed she had been, how vulnerable. Then, the glowering sky had looked down on the possibility of threat.

Today, the sun shone in a sky bluer than Moll's mermaid sea. Amid the lilting music of viols, flutes, and children's laughter, an evil archangel waited to kill the queen.

Taking care, as Robin had warned, I climbed up into the crow's nest. From my perch, I could see the flower-draped carts rattle through three arches of silver cloth, the courtiers disembarking in King Triton's world. Boys mounted on great sea horses brought a chariot made of shells to carry the queen and king to the dais, from which they would watch the masque.

I wondered if anyone noticed that one of the boys looked a good bit older than the others—a wiry page Will had taken into his confidence, a real sword concealed in a makeshift scabbard Robin had designed in the lad's "saddle."

From my hiding place, I could see half a dozen such sentinels and wondered if I had made a fatal mistake in allowing Will to muster them. The man was not the best judge of character. After all, look how he had latched onto me.

Affection for him made my eyes sting. I prayed no bullet or blade meant for the queen would strike him down. My friend made an appallingly big target.

"Do you think Ware might call off the assassination if it seems too difficult to strike?" He had asked me as the morning of the masque dawned.

"No," I said. "Ware fancies himself like Samson driving the greedy Catholics out of England and off of the sea. Saving English pride and seizing the fat purses from men like Buckingham. God will handle trivialities such as Philistines."

Will had cracked his knuckles. "My mother used to say men loved to boast how God was on their side. She always wondered how they felt when they got to God's table and realized that the enemies they were fighting believed they were fighting in God's name, as well. Said if she were in charge of Heaven, she'd take her wooden spoon and whack the whole lot of them on the backside like she did to my brothers and me when we misbehaved." He frowned. "Men willing to be martyrs are the most dangerous of all."

Am I one of those men now? I wondered, peeking out over the edge of the crow's nest. Am I willing to martyr myself to save the queen?

We would soon find out. While Their Majesties were being settled upon the dais, the rest of the troupe spilled out of their conveyances and hastened to their posts. They did well, taking care not to look up at my hiding place and risk betraying my whereabouts to our foe.

As the pageant commenced, I was grateful that I, at least, could see the surrounding area well enough. With the watchman's rattle Will had placed at my feet, I could sound the alarm if necessary so that those stronger and more able could rush to the queen's defense. Not that I wasn't prepared, if necessary. I patted the lump at my waist where my pistol was hidden, shifted the weight of the sword the queen had had a smith make for me.

Never had time crawled more slowly than the next hour, my head pounding, my neck aching from straining to see all angles. But nothing—no one—seemed out of place.

By the time the Mermaid Princess and Moon Lady went to honor the glittering Sun God that clearly represented Moll's father, even I had begun to suspect that Ware might have changed his mind. Or was there a more ominous reason he had not struck? Was it possible he had planned for Dulcinea to escape? Had he fed her wrong information when he'd told her of his plan for this masque? While we had been wasting our time plotting how to protect Henrietta Maria here, was Ware setting up a trap somewhere else?

I shifted my weight without thinking, cursing in frustration as the mast swayed.

Suddenly, I saw it—something askew: the door to the sea serpent's compartment ajar. Boku and Goodfellow had argued for hours over the latch. Goodfellow insisted the adjustments he had made in the design did not leave enough room inside the compartment to include a release for the door's latch. I had even seen Boku's hands tremble at the notion that he could not escape the small enclosure of the compartment under his own power.

The unfastened latch wasn't enough by itself to warrant sounding the alarm, but someone on the ground needed to take a closer look. I tried to catch Will's eyes, warn him to go check the irregularity, but he was turned the wrong way, and the rest of the audience was too transfixed on the spectacle to notice me. The sea horses that had led the procession were circling now, their riders attempting to capture the Moon Lady with silver nets while nymphs wove in and out among them. Their trailing scarves of sea green and blues from cerulean to lapis lazuli created waves that fluttered, spirals of mist rising in the air.

Master Jones struck the tiny droplets of water with lights so bright that they shimmered, and fireworks popped off to one side to draw the audience's eyes away from the ship just long enough to shove the final bit of scenery into place. I saw Sara in her plump salmon-colored fish costume—complete with fluttering silver-stitched fins. She swept up to the queen and signaled so that the sea horse men cast a net over Henrietta Maria, weaving this way and that.

I saw the queen laughing as she was pulled into the game, the king clapping his hands as they brought their captive toward the magical ship. She was awash in a sea of children; a score of them pooled around her, singing and dancing in an adorable choir of dryads. The plumes in Henrietta Maria's helm swept up, red as blood. Unease twisted in me. Somehow, in the dance, the queen had been cut off from everyone save the children and Boku, who was hidden in the serpent's head.

I prayed he would be able to see her, guard her until she sprang into her guards' range of vision again. Robin had assured me the sorcerer could break through the slats of wood and plaster that formed the figurehead if he was needed. I knew Boku was armed with more than his skills in necromancy. He had a thin blade bound into his velvet gauntlet. Swift as his reflexes were, I had no doubt he could best any attacker.

The ship shifted, flinging my perch off balance just enough for me to notice something else I had not before. As the serpent's mouth opened, the void was not filled by the darkness of Boku's skin, but by a pale smear cut across its middle by a black band.

I grabbed for the watchman's rattle, but the noise was drowned out in shouts from the crowd, a spate of fireworks exploding in dazzling colors somewhere behind the king.

Everyone spun to see them, sure they were part of the performance. But I knew better as I saw a pimpled face, a scalp plucked bare in patches—two of the apprentices I had seen at the Saracen's Bane.

I saw something move in the serpent head, glimpsed a flash of what must be steel. Not one of the sentinels was looking at the queen, and I could never climb down the mast in time. I prayed there was another way.

I flung myself against the rail of the crow's nest with all my might, once, twice. The third time, I heard a telltale crack. I felt it starting to tip as the serpent burst open.

Ware charged toward the queen, a knife in his hand. I heard a murmur from the crowd—people thinking it was part of the masque. Then they gasped in horror as they and the guards realized the threat was real. I saw the king leap to his feet on the dais, cut off from his wife by the crowd. The queen screamed, but the tangle of silk waves bound her. Guards tried to clamber toward her but were blocked by panicked children attempting to escape in a chaos of confusion. No one, not even Will, could reach her in time, even if they trampled the little ones.

But I might have a chance. The mast was shifting, falling, the ship's deck rushing up to meet me. At the last instant, I did as Dulcinea had taught me, launching myself toward the figure looming over the queen.

Just as he plunged his dagger, I struck the queen like a cannonball, knocking her out of his way. White-hot pain sliced my right arm, bones in my shoulder seeming to snap.

I rolled and gained my feet, Ware towering over me, his eye patch torn off. Looking off in the distance, I saw Will thundering toward me through a sea of frightened children. I had to buy him time to reach the queen.

I heard the king shouting, glimpsed Charles trying to push through the mass of people as I groped for my sword. Pain seared through the wound in my shoulder, making it impossible for my right hand to draw the sword from the scabbard. I tried to use my left, but my arm was too short and the blade too long to get free, the hilt snagging under my arm. I could see the queen's eyes, dark and filled with terror.

Scorn flooded Ware's face. "Worthless little fool!" He wheeled toward her. I launched myself into the space between them just as Uriel Ware drew his dagger back to strike. I knotted my hand in his hair, using his own momentum to overset him. Had he managed to wound the queen? I could not tell. We tumbled across the ground as I clung to him with the fierceness of my father's dogs when the fight was the most uncertain.

Ware slammed his elbow back into my midsection, my ribs giving a hideous cracking sound. I couldn't breathe, choked as if I were drowning. Triumph filled Ware's face as he shook free of my grasp and turned back to the terrified queen. Blackness swam before my eyes as I groped for my boot top, the dagger hidden within. I forced my left hand to close around it, gave a guttural cry. Ware turned to look at me over his shoulder. I thrust the dagger point into the empty socket where Uriel Ware's eye should have been.

Ware pitched forward, his body sprawling over that of the fallen queen. Blood . . . there was so much blood. . . . Please, God, let it be his, let it be mine . . . not Henrietta Maria's.

I tried to drag Ware off of her, tears flowing down my face, my breath coming in tortured gasps as I fought to keep unconsciousness at bay. "My . . . lady . . . Someone help me!"

Suddenly, Ware was yanked skyward. His arms and legs dangled like a spider's; then he was flying through the air, flung across the void into a mass of yeomen guards.

Will appeared above me, a hazy blur of thick brows, deep-set eyes, and wild hair.

"The queen. Will, tell me she is safe." My voice broke, my right side seeming to be full of glass shards. "God, let her be safe."

The queen cried out to calm those around her, her voice all but drowned out by the sobbing children. "I am unharmed!"

"The queen is unharmed!" Will bellowed above the din of the crowd.

"The assassin?"

"Buckingham's man: Uriel Ware. Jeffrey Hudson cut him down!"

I could hear gasps of relief and astonishment going through the crowd, and, in the distance, the bellows of guards and shouts from the king as he attempted to get to his wife. I expected Henrietta Maria would be running to Charles as well, but her shadow fell over me. I saw tumbled dark curls, felt that soft hand that had not touched me in so long. She stroked the hair back from my cheek. "Jeffrey. You are not supposed to be here! I forbade you to perform."

"I couldn't bear being away from the audience," I started to joke, then said, "Dulcinea betrayed a plot to harm you. I couldn't stay away."

"How did you get to me? When I saw Ware's knife . . . How could you reach me when no one else could?"

"Goodfellow's shoddy workmanship on the mast. He told me it would snap if I leaned the wrong way." It hurt to jest. "Thank God it fell the right way. You must have angels looking out for you." I thought of her father, taken from her by just such a lunatic with a knife. Had Henri le Grande reached down from heaven to aid me? Or was it merely the training I had gained in other performances, the reflexes Dulcinea had nurtured, the times I had watched her with Simon Rattlebones and Inigo Jones, plotting acrobatics to accompany Boku's magic?

"This is no time for jests. Your arm is bleeding and your shoulder is awry."

"A trifling matter, though being able to draw a decent . . . breath might be a pleasant change."

She turned her face away, looking at Will. "How badly is he hurt?"

"I cannot say." The grief in Will's voice told me all I needed to know.

"Henrietta Maria, come away from there. We must get him to a surgeon," I heard the king say from some distance.

I expected Henrietta Maria to disappear from my sight, go to the king. I dreaded the tearing away, all too aware I would never see that beloved face again.

But the queen bent closer to me. "You must not die, Jeffrey. I command you not to die."

"There are some things even a queen . . . cannot decree."

"You flung yourself between me and a naked blade."

I tried to force a smile. "Did I not promise to be your champion the night I burst out of the pie?"

"I have been so dreadful to you! I cast you out, let your brother languish in prison."

"You had good reason to hate me."

"I did not hate you. I could never hate you. When Lucy gave me the letters, she said . . ."

"Lady Carlisle was right to warn you." I swallowed hard, licked my dry lips. It hurt, my chest feeling half-caved in. "I am . . . sorry I betrayed you."

"Why did you do it? Why?"

"Buckingham gave my father coin, forced me. But after the defeat in France . . . Ware took the reins. Went further than even Buckingham dared. Malevolent bastard. He had Samuel imprisoned . . . said he would kill him. But I would not hurt you anymore."

"You might have died."

"I would have laid life down gladly. Because I love you."

"Of course." She brushed the words aside with a wave of her hand. "I know that."

"No, you don't." I drew on my last ounce of courage, knowing I was going to die. What did it matter if I confessed the truth? I would not have to bear ridicule, scorn, or see the withdrawal in Henrietta Maria's eyes. At least not for long. "I do not love you as your servant, Majesty, as your fool. I love you as a man loves a woman."

Her face crumpled. Not into revulsion, but into heartbreaking empathy, the passionate kindness I had been starved of for so long. I could see her search for the right words to say. I did not want to leave her with more guilt, more regrets.

"I know it may be the most fool-like thing I have ever done. Courtiers . . . and servants alike will laugh. But I could not help loving . . . not the queen . . .

but the Henrietta Maria who loved her spaniels, who dressed up for masques with such delight . . . who comforted me when my brother died. I know you can never love me the way I love you. You cannot even forgive me . . . for mistakes I made."

"I can! I will! If I had not been so infernally proud, I would have let you explain. . . ." She pulled me into her arms, like she might have embraced Mitte or little Moll Buckingham or a babe of her own. Agony shot through me, and yet it was worth the pain to feel her against me, the softness of her, the warmth, just as I had always dreamed. "Just wait, Jeffrey. I'll make certain Samuel is freed."

I saw Will bending over us. My friend's face was wet with tears. "Sara found Boku," he said. "Let Boku attempt to treat him. Majesty, there is something he can try."

I saw the magician—a gash on his brow, his hands a trifle unsteady. Ware must have struck him. Dragged him from the compartment he had recoiled from?

The illusionist had a wand in his hand—one of the reeds from the set. Did he intend to work some charm? "The sack that air goes into is crushed," Boku said in that strange accent. "Let me punch this hollow reed through the chest, try to fill . . ."

I saw the king reach down for the queen, meaning to draw her away to let Boku do his work. "Do not leave me, Jeffrey." The queen wept, clinging to me a moment more. "You will be featured in every masque, ride with me on the hunt, play every game of bowls. I have missed you so much, my dearest friend."

"But I am not . . . your love," I said softly. "In every hero tale Will has ever told me, the lady's champion . . . sacrifices himself in her place. Never forget I am . . . honored . . . I had the chance to do that for you."

She drew herself up, looking almost haughty. "I order you not to die. Do you hear me? Who will make me laugh?"

"Your husband. The babes I know will come. Let Lord Minimus go. It is better . . . if my tale ends this way."

I felt a piercing pain in my chest, as if Boku were driving a stake through my heart. His black skin seemed to diffuse into a night sky, blotting out the world.

THIRTY-ONE

•

I was only a little surprised that Heaven resembled Will Evans's room. It made sense in a strange way—this first place I discovered friendship. But a jolt of fear went through me at the sight of Samuel's face.

"No. Samuel, you're not supposed to be dead," I gasped. "The queen promised she'd free you."

"I'm not dead, Jeff, and neither are you. Even though everyone, including the royal doctor, says you should be, *would* be, if it weren't for Boku." Samuel sat down on the bed. The jarring made fire explode in my chest. "Some people claimed it was dark magic, a kind of evil. Father Quintin told them he'd heard of the procedure from some Moors when he was in Spain. It was no more magic than the other treatments the Moors had shared with the rest of the world before the Inquisition burned all their books, decreed it un-Christian to use their methods."

"Just waking up and I get a lecture about how clever Father Quintin is."

"Father's stories were the only thing that kept me sane during those weeks in that horrible cell. Took my mind off the things that evil man said."

I felt a sinking sensation, my greatest fear. "What evil man?"

"Ware."

"Ware?" If Samuel had doused me with water from the wintery Thames, he could not have roused me more thoroughly. "What did the bastard say?" I swore, tried to force myself up on one elbow, but someone had bound my arm against my midsection.

"Don't strain yourself," Samuel said. "Let me help you." He worked one arm beneath my back and lifted me so I could almost sit up, leaning back against a mound of pillows. "How do you feel?"

I arched my brow. "Remember that time you ran out into the street to save that widow's cat when they were driving the cattle through to be slaughtered?"

"You were the one who saved her."

"Only because I wasn't big enough to haul you back by the seat of your breeches and I knew you'd never go back into the cottage unless the blasted creature was safe. Scratched me for my pains. Damned ungrateful beasts, cats."

"The widow was so thankful for its rescue, she got out the Lady statue so we could offer prayers of thanks."

That was the first time Samuel had seen the carving of Mary. I could remember his face, so enthralled. How the widow had let him touch the Holy Mother's face. That was when it had begun—Samuel's devotion to a world he could not see, while I was too concerned about keeping us both alive in this world.

"You leaped into the fray again—this time, from a height that could have killed you. What were you thinking, Jeffrey?"

"That Will was upstaging me in the masque. Can't bear when someone else gets more attention than I do."

"I know that is not true. Well, perhaps a little bit. You paid in blood for being center stage this time. Your shoulder popped out of place and two of your ribs were broken from the leap you took from the mast, or from Ware's pummeling—we don't know which. Boku bound the injured parts to hold them still, give them a chance to heal. He's been putting something made with moldy bread on your stab wound. It has not festered."

"Boku should have made up his mind whether he was harming me or helping me. My last memory is of him stabbing me in the chest."

"He said it was a trick he learned when he was traveling among the Moors. He's traveled all over, Jeffrey, learned so many things. When he blew into the hollow reed, you started to breathe more easily. You were lucky, Jeffrey. Very lucky."

"Not if . . . if Ware . . ." I faltered, more terrified than I had ever been in my life. Samuel loved his saintly Father Quintin so much. How could I bear for my brother to despise me? "God, Samuel, what did he say?"

"He told me everything. Taunted me, told me how you were going to hell for what you had done for me."

I closed my eyes, wishing to Heaven Boku had just let me die. "Samuel, don't hate me."

"For saving me from a life in the shambles? For getting me an education and placing me in the care of the finest man I've ever known? How can you think I would hate you?" Samuel's voice quavered. With what? Love for Father Quintin or sorrow that I was destined for hell?

"I did not know Quintin was a priest. I never would have put you . . . in harm's way on purpose."

"I know that, Jeffrey. When I think of you—spying for Buckingham, trapped here by men like Ware . . . I know how much it cost you, inside. Yet you never ceased trying to make certain I was safe. You sacrificed so much. You shouldn't have done it. If I'd known, I never would have let you," he said fiercely.

"Even you could not have stopped me, brother," I said. "You were . . . the only person who . . . loved me. Until I joined the menagerie."

"I am so glad you found them. I knew something was amiss when several of the guards started taunting me worse than usual. Sharpening their knives and tweaking me about my throat, saying I had best hope they not get some signal. When Havlock explained someone in the menagerie had asked him to stand guard over Master Quintin and me, I guessed you were fighting some battle to keep us safe—Father and Mother, the queen, and me. Even Will Evans. You've spent your whole life smaller than everyone else. Yet, somehow, you are always trying to protect us."

"Must look absurd—a man my size playing hero. Ridiculous, aren't I?"

"No. Brave. Like no one else in the world. Not because of your body, but because your spirit is larger than anyone I've ever met. John always thought so, too."

"I miss him," I said, my chest so full that it ached.

Samuel clasped my hand. "I miss him also. But not as much as I am going to miss you."

A frisson of alarm jolted through me. "You'll not be able to be rid of me from now on."

Samuel picked at my coverlet, his curls catching the light. He hesitated a moment before he spoke. The pause filled me with sinking dread.

"Jeff, the queen has arranged to slip Father Quintin out of the country on a merchant ship. He's going to the Jesuit school in France. I'm going with him."

I started to protest, but I knew it was futile. Samuel would not feel right about leaving this wise man who needed him. "I suppose there is no dissuading you. You might as well help him until he can rejoin the other Jesuits in his order, but as soon as you turn Father Quintin over to them, you can hurry back here. I'm certain the queen will help me find you another tutor."

"Father Quintin can school me best in the ways that I need." Samuel drew a deep breath. "I've decided to take holy orders."

I choked, fought to remember how to breathe, this blow more crushing than any Ware had dealt me. It wasn't my ribs breaking this time, but my heart.

"Holy orders . . . become a priest?" Panic battered dark wings inside me. "Samuel, no. I won't let you do it! Have you seen what happened to your Father Quintin? He can barely walk because he spent two weeks in a priest hole! The courts sent him to Barbados, to the cane fields, as punishment. The courts could execute him because he returned to England."

"If I know Father Quintin, he will come back to England again." Samuel set his jaw, stubborn with a resolve that shook me to my core. "Father Quintin told me about the dangers in becoming a priest. I'm willing to face them. I hope I can show his courage."

His words drove through me, more piercing than the wound Boku had dealt me the day Uriel Ware had died. "If you become a Jesuit, I'll never see you again, Samuel," I whispered. "You'll never be able to come home." My eyes burned and my hands shook, my future stretching out before me without Samuel.

"Of course I will come home. The moment I am ordained."

"Oh, Samuel." There was no point in arguing. I could see it in his eyes. I thought of Tyburn, the scaffold where Catholic martyrs had died among thieves and murderers. I remembered the dried blood Henrietta Maria had kissed. Would Samuel's stain the same hellish spot? It seemed a fitting punishment for what I had done—manipulating the queen into losing the love of her subjects on the road to Tyburn Tree. But Samuel was innocent. Would he pay the price because of what I had done?

Samuel touched my good arm, his face so solemn, it felt as if he were already an ocean away from me. "Thank you for not trying to dissuade me."

I struggled to find a jest, a fool to the end. "When you thought you had the right of something, no power on earth could change your mind. I won't even bother wrestling the power of Heaven. Everyone thought you were the sweet one at the Hudson fireside. You were the most stubborn."

"Jeffrey, speaking of that fireside: Promise me you will go home sometimes to visit Mother and Ann. Father, too. With John gone, and now me, they will need you."

"I am the last son our parents would see if they had the choice."

Samuel winced, didn't even bother denying it was true. "That does not mean they will not be glad to see you."

"Fine. I will visit Oakham whenever the queen's household is within reach of it. I can't have you skipping off to devote your life to God with a guilty conscience."

I saw my brother's eyes grow bright with tears. He was the only lad I knew who had never attempted to hide them. "I will miss you, Jeffrey."

"You'll have plenty of company: saints, martyrs, priests. Why, God alone is three in one. You will be downright thronged with company." Did my bitterness seep through? No. Only my grief.

"Do not jest about God."

Humor drained out of me. "God can forgive me this one small trespass. I am giving Him my most precious possession."

Samuel's face turned pink with both pleasure and embarrassment. "Father Quintin knows ways to pass letters between us when I can send them. I will be very busy. They say the Jesuit regimen is strict."

"They had to make it so, or everyone would be running away from a perfectly lovely future their brothers arranged for them and choosing to become a Jesuit instead."

Samuel smiled. "I am so glad you awakened before I had to leave. I was afraid if you did not, I wouldn't have a chance to tell you good-bye. You see, the packet sails in the morning. Father Quintin and I must be on it."

I felt as if the floor were falling out from under me. But the parting had been inevitable. I should have known Samuel would have been chafing to get at his studies. Besides, the sooner Quintin was on a ship, the less chance he'd be thrown back in prison. I was certain most of the king's advisers would wish the Jesuit behind bars. Many of the people beyond the palace walls would want him dead. I would have liked the priest myself, if it weren't for the fact that his influence might get Samuel killed.

"So this is good-bye." I could not fathom more pain than I felt at that moment.

"It is good-bye for now."

"Wait." I struggled up. "Have Will take you up to my room. In my trunk, my Fairy King costume is there. Bring it to me."

Samuel flushed. "I put it under your pillow for protection. Will is off questioning everyone at the Saracen's Bane, trying to track down any of Ware's fellow conspirators. No telling how long it might take or if he will be able to find them all. Will wanted to put you here in his room until you grew stronger. He worried that one of Ware's men might decide to come after the man who saved the queen. He thought you'd be safer here while he was away. Master Quintin thinks anyone working with Ware would have scattered to the far corners of the kingdom by now. But Will didn't want to take any chances after what happened to Dulcinea."

I wondered if Will would be so determined to guard me if he knew I had been in Buckingham's employ. Guilt dragged at me as I groped under my pillow with my good arm until I found the coarse cloth of my tunic, the lump where Samuel had sewn the holy medal the night before I left for Burley-on-the-Hill.

"Give me your penknife," I said as I drew the garment out. Samuel did as I asked.

With some difficulty, I sliced the lump of cloth free from the rest of the garment. I could feel the hard disk of the medal still concealed. Despite the covering, I could picture the face of Samuel's beloved Holy Mother.

"You need protection more than I do now," I said, pressing it into my brother's hand. "You might ask your Lady for one thing, though, in return for giving her back to you."

"What is that?" Samuel asked.

"I know a woman and her husband who long for a babe more than kingdoms or crowns. Perhaps your Queen of Heaven might arrange for a prince on earth?"

"I'll pray to her. Jeff, I hate to leave you this way."

I tightened my hands on the coverlet, clutched tight so I would not try to catch hold of Samuel, never let him go. "Better not keep God or the tides waiting," I said gruffly.

Samuel embraced me, and I did not mind the pain. I could feel his tears hot on my cheek. They mingled with my own. "Jeff, I could not have asked for a better brother."

"Might have asked for a taller one," I grumbled.

"Just measure the part you take up in my heart."

With that, Samuel turned, hastened away. I knew I would never see my Samuel again.

If he ever returned, he would be changed. A priest. A Jesuit. If he came to England, he would be a hunted man.

I closed my eyes and prayed his Lord and Lady would take better care of him than I had.

≈≈≈

If anyone had told me the queen of England would visit me while I was still abed, I would have scoffed at the notion. I had dreamed of Henrietta Maria often enough, her ivory skin bare, her dark hair threaded through with my fingers, her lips ripe from kisses she returned as eagerly as I bestowed them. In my dreams, she had not been wed to Charles. In my dreams, when I rolled her beneath me, I was tall as Buckingham and as beautiful to look at. She returned my kisses with the same passion I felt for her.

I had done my best to put her out of my mind since I had regained consciousness. She was alive. She was safe. But nothing could ever be the same. We could never go back to the way our relationship had been before the countess of Carlisle showed her Buckingham's letters. Not after my confession at little Moll's pageant.

Even if the queen would forgive me for my betrayal enough to summon me into her service again, I could not bear the humiliation in seeing Henrietta Maria every day, knowing that she knew of my passion for her now.

I love you as a man loves a woman. Time and again, those words ran through my mind. I saw her shock, her empathy. Was she also disgusted? Had her imagination painted a far different picture from mine? A shrunken dwarf of a man—a freak—trying to pleasure her?

I felt sick at the thought that my lady might be repulsed by me, even in her imagination.

So when I heard tramping feet outside Will's chamber door, heard cries of "Make way for the queen" from her guards, I had to fight not to bury my head under the coverlets.

The bedchamber door opened, and there she stood, the dowager duchess of Buckingham, with Lady Carlisle behind her. Those familiar ringlets pressed against the queen's brow, a soft pink gown making her look like spring's first primrose. A blue sash cinched the dainty waist she longed to have blossom with a child.

She looked at me through her lashes, this daughter of a king seeming almost as shy as I felt.

I attempted to struggle out of bed, intending to kneel at her feet, but she closed the space between us, gently pressing me back down onto the pillows. The scent of her drifted over me.

"Do not tire yourself observing formalities on my account, Jeffrey," she said. "I wanted to speak to you in private, explain why no one must ever know of your courage save those who witnessed it. His Majesty has forbidden anyone present at the pageant to mention what happened there. He fears such talk might give other malcontents ideas, hopes of furthering this mad cause. To seize England for true Englishmen is what they claim."

"I am glad Uriel Ware will not become a martyr. He will slip into obscurity and no one will remember him."

"I pray you are not in too much pain."

"I am better every day, Majesty. Are you well? You did not suffer any injuries from Ware's attack?"

"A lump on the back of my head from when you knocked me out of the path of Ware's knife." She smiled.

"I am sorry to have hurt you."

"Do not be. There was a scratch upon the breastplate Sergeant Evans got me to wear. He said the armor was your idea. If I had not been wearing it, if you had not risked so much to come to my aid, I would have died as my father died." She shuddered, and I could see childhood nightmares in her eyes. "While you were unconscious, Sergeant Evans told the king and me everything. How you came to know of the plot against me. It is hard to think the rope dancer was enmeshed in this treachery, even harder to imagine that she is dead. Dulcinea was so young and beautiful. No wonder both you and Sergeant Evans loved her."

"I did not love her. I only let you believe I did in an ill-considered plan to spare my friend pain. She would have broken his heart. In the end, she did. It seems the hearts of curiosities are as brittle as anyone else's."

She turned to her attendants. "Leave us," she said. "I would have some speech alone with the man who saved my life."

The countess of Carlisle and the dowager duchess of Buckingham curtsyed, both women's faces still reflecting the horror of what had happened in the park. What had it been like for the duchess to see an assassin with a knife this second time? See the chaos and violence with her little daughter nearby? What had Lady Carlisle hoped in her secret heart when Ware had attacked? Would she have regretted the queen's death had Ware succeeded, or did she hope for the opportunity to give succor to a grieving king? The countess might as well have been masked as she was the first time I saw her for all the emotion I could read in her exquisite face. I was grateful when the room emptied.

The queen turned back to me, her smile uncertain. "It has been too long since I have had conversation with you, my dear Jeffery."

"We both know why you were silent."

"People who love each other forgive, do they not?" She fidgeted with the watch that dangled from a rope of pearls against her breast. She turned the oval disk over, and I could see a painted image that could only be that of the king.

"I have been receiving reports from all who have tended you these three days. I would have been here to thank you in person sooner except that the king had me practically locked up in a jewel cask until he was satisfied that any who conspired with Ware had been rooted out."

"His Majesty is a wise man to guard such a treasure."

"I pray you are not in too much pain from your exploits."

"I grow better every day. Not that I recommend leaping from a falling mast as an entertaining pastime, nor wrestling a dagger-wielding maniac.

There are far pleasanter ways to spend an afternoon." It was a valiant attempt at humor. She did not show even a hint of a smile.

"You may spend your days however you wish, Jeffrey. You have earned that right."

"Majesty . . ."

"The king will reward you in any way you desire: a fine house far from court, a knighthood. You will never have to worry about coin again. Just ask and that life will be yours."

I reeled at her offer, stunned. I could leave the gawking crowds, the scheming courtiers, the intrigues. I'd be safe from nobles like Buckingham who might seek to use me against the queen. I should have been rejoicing in my good fortune. And yet . . . I pictured it as if it were on the other side of a window, thick glass separating me from that world, distorting its shapes and hues.

The queen plucked at a tear-shaped sapphire that dangled from a ribbon about her throat. "You have earned the freedom to choose your own future," she said. "Is it wrong of me to hope that you will choose to stay with me?"

"With you, Majesty?" I felt as if I was plummeting downward aboard the crow's nest again.

"I need you, Lord Minimus: Your friendship, your humor, your dauntless courage. I do not know what is to come. I know only that with His Majesty and with Jeffrey Hudson, my dearest friend, I can meet whatever the future holds. Will you stay?"

I stared for long moments into a future I had never even dared to imagine. Would I be better off away from the queen? To escape the constant reminder of the love I could never have? Would it not be hell to see her so happy as another man's wife, even if that man was my king?

For a moment, I hesitated, indecision sharp as Ware's dagger. Then, the truth washed over me. Leave Henrietta Maria forever? I might as well rip the sun out of the sky. Whatever it cost me, I could not leave her. I turned my gaze to hers.

"Yes, Majesty. I will stay."

I would have done anything she wished, just to see her look at me as she did now, her heart in her eyes. "Jeffrey, never be ashamed of what you told me when you feared you were dying. I am honored to be loved by you." She kissed me on the lips, one sweet, aching kiss. "May the next woman who kisses you be a love of your own."

—⚬—

I couldn't say how long Will had been gone from the palace, tidying up what remained of Ware's poison. I was certain he would come see me as soon as he returned, knowing I would be grieving the loss of Samuel. The giant who took up so much space in the world, forever thunking into things with his great shoulders or tramping on things with his boat-size feet, had a remarkable gift for treading softly around people's bruised feelings. When he did tap at the door, I bade him enter.

"You are the only man I know who would knock on the door to his own room," I said with feigned irritation from my seat beside the fire. Will's chair, in truth.

It was a ridiculous place for me to sit, with my ribs still sore and my clothes on for the first time in a week. I wasn't about to tell him I had made Griggory lift me up into the giant-size chair, wanting to feel closer to my friend.

"I can imagine how hard it has been for you—seeing the queen, learning Samuel is going to France. To lose a second brother . . . well, I didn't know if you'd welcome company," Will explained.

"You're not company," I told him. "You're the brother I've chosen. It's a good thing, too. I'm going to need someone to manage now that Samuel is gone."

"It seems you are going to have a fair number, since the menagerie is about to grow again, if Rattlebones has anything to do with it. He and the Gargoyle have been trading secrets about how to train dogs."

"Phineas is free?"

"Sara traced the scented cloth Dulcinea found stitched to the queen's petticoat, found the woman who handled the skirt last. Boku burned some sweet herb under her nose and wheedled the whole tale out of the girl. A man working in the kennel let the dogs out to attack the queen. The Gargoyle was in the palace by accident, having come to visit you. Boku is an amazing man. Said he learned the trick from a sultan when he was on some mission to gather scientific nonsense for that School of Night the countess of Carlisle's father belonged to. Confused the devil out of us all, trying to figure out where he had come from. First, he seemed like he'd come from the New World, then Africa, then the Indies—knew of strange religions, Christianity, and Moorish ways."

"The School of Night. Do you think Boku will share their secrets?"

"He is not the only one whose secrets the menagerie is lusting after. We've found our very own wizard with animals. It's remarkable what Gargoyle can make them do. I wished for the queen to meet him, but I am not certain how she would react to his face. Women like to look upon the beautiful, not the grotesque."

I caught him looking at his reflection in a mirror. I knew he had hung it there when making his bachelor quarters into a bridal chamber. He'd no more been able to take the mirror down than he'd been able to stop whittling the toy horse. Will, still cherishing fragments of the family he'd hoped to have.

"I suppose some of us are not meant to inspire the love of a woman," he said softly. "We're fortunate if we get to watch the ones we love from a distance. See them alive. Happy. As you will be able to watch over the queen."

"It feels strange to stay at court, now that she knows."

"That a brave man loved her enough to risk his life for her? Watch over her? Protect her?"

Shame washed through me and I could not bear his praise—no matter what it cost me. "Will, you think too highly of me. You must know the truth. The reason she cast me out of favor."

He came to the front of the chair. Grasping hold of the chair's arms, he hunkered down so he could look me in the face. "Samuel told me enough. I pieced together the rest."

His deep-set eyes seemed to look into me so far that he could see the shriveled parts of my soul. "Ah, Jeffrey, there were signs you were working for Buckingham, just as I knew it was unwise to love Dulcinea. Perhaps I am no better than Her Majesty, choosing fantasies over grim truth, but I would rather see goodness and have someone else snatch it away than to stripe my own skin with a cat-o'-nine-tales made of bitterness and suspicion. Better to give people a chance than to go through life alone."

"The night Dulcinea died, all I could think of was that I was no different from her. I feared you would hate me when you learned how false I had been to the queen, to the menagerie. To you."

"You are nothing like Dulcinea," he said with such fierce affection, I could scarcely believe it was real. "You acted to survive and save your brother's life. When you rode to kill Buckingham, it was to make the queen and Samuel safe. You could not know Ware's hand was moving the chess pieces across the board."

The emotions flooded back to me—the helplessness, the self-loathing, the fear that I would lose this man's friendship, that I had never deserved to have Will Evans in my life at all.

"God, when I learned Ware was behind it, heard of his plans . . ." I shuddered.

"He's dead now," Will reassured me. "He cannot hurt the queen."

"But I still cannot think what he hoped to accomplish."

"We questioned Bartholomew Rowland, the owner of the Saracen's Bane. He said Ware loathed all things Catholic, said they used dark arts to hold decent men in thrall." He drew something out of his pocket. "We found this on Ware's person." He held out a stone. I looked at the impression on it—a strange creature's claw held captive in stone.

"A dragon stone," I said.

"He stole it from Boku's shelves when he was in the menagerie's lodgings. Ware's men said he believed there was some kind of power in such things."

"His father collected them. There was a French woman who loved to study them, as well. Ware's mother thought they were in love. She tried to murder her husband in front of the boy, then fled with him."

"Horrible."

"The true horror came after. She hid him among Puritans, took him to executions to drive his father's sinful nature out of him. When she saw him look at a girl with 'lust,' she put out his eye."

"His own mother?"

"She would have castrated him as well if another Puritan hadn't stopped her."

"Jesus, Mary, and Joseph," Will croaked. "How does a lad make sense of it when his own mother wounds him thus?"

"He must have blamed the woman who loved dragon stones. Add to that the loathing of Catholics he was taught by the Puritans, and the queen embodied everything Ware loathed."

"The men we questioned said Ware thought that once the queen was gone, His Majesty would be willing to challenge French and Spanish power in the New World. The king would see the merit in the East India Company and other such enterprises and be willing to listen to Parliament. The Crown would begin to work with these men who are determined to seize fate on their own terms."

"I wish his reasoning did not make sense. But in some ways, it does."

"When Buckingham was assassinated, the king was furious at men of Felton's ilk—commoners who demanded more than the aristocrats chose to give them. With the duke gone, Ware had to take matters into his own hands. He enlisted the help of those angered by the king's demands for money. Once the queen was assassinated, they planned to compel the king to listen to Parliament."

"Ware expected Charles Stuart to sit down and negotiate with men who had just murdered his wife? They do not know His Majesty at all."

"I fear the king does not know the Commons, either. Ware may have been mad, his scheme so wild that only the most reckless would support it. But there are plenty of commoners who see men like Buckingham— vainglorious fools who are put in command of the fleet, the country, the lives of simple folk. If you could see the arguments they print in pamphlets—"

I shuddered, remembering the broadsheet the countess of Carlisle had given me. Had anyone traced such scandalous printings to the bookshop near St. Paul's and the family that had welcomed Samuel so kindly, provided a haven for Father Quintin?

"What will happen to the Rowlands?" I asked. "I am certain Ware threatened them as he did me."

"I can't say the king is disposed to be merciful to anyone involved in Ware's scheme, but I believe His Majesty would give you any boon right now to thank you for saving the queen's life."

"Then I will ask His Majesty to send Rowland and his family to France. Father Quintin will help them start anew. I only hope there are not other masterless men starting anew, as well. How many others might Ware have spread his contagion to?"

"We cannot know," Will said, solemn. "All I am certain of is this: Things are changing beyond the palace walls. If we hope to protect the queen, we will have to watch, listen."

"Fortunately, you're tall as a house. You can see over any crowd, and I am a most accomplished spy."

Will chuckled, then grew pensive. "Archie said something that troubles me still. He says we had best not celebrate our triumph too soon. It is possible for a king to love his queen too well. Tend her interests rather than his country's. Do you think it might be true?"

I motioned for him to lift me down. Will did so with a gentleness that never failed to surprise me. "Archie is a crabbed boil on my arse," I said. "He can't bear for anyone to be happy."

Will laughed. "Ware's knife didn't bleed the wickedness out of your wit."

"No one wants to deal with a morose court fool," I said, straightening my doublet. "Someone must make people laugh."

"Even when the tale ends sadly." Will crossed to where the little wooden horse stood upon the window ledge. I knew he was thinking of a graceful butterfly dancing upon a rope, never imagining she could fall.

I wished I could reach back into time and rearrange things, give him the happiness he'd dreamed of. But that time was over. Or was it? I remembered the day my father had lifted me onto the duke's writing table and I had lost hold of everything I'd known, set forth on a path I could not even imagine.

I laid my hand upon Will Evans's boot. "Maybe the end of one story is just the beginning of another, Will," I said as he looked down at me. "Maybe this time the giant will win a woman who deserves his love."

Will tipped his head to one side, considering. "Maybe the dwarf will win a lady fair, too."

"With or without a crown?" I challenged. "You know, before I came here, I was a Fairy King."

"It is a good tale—the dwarf and the giant winning love and glory," Will said, his voice warming. "Might as well add a chest of pirate gold. A sea monster or two."

"Shall we go down to the lodgings and see what Boku and the others can add?" I said, knowing I was home at last. "The one thing I am sure of is that the whole world is a menagerie. Every curiosity has a story to tell."

HISTORICAL NOTE

•

What became *The Queen's Dwarf* began with the seed of an idea: the story of royal intrigues entirely told from the viewpoint of a court fool. It grew into a story of friendship, a brother's devotion, and the rocky beginnings of one of the most touching royal romances ever recorded: the unexpected love that bloomed between a fatherless French princess and the shy young man who was never supposed to be king. But what amazed me most while researching the real Jeffrey Hudson's life was that fact was more astonishing than fiction. (Really, if I were going to have my hero kidnapped by pirates, I'd do it once. Jeffrey was seized by pirates twice!)

Jeffrey stood a mere eighteen inches tall during his time at court. A midwife blamed his diminutive size on his mother's penchant for pickled gherkins. Perhaps the Hudson family seized on that explanation because widely accepted superstition claimed such physical imperfection was caused by the devil. In truth, Jeffrey suffered from a deficient pituitary gland. If he were born today, he could easily be cured with injections of growth hormone.

Jeffrey was the son of the butcher who trained the duke of Buckingham's bull-baiting dogs, just as I portray in the novel. However, John Hudson's temperament is a fictional creation, based on my belief that training dogs and sending them into the ring to be savaged would take a certain brutality. Jeffrey's brother Samuel did not become a Jesuit, nor was anyone plagued by the fictional Uriel Ware. But the deep affection between the two Hudson lads was real. Samuel named his first son after Jeffrey, a rarity in a time when the heir was named for the father of the child. Once Jeffrey escaped his time in North Africa as a pirate's slave, he returned to England to live with his brother.

As for Jeffrey's introduction to the queen: Imagine my delight in discovering that Buckingham did present Jeffrey to Queen Henrietta Maria at a banquet at York House by having him pop out of a pie and march up and down the table dressed in armor. Historically, Jeffrey was only eight years old at the time. I beg the reader's indulgence for having added six years in the interest of the story.

It is little wonder Henrietta Maria, the homesick teenager who was widely hated for being French and Catholic, eased her loneliness by collecting "pets," however strange it seems to us now that some of them were human ones. Her "Curiosities and Freaks of Nature" included Robert Gibson (Goodfellow), a gifted artist and miniaturist; Little Sara; Pug, the monkey; and Will Evans, the knock-kneed Welsh giant who became Jeffrey's real-life best friend. The discord-spreading Archie Armstrong came into royal service—as I relate in the story—by stealing a lamb, then pretending to be an old woman in hopes of outwitting the royal hunting party that gave chase. Rattlebones, Dulcinea, and Boku were products of my imagination, but the royal menagerie really existed and had starring roles in the queen's beloved masques.

The early years of Henrietta Maria's marriage to Charles I were tempestuous. The duke of Buckingham held first place in Charles's affections and, with the help of Buckingham's mistress, the countess of Carlisle, plotted to keep Henrietta Maria's influence over the king minimal. Though there is no evidence Buckingham or Jeffrey were agents provocateurs in the queen's disastrous pilgrimage to Tyburn, the damage done to the queen's reputation was real. It resulted in the heartbreaking but necessary banishing of the queen's French household, among them Mamie Saint-Georges, Henrietta Maria's childhood friend.

Lucy Hay, Lady Carlisle, was known as "the killing beauty of the age." She was the daughter of the Wizard Earl, Henry Percy, ninth earl of Northumberland, who was friend to Sir Walter Raleigh and Christopher Marlowe and a member of the freethinking cadre of alchemists, dabblers in occult matters, and scientists called the School of Night. She spent two years imprisoned in the Tower of London at her father's command. The earl was determined she should not mingle noble Percy blood with that of one of the king's Scots hangers-on. Lucy escaped and wed. How did her passion for James Hay fade? That remains to be explored.

My most delightful discovery about Lucy was that she was Alexander Dumas's model for his famed villainess Milady de Winter. Lucy really did steal the diamond studs Queen Anne of Austria gave Buckingham as a love token. Buckingham, as Lord Admiral, closed the English ports until he could get replacements made. Sadly, the Three Musketeers did not take part in foiling Richelieu's plot.

Buckingham's military disasters made him as widely hated as his arrogance, yet King Charles never forsook the man who was kind to him when he was an awkward prince and never expected to rule. After the disaster at the Citadel, Charles welcomed Buckingham back to England, though not in so public a manner as described here. The message to Buckingham's detractors was the same: Only death would end the duke's hold over the king. John Felton was heralded as a hero when he assassinated the duke, much as I have portrayed it in *The Queen's Dwarf*.

Jeffrey's life was filled with marvels. He fought in skirmishes during the Civil War, barely escaping Parliamentarian troops with the queen. He carried out secret missions on Henrietta Maria's behalf and he was sold into slavery by Barbary pirates. He adored the queen and followed her to France, grieving with her when she learned of her husband's execution. Only after he killed a man in a duel and faced execution did he leave the queen's side. Henrietta Maria ordered him into exile to save his life.

Jeffrey's tale is that of an England on the brink of revolution, a time when the old hierarchy of fealty to nobility was crumbling, a never-before-seen group of enterprising merchants and businessmen having made a fortune by their own labor and daring. Yet this daring was often set in contrast to an increasingly harsh religious zealotry that would lead to the closing of theaters, the abolishment of dancing, and the banning of Christmas under the rule of Parliamentarian Lord Protector Oliver Cromwell.

Three books of nonfiction have been a great help in fashioning *The Queen's Dwarf*. *Lord Minimus: The Extraordinary Life of Britain's Smallest Man*, by Nick Page; *A Royal Passion: The Turbulent Marriage of King Charles I of England and Henrietta Maria of France*, by Katie Whitaker; and *Court*

Lady and Country Wife, by Lita-Rose Betcherman, a biography of Lucy Hay and her sister. These fabulous writers made researching pure delight. To see the full glory of Stuart England, I recommend browsing through the works of Van Dyck, paintings in which he captured the fleeting happiness Charles and Henrietta Maria would share. Some of these paintings include Jeffrey Hudson. One particularly famous portrait shows him standing beside the queen, Pug, the monkey, sitting upon his shoulder. I wonder what he was thinking at that moment, this butcher's son from a tiny village in Rutland. Was he thinking of his brother Samuel? The court intrigues forever brewing in the Stuart court? Did he realize revolution was going to shake the very foundations of the England he knew? I doubt very much he was imagining being captured by pirates. But that is another story.

FIC
CHASE   Chase, Ella March.

                The queen's dwarf.